The

Thomas Walker

Thomas Walker

Also In This Series:

Just See Yourself
Now On Earth

Dedicated to the people who keep asking for more.
You are all annoying and single-minded,
...but I look forward to spending eternity with you

Foreword:

The first two books were incredibly well received; but there were two main points of contention: First, some believed very strongly that money is not going to have any place in the New World. In my series, it was viewed as a necessity, but not anyone's priority; for purposes of trade across a global brotherhood.

Secondly, there was some debate as to whether or not there would be 'Undecided' people. It was a plot point; as there was no specific direction on the subject, the position was based on some deductive reasoning.

These two points created some serious discussion among people I knew, and from that came some interesting viewpoints; which was the whole point of writing this series. But while there was some debate; there's obviously no way to find out. The final word on each debate is: This is a fictional novelization of a place that's certain to come eventually.

So after 'agreeing to disagree' with half a dozen people; I then proceeded to write an entire third novel around the most contentious points of discussion. As always, this is just a fictional viewpoint; and I can't wait to find out the parts I got wrong.

Thomas Walker

Book One: Resurrection

Acts 24:15: *"And I have hope toward God, which hope these men also look forward to, that there is going to be a resurrection of both the righteous and the unrighteous."*

Chapter One: James

The Caribbean. 1691 A.D.

James grinned. "We're rich."

Lancewood, his first mate, pushed the cup over to him. "That we are." He looked at the bejewelled cross. "It's beautiful."

"The Cross of Corinth." James said with a blatantly hungry grin. "Centuries old, and worth a whole fleet. They were wise to hide it in with their livestock. With so many cases of pretties in their cargo hold, who would have looked further?"

"You can't keep it." Lancewood said, as though reminding him. "We took enough gold and silver that I was honestly worried the ship was going to go under. But this? They'll put a price so big on your head that you'll never get a chance to sell it."

"I have plans of my own for this one." James promised, and raised his voice. "Smitty!"

The door opened, and Smitty entered the Captain's Cabin, saluting reflexively. "Cap'n?"

James grinned, and held the prize out to him. "Take it downstairs, put it with the rest of the booty." He saw the hungry reverence in Smitty's eyes as he handed it over. "Once you're done drooling on it, that is."

Smitty schooled his expression, and crossed himself automatically as he took the bejewelled crucifix. "Thank you, sir."

"Smitty?" Lancewood called, pouring again. "Have a drink. You earned it. And this is the good stuff."

Smitty glanced at James, who gave him a tight nod. Lancewood was a relatively new addition to the crew, and this was his first run as First Mate. Smitty took his cup of Rum, and toasted them both as he backed out of the Stateroom.

"I'm a little surprised you didn't keep it for your share." Lancewood commented, watching the Crucifix leave. "It's pretty clear what you were after on that last raid."

"It won't go far." James promised. "I'm surprised you aren't trying to get it yourself. It's the choicest piece of pretty we looted. And you picked most of the people we lost. More than I did."

"The Prize is worth it." Lancewood said easily, and poured a little more rum into the Captain's still-untouched goblet.

"You think so? It was a pretty brutal fight."

"And we won." Lancewood insisted. "Isn't that how this works?"

James picked up his goblet, and raised it to him. "Well then. To the victorious dead."

"And to the wealth of the last men standing." Lancewood returned, raising his own mug. But neither of them sipped, eyes on each other.

"Lancewood, are you thinking what I'm thinking?" James said with an icy smirk.

"I wouldn't know what you're thinkin', Cap'n." Lancewood said brightly.

"I'm thinking that after pouring for both of us the second you walked in here… I've yet to see you take a sip." James drawled, one hand resting on his cutlass, the other pointedly extending to pour his untouched cup out on the deck.

Silence.

"Clever, Captain." Lancewood rested a hand casually on his pistol. "I couldn't get you a deal, James. But I don't suppose you'd want one. You'd always rather swing than bow."

"Traitor!" James snarled, and rose to his full height. "I knew you would sell us out."

"No, Cap'n. You didn't. You didn't hire this crew, I did. Most of them, anyway. Half your loyalists died taking *my* new fortune."

"So did a third of the men *you* hired." James snarled. "You know what the rest of them said, when we buried our dead at sea?"

"More for the rest of us." Lancewood nodded. "Nature of the life. We stopped being honorable sailors some time ago. We're Pirates. And Pirates get paid. I'm not looking over my shoulder for the rest of my life. There's nowhere we can go that the Spaniards won't hunt us."

"But if someone were to make them an offer, say half the plunder and the crew that stole it…" James nodded, unsurprised.

"A third, actually. They were agreeable to that. And with most of the crew gone after tonight, it will be enough." Lancewood drew his pistol. "I will do you one favor. You won't be taken in chains. They'll probably string your bones up as a warning to some proper Spanish Port; but by then you won't care."

Lancewood aimed and pulled the trigger. The charge ignited with a huge bang…

And James grinned. "I took the shot out of your pistol three hours ago, Traitor."

Lancewood checked his gun, though it made no difference. "You knew?"

"I suspected." James nodded, drawing his sword slowly; letting the metal screech. "You didn't dicker over your share. As First Mate, you were entitled to more of The Prize, but you didn't even suggest it. It was pretty clear you weren't going to play by the rules."

"Then why didn't you stop me sooner?"

James grinned savagely. "Well, like you said, most of the crew were your pick. Which of them could I trust? After all, it wasn't difficult to tell my *surviving* loyalists not to drink or eat anything you touched. And with all your mutineers out of the picture, the haul is worth the extra work."

From outside the room came the sound of battle, swords ringing off each other, pistols being fired quickly, screams of pain.

"I'm guessing that shot was your signal, eh?" James drew his sword. "Your mutineers think I'm dead, so they're making their move?"

"Even if you win, you won't escape. They're already on the way; and I made sure your cannons won't be worth spit." Lancewood nodded. "You can't win, James. There are more of us than you."

"They won't fight for you if you're dead." James reminded him, and lunged forward swinging his cutlass to kill. Lancewood reared back, but not in time. The blade caught his neck, and the man dropped with a splash of red.

There was the sound of gunfire from outside, and James knew he couldn't linger over the victory.

Out on the deck, there was a battle being waged. Lancewood's men had expected to find drugged or poisoned opponents, and instead found James' men were ready for them. The battle was pitched and desperate, with survival as the prize.

James lunged towards Smitty, his oldest surviving friend. The huge Dutchman had a cutlass in each hand, holding three of them back, as James joined his people.

A cheer went up when they saw their captain. Even as steel rang out against steel; James could see the light dim in the Traitors' eyes. Their Mutiny had failed. Lancewood was no doubt beaten; and that left them without a Captain to fight for.

But they kept fighting. James' sharp eyes saw snipers reloading in the Crowsnest, and tapped Smitty to follow him up to the wheel. It was a mean duel when they got there, the two of them fighting back to back against three.

James took the wheel from one of Lancewood's conspirators, and forced him back with the swing of his sword. "Scarlett, you swine! It was two days ago I saved your miserable hide from a Spanish shot."

The mutineer actually looked sorry. "Nothing personal, Captain. But I got a better offer."

James danced back neatly as Scarlett swung. The blade missed him and hit timber. It bit deep, carving a notch in the wheel; deep enough that the traitor couldn't pull it free, as James ran him through.

"Down!" Smitty roared, and James felt the huge man tackle him from behind, just as the shot from the Crowsnest whistled past them both. James kicked the wheel, still from the deck, and the ship started to turn. The sails turned into the wind, and the ship suddenly lurched as the sails lofted, jerking the crowsnest back sharply enough that the sniper, already leaning out too far, fell from his perch.

The fight lasted only a few minutes more, but not one Mutineer was willing to surrender. Fighting them all down took most of the crew working together; until casualties grew heavy.

The ship had been saved, but there were few of them left; and the Ships Doctor was not among them. The six survivors made their way below decks. Keller bled out while his four friends stood around him helplessly, trying to make sense of the dead doctor's tools. James poured whiskey into Keller's lips for as long as he could, until the wounded man finally gave in.

There was a heavy silence, broken only by Smitty, reading a few verses over the bodies. His Bible had a lot of pages missing, torn out one by one by desperate crew, rolling their own tobacco. James went out of the room to lower the anchor. Five crew left, and nobody at the helm. Even in a light fog, that could be dangerous.

"I don't understand." Smitty said. "If Lancewood is dead, then they must have known that. The Mutineers must have seen you. Why'd they keep fighting?"

BOOM!

It was a warning shot. The survivors all ran up on deck. On the horizon was ship under full sail. A Galleon, flying the Spanish Flag.

"That's why." James snarled. "Lancewood cut a deal with the Spanish. They get us, he gets a cut of what we've taken. They fought to the last man because they had reinf-"

"We have to run!" Smitty said, grabbing for the wheel.

"No. Strike the colors." James said immediately.

His surviving crew stared at him in disbelief. "Surrender?! You have any idea what a Spanish Court would do to us?"

"All too well." James acknowledged.

"They can't arrest us. These aren't their waters." Anatoly argued. "They don't have the authority."

"Which means they'll just kill us all, if we're lucky." James scorned. "Authority comes from the whim of whoever's pointing the biggest gun. But if we turn to run, they'll have us from the stern; and we're dead.

Lancewood told them he'd have the ship ready and waiting. We fight, they'll sink us. We give them what they expect, they'll come right up alongside to board us; nice and slow." James gestured swiftly. "Now there are five of us. You all go below, load everything on the Lower Starboard Gun Deck and be ready to fire all when I give the signal. I'm going back to my cabin to get Lancewood's coat and Hat. They see me on deck, they'll think it's their man, signaling the all clear."

Smitty grinned, swiftly understanding. "And when they stand easy and roll right up next to us…"

"We hole them below their waterline, and they won't be able to give chase." James summed up; keeping his face even. "You'll only have one shot from each Cannon. Make them count."

"Those ships have more than twice our guns, and our numbers are down to less than ten." Anatoly warned. "We might get a lucky hit, but we'll never…"

James drew his sword. "I've cut down five traitorous souls today, Anatoly. My sword is always hungry for more. You have your orders. Would you rather take your chances with the sharks, the Spaniards, or with me?"

Anatoly backed down. "Ayesir."

"Smitty. Lead them below." James turned to go.

Smitty clasped his hand quickly. "Bleed for no Flag."

"Bow to no King." James grinned, despite himself, at the old promise they had made when they started out.

Smitty pulled a medallion on a chain from around his neck and pushed it at his friend. "May St Nicholas hold the tiller for you." He said as he went below deck.

James felt the smile run away from his face the second he was alone on deck. If Lancewood had been telling the truth about sabotaging the cannon, then his people wouldn't have a hope of escaping prison walls.

There was only one option left.

~oo0Ooo~

James returned to his stateroom, and spared a glance at the body of his treacherous First Mate. "This is your fault." He told the body. "You did this to them, not me."

With that, he went to the Captain's Chest and put all his strength into dragging it. It was full to bursting with the choicest pieces of wealth they'd plundered. A King's Ransom in specific prizes and treasures, worth more than everything else in the ship put together.

The Spanish ships were pulling in their sails, spilling their speed. They knew nobody would be firing back. They could take their time.

Time enough for an escape.

With the enemy inching closer, adrenaline gave him strength, and it took only a few minutes to load a boat. It was enough for ten men, so there was just enough room for the chest, and sufficient provisions.

"Sorry, Smitty." James said, feeling bad about it. "But five men can't get this ship to Port. Not with a Pirate Hunter having us by the hip." He would genuinely have preferred another way, but with the Galleon closing in, he couldn't risk it all on such long odds. "You'll forgive me, one day."

His men would buy him time to reach the fog; and with so many bodies after the mutiny, nobody would notice he was gone. *With all the treasure recovered, they might not even look.*

James caught himself on that thought. The Captain's Share held everything he would need... except the Cross of Corinth.

For a tortured moment, he hesitated, before he quickly scrambled back up on deck. He'd have to chance it. The Galleon was close enough that he had to duck

15

behind the desk railing to go unnoticed as he crept below deck. If the last of his crew saw him heading below the Gun Deck he was dead.

James looked at the St Nicholas Medallion for a moment. He wasn't a believer, but there were no atheists on the battlefield, and he kissed the silver quickly.

When he reached the Cargo hold, he could barely move through it for all the loot his ship had taken. Lancewood hadn't been wrong about how much they'd taken. Chests of dubloons, sacks of silver pieces…

It took him several minutes to find the Cross. Smitty had put it at the head of the room, in a place of reverence. James felt the weight of the Medallion around his neck, and wondered if Smitty had prayed when he put this away.

"Prayers don't save people." James whispered as he hoisted the cross, and tucked it safely into his belt. "But this Cross yet might."

"I didn't want to believe it."

James spun smoothly, one hand on his sword-hilt, and found Smitty in the doorway, looking sick. His first real friend, and longest lived shipmate.

Smitty had a sword drawn already. "I didn't want to believe you'd sent us off just to… what? Create a diversion while you escaped? It was ten minutes ago I saved your life, Cap'n."

James sighed, resigned to doing this the hard way. "It was the only way, Smitty. You know I wouldn't leave my crew if I had any other choice. See, I never told you what the plan was for the things I took as my own, and we don't have time now for-"

"Just you and your blood money." Smitty snarled.

"You didn't mind drinking the blood money down when you had a cut." James pointed out. "I meant what I said. It's a long shot, but if you can get the ship away, it's yours; and if you can't, then I can still-"

BOOM! The ship lurched as the other ship's cannons went off.

"Too late." James sighed. "They decided just to sink us after all."

"Yes, it is too late." Smitty lunged at his Captain, sword flashing.

James jumped back, and felt the hoard filling his cargo hold hemming him in.

And then the world tilted as the ship was hit again, harder. James got to his feet first, and darted for the stairs.

There was the sound of metal sliding, and James felt a numbness suddenly growing in his arm. James spun, as blood poured from his arm, his sword blocking the next blow through sheer luck more than anything else.

"I was your oldest friend!" Smitty howled. "I sided with you against everyone! Every time you got us into a fight, I got you out of it." His sword flashed, again and again and again. "You were going to let us all die! And for what?! Your damn gold!?"

"It was never about the money!" James roared back. "I bled for this ship!"

"WE ALL DID!" Smitty struck again.

As he swung, the ship lurched again, without cannonfire. James had spent his life on ships, feeling the ocean beneath his feet. He knew that they'd pulled free. The ship was moving again.

James grabbed a handful of spilled coins and threw them at Smitty, hurrying towards the stairs while he was distracted...

There was a half second of noise that seemed to shake apart the world. James had a flash of the wall erupting with a burst of shattered timber, and flame. Not time to dodge, or even to articulate the thought, just that millisecond of awareness that he was about to die-

James opened his eyes and took a deep breath.

It was a warm sunny day, which was odd, since it was meant to be the middle of the night, with fog rolled in. James found he was laying back on the... grass?

What's going on?

His arm was working again. He was calm. He'd just been fighting for his life, and... He felt like he'd just woken from a good sleep. As he sat up, the hairs on the back of his neck stood up, and he knew immediately that he wasn't alone.

Beside him, but standing a respectful distance away, there were two figures. Both young and healthy, one large and heavily muscled man with dark skin, one caucasian woman. The woman was the single most attractive specimen that James had ever laid eyes on. He'd met Courtesans and Doxies from every corner of the Caribbean and Southern Seas, but this woman was almost supernaturally beautiful.

"Hello, James." The beauty said with a smile. "My name is Karen; and this is my friend Irsu. I imagine you have some questions."

"A few." James admitted.

"Well, let's see what we can do to answer them." Karen said lightly, and James' sharp eyes noticed her putting a green letter into her pocket. "Shall we go?"

"Go where?" James brushed off his clothes, which he discovered were not his own, but rather a comfortable set of non-descript breeches and tunic. The shoes were unlike anything he'd worn before, but noticed the woman wearing something similar in form. "Where am I?"

"The Southern Italian Region." Karen reported.

James' eyes flashed. "I am… not popular with the Italian Authorities."

"They won't be a problem." Karen said with certainty. "That's part of what I need to tell you."

"Are you my Patron?"

"I'm your Welcome Wagon." Karen said. "We have much to tell you, James. Many wonderful things."

James said nothing to that as they started walking, already sizing up the escape routes. She knew his name. However he'd gotten there, his identity was known. If this was Italy, he was in danger.

"Thank you, Irsu; but I believe I can take it from here." Karen said brightly to her friend. "And you have an appointment of your own to keep, do you not?"

Chapter Two: Atxi

Tenochtitlan. 1520 A.D.

"Atxi."

Atxi and her sister looked up from their meal. Huitzilin, the High Priest, had come in to join them. "I've been discussing matters with the others. We need to move up your ceremony."

Atxi felt her heart stop. "But… The calender says another month, before-"

"I know." The High Priest told them. "But our armies will be called to battle soon; and this enemy is strong. We all have to do our part."

Patli had turned to stone. As the elder sibling, it was understood that she would go first. But Patli had her other duties, beyond the ceremonial; and the schedule had suddenly changed. It had been a source of friction in the household, that Atxi was so eager to undertake her duties at the Temple.

Atxi noticed the look being traded between Huitzilin and her mother, swiftly realizing how she had convinced them to let Atxi take her sister's place. "I am ready." Atxi said seriously. "Whatever the gods wish of me, I gladly give."

Huitzilin nodded and turned to leave.

"Priest." Her mother said suddenly. "We had planned to give Atxi a proper goodbye. Her nephew just went to join Tialoc with the other children last week."

"Did he weep?" Huitzilin asked quietly.

"He did." Atxi said softly. "Lots of the youngest weep when their time comes. Most of them don't understand what an important responsibility it is."

"Their tears are a good sign. Tlaloc gives back tears to show how pleasing the Tribute is." Huitzilin came back into the room and removed his mask, looking at Atxi carefully. "Huitzilopochtli chose his wonders with his all-knowing skill." Huitzilin intoned, hypnotic and certain. "Remember that even now, the blessings we're receiving are tiny specks of the glory of the Gods. They are holy beings who put the stars in their position; and yet we are awed by a bountiful harvest, or the song of the birds." His voice was so full of certainty and power that Atxi felt herself grow taller under his gaze. She felt like she had as a little girl, when this man had taught her the story of The Sun People, and how Tenochtitlan had come to be.

"I'm ready." Atxi promised.

~oo00oo~

"I'm not ready." Atxi told her family the next day.

Busy at the loom, her sister was praying incessantly, not pausing her weaving. "If you weren't ready, Huitzilin would not have called on you early."

Atxi glanced at the doorway for the hundredth time, trying to slow her breathing. Her mother fussed with her hair, braiding it again. "Mother, you're going to pull my hair out!"

"I want it to be perfect." The older woman fussed, undoing the braid again. "It's your day."

"It's God's day." Patli shushed their mother.

"It is." Atxi agreed. "I just want to look good for my part in it."

"You will, dear one." Her mother promised. "You look lovely." She rose and went to the other side of their home, picking up the garment she'd been weaving. Patli finished weaving whatever it was, and the two of them together presented Atxi with her new robe. "I stayed up the entire night on this."

Atxi actually choked up as her mother put it around her shoulders. The cotton garment was pure, radiant white, and the lightest, coolest fabric she'd ever worn. It was her ceremonial robe. Her mother had made it for her personally. "It's beautiful."

Her mother demurred. "It's fine for being three weeks early."

"I still can't believe they moved it up that much."

"They moved a lot of things up." Patli confided.

Atxi and their mother traded a secret smile. Patli was their source for all the best inside information; as well as the best gossip. She spent time with the Tributes, and their guards; and the Temple Attendants; all as part of her training. "Tell us why, sister."

"Montezuma has been captured by the Invaders." Patli said profoundly.

Atxi barked out a laugh before she could stop herself. "No, surely not."

"I heard it from one of the soldiers." Patli insisted. "The Tlaxalan and the Texcocan have allied with them."

Atxi felt anger twist in her a moment. "That's why they're in such a hurry to offer Tribute to Huitzilopochtli. Because our warriors have to strike quickly; and they'll need our gods to be strong."

Their mother sighed hard. "The Gods give so much of themselves keeping the darkness away; keeping the rivers flowing and the crops growing. We ask them for so much." She immediately began taking off Atxi's robes. "Go get changed. Don't wear this until you reach the Temple. You don't want to get it dirty."

Atxi nodded, and hurried to prepare. Her mother gave her a tight hug, whispering words of pride and love. Atxi hugged her back. "I'll see you soon." She promised.

~oo0Ooo~

Tenochtitlan was a very beautiful city. Atxi had lived outside it her entire life. The valley waters surrounded their community, with the fishermen gathering their catch, and the farmers binding up little muddy islands to farm corn. Patli walked the causeway with her, heading towards the Guardhouse that would let them into the Temple Courtyard.

"Did you see the way mother and the priest were looking at each other?" Patli hissed, always eager for gossip.

"Try not to think about it." Atxi counselled her.

"I'm just saying, if you wondered how you were put at the top of the list so fast..." Patli winced. "Forget I said that. I know how much you wanted this."

"I do." Atxi agreed. "But I'm not sure prominence is such an issue anymore. If you heard right, and the king has been captured…"

"I agree; they'll be doing everything they can to empower the gods for the next battle." Patli shivered. "There will be *thousands* over the next week."

"Tens of thousands." Atxi said with certainty. "It will be enough."

~oo0Ooo~

They entered the walls, and passed the fine houses of the nobles. The Tributes were being dragged out of them by the Temple Guards. Atxi and Patli waited politely, giving them space. The Tributes had been selected from the Prisoners-Of-War for Sacrifice. They had spent years being purified and revered in luxury preparing for this day.

But almost never did the Foreign Tributes see the value in what they had been spared for. The priestesses that had lived with them kept pace, untouched by the noise as the Tributes screamed at the guards who hauled them to the stairs.

"I wish I could speak their language." Atxi murmured to Patli.

"Some of the Attendants can." Patli whispered back. "They say it's always the same thing. They call us heathens and godless savages."

"Godless." Atxi repeated. "I don't know why they act like that." Atxi said regretfully. "They aren't mistreated during their time here. Some prisoners, I can understand their hatred of us; but the Tributes live comfortably; plenty of food and rest, women to tend to their needs… It's not until their time comes that they even think of their own gods, let alone ours."

"They don't think like we do." Patli counselled her. "Their Priests tell them that we are false worshippers. That only *their* god is real. The Christians think we're monsters because of the Sacrifices. Their Priests don't do that."

"Only one God, and they offer Him nothing? And they call *us* savage." Atxi shook her head. "How can anyone value their mortal flesh so highly? It lasts such a short time."

"They're obsessed with making that time longer and more comfortable." Patli explained. "Or so the priestess' tell me. It's why they invaded, looking for gold and silver to line their nests."

"They go to war over things they can't take with them." Atxi's fingers went to the gold jewellry that tied her soft robes together. "Seems so selfish. Surely the heavens are big enough for everyone."

~oo0Ooo~

The two slipped into one of the private rooms and Atxi breathed deeply, changing into her ceremonial robes. "Mother was right. I don't want this to get dirty."

"It's a lovely robe. Some of her best work." Patli agreed. "She was lucky to get the material. I heard that the cottons are running low. Trade from Mexico is being harried by the invaders."

"That changes today." Atxi promised softly.

"This is where we part." Patli said softly. "I'm happy for you, sister. And a little jealous. Is that alright?"

"It should be you, sister." Atxi hugged her tightly. "One day, it will be. I promise. But until then, you have your own service. I'll never dance at the festival."

"No, I guess you won't." Patli admitted. "But what's coming will be so much more."

~oo0Ooo~

There was a line of people at the steps. The sun was at its highest point, proof of Huitzilopochtli's energy and gratitude for all that the people had done. Atxi was allowed a place of prominence in the line; but she hesitated to be there, running to the edge of the steps. Past the line of stone, she could see Patli, dancing out the story of Tenochtitlan, how it was founded, and how The Sun was born again each day.

She'd seen Patli dance before, of course. Every movement had to be precisely controlled; so they had practised together endlessly. The serpent sway to represent fertility, the low crouches for the harvest, the leaps and twirls to show the soul. Patli was privileged, wearing one of the bird masks that identified her as the Great Sun God incarnate.

"Change your mind?"

Atxi jumped a bit, and looked to see her mother had come to join her. "No, of course not. I just… I wanted to see my sister dance the story of Huitzilopochtli, just once, before I went up there."

"You'll be with the gods, Atxi. You'll see everything."

"I know." Atxi nodded. "But not with you beside me."

Her mother hugged her again. "I'm so very proud of you."

~ooOOoo~

The line started moving.

"Any Gods who may be listening, I pray that you are good, and that you know how much I want to be good too." Atxi said quietly to the sky as she climbed the stone steps. The line moved slowly. "I hope that what I have to offer is good in your eyes, and that you can forgive me for all the wrong things I've done. Thank you for all the good things I've seen and felt; and I hope one day to understand the bad. Because if you can hear me, I know that only good things would come from whoever's listening. Because a cruel or bad God wouldn't hear me."

"Amen." Said a young man behind her. She didn't turn.

The sun beat down on the stone. The line was moving slowly enough that Atxi wasn't short of breath; but the methodical precision of it was nearly mechanical. Atxi could hear the drums setting the beat to her sister's dancing, though she couldn't see it. Far below, the children were being taught about the world. The sacrifices that the Gods had made of themselves to keep the world alive, the Sun reborn every day; the entire universe every fifty-four years; and the war to prevent the end of the world when it came.

Atxi felt so much better as she ascended the stairs. The stone stairs to the Altar were wide enough for twenty men to walk side by side. The stone was solid and unbreakable; the drumming fading as she climbed higher and higher. The permanence of it was a comfort. Though invaders came to their nation; and hostile gods sent their armies, their city of Tenochtitlan could surely never fall.

There was a slickness on the stone, and Atxi could see the blood running down the steps, the fresh mingling with the dried. The Sun's heat never let it last for long before being baked away. Atxi could smell the smoke of the altar fire, consuming the hearts of each Tribute.

"You want some peyotl?" One of the attendants asked her quietly when she got near the top step. "We don't usually offer, but we have some on hand. For some of the Foreign Tributes, it's the only way we can get them still enough to do this properly."

"No, thank you." Atxi whispered back. "I don't want anything to dull my senses. Not for this."

When she reached the top of the stairs, the line in front of her suddenly seemed so short.

And yet, despite all this, the nerves evaporated instantly. She was totally at peace. She'd done all she could, and had no time for more. Whatever was going to happen, she was little more than an observer now.

Time seemed to slow down and she could take in every single thing. The wisp of the smoke, the smell of the fresh blood; the softness of the cotton, the solid reassurance of the stone…

Atxi had never felt so connected the the world. She'd never felt so pure at heart and soul.

The previous Tribute was pitched over the side, and Atxi stepped forward, laying on her back across the Altar, arms and legs extended. The attendants gripped her wrists and ankles. There would be movement, no matter how hard Atxi tried to hold still.

"Have I pleased the gods?" She asked, so soft that

she could barely hear her own voice.

"You have." Huitzilin promised, and raised his obsidian knife high above her; the tip of it slick and gleaming by the firelight, and-

Atxi drew in a breath, feeling wonderful.

The Altar was gone. So was everything else. She was laying on soft cool grass. Surprised, Atxi sat upright. She saw rolling hills, filled with golden colored grass, seeming to glow in warm sunlight. The strong heat was gone; and there was a gentle smell of spices and orange-blossoms in the air.

Atxi was surprised. "What?" She had been expecting to arrive at The Sun, not this... this beautiful place.

"Atxi?"

She looked. She had company. A huge, powerfully built man with dark skin. He was dressed in some kind of clothing she had never seen before; but his expression was warm and friendly. "My name is Irsu." He rumbled politely. "It's nice to meet you."

Chapter Three: Walter

New York. 2017 A.D.

Walter Emmerson was dying. But that was no reason to let his standards slip.

The Hospital at St Augustine's was the most exclusive private hospital in the country, with only the finest doctors. Even their chef was five star. There was no reason for Walter to eat the kind of garbage they usually served in more public hospitals.

But his doctors had put him on a restricted diet. One that took several of the more civilized options off the menu. That wasn't acceptable. Townsend didn't have much appetite, but what little he ate was not about to be hospital food.

There was a knock at his door, and his nurse came in. "Are you up to receiving a visitor, Mister Emmerson?"

Walter blinked. He'd never had a visitor before; outside his staff. "Send him in."

A familiar face entered the room, and nodded respectfully to the Nurse. Walter brightened. Townsend Chalcott Coatesworth was one of his old friends. They'd attended Prep School together, and kept in touch over the years as they built their fortunes; Walter in Construction, Townsend in Insurance; though neither of them were limited to those fields in their holdings and investments.

Townsend came over. "Your hospital has the most attractive nurses."

"The homely ones are downstairs, where the 'cheap seats' are." Walter quipped. "It can make it difficult for them to get a proper reading on my heartrate, but it's quite worth it."

The two men laughed as Townsend sat down.

"Eisenmenger's disease." Walter said softly.

"Never heard of it."

"Neither had I, until they told me I had it." Walter admitted. "I need a heart-lung transplant."

Townsend nodded. "Not the easiest thing to get."

"Oh, I had the donors lined up in less than a day." Walter waved it off. "A word or two in the right ear, and you can get to the top of the donor lists. It's a big world. Someone with the right blood type dies every day. And the list is so anonymous, it's almost impossible for someone waiting for the call to notice they're waiting a few days longer."

"How much did you have to 'donate' to the hospital for that?"

"A new Trauma Centre." Walter smirked. "They'll treat hundreds of patients a day, so…" His smirk faltered. "Of course, that's just what you do. I've spoken to seven different surgeons. They all say I probably won't survive the operation… and it'll buy me three or four years, at most. My excesses have finally caught up with me."

"Four years?" Townsend sat down. "That's um… longer than I've got."

Walter blinked, stunned. "What?"

"It seems time caught up with us both." Townsend nodded. "I'm not just here to visit you. I had an appointment of my own." He looked sad. "It's 'Goodnight, Nurse'."

"What are they telling you?"

Townsend shook his head. "I can get a surgeon by tomorrow, if I put my name forward. I'm not going to."

"Why not?"

"Because I'm eighty six, twice divorced, with no kids… And what's another year?" Townsend looked at the table between them, and reached across to lift the cloche off Walter's plate. "I might have known you wouldn't eat the standard stuff."

"A lobster frittata with a white truffle reduction." Walter nodded. "You should see what I eat for dinners."

"And I'm sure your heart appreciates the flavor." Townsend countered.

"What difference does that make anymore?" Walter shot back. "So, you got a plan?"

"For what comes next?" Townsend grinned. "I've taken an awful lot out of the world… and it suddenly dawned on me that maybe it was too much."

"Yeah?"

"Well, unless they're wrong, and you really *can* take it with you, it's not like I'm saving for my retirement or anything."

"We still showed them, Townie." Walter chuckled.

Townsend put on a brave face. "I'm giving it all away."

"What?" Walter laughed.

"It's not like I need it. When people like us say 'we've lost everything' it's still a hundred times what some schmuck with a shovel can get." Townsend stole his wineglass and took a sip. "The way I figure it, people like us don't do the things we do because we expect to see heaven. Until now, that didn't seem like a problem."

"Don't tell me you're getting superstitious."

"You're not?" Townsend argued. "I never gave much thought to what was in that 'undiscovered country', but it's all I can think about now; since it's all I've got left." He pushed the glass back. "I've done my share of the taking. If my last act is to give it all away… I don't

31

know, maybe that'll do for a legacy."

"Sounds to me like you're trying to buy your way into heaven." Walter commented.

"I prefer to think of it as 'negotiating for the ultimate deal'. Is that so unreasonable, given that the deal is pretty much done, one way or another?"

Walter said nothing to that. He didn't agree, but there was no point arguing.

"Have you spoken to Walt?" Townsend asked.

"My son? We spoke on the phone last night. It… ended, as most conversations between us do."

"Didn't tell him, did you?"

"No." Walter confessed.

Silence. Finally, Townsend broke it. "What did you mean, before? When you said 'we showed them'?"

Walter smirked again. "My first personal physician? He told me I was on a suicidal course, more than forty years ago. I outlived that quack and sucked every last drop out of the good life. *Real* life."

Townsend sniffed. "It's oddly liberating, giving it all away, knowing I'll never have to deal again. I feel like Santa Claus. 'You get a donation, and you get a pony, and you get a new clinic, and you get a new house; and here, have a homeless shelter'. For my swan song, I'm going out with some class."

Walter forced himself to take a bite, let the luxurious flavor roll around his mouth. "Me? I don't plan on going out at all."

~ooO0Ooo~

"Mister Milne." Walter gestured for him to sit. "I appreciate your promptness."

"I'm aware of how valuable your time is, Mister Emmerson." Milne said politely. "Even more so now than usual."

"Indeed." Walter nodded. "You're aware, I hope, that I'm not a man to take fools lightly."

"Nosir."

"And you should also be aware that I've already run off a few sham artists who were hoping to take advantage of my… medical status to run a long con."

"You can be sure, my company is the real thing."

"And yet, you do not advertise."

"No point. We don't have the facilities for the whole human race. And for what we're offering, they couldn't afford it anyway. And to be perfectly honest, there are still some legal hurdles that nobody accounted for. Hurdles that we can clear, but you can't wait for."

Walter nodded. "How does this work?"

"You give us power of attorney, so that we can make the arrangements for your remains. We can either wait for nature to take its unfair and indiscriminate course, or we can induce, in such a way as to improve your odds of revival. It's actually not that different from the way a surgeon can stop your heart long enough to operate or transplant. We just keep you that way a fair bit longer." Milne walked him through it. "Your body will be preserved, and the whole company is kept in various trusts, to insure that the project does not end with any one manager."

"And what's to stop you from just pulling the plug?"

"Your fee will be put into another trust, which pays out at regular intervals. Our legal department is mandated to make sure we are following the arrangement. If we want you to, pardon the phrase, 'live up' to your end of the bargain, we have to act in good faith." Milne brought out a folder, about the width of a small-city phonebook. "Our 'fine print'. For your perusal." Mailne sat back in the plush leather chair. "I think it best for all concerned that you be as certain of our service as we are."

Walter was pleased with that. "Thank you. I shall give it due attention, given what's at stake."

"And that leaves only the unpleasantness of our fee." Milne took out an expensive fountain pen and wrote down a number, sliding the page across the table at him.

Walter read the number. "I've always said, if you have to ask what something costs, you can't really afford it. This, to *me*, still seems like a lot."

"And what else do you plan to spend it on?" Milne countered.

"Yes. 'Your money, or your life'." Walter scorned. "That's what you say when you're mugging someone."

"Or when you work for a private hospital." Milne fired back with a smile. "Walter, we're offering you a chance to cheat death. Something that has never once, in history, been available to anyone. It's not even available now. That's why Cryonics exist. You have it in your power to be one of the few people from our century who could live forever. And really, what's money compared to that?"

"You expect me to live forever with nothing?"

"Not at all. We're a full service company." Milne promised smoothly. "We've made an accounting of your diverse and many holdings, and believe it will be a relatively simple matter to secure them."

Walter sat up straighter, the machines beeping a little faster. If there was a con-game being played, this was it. "You've already examined my portfolio."

"Sir, we don't offer this to anyone who can't afford it." Milne promised. "This is about the future, and securing yourself a place in it. Ask yourself, if this technology had been available seventy years ago, who would have predicted this world? IBM was a company that nobody had ever heard of. Then technology evolved, and they became extremely profitable. Google, Amazon, and Apple? Who had heard of them, even thirty years ago?"

"How long do you expect me to be… under?" Walter asked.

"To beat the death barrier? Realistically, fifty years. Maybe less. Needless to say, people are working on it with due diligence." Milne nodded. "Nobody knows what that world will look like. Oil and Coal were some of the most stable stocks and properties until ten years ago. Now they're in freefall. Technology and market trends changed. You know what became *more* valuable in the last hundred years? The same things that always did. Gold, diamonds, land. They're expensive, but they're the one thing that's future-proof. If you had to keep your wealth someplace safe and reliable for that long, what would you invest in?"

Walter considered that, and turned to the document. "It feels like science fiction."

"It is. But so is eternal life." Milne nodded.

Walter thought hard for a few minutes, but the spike of pain that went through his chest was something he couldn't argue with. "Alright. I accept."

"There is… regretfully, one last hurdle to clear." Milne said evenly. "Your son, Walt? Typically, we don't offer this service to people with living heirs. The kind of costs we're talking about… Your son stands to inherit a vast fortune. And it will be spent in another direction. If you can offer my people assurances that we aren't going to spend the rest of his life fighting for our fee…"

"You want me to disinherit my son?"

"That's your choice, sir." Milne countered. "But we

don't offer 'family deals'. Provision could be made to *include* your son, of course; but he'll either be a major legal hassle, or our next customer."

Walter hesitated.

"That doubt, right there? Either get rid of it or bid me good day, right now." Milne sensed his hesitation. "A thousand years from now, all of us are dust. Except for the ones that find a way to take control of their own death and defeat it. You're charging into the unknown, and the one thing we can promise you, is that you'll be leaving behind the life you knew. How many people can say they faced death on their own terms and *won*? A thousand years from now, everything we did will be meaningless. A thousand years from now, maybe everyone will live forever. But given what it'll likely cost to succeed, you can count on the fact that it'll be the ultimate prize. The number of people in this century who can take a shot at seeing it? More people have walked on the moon. This is a very exclusive club, Walter. And if you have doubts, then I can offer it to someone else. Your choice."

Walter gave a single nod, liking that idea. "I've dedicated my entire adult life to making the world bend to my choices. Death is the only opponent I have yet to beat." He picked up the file. "I'll have my people study this, and make the necessary arrangements. If your fine print is as advertised, I'll be in touch…" Pain lanced through his chest unexpectedly. "Uh. And soon."

~oo0Ooo~

The work took a few weeks. Walter's legal team had taken apart the contracts, and decided it was a legitimate offer. His diverse holdings were liquidated and put into trusts, invested into commodities that would be valuable for centuries.

His doctors had told him that he still had a few

months. Clearing the final legal and financial hurdles hadn't been easy. Informing his son was harder still. Walter wasn't going to be 'that' parent. His son would always be looked after, but 'looked after' wasn't the same as 'obscenely wealthy'; and Walt was raw about it.

Walter had shared these thoughts with Milne, who had told him not to stress about it. There were several people preserved already, and some of them had made provision for their children to be the same.

"Assuming, of course, that they don't crack the problem in his lifetime." Milne had said with a smile. "You may be able to make it up to your boy across eternity."

"If they don't crack it by then, and if Walt can't afford your rates, I'll never see my son again." Walter said quietly.

Milne studied him. "I told you: If you have doubts, now's the time to listen to them, because once we give you the injection, you won't be able to. Immortality is a one way street."

Walter felt another painful spike in his chest. "The pain is constant now, and even my superior breeding can ignore endless pain for only so long. Do it. Now."

Milne stepped out to give his nurses and doctors the go-ahead, and Walter took in a deep breath, letting himself take in the 'last sights' as they began the injection. The silk sheets that surrounded him, the fresh-cut flowers that perfumed the room every second, the gold frames on the impressionist originals that cost a fortune to be moved into his private hospital room.

On the big screen TV, the Business Channel was suddenly filled with a familiar face. Townsend was in the news. Walter immediately turned up the volume.

"...large donations to various social causes. So much so that the Board of Directors at Coatesworth Industries

moved to have him declared incompetent. For more on this, our Financial Editor. Dan?"

"Nothing's like to come of that challenge, since he's being careful to give only his own money. Coatesworth sold off all his personal holdings, and his own stocks and bonds; while releasing his medical records, showing he has less than six months to live. A revelation that has calmed rumors, without making his Directors feel better. Even if they challenge this philanthropy in court, there won't be much left for them."

"Expressions of gratitude and condolence are pouring in from across the world. The new Coatesworth Foundation will provide medicine to thousands of people in low-income areas on a weekly basis, as well as the largest number of privately funded homeless shelters in Europe. A man with nothing to lose, the legacy of Townsend Chalcott Coatesworth is assured, as-"

Walter muted the TV. "Milne, bring my notepad over, would you?" He croaked. "I want to leave a note for my lawyer, regarding the last of my financials."

"Walter, there's almost none of your financials left. They've all been liquidated for this."

"I still have a few hundred thousand." Walter gestured at the TV. "Those people that Townsend is helping? They're..." His chest spiked again. "They're not worth much, and they're easily replaceable. But if they want to spend their tiny lives running around like desperate worker bees, I can at least buy them some socks. It's not like I'll ever have to think about them again, where I'm going..." His breathing started to slow. "After all, none of them could hope to afford a chance at eternal life, right?"

"This is true." Milne said gravely.

Walter scribbled down the note, feeling his pen grow heavy, his grip become slack...

Should I pray? The thought came to him distantly, as his eyes closed and his brain shut down. *I'm not a believer... But now that I'm facing... my own death... I don't-*

The light reaching his eyelids suddenly became warmer and brighter. Walter took a deep breath. The breath came easily and naturally. He didn't open his eyes, as he had learned a long time ago. Always get your bearings before you let anyone in the room know that you were aware of them.

He could sense someone several feet away, not moving. So, someone was there for him. Walter took another breath, and noticed the perfume of oranges and the sounds of birds. The flowers in his hospital room had been lilacs, not Orange Blossoms.

Did it work? He thought to himself, almost hopeful.

He opened his eyes and sat up. It was daytime, and he was outside, in a large garden. There were buildings beyond a grove of orange trees, and a single tower the reached hundreds of stories into the air; though the architecture was something completely foreign. He could see people having a picnic over in the distance, and his vision was sharp enough to notice that there were several children. More than the usual proportion.

Walter was very analytical, and was already calculating what that meant. Why had he awoken here? Were those children patients? Was it a school trip? Hospitals didn't have gardens this size. Only the very high end ones had the luxury of a meditation garden at all...

"Hello."

Walter turned. The newcomer was a young man, about twenty five. Walter sized him up as being an intern, and not one of the doctors in charge. It boded well, that he didn't have a team of surgeons on hand to meet him, and that they'd revived him in a park instead of a Critical Care Ward. "How long?" He asked immediately, and marveled at how steady and strong his voice sounded. It was a younger man's voice.

The young man blinked. "I'm sorry?"

"How long have I been dead?" Walter clarified, impatient.

The young man, not much older than a teenage boy, really; blinked owlishly, and smiled at him. "Well, usually that's the hardest part to get through when we do this."

"I'm sure." Walter drawled. "But I'm not a fool. Now, how long?"

"Well, I looked you up, and you were reported as deceased in 2017. By your calendar, it is now midway through the 23rd Century."

Walter put a hand to his chest. "And my heart? It's… well?"

"Like new; same as every other part." The young man smiled.

Walter looked around. "So, is it just the one thing fixed, or… everything?" He didn't want to appear ungrateful, but the whole point of the experiment was to see how long he could increase his longevity. Some estimates said the death barrier would be broken completely within half a century. If more than two had passed... "By which I mean: How long am I likely to last?"

"Well, that's up to you." The young man said warmly. "But there's no reason it can't last… forever and ever."

"IT WORKED!" Walter threw up his arms and let out a war whoop that got the attention of everyone in the garden. "HAHAHA! IT WORKED! I DID IT!"

Walter beamed at the world, feeling exalted; full of energy and vitality. He'd made death yield to him. All that was left was to…

To what? Walter asked himself in awe at what he'd achieved. *What does one do for an encore?*

Chapter Four: In The Beginning

James didn't know what to make of this. He'd have assumed the woman was lying. It took him no time at all to pick her pockets clean, and he waited until she turned to admire the view as they walked before he could examine his prize. Nothing in her pockets but a green piece of paper with his name on it, and a flat piece of black glass. No money, no papers, no weapon. The book in her hand was a Bible, which surprised him; but he'd heard of how powerful the Church was in Roma.

"So, tell me if these words sound familiar." Karen said lightly as they walked. "'*In the beginning, God created the heavens and the earth.*'"

James froze for half a heartbeat. Her opening salvo was to quote scripture? "I believe I've heard that before."

"Good. That will help." Karen nodded. "I'm about to give you the short version of a very long story; and then we'll discuss where you fit into it."

James nodded. He wasn't surprised. Wealthy and influential people liked putting on airs. Most of them liked explaining 'where you fit' without any input from the actual people involved. If this woman wanted to do the same, he could wait; and keep his eyes open until he figured things out.

"When the world began; it was made as a Paradise. A place where people could live, and never get sick, and never get old, and never be in danger; and never ever die. But there was a 'snake in the garden', quite literally. So when God told His creation to enjoy eternal life, and be his children forever, Satan stepped in and told them that God was keeping them prisoner. I don't know how much you know about what came next, but that was the point where the human race, admittedly a very small group at that point, voted unanimously to be in charge of their own world; and follow Satan's lead in rebellion. They made that choice for their children too."

James listened with half an ear, eyes taking in everything subtly. If she was leading him into an ambush, it was a well hidden one. Irsu had split off from them quickly, apparently with an appointment of his own. James could tell at once that he had been there only for the protection of the woman; which was good, since James couldn't relax around the huge man.

"At that point, God had a choice to make. See, He was in the right, and Satan was wrong, but a challenge had been made, and it had to be answered. Were humans only serving God selfishly? Should God make decisions for people or not?"

"I thought the upside of being God was that you got your way." James pointed out, not really giving it his full attention.

"Before I came here, so did I." Karen nodded at that. "You ever see a Prize Fight? Two boxers in a ring?"

James nodded. There had been such Tournaments on his ship. They helped cool tempers and keep grudges from lingering.

"Imagine someone challenges The Champion." Karen reasoned. "Says he's a liar, and doesn't deserve the Title. So The Champ steps into the Ring with him... And as soon as the match starts, the Champ pulls a gun and shoots the Challenger down in cold blood on the spot. Does that seem like a way to win in good faith? God was in the same spot. He could have snuffed out Adam and Eve; Satan too. But that wouldn't prove him right; it just would have made him a tyrant."

James finally looked at her. "I had a Captain like that once. Disagreement was met with summary execution."

"Did you think he was a good Captain? Someone who cared about his crew?"

James set his jaw. "No."

"Then you also understand the reasoning behind letting the world play out as it did. God stepped back, let Humans make their choices." Karen continued. "What followed was six thousand years of the human race going from bad, to worse, to catastrophic." She slowed her step to look at him. "What you said, about how the point of 'being God' is that you get your way. Do you think the world you know was what God wanted?"

James looked away, unable to meet those flawless eyes. "I stopped believing in God a long time ago. His 'Grand Plan' wasn't one I wanted any part of."

"That was my thought too, back then." Karen agreed, and opened the Bible that had never left her hand. "Now, that's the background. The important part is this: God's intention for the world never changed. Paradise was always the original plan, and as you so correctly pointed out, the point of being God is: Nobody can tell you 'no'. So the world fell apart and became a horror show, but that was a detour. While that was happening, God still had followers. Always a minority, in a world that was at the mercy of evil powers, but he never left his people alone. So, he provided a Ransom."

James froze at that word. "What?" He grated. "A ransom? Ransoming what?"

"Us." Karen noted the strength of his reaction, but didn't dwell on it. "The original Plan was to have perfect people living in paradise forever. How do you start that, when all you have are imperfect people? Scripture says: *'all his ways are justice'*, so he needed a way to balance the scales. We were all stuck with the consequences of Adam and Eve's choice; so how could we pay the price? Consider what was lost: A perfect person created by God directly; who elected to leave God's service. How do you balance that?"

James was listening now. "Very well. How?"

"With a perfect person who elected to *stay* in God's Service, no matter what." Karen told him. "An equal and opposite to what Adam did."

~oo0Ooo~

David and Walter were having the same conversation.

"And it couldn't be done. No matter how many of us lowly sinners tried to earnestly serve Jehovah; we couldn't measure up; for the simple reason that we *weren't* perfect as Adam was." David held out the Bible. "1 Corinthians 15:21,22: '*For since death came through a man, resurrection of the dead also comes through a man. For just as in Adam all are dying, so also in the Christ all will be made alive*'."

Walter said nothing to that, already looking for a way out of the conversation. "Well, this is all very interesting, but what does it have to do with-"

"We're almost there, Walter; I promise." David told him patiently. "You had money back in the day? You tell me: What would something 'perfect' be worth? Not just very good, but actually, *literally* perfect? Like a diamond, for instance? A perfect diamond?"

It was the first question Walter took seriously. "No such thing, in my experience. High Quality and Low Quality to be sure, but perfect?"

"Exactly." David agreed. "Imagine you had a genuinely *perfect* diamond. The only one in the world. How would you replace it? You can't trade something perfect for something imperfect. Not for any number of imperfect, in fact. So when we lost a perfect man, God had to provide one. So he sent his Son. A Perfect Man."

"Why?" Walter pounced. "Why should he? If, as you say, the fault was always ours; then why did God have to go out of his way to provide a balance? If the world didn't want Him, why not let them have what they want and be done?"

David smiled. "Love."

~oo0Ooo~

Axti was getting a similar lesson from Irsu.

"Colossians 1:13: *'He rescued us from the authority of the darkness and transferred us into the kingdom of his beloved Son'*." Irsu read to Atxi. "The whole history of the world has been a case study, in who humans are to obey. Themselves, or Jehovah God. At all points through time, there has been a minority of people determined to do what God asks of them; and on the other side there was Satan, manipulating a world apart from God, turning people more and more ferocious, in an effort to break that minority apart."

Atxi said nothing for a long moment. "You're saying… That my… That our…"

"That the world was *'lying in the power of the wicked one'*." Irsu said gently. "Think of the rivers of blood spilled, the greed that took and took, every passionate religion, every Tyrant that rose to power. All of it was a way to divide the world against itself, and keep turning up the heat." Irsu nodded. "Thousands of years of expansion, advancement, history, and exploitation… Finally leading to the point where the whole world just couldn't survive if things continued. And the whole time, Jehovah God kept his hands off the world and its leadership; just to make that point."

"You say 'false religion', but you're talking about mine, aren't you?" Atxi pushed, not liking it.

Irsu explained gently. "Well, does your faith give a better reason for wickedness in the world?" He pressed.

"That an illness was 'punishment', or 'the will of the gods'?" He turned the book to her again, though Atxi couldn't read the writing. "James 1:13 says: *'When under trial, let no one say: 'I am being tried by God.' For with evil things God cannot be tried, nor does he himself try anyone'*."

~oo0Ooo~

"I mean, just think about what that means, for a second." Karen smiled winningly. "All the people who rage at God over natural disasters, loss of loved ones, crime and punishment, misfortune and accident and … And none of it was God's Will. In the space of five minutes and three scriptures, we just *disproved* how many 'Holy' Men?"

James smothered a dirty grin. "It's as sound reasoning as any, I suppose, but what does that have to do with… well, any of this?"

Karen took a deep breath. "Right. The next part is kind of a big deal, and there's really no way to ease you into it." She opened her Bible again. "Now, I told you that God's ultimate Goal for the world hasn't changed. A paradise where everyone lives forever, as faithful, happy servants; granted eternal youth, and peace, and plenty; with a loving, benevolent God in charge. Christ made it possible for people to live in that Kingdom, forgiven of sins… And now, at last, we are."

James paused. "We are… what?"

"Living in that Kingdom." She turned the Bible to him. "Revelation 21:4. *"He will wipe out every tear from their eyes, and death will be no more, neither will mourning nor outcry nor pain be any more. The former things have passed away."*

James blinked again, slowly. "Miss Karen…" He said seriously. "Where am I?"

"You are now in that Paradise. God's promised return

to Eden." She was watching him carefully, waiting for his reaction. "Welcome Back."

James thought back, trying to process. His duel with Smitty had left him wounded. But Smitty was a Believer… He'd told James a few scriptures. One or two that Karen had read to him. He ran a hand along his side; where Smitty had stuck him. There was no pain, no scar… James had all sorts of aches from old injuries. They weren't there now. "I… I'm dead? Am I in heaven?"

"You are not in heaven. This is Earth. You were dead. You aren't anymore." She tapped the scripture in Revelation. "This prophecy has come to pass." She put the Bible away. "As we've established, God's goal was for humans to live forever on earth. Why would he take people to Heaven? Heaven was never part of the plan for human beings. You've heard the Lazarus story, yes? Jesus said the day would come when everyone would hear his call, and leave their tombs. For you, *this* is that day."

James started to say something cutting in return, and her hand flashed up to lay a finger over his lips. "Big moment, I know. Take a minute before you say 'no'."

James did so. The woman was far too attractive to be human. James had heard tell of the Sirens, luring sailors to their death on the rocks, but he'd never believed such things. Certainly, a Siren never preached the Gospel.

Does that make her an Angel, then? James asked himself carefully.

When they reached the small township, that thought vanished. Everyone looked like her. There wasn't a single person older than about twenty five, all of them looking flawless. James was surprised. Even in the most exclusive places, with the most money and the best doctors, there was always a few people with blemishes.

It was why they made their faces up so heavily. He didn't see any rouge or face powder here; for the women or the men.

There were no bad teeth, or thinning hair, no sign of the pox, or plague… In fact, there were no doctors or signs of illness at all. Even in communities with no Plague, there should have been some beggars asking for cash. James couldn't remember the last town he had visited without someone trying to peddle a curative of some kind...

James shivered. There was something very wrong with this place.

~oo00oo~

"Are you very sure?" Axti asked, yet again.

"Quite sure." Irsu promised. "I know, it's not what you expected; but I assure you that every word I've said is the Truth."

Atxi was trembling. "The Christian God?" She breathed. "It was the Christian Conquistadors that came to slaughter my people. I served the Gods that fought *against* them. There's been a mistake! I'm not meant to be here! I was to be with Huitzilopochtli!"

Irsu looked sympathetic. "Atxi, this is going to be hard for you to hear, but that was never a possibility."

Atxi glared at him. She had never been an angry person, but this was pushing her.

"I know it's not a comfort right now." Irsu told her. "But I'm sure you can appreciate how many people have been through just such a shocking revelation as this. I was too. The Gods I worshiped were long forgotten even before *you* were born, let alone any of the people who welcomed me *here*."

That caught Atxi off guard. "Really?"

He smiled sadly. "It took me a long time to shake my

fear of Hathor. Her vengeful hunger for human souls was said to be terrible. But in time, I came to see the world, and what I had believed, for what they really were."

There was silence as she considered his words, looking around. It was a beautiful day. She had grown up in a country with jungles and swamps alike, and this one was much more open. But the sky was far more vibrant, the green plants were leafy and healthy in a way she'd never seen… There were animals here and there; all looking relaxed and friendly. There was a real sense of peace and harmony.

"I don't believe you are lying." She said finally, considering him carefully. "But that doesn't mean you're right. You are, quite honestly, quite earnestly, telling me that everything I believe is wrong. Everyone I know and trust would say the same about you. When two honest people give opposite stories, how do you choose? How do I know which holy man is in error, if neither of them are being deliberately dishonest?"

Irsu nodded. "I understand. Atxi, the thing you have to understand is that I don't have to convince you. Nor am I trying to."

Atxi just looked at him. "Everything you've said to me since we met has been trying to convince me."

Irsu smiled warmly. "Heh. I suppose so. But for all the… the joy that this world brings, the thing you have to remember is that nobody can tell you what to believe. If you decide you want nothing to do with us, we can't force you."

Long silence.

"This is a test." Atxi said finally. "Huitzilopochtli is testing me. Testing my loyalty. I don't know why having my heart cut out wasn't proof enough of my faith, but-"

"Having your WHAT?" Irsu was stunned.

~oo0Ooo~

On the whole, Walter was more pleased than annoyed. He felt better than he'd felt in years. The new century had apparently broken the death *and* the aging barrier completely. The number of people he'd seen who looked older than thirty could be counted on one hand. The air smelled sweet, and as far as he could tell, there was nobody begging for money, or trying to sell anything to passerby.

The one confusing point was his guide. The boy couldn't be more than twenty-five, *if* that; and he was apparently something of a religious nut. By itself, that wasn't a concern. A lot of the high end private medical centers were religiously backed.

Walter was only half listening to the kid's pitch. The idea that God had taken over the world and made it a Paradise was laughable. If the actual Lord was running the earth, there would be far more churches and religious icons around. Walter hadn't seen one Cross or Saint anywhere since he'd woken up. "So, Mister Thorne-."

"David, please."

Walter nodded. "David, then. It's clear I have some catching up to do. If you could direct me to the nearest bank, I can start to get my bearings; figure out where my holdings stand..."

"You think your account is still open after almost three hundred years?" David smirked. "All financial institutions were brought to ruin on A-Day."

"Glad I missed that day, then. In any event, I had prepared for it." Walter shivered. "My people were under instruction to liquidate everything upon my preservation, and transfer it into gold. That way, whatever form the currency took, I'd always have a top commodity."

David blinked slowly. "Your 'preservation'?" He

shook his head. "No, never mind. Gold won't help either. The whole system collapsed. Economic, political, even religious. Nothing outlasted A-Day except us."

David stared at the young man, brain refusing to process that, before he waved at the street. It may not have been a full on Metropolis anymore, but it was still a civilized township; with technology and buildings, and public works. "Then… who pays for all this?"

"Well, we do. Savings Banks are still there, given how long we live. But money is something of an… optional extra."

"Money. Optional." Walter repeated. He recognized all those words, but the sentence made no sense at all. "As in… optional?"

~oo0Ooo~

Irsu brought her to the Centre, and Atxi saw the tables. They were full to buckling with a huge array of food. Despite herself, she breathed in deeply. The spices and herbs were scenting the air, and the delicious aromas of fresh baked bread, and ripened fruits warred for dominance. Axti inhaled so much she almost coughed, trying to get more of it.

But as nice as it was to be there, Atxi was confused.

"Tialocan?" Atxi said, uncertain. "Am I in Tialocan?"

"No, this is New Roma." Irsu told her.

Atxi shook her head. "No, I mean… I was meant to go to the Sun. Tialocan is where the Water God lives. Tialoc takes his tributes to his Realm." She gestured at the table. "There's always food, and it's always Springtime, and there is always peace. But I wasn't taken by Water. I was meant to go to-" She stopped suddenly, seeing everyone looking at her with…

With what? She asked herself. She saw a long row of

people. All different skin colors, though they were all healthy, and all young. And everyone was smiling warmly at her; though it was clear they'd heard her words and didn't understand them. It certainly seemed like the Region of Tialoc, though she supposed she had never thought what any of the Thirteen Heavens should be like on her first day there.

"Everyone, this is Atxi." Irsu made introductions. "She just arrived half an hour ago."

The people along the table were suddenly looking at her with a strange mix of emotions. Some that had heard her speaking before now showed abject pity for her. Others were excited. All of them wore one kind of smile or another, both happy and sad; but all of the sadness seemed to be for her, rather than from any of them.

Irsu guided Atxi to a seat. "Please, help yourself to anything."

Atxi sat, and someone put a plate in front of her immediately. People were sneaking peeks at her, and she was sneaking peeks at them. They didn't look like her. She wondered if Tialocan was open to foreigners too. They had their own gods. Irsu had told her about his own, and She knew that some Foreign Gods refused to accept worshipers of others...

"Hi." A pretty woman with odd eyes sat beside her. "I'm Kasumi. What do you think so far?"

Atxi looked over the table. One or two fruit platters were familiar. There were some dishes that almost looked like the sort of thing her mother would make, or at least the same ingredients... But they were very few. "I don't really recognize much."

"The Gods you mentioned are Aztec. I don't imagine there's a lot of International delicacies on your menu." Kasumi said with a smile. "I'll walk you through it." She started pointing out things on the table, in all sorts of serving bowls and platters. "We have… French Onion Soup. Over here, from Italy, we have Pasta dishes, with an olive and tomato sauce… And this is called Paella, from Spain."

Atxi scowled at the dish in question. The reaction was immediate and automatic.

"But first, try this." Kasumi slid a small brown square onto Atxi's plate. "Usually, you have this as a treat at the end of the meal, but I think we can make an exception."

On the other side of her, Irsu chuckled. "I think we can consider today's lunch to be a celebration." Everyone was beaming at her, and Atxi picked up a spoon automatically. "It's not every day you come back from the dead."

She started to take a bite, when that comment made her freeze. Irsu had mentioned something like that before, but she hadn't really processed it. She was in the next world. How was that 'coming back'? She looked back at the odd food. "What is it?"

"It's called 'fudge'." Kasumi said with a smile. "Your accent and references say 'South American', so you've probably had cacao beans before. This is what we do with them in this world."

Atxi took a careful bite. She went still when it hit her tongue. Then she took a much bigger bite. "I *am* in Tialocan!" Atxi breathed. "A table laid by the gods!"

Kasumi smothered a laugh. "Well, one thing at a time."

Atxi inhaled the chocolate treat quickly. She noticed the rest of the table smiling at her. Their expressions were so earnest that she almost smiled back, but she was still unnerved.

~oo0Ooo~

"So, let me show you around. We can start there, at

the Centre." David said with a smile.

Walter started moving, feeling an easy pace and strength in his limbs that he hadn't felt in years. After a few moments, he realized he was alone, and looked back. David was coming along behind him, in no particular hurry. "Is something wrong?"

"I was about to ask you the same thing." David said with a knowing smile. "Are you in a rush?"

"Well, no…"

"There's plenty of day left. Time is on your side now. There's no hurry. Look around, breathe deep." David enthused. "Seriously, Walter; take it all in. You're in a world where there's no crime, no poverty, no violence of any kind. There's nobody sick, nobody starving."

"However did you manage it?" Walter asked, marveling. A cure to his heart trouble was one thing. Breaking the Death Barrier entirely would have been the ideal, but if this utopia was as advertised, Walter had cheated far more than his doctor's prognosis.

"Well, that's the really important part, isn't it?" David said, and pulled out his Bible again. A book that Walter had instantly recognized, even centuries later.

"Oh." Walter's eyes flashed, just a little disappointed. "I'm sorry, I'm not really a churchgoer. Not habitually, anyway."

"Most people weren't, in your time." David nodded. "Or so I am told, I wasn't there."

The comment made Walter's sudden healthy heart tick a touch faster. David's 'lesson' implied that the Church was a more common thing, now. If religion was a big part of the world of the future, then something fundamental had changed. Walter was trying to process that, and almost missed David's next comment.

"Remember, Jesus did very little of his work in a

Temple. He went where the people were. There was a time people like me went door to door. Nowadays, we don't have doors for newcomers at first. You'd be surprised how many of our people learn the most over a cup of coffee, or at a picnic." David smiled. "My dad taught me over a card game. You'd be amazed how many scriptures a kid can memorize for thirty points." He looked the question to Walter. "Of course, I'd imagine you'd prefer something a little more grown-up?"

"Thank you, no." Walter said politely. "It's clear I need a pretty extensive catch-up, but I'd like to start with more practical matters."

David just smiled. "You'd be surprised how practical it is, these days."

A comment that did nothing to lessen Walter's concern.

~oo0Ooo~

James didn't know where he was. He had no idea how he had been in a fight for his life, a mile out to sea; and then woke up here, in an apparently Italian Province; with this woman as a guide.

James was a pirate. When he was being lead somewhere he didn't plan for himself, it was usually a deathtrap, and he'd already fallen for one of those today.

"Now, these people heading in? They're from a local congregation, but not our own." Karen kept a running commentary as she gave the tour. "There are over a dozen congregations in this area, so the meetings run day and night. The Community Centre is where we hold meetings, classes, studies, public events… and of course the Dormitory. We can have lunch while these people have their meeting, and then we can do the same."

James saw she was leading him to a crowd. A crowd meant lawmen. A crowd meant witnesses. A crowd meant plenty of people who could trap him. So he had to escape. And since he wasn't armed, and had no backup, there was only one way to do that.

James cocked his arm out to Karen as a gentleman, and she took it with a smile. He dug his arm closer, holding her wrist. If she wanted to make trouble, it wouldn't last.

She didn't even blink. "James, you haven't heard a word I've said, have you?"

"I heard every word, I just don't believe it." James said, keeping his face polite for those nearby. "And I don't believe you do either."

"No?"

James gestured at the Community Centre, and the crowd of smartly-dressed people threading their way into it. "I don't doubt that's the religion here, but it's not like everyone is devout. The world doesn't work like that. I've been in places where folks are locked in stocks for taking the lord's name in vain. They're the same places where Bishops would tell me which brothels were most discreet."

"Not anymore."

"Trust me, Miss Karen. People are made of their sins. The veneer of civility is thin at the best of times, and if you've made it thicker, it just means the sleaze is deeper and stronger beneath it. So, no. I won't be attending your Sermons."

Karen glanced at him. "Let go of my arm, and I'll make a bet with you. If I can convince you that the people here are genuine in their feelings, and not just going through the motions, then you stay for the Meeting. If I can't, I'll walk you outta here."

James thought for a moment. "I'll take that bet. But how can you do that?"

Karen gave him an unsettling smile, and suddenly started to sing. *"We thank you, Jehovah, each day and each night-"*

James actually took a step back at the sheer unexpectedness of the move. But what shocked him more, was that almost a hundred people suddenly started singing along.

"That you shed upon us your precious light.

We thank you that we have the privilege of prayer,

That we can approach you with ev'ry care."

James looked around like he was surrounded by people from another planet. For the first time, he really looked at their faces. He'd noted their clothes, checked for weapons and signs of wealth; but this was the first time he'd looked at their faces.

They were smiling. Actually smiling. Actually happy. James had smiled like a shark in a knife-fight, and he'd kept his best poker-face on when staring down lawmen in five different nations. He'd lied to the very worst of the very best.

And these were total strangers breaking out into song. Karen had stopped, just watching the crowd with him. It hadn't been a few people playing along with the pretty lady. They hadn't stopped their steady walk into the Centre. They just… wanted to sing along.

"We thank you, our God, for the honor to preach

About your great name and the truth to teach.

We thank you that soon all earth's woes will be past,

While your Kingdom blessings, forever last."

Karen took his hand, and led him into the Centre. He didn't fight it. "These days, it doesn't take much. It's a miracle, and everyone gets to be part of it." She said to him quietly. "You walk around with a song in your heart, it doesn't take much to get it out there."

~oo0Ooo~

Accepting David as his guide was an easy decision. The young man couldn't be older than mid twenties, and his expression was far too trusting and naive. There was no chance that this man was going to try and con him out of anything. Walter had traveled internationally many times, and knew how to spot a hustler. Any undesirable sort could become his guide, and choosing a fresh-faced young man with Caucasian skin that spoke excellent English was always Walter's preferred choice.

There was a song being sung outside, which surprised Walter. He'd seen church meetings before; though he'd rarely attended. Some of them had singing groups to draw attention from passerby, but from the sound of it, lots of people were singing impulsively. It was odd, but not unpleasant. If the crowd was singing along, then it meant they were happy; so it wasn't likely to cause trouble.

The Ministry Centre was clearly the heart of the small town. Walter explored as David checked a notice board and left him to 'take care of a small matter', suggesting Walter look around and 'enjoy a meal outside'. There was a main auditorium, with hundreds of chairs facing a stage, but there were several other rooms too. Smaller meeting rooms, some that looked like classrooms. The library intrigued him. It was open to the public, with all manner of reference books, some religious, some secular; and multiple terminals.

Walter went to the terminal, which was enough like a computer for him to use it. He looked up his Firm. There was no trace of it. He looked up his bank. No trace of that either. He looked up his family members. He found their names, but they were listed as 'Deceased', which he learned, with some deduction, was different from whatever he'd been. Whoever these people were, they didn't except his son to be 'raised up' as Walter had been. His father and mother, listed as 'Pending' were also not among the living, though it seemed the people here thought that would change.

With the initial search for the familiar a bust, he suddenly realized he was hungry; and went looking for a cafeteria. He found a long table, outside in the Plaza. The Centre had three wings, the building shaped like a flat 'U', with a garden in the middle, where there were almost twenty people. Walter came out just as they were all leaving, apparently having finished their lunch.

Still, there was plenty of food left on the serving platters, and Walter found a clean plate; helping himself.

The food was unbelievable. If Walter hadn't believed he was centuries ahead of his time before, the food alone would have convinced him. It was a five star meal, and Walter was halfway through seconds before it dawned on him that he was eating the leftovers.

He went inside, and found everyone from the table washing dishes. Someone looked at him inquiringly, and he moved on quickly, before he got handed a dishtowel.

~oo0Ooo~

"Who was that?" Atxi asked as the older man ducked out. It occurred to her that he was the only one who looked older than any of them.

"Don't recognize him." Irsu admitted. "But you're not the only newly Returned one. Twenty thousand per day come back."

Atxi nodded, and looked around the kitchen. There were things here she didn't recognize. Everything was shiny and smooth. Every countertop, every shelf was made of some kind of metal. The Aztecs had the gift of metalworking, but she'd seen nothing like this before. The lights fascinated her. She knew this room was where the incredible food came from, but she had seen no sign of anything she recognized.

The others let her look around, opening every cupboard, looking at the produce, of which there was plenty. There was more variety in this place than in any of the marketplaces Atxi had grown up with. Even the Temples had nothing like this. It was more than just the amount of produce: It was all new. Everything seemed fresh and crisp; so full of flavor that Atxi could feel her tongue tingling from the smells alone.

"Psalms 145 says *'You open your hand And satisfy the desire of every living thing'*." Irsu said to her gently. "And that includes you."

Despite herself, Atxi smiled. "Sounds lovely." She admitted. "Though I have no idea what any of this means for me."

"Well, we have a meeting in about twenty minutes; so you can get to know some of the people, hear a little more." Irsu smiled. "And after that, I'll show you to your room."

"My room?" Atxi repeated.

"Did you think we were just going to leave you homeless?"

~oo0Ooo~

Walter went looking for a bathroom, and found one in short order. There was a mirror there; and he took a look at himself. The clothing he wore was a simple tunic and pants. Comfortable, modest, and durable. More than anything he'd ever been issued in the hospital; but with none of the style or silks that suggested money.

And then there was his reflection itself. Walter still looked about the same age, but… He was wearing it so much better. The greying hair, lines around his eyes were still there… But full of vitality, with no trace of illness. His capped teeth were restored and natural. His glasses were not needed. He felt like he could run a marathon. His age felt skin deep, and his skin was without blemish.

(**Author's Note:** *In the previous two volumes, I'd made it clear that those who do not accept God into their lives, even in Paradise, do not have eternal life. The reason for this is two-fold. One: It seems logical, as it follows the example set by Adam and Eve, the only two people who rejected God while in Paradise already. After their rebellion, they grew old and died, but did not die immediately. Two: It gives everyone a practical way to acknowledge that they have to make a change in their lives. Our publications note that as ruler of the New World, Jesus would have the authority to remove opposition; but there's nothing to indicate how. As I'd already committed to this method in my own series, I had to account for people resurrected, after having died at an already advanced age; since there's no indication that people will be Returned at a specific age. To quote Job 33:25 'Let his flesh become fresher than in youth; Let him return to the days of his youthful vigor.' Return. Not arrive.*

This is the best result I can come up with; though it is mainly my own invention; based on some Biblical references; and some deductive reasoning. In the last two books of the Series, it's not a major plot point. In this one, it's almost the central theme. Whatever the true method turns out to be in Paradise, we can be sure that all people will have a proper chance to make an informed decision; and it will be handled with Compassion and Justice.)

Walter was growing more confused with each passing hour. He believed what David had been telling him about the passage of time, and he'd gone to sleep hoping to wake up in perfect health; even if it took centuries. But the world he'd woken into seemed a blatant contradiction. Advanced technology, but no money? World peace, but no law enforcement? Religion as a world power, but no churches? Amazing food, but no charge?

He heard one of the toilet cubicles open, and saw David come into view, wearing a pair of rubber gloves, and holding a toilet brush. "Oh, hi." David said with a smile, heading to the next cubicle. "You found the Cafeteria?"

"I-I did." Walter was staring after him, thoughts derailed. "I missed the serving, but there was plenty there. The food is excellent, by the way." *He's scrubbing toilets? This is my guide?*

~oo00oo~

David followed Walter out to the lobby, and put his cleaning supplies away; as people started threading into the main Meeting Area. David walked around the auditorium a bit, letting Walter get a sense of the space. "Anyway, the meeting starts in another half hour. Time enough to start your Induction."

"No, thank you." Walter said immediately.

"Oh, I promise; the first lessons are really very simple. A few minutes at mo-"

"Yeah, I won't be available." Walter said promptly.

David looked patiently at him. "I'm not trying to force anything. You've been here less than three hours. I promise, we won't tackle the religion issue until you're ready. But the meeting will cover a lot of things you're not familiar with; so an induction is a smart move. Consider it a primer. A glossary, even."

"No, I mean I won't be studying with you." Walter told him. "Nothing personal, but if I'd known you were the Janitor around here, I would have waited for someone more qualified."

David's lip twitched, just a little. "I see." He said with suppressed mirth. "Well, if you'd like to study with someone else, that's no problem. All the 'qualified' people around will be here for the meeting. I can introduce you to the Elders. Any of them would be happy to study with you."

"That is acceptable." Walter said, when he suddenly noticed something. It wasn't clear what drew his attention, but it finally dawned on him. The man who just walked in was the only other man who seemed older than thirty years.

~oo000oo~

James noticed the older man standing closer to the stage. "What about him?" He asked Karen.

Karen followed his gaze. "Ooh. Another newcomer. From the way he's scanning around, probably a recent one, too." She seemed unconcerned. "You'll see two or three at every meeting, James. Thousands of people a day are coming back from the dead, and that rate is accelerating as the world fills up with people to meet them."

James felt that explanation wash over him. He didn't believe it, after all; but it fit with what she had been telling him so far. You spotted a lie by looking for contradictions in the story, and she hadn't given one yet.

The meeting began soon after. James found a seat towards the back. Karen supplied him with a paper Bible, though he noticed she followed the program on her Device. When she pulled it out, James put a hand to his pocket automatically, and found it gone. Somewhere between entering the Centre and sitting down, she'd stolen her property back, and he hadn't noticed.

She smiled at him innocently until the prayer started, and she bowed her head.

~oo000oo~

Walter had worked with some Church-Run charities before. They were usually pretty generous, since they weren't using their own money. He couldn't tell who was funding any of this place. There were no logos or posters about. The Centre had pictures in the hallways, and all of them impressive; but there were no portraits of benefactors, no statues to honor anyone.

When the music started, he'd had a Bible put in his hands instantly, the words to whatever hymn they were singing were projected on an advanced display like something out of a sci-fi movie.

The prayer came, and everyone bowed their heads. Walter took the unobserved moment to examine things quickly. The Bible had no publishers mark or barcode. There was a notation of which printing it was, and the year suggested it was indeed centuries after his time.

David sat next to him, until the speaker made introductions. "Today's Public Talk is from our own Presiding Overseer, Brother David Thorne; on the topic: 'We Can Do Nothing Against The Truth'."

Walter was stunned as David stood up and made his way to the stage. It defied common sense. *So is he a Janitor that gives Sermons? Or is he a 'Presiding Overseer' who scrubs toilets?*

He was so wrapped up in that question, that he only heard half the talk.

"Consider the long history of all the attacks that Satan made on God's Purposes for his people. For almost four thousand years, a Messiah was promised, according to a specific bloodline. And the whole world, under Satan's control, sent armies, false teachers, and many attacks; all to break that family line. When Jesus was born, all the babies in the town were targeted. Jesus himself was martyred. But everything that Satan did was prophesied; including the time Jesus' parents had to flee the country, and the events of Jesus death, even the most unusual details of his execution. Things that Jesus had no control over." David let that sink in. "Over a hundred prophecies to identify the Messiah, and Satan was personally responsible for some of them coming true; no matter how hard he tried to do the opposite."

Atxi couldn't figure out the meeting. Her people had taught about the gods all the time. There had been many festivals and ceremonies. This was like none of them. There was nobody to act out the story of Jehovah, no altar for them to worship at...

"In the modern day, we saw the same thing. The Bible was banned for centuries; and what followed was a determined effort from honest seekers of truth to protect their Bibles by spreading copies of it to many different lands. Attacks from political parties backfired. All the governments that made it their business to oppose God were brought to ruin. All the financial institutions that worshiped only their own money were left destitute. All the false religions that offered service to idols, or even hypocritical false service to the Christ, were left empty by peoples that lost faith in them. All these were shown up as being failed models to live by, even before A-Day. Billions of people, dedicated to making their way in a world that was falling apart."

James looked around, thinking. There was no security. No stained glass. James was used to shipboard services. The crew would assemble by rank, as it was done in regular churches. The town leaders would get the front row; the poor would assemble on the balcony, since they had nothing to put in the collection plate.

"Brothers, aren't we grateful to have a God that is is so merciful and loving, that even those *opponents* are now having their chance to find the truth. With their world gone, we are all seeing, for the first time, what the world could have looked like if Jehovah had always been in charge of it. A world where money isn't more important than people, or where corrupt leaders can't hurt the innocent, or where false prophets can't mislead the masses. Everyday we thank Jehovah God for giving us all this second chance. A lot of us didn't even know we needed one; but no matter how noble, or how selfless our goals, could anyone have seriously planned to live forever with the people we love?"

Walter twitched at the thought; because it suddenly dawned on him: When he'd made his plans to live forever, he never thought to take people along. Not even his son. Walter took a moment to remind himself that he wasn't staying. These people could say what they wanted; and believe in whatever manner suited them.

~oo0Ooo~

Atxi had almost fled the Hall when the meeting was over. She moved away from the people, looking for privacy. She only had it for a few moments, before Irsu found her; but it was enough for her to get herself under control. He sat beside her, a respectful distance, not reaching out a hand, or crowding her thoughts.

She didn't know how to start a conversation either, so they just sat. The sky was clear and the air warm. There was a sweet smell of some ripe fruit on the breeze, but she couldn't tell from where. Since walking up, she had seen several fruiting trees, planted everywhere, even in the middle of the footpaths. Nobody seemed to own them, and the orange-blossoms were sweet perfume.

"False prophets misleading masses." Atxi said darkly. "He was talking about me, wasn't he? Me and Huitzilin and my sister and…" She trailed off.

"Truth can be a hard thing to learn." He said gently. "But it's almost always better than a lie. Especially this Truth. This one above all else."

Atxi said nothing. He didn't push.

Finally, Atxi shook her head. "No."

Irsu sighed and gave her a nod. "I know it's a huge thing to be hit with. It's only natural to reject it out of hand, at least at first. But if I may offer you one word of comfort: The Religious Wars are over. All wars are over, in fact. This is a place where nobody will ever harm another over believing differently, or over anything else. And not only will there never be war again, but all those who have fallen, including you and me, will get to live in Paradise. For most people, that's good news."

"Most people weren't like me." Atxi said firmly.

"Ohh, you'd be surprised." Irsu told her. "Millions by hunger. Millions by war. Millions by illness. And a whole lot of them begging one god or another for help. But all of those people are now here, in a place where they'll never have to face war, or hunger, or disease. A place where the Truth is everywhere… And it's Good News."

Put that way, Atxi felt a tear gathering in the corner of her eye. "I… I can't."

"I know." Irsu pointed out at the visible people. "Go to anyone you meet and ask them: 'What convinced you?' They'll all know what you mean; and they'll all be happy to tell you. The entire world has this huge, common thing. And for once, it's something wonderful." Irsu smiled at her. "The time will come when you'll be able to answer that question too. Be patient with the world, Atxi. Nobody says you have to make a decision today."

~oo0Ooo~

As the Meeting wrapped up, everyone broke up into conversations. David had a few matters to attend to, and Walter found he had nobody to talk to. But his isolation didn't last for long.

"You must be Walter." A man said with a smile, offering a hand to shake. "I'm Hitch Thorne. I believe you were met by David. He's my son."

Walter shook the hand automatically, but couldn't help the lingering look. This man looked to be the same age as David exactly. In fact, everyone seemed to be of similar ages, except him and the other 'older' man who was sitting beside a beautiful young woman.

Hitch Thorne let Walter look. "Trying to figure it out?" He guessed. "I've seen the reactions of almost a dozen newly Returned Ones. You're wondering if I'm secretly David's twin brother, working on some Long Con with him?"

"I don't think it's a con. Not a deliberate one, anyway." Walter admitted. "Earlier, I had thought that maybe this was a trick. Telling me I was centuries out of date, so that I'd call my bank and give them all my personal details."

"But now you don't think so?"

Walter gestured at his face. "There's nothing fake about this. I don't look that much younger than I did, but a lot healthier. I remember where I was before this. I can feel the energy in me. It's not a dream, or power of suggestion."

"No, it certainly isn't." Thorne agreed. "But you still seem to be more confused than interested."

Walter sent a look over to David, who had finished his business and wandered over to them.

"You can ask." David said with a smile.

"Why are you sweeping floors and scrubbing toilets, if you're in charge here?" Walter demanded, disbelieving. "Isn't that the sort of job given to maintenance staff?"

"We're all maintenance staff." The elder Thorne put

in. "We share all the duties here."

"I understand the principle, but what I mean is, you can delegate that sort of menial labor."

David gave him a look. "Walter, the lowest man in the hierarchy of this town is you. You've been here a total of four hours. Would you like me to hand you a broom and 'delegate'?"

Walter had no answer to that.

~oo0Ooo~

"How many 'newcomers' like me were in that Meeting?" James asked Karen as they walked towards the Dorms.

"At least a dozen who have come back in the last few months. People who are there for the first time, like you? Maybe three or four."

"And you decide to tell them that everything they did in their old lives was pointless, and a waste of time? You sure know how to make friends."

"Perhaps not the easiest topic to introduce you on." Karen conceded.

"No, I get why you would." James shook his head. "On a ship, when you have to break in a new man, the hard part isn't teaching him how things are, it's getting him to stop all the different things he learned elsewhere. I'd rather a cabin boy who'd never sailed before, than some lubber who thought it was right to tie a knot the wrong way."

Karen grinned. "I agree. In fact, the hardest part of teaching someone the truth is to unlearn the lies."

~oo0Ooo~

There were three Dorms. One for the men, one for the women, and one for temporary residents. Atxi had asked Irsu what that meant.

70

"Not everyone stays here; and not everyone's a Returnee." He explained. "Reunions happen every day, and those Returnees need somewhere to go. Plus, travel is a very popular pastime. Practically everyone is on the move. The Dorms double as a Travel Hostel for people who are visiting from all around the globe."

Atxi nodded, but she had little experience with long-range travel. 'The Globe' was a foreign concept to her. "Reunions." She picked out the key word. "Is my family here too?"

"Well, let's find out." Irsu said brightly.

~oo0Ooo~

Irsu called it a 'Computer Terminal'. Atxi had never seen anything like it, but she couldn't take her eyes off the moving screen. It was magical. Even a little frightening.

Atxi couldn't understand the writing on the screen, but Irsu was happy to explain as they went. "Everyone's looking for someone in the world. We have no word on when or where people are Returned, so it can hard to find people in any logical order. When that happens, we put our names in the Database. Sooner or later, we find someone we want to see."

Atxi did several searches. Her mother. Other relatives. The girls in the Temple Courtyards… None of them came back with a match.

"It happens." Irsu said, unconcerned. "People are in groups, for the most part. There's overlap, but most people are only close with a small group. Family, friends, co-workers… If you're the first one in your Social Circle, then it means the rest will be back one day. Leave your details. Someone will contact you eventually. You can also flag other names, so that you get an alert when any of these people come back."

She didn't understand all those words, but Irsu was

able to talk her through it. Then the Terminal beeped at her. The unfamiliar sound made her jump, and Irsu tapped at the Screen. "Well. Someone flagged your name." Atxi didn't understand, so he spelled it out. "There's someone out there who's been waiting to meet you. Someone you haven't looked for."

Atxi was intrigued, running through a mental list of everyone she knew. "Who?"

~oo0Ooo~

"Drew Thorne, nice to meet you, Miss Atxi. May I call you that?"

"Just Atxi." The Aztec told her, clasping her extended hand automatically. "It's my name, after all." She looked the woman over. She was older. Everyone in the Hall seemed young, but this woman seemed mature. There were a few thin lines here and there, a little extra weight along her jaw. She was still as healthy and energetic as anyone Atxi had seen since waking up, but there were signs of age on her face.

Why her? Atxi asked herself. *Why is this woman... mortal?*

"Anyway, you're probably wondering why I flagged your name." Drew said brightly. "It's like this... I'm an anthropologist."

"I don't know the word." Atxi answered; through this was nothing unusual. She only understood about a third of the terms she'd been hearing since the Meeting started.

"I am a 'professor'." Drew clarified. "Or a 'scholar' if that sounds more familiar. A 'teacher'? 'Educator'?"

Atxi nodded. "Yes, I understand."

"My work, since I was about your age, was to spend my career in two tasks: First, I was teaching students about other cultures and nations; and secondly; I was trying to learn more about them, for others to teach later on. You have been told, I'm sure, that time has passed since you were last... around?"

Atxi nodded. "Not sure I believe it."

"Well, that much I can vouch for." Drew told her. "The Aztecs was one of the cultures I studied. Your friend Irsu? Him too. I also studied the Egyptians. I've been back almost twelve years now, and it seems to be a rising concern: Finding common ground between people who lived centuries apart. Back in my old life... I sort of built my career around you and Irsu *specifically*. Your Temple robes, and his mummified remains, in fact."

Atxi nodded, a little unsettled; but that was nothing new for her lately. "So, you want me to... what?"

"I've been working on a book about various ancient cultures. A reference guide, really. I'd like your help to complete it."

"I'm not a teacher."

"You don't have to be, my dear." Drew promised. "All it will involve is us talking about the world you came from. I'll tell you what we know, and you'll fill in the blanks; and correct us on any mistakes."

Atxi held up the Screen that Irsu had given her during the Meeting. "Are you so sure you don't have the answers already?"

"Things get lost. History keeps moving; sometimes at a breakneck speed." Drew explained. "Things get stolen, things get lied about. After a century, it all shakes out until an 'agreed on' story is the best history you can find." Drew looked distant for a moment. "The sheer number of things that we took as fact, and only now realize we had it entirely wrong..."

Atxi shivered. Some of those things they had 'entirely wrong' included her.

Drew came back to the moment. "Can I ask, what do *you* think of the Meetings?"

Atxi wasn't sure how to answer.

"You can tell me the truth." Drew said, discerning her hesitation. "I haven't joined them either."

Atxi filed that little tidbit away, and gave her answer. "It's nothing like the story of the gods that we have back home. My people would not only tell the story of wars and victories and loves and losses that our gods are heir to; we would act them out. People would spend their lives taking on the image of our gods, and making sure that everyone who watched them dance could feel the fervor that the gods demanded." She gestured. "These people speak of eternal life, but to an Aztec, living a long life and dying 'by natural causes' is a disgrace. We give ourselves to the gods long before that. We had to. Our gods burn themselves up providing protection, food, shelter… We have to give back to them. We give everything. These people are… so very tame."

"Oh, they take it seriously." Drew confirmed. "More than anyone I knew in my life, back before. But they're more reserved about it." She smiled warmly at Atxi. "I have a million questions. I know you're new here, but it was my life's work, to try an understand people like you; from what little we knew."

Atxi looked over sharply. "What? Why 'little'? What happened to my people? This world knows everything, or so it seems from your technology. How could my people have been *forgotten*?"

Drew winced, kicking herself mentally. "I… I don't…"

Atxi forced herself to stay calm. "Tell me, please."

Drew lead her off a bit, away from other people. "It's… I mean, we don't have a lot of details. During those centuries, it was custom for reports to be vague when saying something negative about a leader, and so some of the facts are in conflict… And of course, I don't know exactly where or when you were…"

"Miss Drew." Atxi cut her off. "Please. The last I heard, our king was being held hostage by the Spanish, and…"

The older woman sighed hard. "Cortes killed Montezuma the Second in 1520. What followed was an Aztec victory that drove Cortes and his people out. History remembered the battle as 'La Noche Triste'. The Night of Sorrows. Cortes ran for it, and your people gave chase; he counterattacked and made alliances with your political enemies… A year later there was a smallpox outbreak, and Cortes led the Spanish-Tlaxalan-Texcocan forces; and laid siege to Tenochtitlan."

"No…" Atxi breathed in horror. "How did the siege end?"

Drew clearly didn't want to say.

"TELL ME!" Atxi nearly screamed.

Drew finally gave it up. "The Spanish got reinforcements in July 1521. About a month later, your people made their last stand at Plaza Mayor… And failed. The Aztecs surrendered in August 1521; and-"

"And the Spanish started looting and pillaging." Atxi covered her face with her hands, weeping. "We lost. We lost the war. Our Gods couldn't save us." She looked up desperately. "Is that why I'm here? Was Huitzilopochtli slain too? Can your God do that? Were the Thirteen Heavens *routed*? Did your Jehovah take my soul from Huitzilopochtli by force?"

Drew bit her lip. "The… The first missionaries from Spanish territory didn't arrive until 1624, but… Yeah, they started bringing your people 'into line' with Christendom." She leaned forward. "Atxi. My husband is quite insistent on this point. *They* were wrong too.

Christendom was spread across the world on the tip of a sword for centuries; but that Church was beaten into the dust and scattered away to nothing. He was there when it happened. It was centuries later, but your people were avenged. The Conquerors, the Churches… all the blood-guilty are gone."

Atxi couldn't speak, fallen to her knees in grief. Her people had lost the war. She knew what had followed. Pillaging and executions and enslavement for anyone who didn't have the Conquistadors features or language… She could picture it happening so vividly.

Patli… Atxi cried out in her mind. *Huitzilopochtli couldn't save you?! What happened to you, sister? Were you fed to our Gods? Or were you taken prisoner? Claimed by some soldier as spoils of war?*

"I'm… I'm sorry." Drew said finally, stricken. "All these things… they happened centuries before I was born. I read them in a book. I wrote the words on a chalkboard. I forgot for a moment that I was talking about your people."

Atxi was still staring through eyes filled with hot, helpless tears. *Huitzilopochtli!* She wept silently. *Answer me! Tell me this is all a lie! Tell me this world is wrong, and you are there! Please?!*

The only answer was Drew, whispering apologies, trying to get through to her, trying to make the young woman hear her again.

"Atxi…" Drew began, and Atxi suddenly realized how hard the pale woman was trying to be nice. "You're here. You're alive. I haven't thrown in with the Witnesses yet; but the man who gave that talk today? He's my son. And I don't know what other force than a god can raise the dead, but I can tell you with some certainty that the 'Resurrection' is really happening. More than that, I'm not sure. As proud as I am of my son settling into a leadership role, having the respect of his peers and-"

"Why haven't you?" Atxi asked suddenly, struggling to her feet. "If you believe that this is real, why haven't you decided to be part of their world, yet?"

Drew bit her lip. "Don't tell my son? Or his father?"

Atxi nodded. An easy promise to make, given that she hadn't met either of them yet.

"As much as this world has to offer, including bringing people like you and me back from the dead... The Aztecs had such passionate faith. The Egyptians and the Romans built such incredible structures. The Greeks had such fascinating art and culture... All of that is gone. I'm an anthropologist. Studying the cultures that had come before was my passion in life; trying to understand what was unique and wonderful about every page in the history book. The people may be back, but their culture isn't. You're not the first Aztec I've met and interviewed, Atxi; but in this world, you'll never see faithful Temple Priests dance out the story of Huitzilopochtli again."

Atxi felt a sick thrill go through her. She believed every word Drew Thorne was saying. Her world was gone, ground out of existence by the heel of the conquerors; and forgotten by time. She'd lain on the altar, knowing that she'd never return to the Temple. But the idea that nobody ever would again...

It was all gone. All of it.

No. Atxi felt her heart give a solid thump, and then start beating triple-time. *No! If I am indeed the last of my kind, then I won't let them grind me away too!*

"Drew?" She heard herself say. "Thank you, for believing that something of my people was worth keeping. So far, you're the only one who has tried to see what we were, and to see my life for what it was. And yes, I'll give you all the answers you can ask questions for, but I hope you'll understand that I can't just yet." She wiped her eyes. "I have to think on… well, many things."

"Of course." Drew didn't push. "Contact me when you *are* ready."

Chapter Five: Out Of Date

The Centre had several meeting rooms, which meant it also had corridors. Walter was walking through one slowly. Each corridor had artworks, some elaborate, some very innocent and childlike. But the current hallway was something like a museum. There were half a dozen glass cases mounted on the wall; and in each one was a familiar item.

A pair of reading glasses. A set of dentures. An asthma inhaler… All these things were at least a century or two old, complete with a little reference cards to describe what each item did, and why it was needed.

"You're not imagining it." A man said lightly. "They're museum pieces now."

Walter jumped a bit, emerging from his thoughts. "I always knew the 23rd Century would be free of such things. I didn't expect anyone to keep them like this."

"This one was my idea." The man said, and Walter noticed he was holding a Bible with the name 'Alai' embossed on it. "More people have been convinced of 'no more sickness' from this hallway than by anything we could tell them."

"I'm sure." Walter smiled.

"You don't remember me do you?" Alai commented.

"Should I?"

"No reason you should." Alai smiled. "I was a waiter at the East Hampton Yacht Club." He said with a grin. "This was years before A-Day. Years before I heard you'd died. It was that Fundraising Gala for renovations to the Club. I was fetching drinks for your table, I got the order wrong, and your 'guest' for the evening laughed. You didn't like them laughing, so you had me fired."

Walter felt a trickle of fear reach him. He'd faced

people with a grudge against their superiors. But in this world he'd observed no police, or private security. For the first time, he was facing that kind of opposition without his protection. "Yes. I remember that."

"One thing I never got, why were you angry, even though they were laughing at *me*?" It wasn't an accusation, just a honest question.

Walter found himself answering reflexively. "It was a loss of control. A loss of face."

"Ah." Alai gestured around. "Well, obviously I'm fine with how things turned out. Nice to see you again."

Walter watched him go, surprised. He wasn't expecting that. He'd been bracing for an attack, or at least a lecture, something holier-than-thou.

David and his father, watching the whole conversation discreetly, fell into step behind Walter. "Sixty three thousand homeless people in New York City at your time, and you held a charity fundraiser to make a nicer house for your Yachts?" Hitch said, as though not believing it.

Ah, here comes the holier-than-thou. "You must hate me very much." Walter nodded, expecting it. Jealousy was something he'd known how to deal with his whole life. Like it was evil to be rich.

"Why would we hate you?" David asked, completely guileless.

Walter blinked. He was serious. "Well, you're more evolved than most, then."

Hitch shook his head. "No, what David means is: What would our motive for disliking you be? All those Country Club guys? The ones that made it here are all in your boat. All the homeless people who died alone on the streets are designing their own homes. It's not like anything you did has negatively impacted the life we have here. Anyone that did have a grudge, legitimate or not, has had the scales balanced and been given the same offer of eternal life that you have. That man who you apparently knew briefly, did he have any hatred in his voice?"

"No." Walter conceded. "In fact, if I had to pick a word, it would be… amusement."

David nodded. "When I was a little boy, I went back to the ruins of New York for an afternoon with one of the older sisters. I couldn't figure out why you might seal up a priceless painting in a vault where nobody could see it, or what a 'gun' was, or why seeing a shootout would be entertaining on a screen." He shrugged with a genuine smile of amusement. "Trust me, Walter: A lot of your world is hilarious, now that it's not hurting anyone."

Walter took several minutes to digest that as they walked.

"David." Walter said suddenly. "I… I apologize. What I said about how you should 'delegate' the menial tasks? It seems I have behaved… improperly. Such impropriety is beneath my station, and I beg your pardon."

"I accept your apology."

"In fact, to be honest, I don't know why I'm reacting like this."

"Culture shock." David said with a sage nod. "I've seen it before. I was raised in this world, my brother. It's like when we were walking to the Centre, and you noticed you were casually walking three times my speed."

"David, I get that you've never known different, but try and open your mind, just for a moment." Walter scoffed. "There are only two kinds of people in this world. The people on top, and the people being stood on."

"What a terrible way to view the world." Hitch said with an almost nostalgic smile. "I've heard it said that people of your generation worshiped money. But it just occurred to me what that must mean for someone like you. You were a high roller in that world. People flocked to you to find out where the money was going, and how to profit. In your 'religion', you're a Cleric."

"I know that everyone expects me to break, eventually; but I won't." Walter said with certainty. "Religion is a fairy tale to give the desperate a sense of place. And I already know my place."

"Well, first of all: I don't appreciate the term 'break'." The Elder Thorne said pointedly.

"Fair enough, would 'convert' be better?"

"Conversion is just a fancy word for 'changing your thinking'." Thorne said. "And almost everyone alive has had to do it at some point; even before arriving here. Our faith was a lot simpler. An understanding that it wasn't the way we were meant to live, and that sooner or later, God would do what people can't, and fix it." He gestured across at the Hall, and all the congregation who were sneaking looks at him, and at the other newcomers. "All humanity is undergoing a conversion right now; and you aren't immune to-"

"Humanity is my business." Walter quoted derisively. "I am not a character out of Dickens' Christmas Carol."

David looked confused. "What's 'Christmas'?"

Walter just stared at the man blankly.

The elder Thorne stepped in with a grin. "You'll have to excuse my son. He was Resurrected, as you were, but for him, he was so young he remembers very little of the Old Days." He glanced over. "Walter is referencing an old story that was fairly popular in the modern era of

OS. A wealthy, but cruel-hearted miser is visited one night by three spirits who show him the error of his ways. By the end of the story, he has vowed to change his life; and become a good man." Thorne chuckled a little. "Irony of ironies that an old Christmas Story is actually a fairly accurate metaphor for the current world situation."

"And I object to the term 'cruel-hearted miser'." Walter countered.

"It was your metaphor." David reminded him. "But whether you want to change your thinking or not, surely you've reached some conclusions about everything you've seen and heard since arriving here?"

"David, I don't even know where 'here' is." Walter scorned. "I don't claim to understand all of this, but I don't have to; because it Doesn't. Make. Sense." Walter let that point hang in the air between them for a moment. "And when presented with a question I don't immediately have an answer to, I'm not prepared to throw away my wisdom, my experience, my reason-"

"Your privilege?" David challenged. "Because I imagine a man like you might have trouble with what he was hearing me say on that platform today. A man who is supremely proud of his legacy? Might not approve of the idea that God brought everyone back down to earth."

"You bet I don't. There's a reason people like me were the first ones on the lifeboats when the Titanic sank."

"True. But there are some people who might call that unfair." Hitch observed.

"Those people are the ones who got left to drown." Walter countered, matter-of-factly. "If some anti-money hippie ever got handed a billion dollars, do you really think he'd give all of it away to the needy?"

"Well, you tell me. You did the same thing in

reverse." David quipped pointedly.

"And by the way." His father added with a slight smirk. "Just so you know, if you plan to use that Dickens Story as an example, just remember that in that story, Marley and the three Spirits that haunted Scrooge were the real deal; and he *did* make a change… And his life was far better for it."

Walter said nothing to that, so David and his father left him alone on that thought.

"Bah, Humbug." Walter declared finally.

~oo0Ooo~

Atxi had stormed away from Irsu and Drew and the Meeting Hall for no reason, other than to be away from them for a while. She walked for almost an hour, before she realized she had no idea where she was.

It was the only township on this road, so it wasn't hard to find her way back.

Irsu was there, with a covered plate. "I figured you'd be back when you got hungry."

Atxi nodded thickly, and sat down to eat. "I'm hungry, tired, my feet are aching…" She ate a few more bites quickly. "So it isn't a dream. And it's not where the Gods live. There's no hunger and thirst there." This much she had become certain of.

"This is the flesh-and-blood human world." Irsu agreed. "But it's a very nice one."

"I was meant to be with the Gods." Atxi bit out, betrayed.

"For what it's worth, all those Christian Soldiers who came marching on you in the name of their own idea of Christ? They were all expecting Heaven too, and when they get here, they'll have the same choice to make. There's no special treatment for anyone."

"Because humble man can't do anything against

God." Atxi fumed. "And we're meant to accept this as an act of love?"

"Would *your* God care to resurrect people who died to strengthen a rival?" Irsu put to her. "Your people believed that human sacrifice made their gods stronger. If we were living in your afterlife now, would the thousands of millions who followed Jehovah be given a Resurrection at all? Are any of the Aztec gods so generous?"

"Why should yours be?" Atxi shot back. "If my gods wouldn't bring back their enemies, why would yours?"

"Love." Irsu said simply. "I've met a hundred people from half a dozen different eras, Atxi. Not one of their many gods showed concern and love for people who believed in different heavens."

"If your God loved me, he would have let me go to The Sun!"

"Atxi, you talk about it like there were multiple options on an Afterlife. There aren't. This was it. This was always it, even when you were told different. If you were *able* to go to an Aztec Heaven, why did you wake up in a Christian Kingdom?"

Atzi thought for a moment. "I don't know, yet. I've been thinking on it for a while." She said finally. "My kingdom is not so… prejudiced against other gods as you are. Each of the Gods had their own Kingdom, and while your God may be jealous, my holy men never begrudged their enemies getting to their own gods. I never doubted any of them then, so why should that change now?"

Her guide smothered a laugh at that. "You think your soul took a wrong turn? Went to the wrong afterlife?"

"I think my faith is strong enough to endure one day that I don't understand." Atxi told him. "Have you never had a day when you asked your Jehovah 'why?' and got no immediate answer?"

"I would have to admit that's true enough." Irsu conceded.

"So what makes yours any more real than mine? Your God forbids people with other faiths getting where they want to be. Mine doesn't. Who says Tialocan isn't waiting for me to arrive right now?" Atxi countered, finally feeling like she'd put it into words.

He was silent a long moment while she kept eating. "When you're finished, I'd like to show you something." He said finally.

~oo0Ooo~

Walter came into the library. David was there, head bowed over a Bible. Walter stood at the door and waited while David finished his prayer. When the younger… younger-*looking* man opened his eyes, Walter spoke. "I know I had a privileged life, David." He said quietly. "I know I had it better than anyone else. It wasn't because I was a bad person. It wasn't because I didn't care. It's because I was born to it. My father was bankrupted, worked his way back to wealthy. It's not luck. Wealth and privilege is a matter of my bloodline. I cannot refuse it, anymore than I can refuse to have my father's blue eyes. It's a fact of my life."

"You think you were destined to have prestige?" David found that amusing. "Like you were better than us by divine right?"

"It's not a joke, it's a provable statement. People like me, like my father… We could write laws, move mountains, have anything we wanted. Other people couldn't feed their families. If they were any better than that, then they'd have *been* better than that. It's that simple. The fact that I did it means that it was my right to do it. If I wasn't meant for better things than anyone else, I wouldn't be *able* to point to my life and say it was better than theirs. And it was. It always was. There are self-made millionaires. People who rose from nothing through hard work and sheer talent. I never begrudged any of them. You know how you can tell the Apex people? They're the ones on top."

David looked at him. "But… you're not on top."

"I think we can both agree that's not by my choice." Walter reminded him. "It's hardwired into me, to be the cream that rises to the top. It has been that way for my whole life, before this commune you've somehow built." Walter stepped forward, genuinely begging David to understand. "It's not wrong to acknowledge that. It's wasteful to pretend I'm just another worker bee. It's a waste of my talent, and my breeding."

"Aristocracy." David summed up. "The natural superiority of the high-born. I thought by 2016, that view had faded."

"I know it's unpopular to say so, and I wouldn't, except between friends." Walter told him.

"Is that what I am?"

"You are the head of your Congregation, and your God had you waiting to meet me, the moment I arrived. Of course that's what we are." Walter had reconciled that much. "I've never treated anyone as less than they were. And neither have you. I've noticed you treating everyone, even a total stranger, like a part of your family. A fine quality, to be sure. But ever since I got here, my life has been less than it should be. Less than it always has been. It's basic nature."

"The strong prosper and the weak get eaten." David sighed, so sorry for him. "Walter, we live in a world where even the lions don't hunt lambs anymore."

"But they are still lions." Walter reminded him, as though that proved everything. "And pretending they are lambs is to insult them. To make them less than they are."

David stood. "Come with me."

~ooOOoo~

"What is it?" Atxi asked, intrigued.

"The Tree." Irsu said warmly. "As in, 'The Family Tree'. Pretty much everyone that has been Returned has put their details in here."

Axti stared in disbelief. The sun was going down behind them, and the Wall was lit up by the cheery glow. Atxi wandered over closer to it, peering into it. The wall was nothing but names. Millions of names. The Wall was almost twenty feet high, and hundreds of feet long; and the names were small and neat; drawing the whole human family. As intricate as it was, there was plenty of room for far more names to be added.

"It's amazing." Atxi declared finally.

"You know where this started?" Irsu asked. "With the opening page of the Gospels." He pulled out his Bible and showed it to her. A row of names that meant nothing to her. "From Christ to Adam." Irsu pointed at The Tree. "You can follow that bloodline here, along with all the others."

Atxi nodded.

"Somewhere out there is the first person who told you that your gods needed human sacrifices. Somewhere out there is the first person who ever said it to anyone. Were they trying to start a religion? Get some money? Eliminate an enemy? Who knows? Sooner or later, maybe you can ask them yourself. But there will be a long line."

Atxi said nothing.

He came over beside her. "When I first got here, I didn't know who Ra first spoke to, or what Hathor found so appetizing about humans." He pointed to the wall.

"But I can tell you the entire timeline of the Judeo-Christian Faith, including the people, by *name*, that Jehovah first called 'friend'." He squeezed her hand, and rose to go. "The thing about the truth? It gets easier to spot, because it just makes more sense, the deeper you go."

Atxi said nothing to that.

"The truth is not hard to find anymore, sister. You, quite literally, gave your heart away. I can understand needing some time when presented with the opposing view." He told her. "You'll have all the time you need to make a decision, Atxi. You won't be restricted from any information, any evidence. God gives freely of whatever people need."

"Except for the Temples." Atzi remarked, mostly to herself.

"Those are things people don't need anymore."

"And if I had said the same thing to you?" Atxi challenged. "If you had come to my paradise, instead of me to yours?" Having said it, she suddenly felt on firmer ground. "In fact, what if that had happened? Jehovah is a God I've never heard of. Christ I know only through the invaders. If you had been taken to some Afterlife run by a God you'd never heard of, and then told your own gods were lost to you, how would you react?"

Irsu took the question seriously. "Forty five years ago, I *did* have to make that leap." He said. "My gods were long forgotten by the world. The thing that took me the longest to figure out was that there weren't other options. You talk like there are a thousand Afterlives, lined up for people to go into the one they pick." He gave her a sympathetic smile. "There isn't any other place. You have been dead for centuries and centuries. Did you have any say? A long dark tunnel with light at the end? Were you aware of the passage of time at all?"

"This is worse than telling me I'm in the wrong place. Now you're telling me I was always chasing a lie?"

"You, and thousands of millions of others." Irsu said.

"How am I supposed to just…" Atzi waved a hand vaguely. "How do I start again, with nothing?"

"Not with nothing." He promised her immediately. "With a home, ready to be arranged however you want it. With food, healthy and plentiful, for as long as you need. With the truth, and many people eager to tell you how wonderful it is. As starting over goes, it's not the hardest landing you could have had."

"In my head, I understand that. But I don't recognize anything. None of this." Atxi said softly, tears forming. "I was to join the gods, in the Great White Place. I gave them my heart. And I think my mother seduced the High Priest to give me and my sister that opportunity, and it was all a *lie*."

"I know."

"I gave my life to them. We all did." Atxi hissed. "Our children were named by the Diviners. There were festivals every week to every God we had a name for. When the Spanish came to conquer, they sacrificed over eighty thousand people to our War Gods, strengthening him for a victory."

"And all of them will live again." He told her. "Every single one of them. Every woman and child, every flayed prisoner. Remember, most of them warred on your tribes in the name of their own gods."

Atxi heard that, and felt her knees go weak. "If it's true… If you're right… Then it's all such an unholy joke. All our lives. For generations!"

"And now it is over." Irsu said seriously. "If this is making you angry, just remember that all those lies had one thing in common: They were all told with God's signature. They gave him the blame; for all of it." Irsu pointed at the far end of The Wall. "You see that there? Where all those lines just stop? That was the moment where God suddenly declared: No More. And every name before it got a do-over with a clean slate."

"Not that clean." Atxi said. "I can't even figure out the calendar anymore."

"True, but to be fair, you've only been here a day." Irsu reminded her.

Atxi seethed a moment. "When I was born, the Diviners gave me a name. The Calendar was drawn according to the gods, and no event, from marriage to schooling, to planting, to harvesting, and everything in between… Every single moment of our lives was drawn around them. Every one of our people, from Emperor to slave, lived their life according to the gods. The Priests said that the gods, hundreds of them, sacrificed themselves bit by bit, to make our lives possible…" She rubbed her eyes. "Your world can offer me everything except the Temples. Without that, I don't know what I am."

"Whether you are eating or drinking, or doing anything else; do all things for God's glory." Irsu quoted scripture.

"I've heard those words before." Atxi bit out.

"Yes, I imagine you have." Irsu sighed, and gave her a nod. "I've thrown a lot of heavy ideas at you today, I'm sorry if it was too much too soon. Take some time. We have all the time in the world."

Neither of them noticed, but over at the other end of The Tree, David and Walter were having the same conversation.

~oo0Ooo~

"When the Old System ended, I wasn't there." David said. "What I know of that world all came after the dust settled. I saw the ruins of it. Saw the bones of it. And it was already long gone. We're cleaning up the world so fast that the cites are all but dots on a map that nobody uses anymore. The rest will be restored in time." David gestured. "The only thing of the Old Days that is guaranteed to be here? The people."

Walter was impressed by the Tree. The amount of effort that had gone into it was mind-boggling to him. "I know people who would brag about their family line, going all the way back to the time of the Fair Traders, or the Mayflower…"

David nodded. "Walter, all those 'natural born superiors' you talk about, all those 'noble bloodlines'… They're all on this wall. Or they will be. The people who are listed here, they're all here in the world, right now. Your name will be added too; if you want it there." He took a breath. "Trace them all back. Every Knight and Duke? They all came from somewhere. Before there was an America, there were English immigrants. Before there was an England, there was a Roman or Celtic tribe. Before there were Romans and Celts…" David waved at the whole length of the wall. "Trace it back, Walter. Nobleman or Commoner, we all came from the same blood once. How is one descendant 'naturally superior' to another when we all come from the same source?"

Walter looked at the wall, humbled by it, though refusing to let that show on his face. "I was named for my grandfather. Who was named for his grandfather. Who was named for his great-grandfather. You say to me that all of us will be here at some point…"

David nodded. "Hang in there, my friend. Everyone on this wall also had to shake a few deeply held truths. You think it's hard to deal with the idea of new social structures, try explaining all this to people who thought the Earth was flat."

Walter sniffed, forced to concede that one. "It's not quite the same thing. Your talk this afternoon... David, I'm starting over with nothing."

"Well, if it helps, so did the True Believers." David offered. "My father was there when the Old Days ended. No homes to go back to, no jobs waiting... But they were happier than they'd ever been." David waved at the wall. "What you said, about being the first ones on the lifeboat when the Titanic sank? Look at the Tree again. There are no titles written down here, no accolades, honorifics, doctorates... The only thing God pulled out of the Last Days were those faithful to him."

Walter filled in the unspoken thought. *Aristocrats weren't saved when that ship sank.*

"Take it as a hint of what's important here." David said. "My father certainly did. God didn't save the infrastructure, the buildings, the artworks, and least of all the money. God saves the people."

Walter said nothing to that for a while. "I know the old days were unfair to many. And I know that I was on the higher end of the seesaw. But I imagine it must be easy for you to tell me I'm unworthy, as you happen to be in the superior position now. What you just said, about how it was easy for the Survivors to leave things behind and learn the new rules? I could have said the same thing about my old life. It was easy for a rich man to get the best schools, the best home, the best security..." He gave David a canny look. "Now that the scales have shifted, it's easy for you to be so high above me."

"You don't get it." David sighed. "We aren't above anyone. We're just older than you, and we've been doing this longer, and we found out what matters."

~oo0Ooo~

Atxi stared at the ceiling for hours. Irsu had walked her back to the Dorms. The people there were like her, and she was glad for it. None of them knew much about this world, and not all of them were thrilled to be there.

Atxi's arrival had caused something of a stir. But the woman who ran the Women's Dorm was quick to shoo them away. "Give her some privacy!" She told them. "She's having a big day."

"I am, aren't I?" Atxi sighed, overwhelmed.

The Dorms were pretty uniform. Atxi didn't recognize the style at all. There was a balcony, common to the rooms on this level. Atxi went out, looked down at the plaza on the ground. There was a garden, and a table with food and drink. There was a firepit, the only thing Atxi recognized, and several people gathered around it.

Layla, the woman who ran the Dorm, was like everyone else in this world, older than she looked, totally calm and endlessly patient. A few of the women in the garden plaza were borderline clinging to her, asking permission for every little thing, full of questions that even Atxi could tell were pointless and trivial.

And yet their Host took all of it in total stride.

"You're not the only one having a big day." A woman's voice said.

Axti jumped. She'd been lost in her thoughts, watching the women in the garden that she hadn't noticed she had company. At the balcony table, the woman with the oddly-shaped eyes was there again, pouring a dark, aromatic tea over a beautiful clay teapot. "Please, join me." The woman said. "You may not remember, but my name is Kasumi. I've been in this world a while now. The Dorms always have rooms free for Travellers."

Atxi sat, looking at the woman carefully. She couldn't stop staring at her face.

"Never met an Asian before?" Kasumi guessed.

Atxi shook her head.

"Well, I've never met an Aztec." Kasumi said with a smile. "But such is the world we live in." She was pouring the tea again, this time over the pot, distributing it evenly. The tea ran off it into a pan, and Atxi could suddenly tell where the lovely color of the ceramics came from. Kasumi then shifted the tea expertly into two cups, and slid one over. The process was very well practiced, ceremonial.

"There's a question I ask every newcomer I meet." Kasumi sipped from her cup. "What would you do with eternal life?"

"I don't know." Atxi admitted. "I've never thought about it before."

"Well, what did you plan to do, when you reached your own idea of the Afterlife?" Kasumi pressed. "My own people believed in Ancestor Worship. Others, reincarnation. There are a hundred different views on the Otherworld. Does it strike you as significant that we *all* came here?"

Atxi was silent a long moment. "The people here are smart. The children are quicker at things the Scribes had to do. If they decided to try and confuse me, if they decided to lie to me... I'd never be able to stop them. They have me half believing their story already, and it's only been a day. I don't have a chance!"

Kasumi chuckled. "I've been traveling for a long time, Atxi. Something I've noticed? People like to talk about things they care about. Things they're invested in." She gestured at the cup in her hand. "I could go on for an hour about this teapot, of all things. Faith is the one thing that unites all the people who belong here. In time, you may find you share it too. If not, that's up to you. But there are plenty of people who are passionate about teaching, about learning, about helping. It would not be difficult to find a teacher. And I don't mean teaching about God. There's plenty to learn; and you can set your own pace, ask your own questions."

Atxi bit her lip. "I... I would like to do that."

Kasumi smiled at her like a daughter, actually tearing up.

Atxi pulled back a bit. "What?"

"Nothing." Kasumi said softly. "Just... Thinking about how lucky we all are. I was so young when I died. I never thought I'd get to live and do anything *at all*. I know you're not there yet; but I envy you, Atxi. The things you'll see? You're just at the start of the greatest story ever told."

Axti shivered hard. She knew Kasumi meant it to be nice, but the intensity she was getting from all these people... This world was scaring her.

Kasumi could see that she had pushed too far, and pulled back to a safer topic. "So. Figured out your room yet?"

"I've never seen a room that has light without flame, or its own well-water." Atxi admitted. "It's overwhelming."

"The sink?" Kasumi guessed. "Yeah. They were around in my time, so I at least recognized more than you did. For me, that made the things I didn't recognize seem stranger. My first day back, I felt like something was wrong with the world. People from your era? They figured the world was a dream, and what's a minor bit of 'magic' like lightbulbs compared to that?"

Atxi nodded, still more overwhelmed than impressed. "The rooms *are* magical. Even the High Priests didn't have 'lightbulbs' that could make a room as bright as day after nightfall." She confided. "Layla says that the room is mine for as long as I need it, and that eventually I will want something better for myself; as I learn my way around. This is what you offer to a stranger, for free? Until 'something better' comes along? This world must be very full of miracles, to pass them out so easily."

~oo0Ooo~

Walter looked around the Dormitory room. "Well. This is unacceptable." He declared immediately.

"These are the standard rooms, Walter. Everyone builds their own home eventually, to their own specifications." David said patiently. "If you want a Five-Star Suite, I'm afraid you won't be able to-"

"No, I understand that these Dorms are complementary, and temporary." Walter nodded. "Free accommodation is basically a nice way of saying 'refugee camp', and I'm sure this place is quite a bit nicer than most halfway homes they put transients in, but it's hardly appropriate for me."

David said nothing, but his eyebrows climbed to his hairline.

"I made arrangements." Walter said, not for the first time. "I have resources; if you'd kindly tell me where a person can access them. Stocks, bonds, precious stones, gold. I have an extremely diverse portfolio, and even if the market changed shape a hundred times in the last two hundred years, I assure you, I can afford a hotel room." He drew himself tall. "And a very good one, at that." He gestured at himself. "I mean, look at these clothes. They don't even have a brand!"

David didn't even blink. "When I was a little boy, this world was fifty years past A-Day. I went as an apprentice to what was left of New York City. When I needed a bathroom, my teacher levered open a safe deposit box and gave me a roll of hundred dollar bills to use as toilet paper. 'Good for one use', she said."

Walter blinked, brain jarred by the blasphemy.

"That was over a century ago, and I haven't handled cash more than twice since then." David continued. "And as for the clothes…" David drawled. "Trust me. You've heard of the designer."

Walter was about to respond with something cutting, when one of the doors behind them opened and a teenage girl stuck her head out. "David? I thought that was you!"

David made introductions. "Walter, this is Mariah. She was Returned a week ago. Mariah, this is Walter; it's his first day back."

Mariah beamed at Walter, and threw her arms around him. "Welcome back! Isn't this wonderful?! This place is amazing! Have you tried the food? Have you been to a meeting? Have you looked up your family? Mine aren't back yet, but I know they will be! Have you seen the rooms yet? It's amazing! It's real! It's all real! God is real! No more evil!" She spun away from Walter and gave David a similar hug. "David, I never thanked you! I was just too stunned, I didn't realize!" She was talking a mile a minute, tears streaming down her overjoyed face. "I've never had a bed before, let alone my own room! The rooms are so nice! There's no cracks in the walls, or holes in the ceiling, or… or anything! Thank you, David. Thank you! Thank God for you, and Thank You, Jehovah God!"

David hugged the young woman warmly, and bid her goodnight. Enthused, Mariah hugged them both tightly again and backed into her room, tears rolling freely as she shut the door. Walter hadn't moved an inch through the whole emotional speech. David just regarded him quietly. He could have said it. He didn't have to.

Finally, Walter spoke, with as much dignity as he could muster. "How do I get a place of my own?"

David nodded. "I can come by, day after tomorrow, show you how it works."

"Thank you." Walter said, and went into his room.

~oo00oo~

Two days later, James noticed the older man from the Meeting wasn't in class. He had been an early riser, making use of The Database to fill in the blanks and answer questions, as they all did. There were several locals in the classroom, helping people with their searching. Not everyone knew how a Terminal worked. James had spoken a language fairly close to the modern day, so he at least recognized letters on the keyboard. Others didn't understand writing at all, and needed to speak their questions to the Terminal; getting the answer spoken back.

The young woman was there every day. The Aztec that had caused something of a stir. James noticed Atxi glancing over at him frequently, and he liked the attention, of course; but he had far more important things to figure out first. James had kept his own heritage quiet; just on principle. But after figuring out the simple commands on the Terminal, he'd been asking questions non-stop. The word 'Pirate' was known to history, for a dozen different reasons. Some viewed his era as exciting and romantic, others as ugly and full of violence. James believed they were both right; and he was glad to have kept it a secret. The 'Age of Piracy' was long dead; and all the people James knew who were like him had also been swallowed by time. He searched for the name of his ship and found little trace at all. He searched for his crew and his family, and found them all listed as 'Pending'.

Then James searched for 'Lawman', 'Police', and 'Navy', and found something even more interesting. There didn't seem to be any.

That was all James needed to know, and he immediately left the Centre.

~oo0Ooo~

Atxi nudged Kasumi and pointed out the empty desk, and the abandoned Terminal. "He didn't come back."

"The other Newcomer?" Kasumi glanced over. "What's your interest in him?"

Atxi flushed. "Not 'interest' exactly. But there are only two or three people here who aren't... like you. If he's like me, then it stands to reason he might have some of the same questions..." Atxi went silent, staring into space for a second.

"Pay a penny for <u>that</u> thought." Kasumi observed. "What's wrong?"

Atxi continued staring at nothing for a long moment. "My first day here, I met a woman named Drew Thorne." Atxi said finally. "She had my name flagged in the Database. When that 'Blue Letter' showed up, she heard the name was listed, and was waiting for me."

Kasumi nodded.

"How did she know my name?" Atxi demanded. "I died centuries before her time, or so you'd all have me believe. She said herself that she never knew anything about me for sure after a lifetime of studies. I know for a fact that the name of one Temple Girl was not recorded anywhere. Certainly nowhere that would survive the end of my civilization and several hundred years in between. How did she know my name?"

Kasumi considered her answer for several moments. "Someone told her your name. Someone who knew that the subject of Sister Thorne's study was... well, you."

Atxi bit her lip. "It wasn't anyone in my family. I already searched for them. They aren't back yet." She turned back to the Terminal. "Aztecs used Pictographs more than writing." She thought aloud. "I have no idea how to spell names."

"Much of the Pre-Modern Human Race didn't have schooling. At least, not in any useful way for Terminal operation." Kasumi nodded. "But the Database is designed for people like that too. Let's get to work."

~oo0Ooo~

James had been sitting in an unobtrusive spot near the Docks for hours, examining the boats, and the security. As near as he could tell, there was no security at all. Not even a patrol. A sailor welcome in many ports, and infamous in many others, he knew enough of several cultures to recognize this as ridiculous.

The people here made no effort to restrict access to information about the world, which struck James as naive. For explorers of his time, the hand-written charts and rutters were among the most valuable items a Pilot-Navigator would keep locked away.

This world had a hundred different maps with a thousand different measurements, and available to everyone who knew how to read them. His study of modern ships showed that even the sails and mainmasts weren't needed anymore.

A ship that can sail against the wind? James had thought it to be a miracle, and proof enough that he was indeed a man out of time. But that was a question for another day.

His search had told him about surveillance cameras and bio-metric scanners, along with a hundred other things he couldn't begin to define; followed by a lengthy explanation of how wonderful it was to never need such measures again.

James watched the Docks for a long time. He wasn't sure he believed any of what he was hearing, but if any of it was true, this was going to be the easiest job he'd ever done.

The ships in dock were sleek and metallic and looked to go faster than anything he'd ever seen, even while sitting still in the dock. He'd spotted a sleek sky-blue-silver Yacht, almost the size of the Stargazer, and he wanted it so badly he could feel himself drooling.

~oo00oo~

Huitzilin was not an uncommon name among the Aztecs. It took Atxi a few tries to be sure she had the right man. But there was a picture included, which left no doubt. It was him.

Six years before she did, the High Priest had come to Paradise.

The thought made her hands quiver for a moment.

"Are you going to get in touch with him?" Kasumi asked. "His contact details are there. You could talk to him right now."

"No." Atxi said seriously. "I think this has to be done in person."

"Well, you have time." Kasumi said with a smile, unaware of the storm gathering in Atxi.

~oo00oo~

With a final glance around, James made his move, darting out towards the Docks. The ship he wanted was unoccupied, unmanned; and-

"Take me with you."

James jumped. The girl from his class was suddenly right there. "What?"

"You're stealing a boat? I need to go somewhere." Atxi said firmly. "Take me with you."

James gave her a lingering look. The company of an attractive woman was never a bad thing. "You're lucky I'm not superstitious. There were some very specific rules about having women on board, back when I last sailed."

"Who's going to complain? We'll be the only two people on the ship."

~oo0Ooo~

Taking the ship was easy. Almost too easy. James actually wondered if it was a trap, or if he'd stolen a ship that wouldn't sail.

But after a few minutes of experimenting, they'd figured out the controls enough to get them away from land.

"What do you think of what they're telling us?" James asked finally. "About… all of it?"

"About Paradise? I don't know. To be honest, this world was similar to what I was expecting, in every way except for the people. But I haven't been able to catch them out in a lie. Not yet." Atxi admitted. "What about you?"

"I don't believe in benevolent gods." James shook his head. "Every church and temple I've ever seen, in all my travels? They're all after money, or loyalty, or in your case; blood. Power and Evil are the same thing. The more power you have, the more evil you become."

Atxi felt an odd need to defend her old Temple. "I don't believe that."

"Believe what you will." James didn't push her. "But if someone has power over a small staff, he will be harsh and unkind to them. If a man has command over a farm; he will fleece his customers and work his servants to death. If a man has rulership over half the world, he will burn the other half to the ground for more. I've seen it everywhere I've ever lived; and I've defied power wherever I've gone. Power is the ability to hurt people; nothing more."

"Wherever you've gone." Atxi repeated. "You've never been here."

"No, I suppose not." James had to admit that. "But it can't be that different, can it?"

Chapter Six: The Secret Of Eternal Life

Atxi hadn't stayed on the ship long, needing transport to a specific destination. James hadn't minded. He was still getting to know his new craft, and didn't need anyone interrupting.

She handled smooth as a dream, and she nearly skimmed the waves like a skipping stone, she moved so fast. With no mainsail, there was an amazing field of vision, and according to what he'd learned about solar cells, it could conceivably run forever; but they ran so silent he could-

The engines stopped suddenly.

James froze, disturbed. He was far enough out that he could barely see land. There was nobody to help him, or arrest him for the theft.

He spent half an hour staring at the engine helplessly, before he discovered that there was indeed a sail. The mast was retractable; another impossible innovation, but he was happy to get her powered by the wind again. Alone, it took him several hours to rig up the mast; when he suddenly discovered he wasn't alone anymore.

"Hallo!" A voice called across the water.

James looked. A smaller Yacht had apparently caught up with him, pulling alongside. There were two familiar faces on board. Karen and Irsu had given chase.

"Your ship has a kill-switch. It's not a security measure. It's a safety feature, specifically to prevent it from sailing away with nobody at the tiller. This class of ship is solar powered. It could go clear over the horizon without anyone at the wheel; so if someone forgets to switch everything off when they leave..." Karen explained by way of greeting. "Even in this world, accidents happen. Can we come aboard?"

James wasn't sure how they'd found him, or how they'd switched off his ship, but he knew there was no chance of escaping. His newly discovered sail would never outpace those silent engines; and he lowered a rope ladder for them. He was expecting to see a squad of lawmen with chains, but it was just her and Irsu. Not that James was any match for the huge man. But from the look he sent around the Yacht when he hauled himself aboard, he had other things on his mind. "Where is she?"

James set his jaw, hand setting automatically at his belt, looking for a cutlass that wasn't there. "I didn't take her against her will, Big Man."

"You would not have been able to." Karen said, unconcerned. "But you both vanished without saying a word, so it was a fair bet you went together."

"I dropped her off this morning, back at Madrid." James told them.

~oo0Ooo~

Atxi had never traveled in her old life. The last place she would have gone was Madrid. Spain had invaded her land, and apparently conquered it. The Terminal told her that the war was long forgotten, by all but the people who had been there. But here she was, walking the streets of a city she'd never been to; the capitol of a land she had dreaded.

And everyone was nice to her. There was no language barrier, no confusing money; and directions came as fast as she could ask for them.

The Meeting Centre in Madrid was just like the one in New Roma. In fact, it was the only building Atxi had seen that looked identical to any other; so she already knew her way around. The difference between this and her own Temples was jarring. No guards, no fortifications…

And then she heard his voice. That same deep, rolling thunder that rang with authority. Huitzilin was here. She followed his voice to one of the main meeting rooms, and there he was, addressing another congregation. Like the one in New Roma, they were ever-young, dressed smartly, flawlessly healthy, and watching with interest as Huitzilin taught them.

Atxi stayed in the doorway, hiding behind the door. He couldn't see her. He hadn't changed a bit. His wardrobe was different, and his 'larger-than-life' bearing was the same, as he captivated the room.

"The plagues of Egypt were chosen carefully!" Huitzilin was declaring. "Egyptians had hundreds of gods. Gods to make pure the Nile River, which was struck with blood! Gods for the animals, that were cut down all at once! Gods for the insects, who devoured and sickened! Gods for the Sun and the Moon, and all of Egypt was in darkness... except for those that praised Jah!"

Atxi felt sick, listening to him.

"Jehovah chose his wonders with his all-knowing skill! He chose attacks that showed the false idols of his enemies to be hollow and helpless. Remember that even now, the blessings we're receiving are tiny specks of the glory of God. A being who put the stars and galaxies in their position; and we are awed by a bountiful harvest, or the song of the birds, or clothes that don't wear out."

They were almost the exact same words he'd used to declare the greatness of Huitzilopochtli. Atxi could take no more, storming out.

What is he even doing here, if Jehovah rules this world? Atxi asked herself sickly. *What am I doing here?*

(Author's Note: *There has long been speculation as to who would be excluded from the Resurrection Promise. We know, from Hebrews 10:26 that not* *everyone will return. The 3/15/06 Watchtower states: 'We must be careful, though, not to speculate on whether a certain person will be resurrected or not. This judgement belongs to God.'*

In this story, the goal is to explore the reactions, and some of the obstacles involved in a Global Resurrection. Also, it's worth noting that Atxi, as well as Huitzilin, predated the rise of Christendom in their own time. Also, Page 73 of the 'Bible Teach' Book states 'He will never resurrect those whom he judges to be wicked and unwilling to change', but I've chosen to give truly ignorant people the benefit of the doubt as a general rule, for purposes of this story.)

~oo0Ooo~

Karen had stayed with James. Irsu had taken their smaller yacht and headed back towards Madrid.

"I'm told you skipped out on the Classes." Karen said to James without looking at him. "Picking up your trail was fairly easy once I thought to head for water." She tapped the railing. "And even easier once I found the confused looking man standing in front of the empty spot at the Docks." She didn't look angry. "I figured you'd be looking for an exit, but I thought you'd wait until the classes were over, at least."

"You aren't responsible for me, Miss Karen." He paused. "I don't actually know your surname."

"No, you don't." Karen admitted. "Because we were never properly introduced. Because you and I didn't meet at a party. I was assigned to greet you when you were raised from the dead."

The pointed nature of the comment was not lost on James. His arrival was the one point he couldn't argue with. He remembered fighting Smitty. He remembered winning. The thought was like a knife in his gut. Smitty was his best friend, and he didn't even have the Prize anymore. "I left the Classes because I-" He broke off, looking to phrase it right.

"Because you didn't want to hear what they were saying." Karen said, unsurprised. "Been there." She glanced around. "You stole this boat, James."

James considered his answer for a moment. He had a ship now, and Irsu had left them. There was no impending trap to escape. "I've stolen lots of things." He said tightly. "I was a pirate. I stole things, I killed people, I shipwrecked people, and that's not even counting the swearing, wenching, and drinking that was how we spent our leisure time."

"And then you died." Karen didn't even blink at his confession. "And now you're here, in a place where Pirates don't exist, and nobody cares what you used to be. And you *stole* this boat, James."

James stared at her. "It's a ship that can go against the wind, and be piloted Solo. You have any idea what that would have been worth to someone like me back in the day?"

"I can imagine." Karen agreed. "But it isn't yours."

"I am a Pirate." He reminded her. "What did you expect me to do? Ask nicely?"

Karen was silent a moment. "I wasn't there." She said finally. "When A-Day happened, there were many places where being a Believer was against the Law. I wasn't there when the order came for all the faithful believers to find each other and wait it out. But I met a guy once who was in prison at the time, unable to make it to the Meeting places. So the brothers in Prison all found each other, and waited it out in the same cell. Just believing what we believe was illegal once. Back then, the brothers did some good work in jails. Half the Bible was written from a prison cell. Nobody cares what your career was then. We care about the now. And you fell back into crime right away."

"What else do I have to fall into?" James charged her. "The Ocean and violence are all I'm good at. I need a ship for one, and an enemy for the other. I found the first. I'm not looking for the second. Not today."

"Mm. Well, as it happens, there's a relatively easy solution." Karen told him. "I bought it for you."

He blinked. "What?"

"Once they figured out it was stolen, they checked for newcomers; since the locals aren't thieves. Once they figured out who likely took it, the builders went looking for a way to walk this back. I was your Welcome Wagon, so they consulted me. Your kin aren't back yet. So I found Brother Claudius Caine; who owned, and personally built this ship. He makes a living at it, you see. He gave me the Transponder on your GPS, and in return, I agreed to buy this ship for you."

No lawmen here. But it took her no time at all. "You can toss that kind of scratch down so easily." James scoffed. "You never told me you were rich."

"I'm not. No more than most people are." Karen shook her head. "But I can pay, with time. Everyone has some income now. Enough to cover the cost of living comfortably. A few coins per month, over a few centuries…"

"And your man Caine is alright with that?"

"He knows he'll get his money eventually. He can afford to wait, just as I can. We worked out a very reasonable payment plan; with a fair amount of interest, given that it's basically a gift for the first few decades until it's paid up. Do your part, and keep this thing in reasonable condition, would you?"

James just shook his head. "And all this is easier than just trying to get his ship back to him?"

"Your ship." She corrected him.

"What?"

"I bought it for you. I have the paperwork to prove it, if you want to see it." She reached into her vest and pulled out the page. Sure enough, it named him as the owner/operator of the ship. "All she needs is a name."

"WHY?!" James was floored. "Why not just…"

"Call in the law? James, we have no prisons here. No criminals either, come to that. You did it because you're new, and-"

"No, I mean… Why is everyone so alright with just letting me go? Why go so far out of your way? Why spend your money on someone you barely know? In support of something you don't agree with?"

"Because everything you took, Brother Caine can replace with time. And the money I spend? It's not like I need it urgently elsewhere. What we're hoping to save is far more than our money. It means your life, more than our coin."

"Which still doesn't explain why?" James insisted. "Surely, there was an option other than…" He broke off. "I don't like owing people, Miss Karen."

"You can learn a lot about someone by what they reach for first when they come back from the dead." Karen smiled. "The Believers immediately want more information about the God that returned them to life. The majority look up their family first. You? Your first move was to steal a boat and get out on the water." She gave him a canny look. "Do you even have a destination?" She shrugged. "I figure having a ship is the first step you'd make towards anything of importance."

"None of which obligates you to buy me one." He pointed out. "Will this thing even hold together for that long? You could be paying this ship off for decades after it's stripped for parts."

"Check the agreement again." She told him bitingly. "The ship is yours until you die, then it goes to me. I can sell it on, or trade it back."

"I thought everyone lived forever now."

"Everyone has the chance to live forever now." She corrected him. "But there's only one Source of Life in the Universe. If you accept what He's offering, you'll live forever too. Not only that, you'll be an honest man. Honest enough to repay me, I'm guessing. If not, then I can get the boat back. After."

He looked at her, askance. "That was almost practical enough to be the sort of thing I would do."

Karen grinned like a shark. "Well, if it helps you feel more at home, Old Man."

James scoffed. "Must be so easy for you. Say a few words over us, and if we happen not to agree, we die; and you can blame us for it."

Karen swatted him. "You bite your tongue. You have no idea how hard it is."

"Yes, I do. I lost people."

"You lost people in a world where nobody could be saved. We lose people now, in a world where everyone can be with us for all eternity, it's just a touch different." She bit out. "And I thank God every single day that I didn't lose anyone close. But not everyone is so lucky."

James said nothing to that, but his eyes made it clear he wasn't there yet.

Karen spelled it out for him. "What's more valuable? A life you can't keep, or a life you can't lose? And the answer is: Neither. They're both irreplaceable. But to lose it is a tragedy, since there will never be another one of any of us. Imagine losing something priceless, when you could have had it forever."

"I don't imagine I'd want to keep anyone forever." James countered. "I wasn't exactly surrounded by dearly beloved."

"Galatians 5:22 says *'The fruitage of the spirit is love, joy, peace, patience, kindness, goodness, faith, mildness, self-control. Against such things there is no law'*." Karen quoted. "The only people left are the ones with that spirit. I could do worse for people to spend eternity with."

"You don't really believe that, do you?"

"Have I said or done anything to make you think I don't?"

"It's impossible." The old pirate said simply. "It's an impossible standard to meet. It's unnatural, it's unfair, and it's not possible to get there."

"Millions have. Thousands of millions will, by the time we get there."

"It's impossible. I get that it's the party line, but it's not really doable. So I'll make it easier for you. I know you're responsible for me, and you've done right enough, so I won't embarrass you. Well, beyond stealing the-"

"You know what I did, back in the day?" She interrupted. "Before this world? I was a supermodel."

"I don't know what that is."

Karen had already tapped at her device, and brought up a picture. Pictures instead of paintings were new to James, but he'd figured it out fairly quickly. This picture was of Karen, wearing lacy underwear, and nothing else. It was the first risque thing he'd seen since waking up on the beach, but it didn't appeal to him the way any of the whores did back in the Pirate Coves.

Karen let him look, unashamed. James couldn't help the way his eyes flicked back and forth between her, and the picture. She looked… ill. Her skin was pale, eyes darker and smokier. She looked malnourished, even unwell. Even in that state, she was pouting provocatively towards the camera, luxuriating on silks; as her bones stretched her skin.

Karen waited, letting him look. After a while, she tapped the image, flicking to another shot. She was dressed in this one; in some rich purple fabric that still managed to be borderline obscene, though the dress was heavier and dragged along behind her. "Curves and weight was the style in your time. In my generation, thin was 'in'."

"Thin? I can see your skeleton." He said finally.

"Yup. I was so weak from hunger for that shoot that when they dressed me in that outfit, I couldn't stand up straight enough, so they lay me flat and held the camera over me like I was standing. I was a human clothes-hanger. Half the girls in the business were getting surgery, using drugs to stay thin... The agency that got me work had doctors on call to keep us vertical without feeding us. I wanted out. So I found a man who liked having a model for a girlfriend, and left that industry behind. I was glad for it. I was able to live like a human being, and eat actual people food instead of birdseed. Then I hit thirty six, and suddenly my looks weren't enough. So I had to... I mean, if I wasn't the youngest and prettiest, then-"

"You had to be the nastiest." The pirate smirked lecherously. "You should see some of the older ladies in the bars of Tortuga, luv. I know how it is."

"Right. I drank, snorted, and smoked whatever it took to stay at all the worst parties. This world is hard to shock, but I when I woke up, I didn't have to dance for it anymore. I told them that I wasn't exactly living a holy, sanctified life. I figured resetting the clock might have been enough. Money wasn't an issue, and I figured the way to handle living 'chaste' was to find a guy who wouldn't mind if we discreetly bent the rules. Wouldn't be the first such relationship I was in." She gestured. "Since you got here, have you seen anyone who isn't gorgeous?"

"Not since I woke up."

"Right. I made my living being a fantasy made flesh. I was out of my league here, and it scared me to death. I knew I couldn't make it either."

"Nobody could."

"No, see... That was the hardest part to figure out. " She told him quietly. "Back when I was a model, I knew a few of the girls who figured out their 'retirement' by looking for a meal ticket. They would agree to provide company now and then. Businessmen old enough to be my grandfather, politicians with wives and kids; even the odd clergymen offered. Discretion was all they cared about. So I thought the same thing you did. The sleaze had to be there, just better hidden. It took me a long time to realize that these guys actually meant what they were saying."

"Are you telling me..."

"It's not an act. It's real. I've been alive for almost seventy years, because I got there too." She pointed at her face. "How old do I look? I'm almost twice your age, and you're already getting grey hairs."

"It's impossible!" He insisted. "Nobody can live up to that!"

"You say 'nobody' but what you mean is: You don't think *you* can."

James rolled his eyes. "Oh, alright. Give me the speech, about how I can do anything, and-"

"Not at all." She didn't even blink. "Lots of people don't make it."

He froze. "What?"

"Yeah. Didn't anyone tell you that part? A lot of people just won't make the leap, and they fade out like they always have at every other point in history. People who die young get to grow old. Even people who died of old age, back before? They get a lifetime enough to decide." She gestured. "Look at you. You already have those little wrinkles around your eyes. My clock has paused. Yours is still ticking."

He stared.

"Millions of people have been brought back, Cap'n. And some of them have grown old and died. Less than you'd think. Most people accept the world for what it is. You? You never accepted the rules of the world around you. And if I'm honest... I don't think you'll make it."

"Really?" He almost laughed.

"Really." She nodded. "I've only been in your company for a short time, but everything I've seen of you tells me you'll die before you accept anyone as your God. I hope I'm wrong, and to be fair, plenty of people said the same about me, and I made it. And more importantly, Jehovah God himself will help you, if only you'd ask. But it's your first week here; and you've skipped out on the people offering to show you the world, and stolen valuable property. It's not looking good for you thus far, Pirate."

James was about to answer, when there was a sudden blast of spray, and Karen let out a delighted shout.

A whale had just breached, arcing into the air, and crashing back down with a big splash.

Karen laughed, thrilled. "I've never seen one in person before."

James watched the whale cavorting about for a while. "I have." He commented. He and his crew had take in some extra cash harpooning them; but he didn't mention that as the huge creature came up to the motionless ship gracefully.

Karen, meanwhile, was rushing to the edge of the ship, leaning out to get a better look. At a slower pace, James went to join her. Karen had climbed out to the side of the ship, able to reach down enough to trail her fingers in the water.

It sent up a jet of spray again, rolling sideways to look at them. Karen was close enough to rest a hand against its leathery skin.

At the railing, James had looked into the eyes of these creatures before, but only after they'd been harpooned to death… "It's not scared of us." He commented.

"He has no reason to fear anything." Karen said, and he observed her a moment. She was maintaining her balance perfectly, one hand holding the railing, one bare foot against the outer hull of the ship. A precarious pose, especially with such a huge animal an inch away; but she was holding the position flawlessly. He had no doubt that she could have stayed there for hours if she'd had a mind to.

The whale's low song rang through them enough to make their insides shake, and the Whale lifted out of the water enough to nudge her hand; before he sank into the water, out of sight. Karen giggled a little out of simple happiness, and pulled herself back up again, one handed; rolling backwards over the railing and onto her feet.

She's never been on a ship before. A sailor has to have fish-hooks for every finger and toe, and this woman can do things that nobody on my crew would even attempt.

And she'd already made the point that she was more like him than he gave her credit for. Or at least, she had started that way.

He was silent a moment. "How did you make it?" He asked finally. "How did you make the change?"

"You lived in the gritty side of your world. Me? I lived in the fantasy. I know exactly how fake the surface can be, because in my world, the 'surface' was all there was. I had ten year old girls telling me that they wanted to look like me when they grew up, and they didn't get that I was debating whether or not to have some ribs removed to keep my waist. So when I woke up in Utopia, I knew where to look for the darker truth. I found it. The dark truth is that some people just won't do it."

"It's not-"

"Not your fault. I know. I told myself that more than once too. Everyone knows the facts of living forever, and everyone who accepts them is happy. And they live forever. And everybody knows that some won't do it, and that it's not up to any of us what others will decide. But the game isn't rigged any more. There's nobody to blame. All the crazy or unwholesome I did? I did it because that was the world, or because I needed the money, or it was just 'the way things are' or even just because it was fun. None of those reasons exist anymore. The truly terrifying secret of eternal life is that it isn't a secret at all."

The Captain said nothing.

"You may figure that out in time, Pirate. You may not. Either way, it's entirely your choice now. You can't put the blame for it on anyone else. Not ever again. This is the one and only choice that nobody can try to influence: What you think when you're alone." She put the piece of paper in his hand. "You have a home now. One that you can take with you wherever you wish to go. Do as you will with it, and go wherever you need to go so you can make your choice."

~oo0Ooo~

Atxi wandered away from the study group in a kind of daze. She'd gotten enough fury pounding through her veins to storm all the way here; and the fury had vanished the minute she heard him speak.

Huitzilin had changed sides. After a lifetime of other people's sacrifice… of other people *being* sacrificed at his hand, herself included, he'd decided to find a new God.

Is that why he's here? Did he surrender to the Conquistadors? Did Huitzilopochtli find his offerings to be unworthy? Did Huitzilin stop me from reaching The Sun?

The questions kept boiling in her brain until she felt sick.

"You need ice-cream."

Atxi blinked, coming out of her thoughts suddenly. "What?" She blurted, unsure.

The Man was wearing a neat, white suit; and had a box on wheels in front of him. Atxi had never seen anything like it before; but that was nothing unusual. She didn't recognize anything at all.

"You seem to be dealing with some heavy thoughts." The man said kindly. He lifted the lid of the large box in front of him, and Atxi could see steam rising from the shock of cold air. She'd never seen anything like that before; and the man reached in with a large spoon, scooping something together for her.

"I'm told it's a common thing." Atxi admitted to him. "And I just wandered away from all the people in the world that I know, trying to find a familiar face… Only to find out he was the least recognizable thing yet."

The man didn't blink. "Yup. Like I said. Heavy

thoughts." He held out a cone. "Here. Enjoy."

Atxi stared at it. "What is it?"

"Never seen ice cream before?" The man seemed oddly eager. "How long have you been back?"

She took the cone. "Only a little while." She noticed some children in the park with ice cream cones of their own, and followed their example. "I was in a place called 'New Roma', and- OhThatIsAmazing." She forgot Huitzilin completely and devoted her whole self to the treat. "It's like the fudge, only..."

"You're right. The flavor is called 'Mint Choc Fudge'." The man said with a smile. "I love that look. I've been making ice cream for people for almost forty years. Been back for three; and picked up my career where I left off."

Atxi didn't respond, savoring the treat. He stepped back, let her finish. When every last trace of it was gone, Atxi looked to him. "You came back too?"

"Most of the people in the world did at some point." He nodded, and held out a hand. "I'm Larry."

She stared at the extended hand, before doing the same. "Atxi." He clasped her hand briefly, and released her. "How did you react, when you got here?" She asked carefully.

"Oh, I knew it was coming. I was a brother long before A-Day." He gestured at the Ice Cream cone she was chewing through. "God's people in ancient times were waiting for this world. They would have expected the spiritual food, but none of them could possibly have expected videos on tablets. Or airships. Or Ice Cream. That thought excited me when I first learned about this world, because if something like Ice Cream could take an ancient believer by surprise, what wonderful thing will surprise the modern believers?" Larry smiled at her. "People who knew things like Ice Cream could exist?"

Atxi had to admit, the things she'd seen had been so far beyond her imagination, that she'd assumed it couldn't be real.

Is it like that for everyone who comes here?

~oo0Ooo~

James said nothing as Karen lowered a boat to leave. The Yacht had a few inflatable boats for landing. Karen had taught him how to inflate one, and pack it away; and then took one to get back to shore. He'd offered to turn back and drop her off; but she'd refused; and he didn't argue the point.

Despite himself, he felt more affinity with her than anyone else. Even in the old world, when he'd understood the rules, people had hidden what they really thought. Finally, he was getting instruction from someone who talked straight.

As the smaller boat sailed back towards land, the thought came to him. *There's a reason she was there to meet you when you... woke up.*

He shook that thought off, and looked to the deed on his ship. It was his. Legally. He'd captained two ships in his life. This one, and the *Stargazer*, which he got by leading a quick mutiny against the most hated Captain he and Smitty ever had.

This one was a gift.

I will pay her back. James decided suddenly. *I have a ship now. I can make my way. I pay her back, and then we're even.*

But I don't have a crew. And Piracy is a dead business, if there are Guardian Angels breathing down my neck every second.

"Then again, I suppose if this is a world where you can buy a ship for tuppence and agree to owe the rest, there might be an honest way to make a living." The thought stayed with him for a few moments, until a familiar grin split his face. "Then again, there's a far better way."

He immediately went to the Terminal in the Captain's Cabin, and called up his maps. The Screen was unlike anything he'd ever used; but this was a world full of people who had never heard the word 'computer' before, so the technology that had become so ubiquitous had to be incredibly intuitive. With a little work, he'd brought up an ocean map.

"Let's see... I was here... We called all stop in the fog after ten hours, so The Spanish Fleet caught up to us... here." He tapped at the screen. "The *Stargazer* would have sunk there. Full to bursting with treasure; waiting at the bottom of the ocean."

With a little more trial and error, he had charted a course.

The Ship had been all he needed to finish his mission. He gripped the wheel, which was far less of a central figure on the bridge than the last wheel he'd held to steer the *Stargazer*...

Thinking of the last time he'd held a ship's wheel gave him a spike. Smitty, giving him the St Nicholas medallion; before they'd fought to the death...

"The *Nicholas*." James said quietly to his new ship. "That's what I'll call you."

Chapter Seven: Time To Think

Atxi decided she would return to the classes. She wanted to learn how to read the local writing. She wanted to learn a lot of things.

Some things she was specifically against learning.

Atxi had settled at one of the public picnic tables; and spent most of her night asking her little device questions, and getting answers. It was oddly exciting, just having all that information come so easily.

She had been so involved, that when Irsu sat down across from her at the table, she didn't notice him at first. When she did, she jumped. "Oh." She said, embarrassed at how easily she'd been caught. "I was coming back. I... don't really have anywhere else yet."

Irsu smiled a bit. "That'll change. You've only been here a few days. It's a lot to process. My job isn't to convince you, it's to welcome you. But I figured you might be... worried, or unsettled; and I wanted to help you get past that stage."

Atxi nodded. "I've traveled more in the last day than I did in my whole life before." She admitted. "This little device says that it's barely a drop of how big the world really is."

"Travel is good for you, Atxi. Gives you perspective. My advice, look at the world. I mean really *look* at it. The graveyards are getting smaller, and the gardens are getting larger. Name one time in history where that has been true."

Atxi bit her lip. "I can't."

"You and I grew up in a world where the dead outnumbered the living. We now live in a world where the reverse will be true. Where kindness will be universal instead of the exception. A place where there are no wars, and no weapons to fight with anyway. I know it's asking you to take an enormous leap, but it's a very wonderful life. If you can make that leap, you can live forever and never fear anything. Does this sound like a bad offer?"

"No. But I don't-"

"I know." Irsu shushed her gently. "But in a month, a year, a decade, you might feel differently. Take it from a guy born in Ancient Egypt. Everything in this world is made better by time."

Atxi set her jaw. "I saw him, Irsu. The last time I saw him, he was standing over me with an obsidian dagger, chanting his loyalty to Huitzilopochtli, and now he's here; lecturing children so earnestly on how your God is the only true one."

"Did you tell him that?"

"I didn't have the nerve to talk to him. If I tried I might have attacked someone." Atxi said darkly. She didn't shout. She didn't thrash about or punch at anything. Her voice was low and icy and full of loathing. "How dare he? He can pick up a new truth so easily. The Shaman do the praying, and the soldiers do the killing, and people like me do the dying; and all in the Name of The Gods!" She clenched her fist so tight she felt her palms bleed. "I hate them all, Irsu. I know that's not what you want to hear, and I don't doubt you're as earnest and faithful as I was when I begged the gods to find my still-beating heart an acceptable snack." Tears were rolling hotly down her face. "And I don't know who God is anymore, but I hope He hates them as much as I do."

Irsu looked at her, his expression was naked pity. He looked so openly crushed that she almost wanted to hug the seven foot man, the way she'd cradled the toddlers in her old life.

"I didn't tell Kasumi I was going. I'll call her now." Atxi nodded and walked off, grateful to change the subject.

But she couldn't help but glance back. Irsu was the first face she'd seen since Huitzilin and he'd been nothing but gentle and kind to her. She didn't wish to hurt anyone, or even offend his beliefs. But she was never going to sort out her faith by doing what Huitzilin had done.

Irsu was still there, head bowed. Atxi knew instantly that he was praying for her. She wasn't sure whether to be grateful, or outraged.

~oo0Ooo~

Walter left the Dorms early, and went to look for breakfast. Traditionally, he started his day before dawn, to get a jump on the news, paperwork… It took him several minutes to remember that he wasn't employed any longer.

Walter realized he was excited. The Dorms were clearly the landing spot for Newcomers. Actually getting your life started didn't begin until you took control of things. It was why he had tried to find his assets right away. If he had to start with lodging over fortune, so be it. He had time for both.

When he went to the tables, there was no food set out yet. He made his way toward the kitchen, knowing that the bakers and chefs were usually up earlier. There'd surely be someone to take his breakfast order.

He was right, but the atmosphere in the kitchen was very relaxed. There were people kneading and shaping breads and pastries; slicing fruit and squeezing fresh juice. There was a strong smell of freshly baked bread, and freshly brewed coffee.

"Morning." Someone said when they saw Walter come in. "You're up early. You a baker yourself?"

"I am not." Walter said politely. "But I am something of an early riser. I was wondering where a person could get some breakfast."

"It hasn't been taken out yet, but there's plenty on the platters already. Help yourself." The woman gestured over to the larger countertops. "You need anything, call out. I'm Layla."

Walter did so, finding the trolleys piled high with food, waiting to be served. Not everything. The eggs were still being prepared, the toast hadn't been toasted. But there were fresh pastries, plenty of fruits, and the coffee was freshly percolating. The smell of cinnamon was so sharp that he felt his stomach roar; and he took more than he needed.

When Walter went outside to the Plaza, it wasn't as cold as he thought it would be. He chose a spot that gave him a view of the doors, and began examining the pastry he was eating. It was light and warm and soft; but the flakes didn't stick to his fingers. A five star kitchen would be hard pressed to put this together in huge quantity.

The Centre was built in a flat U-shape, so he had his back to the dawn as it started. Walter didn't turn to look, but noticed suddenly that he wasn't alone.

"I remember I always got up before dawn when I was little." Layla said, facing the opposite direction, enjoying the sunrise. "When I got older, I was less and less excited at the idea of starting another day and started sleeping in. The world now is more or less in two camps. The people who want to see the start of every new day, and the people who luxuriate in the fact that there's no rush to get up."

Walter was still focused on his Device, and didn't answer. She didn't press him; and they sat that way. Her facing the sunrise, he with his back to it.

"You can take that in there, when you're done." Layla said politely, and promptly did the same, taking her tray with her, back into the kitchens.

Walter finished off his plate and cast about for a busboy. There wasn't one, but the dawn was only just ending, so he imagined it was early for the minimum wage types to be on hand for their jobs.

He took his tray back into the kitchen, where the spread for the morning meal was now assembled, being carried out to the large serving table in the Dormitory Garden. Layla saw him coming in and waved him over to join her at the sink. She had a scrubbing brush held out to him by the time he reached her.

"No, I won't be doing that." Walter said with an outright laugh.

"Why not?" Layla challenged. "You get served a free meal, the least you can do is clean up after yourself. It's a nice thing to do for the people who have been up for three hours baking fresh rolls."

"I am not a dishwasher." Walter said pointedly.

"We all are. The work gets done when it's needed."

"Seems like good sense to me. Contact me when there's something for me to do." Walter said politely, and left the kitchen; shaking his head at her foolishness.

~oo00oo~

James had been afraid to leave the bridge of his new ship, which he could tell was more of a Private Yacht. Karen's comment about the 'safety feature' rang true. This ship barely *needed* anyone at the helm.

James had to take inventory. He was a pirate. He knew how to avoid the attention of authorities... except he hadn't seen any since waking up.

He knew how to escape chains and prison walls... except nobody was trying to keep him trapped.

He knew how to provide for himself and quietly procure supplies… except nobody was denying him anything he clearly needed.

He knew how to hijack a ship… except one had been provided for him as a gift.

~oo0Ooo~

David arrived at breakfast with the rest of the Dorm. Walter was eager to get started, but David assured him there was nothing to be done until after breakfast. Walter, expecting a real estate office, or other such amenity, agreed that business hours were best.

After breakfast was Morning Worship. A man that Walter hadn't been introduced to lead the service. It was relatively simple. He stood up and read a scripture, then gave commentary on it.

The speaker called for someone to read the scripture. Walter had a Bible put in his hand, open to the correct page; and it came so quick he didn't even see who gave it to him.

"Proverbs 16:3 says: *'Commit to Jehovah whatever you do, and your plans will succeed'*." The speaker declared. "Today, more than at any point in history, we have proof of this scripture. But even when times were at their worst, none of Jehovah's prophecies or promises failed to come to pass. Not one. Jehovah cannot fail. If it was possible to defeat his plans, then he wouldn't be God. Today, everyone is making their plans for eternal life. Those plans are many and varied, and as diverse as the people we meet here. But we remind each other, and ourselves, to make our plans according to Jehovah's purposes, because as long as we commit to Him, our plans will succeed. Not because of his blessing, but because His are the only plans that are guaranteed to work."

"You don't agree, do you?" David asked Walter

quietly.

"No." Walter admitted. "I get the idea, and it sounds like sound logic, at least for a religion. But I've discovered that a person's success is measured by their will to keep going, regardless of what others think.."

"Even if they are in the wrong?"

"Right and wrong are measured by success." Walter told him. "A million people tell you that you can't do something, and then you do it, you've proven yourself to be right."

David gave him that look again, though less so than usual, before he answered. "Once we're done with breakfast, I'll show you how people get a new home constructed."

~oo0Ooo~

David had a car. The model was unlike anything Walter had seen before. There was no manufacturing label, and the top was open. There was room for about six people, and as David drove, with Walter in the passenger seat, they passed several people, walking in the same direction. David pulled over for all of them; and the vehicle was full by the time they reached their destination. Walter very carefully said nothing to picking up hitchhikers; hoping David knew them all. They were all carrying tools or baskets.

The construction site was in an open space; well back from the road. Walter hadn't seen any high-capacity construction yet, and wondered if the whole world was these little towns now. There was a good hectare or two of open land around the half-built house, which was a modest family size.

As David pulled the car to a halt, everyone climbed out and got right to work. Those with baskets were unpacking food, those with tools were heading inside to get started. There was no debate, no loitering. Everyone was happy to see each other, knew each other by name...

Another vehicle pulled up, and the driver opened the trunk, to reveal a collection of handheld tools. Walter didn't see a line forming, but they were passed out in seconds, and work began almost instantly. Nobody blew a whistle, or punched a clock. They just showed up and got to work.

David led him into the half-finished house. One room was more or less done, though unfurnished. In this room was a man with a larger Device, and a woman with a happy smile on her face. "Walter, this is Danny. He's our Site Manager, so to speak; and this is Hannah, our host. It's her house we're building."

"*We* are?" Walter repeated.

"We are." David blew past that. "Danny, Walter is new here. Can you show him a bit about how it works?"

Danny held out his device. There was a 3D model of the house they were in. "Most people have never had the chance to design and build their own home. I work with them like a police sketch artist, working out things they care about, things they're interested in, how to improve their ideas and make them realistic..."

"That's design, how does the house get built?" Walter asked. "I mean, where do these builders come from?"

"Oh, this is the congregation." Hannah put in blithely.

Walter blinked. "I'm sorry?"

"Once we sort out the design, we put up the locations and dates on the local congregation notice boards. All the congregations in the area find out who needs something built or repaired; and people show up."

"Must offer them pretty good rates." Walter commented, looking around the house. "But you're fairly lax in your timekeeping. I assume you pay by the day instead of the hour."

"They're volunteers." Danny said, not looking away from the design.

"What?!" Walter stared at him, trying to decide if he'd misheard. He looked to Hannah. "You're getting your house built by amateurs."

"Oh, we're trained. We have on-the-job training in every field. Remember, a lot of these people are still experimenting with their own home designs, or making changes to the places they have."

"Plus, if there's something put together wrong, they catch it." Hannah nodded. "Those with degrees and professional qualifications inspect every site; make sure everyone knows what they're doing; make sure it's all being done safely."

"And Hannah is one of those people, too. She's been checking the wiring on over a dozen properties in the Region. She's finished her regional tour with the Building Committee, which means her own home just became a priority." David put in. "And speaking of, where would you like to start?"

"Start." Walter repeated, trying to comprehend that.

"Yup. Electrical, or plumbing? You'll need both if you want to help; and it'll be wise to have some practice under your belt when you build your own place."

Walter just looked at him. "You're funny." He said flatly.

"Do a good job this morning, and I'll spend the afternoon helping you design your own place, for when your turn comes up."

"Walter, you asked how a person got their own home. This is how." David told him lightly. "Everyone helps us build our own place, we help each other in return."

"David." Walter said plainly. "When a predominant man is presented with plumbing, the only skills he needs to master is how to turn a tap, or flush. I had both those skills sorted some time ago. Manual Labor is not what I do. You understand, I'm sure."

David was already strapping on a toolbelt. "Well, that's up to you, Walter. Me? I'm going to help my friend get a home."

~ooO0Ooo~

People kept arriving for over an hour, and nobody was leaving. Walter wasn't about to hike all the way back to the Dormitory, and he had nothing to do there. David hadn't been joking, it was clear, but Walter wasn't about to grab a hammer. He wouldn't know which end to hold anyway.

But he took the opportunity to observe. Walter had been on construction sites before, as an Assessor, or as an investor, being shown what his money was getting. This worksite was different. Everyone was chatting eagerly, there were kids helping out; and it took him a moment to notice that nobody was using profanity, which had to be a first for a construction site.

Once it became clear that Walter had no intention of helping out, he'd been handed a jug of fruit juice, and he made the rounds, providing refreshments to workers. He'd accepted that because it gave him a closer look at what everyone was doing, and let him speak to a few people. There were people being instructed in how to handle electrical wiring, how to lay and seal pipes together, how to tell a load-bearing wall, or how to use a power-tool properly…

It was as much training as construction, but they were getting through it so fast Walter was in disbelief. He was watching the house come together almost as quickly as he could move between rooms.

"Where are we at?" Hannah asked the room as Walter brought the jug.

Danny checked his Device. "We're short of gravel. We need some more to mix up the amount of concrete we need. There's no point starting on that until we've got it. The cement has to be poured in one complete piece."

"Agreed." Hannah nodded. "Also, someone sent us way too much topsoil. There's no use for it here; and if we don't lay it somewhere, it'll all get trod into the ground or blow away. Twelve tons worth."

"Twelve tons?!"

"A truck got sent to the wrong site. It was loaded up, and dropped its cargo before anyone sorted the mistake."

"We'll work it out." Danny said with certainty. "People are building all over the place."

~oo0Ooo~

"What about people like me?" Walter asked Hitch quietly at one point. "I don't qualify, because I'm not one of your Congregation."

"Not yet." Hitch sipped the drink Walter had brought, wiping sweat from his brow. "Back in OS, by the end, disaster relief had become a major part of the Organization's work. You weren't there for the last few years, but there was just one place after another being demolished by earthquakes, tornadoes, floods, wildfires… Day after day. The Building Committees went global, restoring places of worship, restoring homes… You're right; we prioritized our people first, but we didn't turn away anyone in need. We helped everyone we could back then." He handed the cup back. "Your place? It'll come. But right now, it's-"

"Low priority?" Walter said archly. "Do you have any idea who I am?"

"The only man here who refuses to help lift a pre-fab wall?"

"I don't 'lift'." Walter said plainly. "For all your talk about 'everyone being equal' and nobody being 'above others', it took me less than a day to find your own 'class distinction'." Vindicated, Walter turned to go, chin up.

Hitch caught him by the shoulder. "Walter, this world has an Authority. Like any government, it has responsibilities to its citizens, it has opportunities for newcomers, and it gives blessings and rewards. You're asking for all of the benefits, and none of the responsibility. For all your talk about how 'this world can't work', you still want it to work for you, and ask nothing in return." He shrugged impishly. "Did it take a day to spot our hypocrisy, or yours?"

Walter said nothing to that.

~oo0Ooo~

After a few hours, Hannah let out a loud whistle, and called everyone together for lunch. David prayed over the table of food, which was typically varied and enough to feed an army.

Hannah had taken the opportunity to thank everyone for their effort, and express her gratitude. Walter listened to her do it. He'd organized construction before, and never been so personal in his thanks to the contractors.

Walter had slowly approached the table, and someone put a plate into his hands before he even joined those sitting down. There was a huge spread. He took a few bits of everything. The only other place he'd eaten since arriving was the Cafeteria, and it suddenly hit him. "No meat dishes." He observed aloud to David, though Walter noticed the comment drew some attention. "Did I say something wrong?"

David shook his head. "No, but asking about the meat

sort of 'outed' you as being new. It's the sort of thing most people observe on day one."

"So Vegetarian Food is the norm." Walter surmised. "How ghastly."

"I've heard that from several Returnees." David chuckled. "I don't believe I've ever eaten meat before. Proverbs 15:17 says *'Better is a dish of vegetables where there is love than a manger-fed bull and hatred along with it'*."

"But what if I wanted a Prime Rib anyway?" Walter asked, already mourning the Michelin Star Diet he'd always had.

"More than love?" David asked, surprised by the question.

"Sure, why not?"

David just looked at him. "You realize that you just said that out loud, right?"

Walter said nothing to that, and everyone ate for a few minutes. There was nobody arguing, no pushing for a better seat... "You know, I have to admit, the people here work faster and better than any contractors I've ever hired." Walter said finally to those seated around him. "I've never seen anything like this before."

"No, I'm sure." Danny said. "I was part of the RBC, back in OS."

Walter nodded, though he had no idea what any of those things were. He was about to say something more when a large truck rolled up. "Hey there!" The driver called. "I'm coming from a Restoration project on the far side of Roma. I was told to ask around the Building Sites on my way to the depot; see if anyone has any topsoil."

Hannah sent a look to Danny. "Did you...?"

"No, I didn't call anyone." Danny said with a wide grin before he called back to the driver. "How much you need?"

"About twelve tons worth." The Driver called back.

Hannah laughed like it was the funniest thing she'd ever heard and rose from the table. "Bring the truck. We can hook you up."

"On the way back. I've gotta take this truck back to the depot first, drop off the load."

"What are you hauling?" Danny called.

"Gravel. We've been emptying out an old mine; and need to get it somewhere useful."

~oo0Ooo~

"You know I'm not believing any of it, right?" Walter scorned once the swap was done. "Seriously, that's the most blatant setup I've ever seen. You had to have called him."

"I did not." Hannah promised. "I have my Bible handy if you want me to swear on it."

"Walter, back in OS, these kinds of 'little miracles' took place all the time during construction of Bethels, Convention Halls…" David shrugged. "The whole world is running this way now."

"I don't buy it. God being generous, I get that. But the work you're doing is so inefficient." Walter said pointedly. "I mean, look at the site! If you built a full subdivision here, you could get a hundred homes built a lot faster than just one at a time on acre allotments. Can you even get these people together in any kind of regular way?"

"You *are* new here, aren't you?" Danny said with a wry grin. "The reason we don't build whole communities before the people arrive, is because we all design and build our own homes now. Everyone has a different dream home. Doesn't work for mass production"

Walter stared. "You *custom-build* every home for every person who joins your church, with volunteer labor, and you don't charge them for *any* of it?"

Half a dozen people had their devices and Bibles out already, all of them showing him the same verse. "Isaiah 65: 21,22: *'They will build houses and live in them, and they will plant vineyards and eat their fruitage. They will not build for someone else to inhabit, nor will they plant for others to eat'.*"

"If it's part of prophecy, how can we charge money for it? You can't demand payment for what God promises to give."

"And what better way to make people feel at home, than to give them a home they can feel at home in?" David added. "How can you feel like a place is yours if it's designed for a hundred other people?"

"It can't work." Walter declared instantly. "You just cannot succeed like that. It's impossible."

"Why?" The man asked, enjoying this.

"Because if people can have any place they want, they'd all choose a palace, and get one for free."

Danny gestured at the day's work. "We aren't building a palace today. In fact, I've never built one. There are the Teaching Centres, and the Convention Halls, but those are spaces for thousands of people. Beyond that…"

Walter looked back at the newly built house. "I guess I just assumed Hannah couldn't afford…" He trailed off, trying to process this.

"Couldn't afford something bigger? She didn't pay anything. A dwelling is part of the 'guarantees' list, like food, and clothing, and safety. Nobody charges for these things, because they're basic needs."

Walter turned to Hannah. "So why didn't you go for

a third level? A bigger garage?"

"Why would I need one?" Hannah asked, her tone suggesting the logic was simplicity itself.

"And what about me?" Walter countered. "Assuming I… qualify: What if I wanted a palace?"

"It'd take a lot longer to get it finished, and be a lot harder to maintain. Besides, some people insist on a small cabin, or even a Yurt, so it all balances out in the end."

"You don't offer maintenance?"

"You saw the Hall, we all do our part for the common areas. Why not take care of our own places ourselves? We're all trained how. It's how we can help build homes for the newcomers."

There was a lull in the conversation as another platter of food was put in front of them, and everyone ate. David brought a cake over, and sat down.

"That cake is excellent." Walter tried again, from a different angle. "Better than five star."

"And that's from a man who ate a lot of five star food." David put in to the table at large. "The sister who made it will be glad to know you think so."

"I did less work than anyone else here." Walter challenged. "I haven't taken any of your classes, nor do I plan to. But nobody pays for this food. So aren't I cheating you out of the feast you earned? If this is all gratuity, shouldn't you be sending me away from this table right now? I'm eating as much as you guys, and haven't produced half the results."

"Have another piece of cake." David said easily.

Walter rolled his eyes. "You can't possibly expect to succeed like this." Everyone in earshot was smiling, trying to hold back outright laughter. "Will someone please explain the joke?!"

"Walter, you keep saying 'we can't succeed'." David explained. "The reason we're all finding that amusing is because we *are* succeeding. Just being here is the Prize. We, all of us, consider this the ultimate 'win' that a person can get."

"I'm here." Walter pointed out. "There's more to it than just showing up, surely?"

"You mentioned this site seems odd." Hitch put in. "For people who worked on the Regional Building Committee back in the Old Days, this is actually the more familiar stuff. Food's a little better, and the workers are in far better health, but back in the day, they did this at every 'work day' around the world."

Walter looked around again. "It's hard to imagine people working like this… back then."

"But not here?" David asked with a smile. "Are you saying there may be something different about this world?"

Walter's face hardened at the slip. *Keep your guard up, Walter. This place is smarter than you think.*

Book Two: Promises Kept

Joshua 21:45 *"Not a promise failed out of all the good promises that Jehovah had made to the house of Israel; all of them came true."*

Chapter Eight: Learning Curve

Days passed. Walter took the classes on construction and maintenance, but he only listened with half an ear. In truth, he was looking to see who the best contractors were, how they were paid, what companies they consulted for…

And he found nothing. The people who were leading the classes all knew their stuff, and their credentials and experience were readily available to anyone who asked. In small groups, they taught each aspect of construction, from laying plumbing, to wiring solar panels, to working power tools.

Walter hadn't noticed it at first, but the people here were sharp. They asked intelligent questions, they weren't too shy or timid to handle the equipment; and they barely took notes. David had noticed his reaction and ascribed the mental discipline to 'growing perfection in mind and memory'. Walter had been expecting something like that. After all, he'd expected science to break the death barrier, so improving faculties and ability was a relatively minor miracle.

He was also able to observe how people found help for maintenance of their own homes. The classes ran, day after day; and someone would quietly come by and outline a problem they needed help with. A senior student would volunteer, and they'd go back with the person in need. Often, one or two new students would go along with them. Walter was invited along once; but didn't have much to add. A lunch spread was put out for the two or three volunteers, and Walter had never felt more out of place.

"A lot of people don't ask for help." David had told him. "They go to a lot of the classes, help out here and there; and the only thing they ask in return is the materials. It's not uncommon for some people to want to build their own places solo. It's a point of pride, for some."

Walter was still tapping at the Terminal. "It just doesn't feel… safe. It still feels like amateurs, being taught casually, and then just asking around. In fact, that's exactly what it is. Doesn't seem right, for constructing a whole world."

"We're safer than anyone has ever been." David said simply. "And the only point you got wrong was how 'casual' it appeared. Trust me, people are paying attention. They're acquiring life skills for their own homes, after all." David looked over Walter's shoulder a the Terminal. "Who are you looking for?"

"My old business partners. If you're serious about 'everyone' coming back, then I have to take advantage of the 'talent pool', and quickly."

"Why?"

"There is always an Apex, there is always a Lower-Class. It's a basic law of nature. You have a civilization here. There has to be poor people, and there have to be wealthy. And if there's no necessity in money; then the currency is something else. Reputation, rank, number of pets for all I know. But someone makes a choice about how the world is to work, and then others are put to work making it happen. That's the way it's always been, that's the way it's always going to be; that's the way it is."

David studied him a moment. "You know what? I'd like to get my father in on this conversation? He's a Tribulation Witness. I think someone who was there on both sides of the The Big Day might speak with more… authority on the subject."

Walter nodded, pleased. "I agree."

~ooOOoo~

Atxi was starting to figure out how things worked. The Centre had several classrooms, all of which had access to huge varieties of information. Each classroom was more or less the same. An auditorium shape with seats in a semi-circle, elevated to give everyone a view of the teacher. Some of them were even outdoors; but they always included the Terminals. Atxi had been watching clips and recordings without limit, putting together a huge puzzle in her mind.

Atxi noticed a buzz around the Dorms that she hadn't heard before. There was a sense of anticipation in the air. She asked Kasumi about it, and the Japanese woman smiled. "A friend of mine is coming through with her family later today. Her name is Isobel. She was Returned a few years ago, found her family again. They live in Caravans, on the move. They've seen more of the world than you have; and they make their contribution by making deliveries."

"I thought communications were instant now."

"They are, but just as we have people from the whole timeline here, we have technology from all eras too. Most people will always prefer a letter. A letter from someone is a very powerful thing, Atxi. It's something they held in their hands when they thought of you. It's a captured, preserved moment of what they wanted to say to you, and never say out loud."

Atxi did a double-take at that little speech. "Who are *you* writing to?"

Kasumi coughed a bit. "Just a friend."

~oo0Ooo~

"Why would I be in this part of the world?" Atxi asked. "It took some doing, but… I'm in Europe. I was born, and died in South America. Is that what you call it?"

Kasumi nodded. "We haven't figured out the order

143

yet. But every Returnee is met by someone, chosen by name. I've heard tell about families being reunited, lifelong friendships, even relationships being started."

"Really?" Atxi blinked, thinking of Irsu.

"Don't read anything into that." Kasmi said, reading her mind. "A lot of the time, the pick is as beneficial to the Greeter as it is to the Returnee." She could see Atxi wasn't that convinced, and kept going. "Back in OS, there were fairly specific rules for JW's about what was 'appropriate' between men and women. A single brother or sister usually had a third party present. It wasn't any lack of trust, but it discouraged gossip; and make sure others were not made to feel uncomfortable in any way. In this world, nobody's 'unchaperoned', ever." She gestured at the sky to make the point. "But the truth is, we've finally managed to close the gender gap in a lot of ways. The friendships you make here can last, literally, forever; regardless of gender or marital status."

Atxi thought for a moment about the gossip surrounding her mother and Huitzilin. "I hope so."

(**Author's Note:** *There's no specific passage in the Bible to speak on this subject. In 'Just See Yourself', I had unmarried pairs spending time together unsupervised. At first it was purely as a storytelling device. I find that male/female interactions have good rhythm; even platonically. I made a reference to the fact that in the New World we're never 'unsupervised', ever; but it wasn't a major deal.*

When I wrote 'Now On Earth' I continued the pattern because it was useful as a tool to answer specific questions, like the return of a marriage mate, even centuries later; or to consider the generation gap; like when a man from the 1300's has trouble with the idea of a woman professor.

When writing this book, I seem to have fallen into the

same pattern; this time based on personality conflicts. I wanted to make it clear: Nobody behaves inappropriately in these books, and there is no specific scripture to address the issue, but in the New World according to my imagination, a person is met and taught by whoever has the best chance of getting through to them, for any reason; totally independent of gender or marital status. I'm not pairing up my characters; I'm building mentor/ee relationships and friendships that are not concerned with taboos of any culture in any time period.)

At that moment, a call went up, and Kasumi smiled broadly; leading Atxi outside.

A row of large covered wagons came up, pulled by large horses. A dark haired woman in a homespun dress jumped down lightly. "Hello, everyone!"

There was, as always, a large reception of people. Atxi could tell at once who the newcomers to the world were, because they were hanging back a bit. The experienced brothers were all coming closer, embracing the people from the caravan.

Kasumi was in the latter group, and pulled Atxi along with her. "Isobel!"

"Kas!" The dark haired woman wrapped Kasumi in a tight hug. "I thought that was your name I saw on those envelopes. Last I heard, you were in Australia. Don't you ever sit still?"

"Look who's talking." Kasumi drawled. "I have post?"

"Two for you, Kas. One from your mom, one from Hugh. I won't make mention of the fact that you told them where to find you; and not me." Isobel made the delivery. "Don't you and Hugh talk by Holo every day?"

"Not every day." Kasumi shook her head, totally guileless; before reaching for a letter in her own pocket.

"Oh, and I have one to send back to Hugh, too."

"You're rhyming." Isobel teased.

"It's his name." Kasumi hissed, a little embarrassed, and Atxi suddenly found that she missed her sister very much. Kasumi noticed her reaction, and made introductions. "Isobel Baptiste, this is Atxi. She was only just returned a few days ago."

"Really?" Isobel grinned at Atxi. "Feel like you're trying to swim up a waterfall?"

"Something like that." Atxi nodded.

"We've all been there, Sister." Isobel promised. "Remember, this is the easy part. The hard part is: you can't claim ignorance forever." She smiled wider, showing perfect teeth. "But the very best part? Is what happens after that. Believe me, I know."

"Isobel was one of my Blue Letters." Kasumi explained. "She only made her choice recently; and then her family came back."

"None of my family are here." Atxi murmured.

"They will be." Isobel promised. "And when they are, you'll be like me: The only one in the family that can tell them what's happening. I've met a few families where it happened in that order." She smiled a bit. "Funny, but I never thought my da would listen to me about something like this."

"How's that going, by the way?" Kasumi asked.

"Better than I thought it would. "Dad's not used to having people throwing a party every time our Caravan comes to town. That alone is proof of God to him."

Atxi started to say something, when the dark-haired woman ducked back into her Caravan, and emerged with another letter. "Atxi. I thought that name sounded familiar. I have post for you, too."

"I've been here less than a week." Atxi blinked.

"Who could be sending me things?"

"I would never read your mail, sister." Isobel promised. "But I do know where it came from. There was a man with a nice looking ship who ferried me out to the Islands so that I could make a few deliveries. When he found out where I was going, he asked me to deliver one to you."

"James ferried you?" Atxi repeated, oddly pleased to know the Pirate was still in the area, and taking on jobs.

"I think that was his name, yes."

~oo0Ooo~

Hitch Thorne sat with Walter as David made them coffee.

"I wasn't even a little bit interested in the Jehovah's Witnesses when David was born." Hitch explained. "Then the accident happened, and I lost my kid and my wife at the same time, spent six months physical therapy trying to use my hands again…" Hitch looked over. "Actually, come to think of it, it was your legal firm that represented the hospital."

"What?" Walter blinked.

"When the Insurance Company tried to refuse payments, your firm was the one telling the Judge that my 'Red Dye Allergy' was a pre-existing condition that disqualified me."

Walter scowled. "Look, before you-"

"Hey, I'm not mad. It's not like you kept me from getting here. My wife and kid are back; what else is there?" Thorne waved it off instantly. "But there I was, bankrupt, limping around my house, trying to pack my kid's teddy bear and my wife's make-up kit into boxes; about as done with life as anyone could be, when…" He rapped his knuckles on the timber armrest of his chair.

"That's when they found you?"

"Yup." Thorne nodded. "And I told them to get lost. I told them with a powerful amount of cussin' mixed in, and slammed the door hard."

Walter laughed.

Thorne nodded. "I wasn't about to let anyone take advantage of my misery to get a donation to anything. But the magazine they were holding had a question on it: 'Why?' written in big bold letters."

"The Eternal Question." Walter nodded.

"I shopped around in a dozen different churches, temples… Trying to find an answer that made sense. Not a fairy tale, not something that would make me happy. I wanted something that seemed like actual fact." Thorne snorted. "Every single one of them had some variation on 'God's Plan' as their reasoning; or even 'God's Punishment'. If my wife had some secret sin worth killing our son over, I had no idea what it could be. One or two even suggested it was punishment for something I did, myself."

"I never thought much of that, even before I found out I was dying." Walter agreed.

"I mentioned this to some people I worked with. I was lucky to get a job bussing tables, with my arms messed up, but when I told them about the 'punishment' angle, a co-worker showed me James 1:13. *'For with evil things God cannot be tried, nor does he himself try anyone'.*" Thorne shook his head. "Imagine my shock when I found out my co-worker was a Witness."

"Their message appealed to you more?" Walter guessed.

"I told you; I didn't want 'appealing'. But it ticked all the boxes. A loving God, a rational explanation for evil, and a hope that didn't involve sitting around on clouds in places I had no interest in going." He sipped. "And more importantly, they had focus."

"Focus?"

"Ask any JW, and I mean any of them *in the world*, what kept them going in their bad days, and they'll all have the same answer: Hope for the Future. The message they preached kept getting more and more hurried and pointed, the closer and closer we got. I'd never seen a Church tie themselves to a timeframe that tightly, or put all their hopes on one thing only."

"What was it?" Walter asked, honestly not knowing.

"All this." David put in. "The world we're living in now."

Walter almost answered, eyes going dark and distant again.

"I know. It still seems like a naive dream to you. Truth was, it seemed that way to me too, once. Back in OS, the Witnesses were told to always 'keep their eyes on the prize'." Thorne explained. "But back there, and back then? The Prize was so far out of our experience, it was almost impossible to do that." He gestured at Walter. "I told you, I wasn't looking for a fairy tale. And at the time, promises of Eternal Paradise seemed to fit that bill. Then an Elder told me to look at what I had seen already, and compare that."

Walter frowned. "I'm... not sure I'm following."

"JW's had the shortest learning curve." David put in. "People who arrive here have to deal with the fact that nobody uses foul language anymore. The JW's didn't have that problem, because cleaning up their language was part of becoming a Witness."

David's father nodded. "Racial bias, gender bias... A lot of points in history, these things were a matter of law, let alone a taught behavior. Telling a former slave that he is equal to his former master, and vice-versa, under God's Rule? A hard thing for them to wrap their heads around, but the Witnesses didn't have that problem."

"Money was a bias too." David added. "I told you that my father and his Generation came into this world with less than what they could carry. So did you. But the world back then would have trouble with the idea of the Overseers taking a turn scrubbing toilets like everyone else." This comment was said with a smile, but Walter winced at the point being made. "The Witnesses didn't have a problem with it, because they were following that policy long before coming here."

"Political bias." Hitch ticked off on his fingers. "Plenty of people want to know who's in charge now. A King, a Queen, a General, a President... Plenty of people identify themselves by whoever they voted for, or what issues they cared about. The idea that there are no countries left is hard to wrap their heads around. But the JW's didn't have that problem, because they were already practicing that neutrality."

"You can pretty much pick your division. Military Stance, Religious Denomination, class distinction, even favored sports team." David summed up. "The Witnesses had a very different view on all of these things, long before God put his foot down and put the world in whatever order He had intended it to be in."

"And there was a learning curve for us, too." Hitch said quickly. "A lot of us expected Paradise to look different, be organized a certain way... But in a very real sense, JW's had been training their people from the first study on to be ready for this world, by living as closely as they could to its rules before they ever got here. But this world works, Walter." He spread his hands wide to Walter, making his case. "We know it works, because it's been how we've done things. Even in OS; we lived according to our beliefs, and it worked amazingly."

"Well... Then how does it work?" Walter demanded. "I mean, who pays for all this? Hard work isn't fun;

that's why it's called *work*. If work was fun, you would have to pay for it; instead of *being* paid for it."

"Donations, mainly. Most people donate time and effort. There is still money, but cost of living is nearly non-existent once you're established, so people don't mind donating their surplus. Everyone gets trained in construction, since they build and keep their own homes too. Money is for luxuries that go beyond enjoyment of the world itself, and the company of the people in it."

"But where do you draw that line?"

"That scripture everyone showed you about building your own home? That was a promise in scripture. So was food, life, health, clothing, spiritual provision… Some things were added to that list by our own choice when we were setting up the world; including transport, communications…"

"To illustrate; if you want to travel, you can. Lodging will be provided for you in every community. Nowhere is off limits. There are no borders or papers required. But if you want to travel by private plane, you're going to need to find one and work out a deal to use it."

"Right, but what is the source of these… guarantees?" Walter pressed. "Someone's responsible for keeping the lights on and the water hot. Where does the funding or the provision come from?"

Hitch looked at his son. "Should we show him?"

"I don't know. The shock of it might do him in." David said wryly.

~oo00oo~

Atxi hadn't met Walter yet. But they both stayed in the Dorms. So while the house was being built, she helped Hannah with some of her chores. The woman kept bees, near an area they were using to plant trees.

"I don't know if the Aztecs had honey as part of their

diet…"

"We do. Did." Atxi nodded easily. *How can they not know?*

Hannah handed Atxi a crate full of wooden frames. "Good then. Come along."

Atxi hadn't seen anything like the bee-hives before. Two dozen large wooden boxes, that stood straight as she did. And a cloud of bees buzzed around each of them. Atxi recoiled instinctively, but Hannah walked straight through the bees with a smile.

Hannah wasn't wearing any protective gear, or using any special equipment to protect herself; but she didn't hesitate as she levered the nearest case open, and started sliding out wooden panels, thick with beeswax and dripping with fresh honey. Atxi took them one by one, and handed a fresh wooden panel back. Hannah swapped them into the hive, and moved onto the next one. Atxi could see the bees circling her, but she waved them away like they were harmless flies.

Hannah noticed her scrutiny. "Back in OS, I helped out on a city farm that did this once. They spent ages suiting up before they went out to the hives. Trust me, this is better."

"You're not worried about them stinging you?"

"Nope. And they're not worried about me swatting them." Hannah smiled at the bees as she lifted the lid on the next hive.

"Does your God protect them all?" Atxi asked, genuinely curious. "I know you don't hunt or slaughter animals; but does that extend to killing insects?"

"I'll be honest, I haven't heard anything official on the subject." Hannah said lightly. "But I do know that there's a verse in the Gospel about how *'not a sparrow falls without God's notice'*."

Atxi waved a hand back and forth. "But what if you accidentally squish a bug now? Is that a sin?"

"People still make mistakes, Atxi." Hannah nodded. "But isn't it terrible when a simple mistake you don't even think about costs you some terrible price? Something you can't take back or make right? Well… We don't fear those mistakes anymore."

Hannah turned back to the hives, and Atxi felt the Device she'd been gifted buzz in her pocket. She had a new message.

~oo0Ooo~

An hour later, the frames had been stripped of the wax, and had the honey spun out by hand-cranked centrifuge. The tank they'd been spun in was polished metal. Atxi had seen metalwork before, but nothing like this.

"Want to try some?" Hannah tempted, when she noticed Atxi's pensive expression. "Something wrong?"

Atxi lowered her voice, keeping private. "When I first got here, I got a message from a woman named Drew Thorne. Said she was an antropoi… and anthropis…"

"Anthropologist."

"That was it." Atxi nodded.

"How can you say 'Huitzilopochtli' so easily, and trip on 'anthropologist'?"

Atxi waved that off. "I got another message this morning that I don't understand, while we were out with the bees. I can follow most of the writing now, and it's someone who says he's a 'Movie Director'. I don't know what that is."

Her head tilted. "A Movie Director called you?"

Atxi pulled her Device out to show the message. "Said he was planning a movie about my time period, and he wants to know, once I'm 'settled in', if I'd be willing to visit his planning sessions and tell him what he's gotten wrong." She put the device down. "What's a 'Movie'?"

"Those moving pictures they show on the Screens, and at the Meetings? Imagine one that goes for a few hours and tells you a story." Hannah explained. "It was a huge industry back in OS. Thousands of people, telling thousands of stories to millions upon millions of people watching."

Atxi struggled to grasp this. "I can't imagine."

"You don't have to imagine." Hannah said warmly. "We have movies here. I'll call a movie night, have everyone around to watch with us."

"Why are all these calls coming in so fast?" Atxi simpered. "I don't know anybody."

"Atxi, right now, you're disconnected. This is a world where people prize their connections to each other. They will save your life."

"Can movies do that too?"

"In a way." She promised. "I remember, back in the first century after A-Day, there was some question about entertainment. A lot of it was bad stuff. Trashy stuff, really. We wondered if anyone would bother with making movies again, but the truth is people make movies for the same reason they make music. Something in them wants to get out."

"Even 'trashy stuff'?" Atxi challenged. "I didn't think this world tolerated such things anymore."

Hannah laughed. "I remember when some of the Ancient Romans came back, and asked what we do for entertainment. We showed them movies, and they were bored. I asked Flauvius what they did to kill a weekend when he was around. He told me that he knew where all the best Orgies were, and on special occasions, he'd take his kids to the Colosseum and watch hungry lions rip apart the early Christians. What can I say? No matter what our own standards are, this world is hard to shock."

~oo0Ooo~

Walter had followed David and Hitch to a large room at the Centre. Unlike every other room Walter had seen so far, this one had a door that stayed closed. But it wasn't locked, and David led the way in. With all three of them, it was actually a little cramped. There were rows of boxes, each of them only the size of a breadbox. Each one had a number on the front.

"This is the most basic way to do it." David explained. "Most of it is handled digitally. We have banks and such, and it's possible to set up automatic transfers. A basic wage handles the cost of living expenses, and you know that most of the living needs are freely given, or very cheap."

Walter looked over the boxes carefully. "What are they?"

"Contribution boxes." Thorne explained. "Back in OS, the Witnesses handled all their expenses by voluntary donations. They never passed the plate around, because that would let the others in the Congregation know how much they were or weren't contributing." He gestured back at the end of the room, where the doorway was covered by a heavy privacy curtain. "You'll notice there's nobody observing us now."

David gestured around the boxes. "Each of these has a cause to support. Farmers need equipment, here's their fund." To illustrate the point, he dropped a few coins in the box. "And over there, wages for laborers. In a world where people don't have to work all their lives just to keep from starving to death; the hard labor jobs are actually the most profitable."

Walter just shook his head. "Are you serious?!"

"You said it yourself. If work was fun, they wouldn't pay you for it." Thorne smiled. "I was there at The Conference when we hammered out the economics of this world, Walter. I remember someone, I think it was Benedict, gave the final word on the matter. He said 'Hunger has been our motive for far too long'." He gestured around. "People will support a cause that they care about."

"Why would people care about any of these causes?" Walter scorned, finding that idea offensive. "The reason money and power were the same thing? It's because it defines your responsibility. If it's not your job to dig ditches, you won't get paid to dig ditches. You think people are going to dig them anyway? Self interest is the only cause that motivates people. That's why there are so many laws regarding taxation."

"There *were*." Hitch corrected absently. "How much easier it is, in a world where everyone is just... honest about such things."

"Walter, isn't it in my interests that the storm drains never overflow?" David countered. "Isn't my world a better place if there's music? Isn't my life more fun if there's variety? Isn't it in my interest to live in a world where everyone has everything they need?"

"Of course it is, but the reason there was taxation at all was because people didn't know what was needed, and didn't care enough to check, either."

"Not anymore." Hitch explained. "Everyone is informed of where their money goes when they give it. The Cost of Living is significantly lower in a world with no armed forces, or nations and politicians at all. Ditto for medical care, funerals; police and security of any kind..."

"Every year, we get an accounting of what's been

spent and where. It's a public announcement in each community." David added. "What's needed for the general public, like the Meeting Centres and the plazas, or a library? They have their funding from one of these boxes. If there's something specific a person wants to contribute to, they can add a note telling the people responsible what it's for. We're all taught how to maintain our homes, that includes our budget. There are still banks, of course. People who live forever know the value of saving for something long-term. We just do the math and figure out what's fair to give to whatever cause is in need."

"Just like that?"

"It's not a new idea." Hitch put in. "Back in OS, a lot of non-profit places like museums and charities had contribution boxes of their own. This is just an upgraded version of that." He gestured around. "Infrastructure, like power generation and water? Most of that is broken up by household. You'll have noticed that every home has its own solar panels and such. Things that can't be done at a household level, like sewerage infrastructure, or communications; they also have funds that everyone can contribute to."

"Seems like a lot of baskets to put your eggs into." Walter commented.

"But everyone adds something." David countered. "It's a basic fact of life: People will perform a task that *needs* to be done; they'll spend more time on something that they *want* to get done; and they'll spend their leisure time on what they *love* doing. If something isn't necessary, important, or enjoyable; then why do it?"

"People aren't going to give away money if they don't have to." Walter said, yet again, and with unwavering certainty. "Especially to people they don't know."

"We always have." Thorne countered immediately. "Back in OS, where being homeless and hungry were very real possibilities; the Society told us where our contributions went. There were no fees or dues for being a JW. They showed us footage of Conventions being organized, the printers rolling every day... Disaster Relief, in particular. Something that never stopped getting more and more expensive as the world started coming apart." He gave Walter a hard look. "Cost of living then was ridiculous. Depending on where you lived, it was virtually a death sentence to get sick, or to lose work. But not once, in an organization that prioritized spiritual learning over financial security, did the funds for our brothers ever run out. Not for a second. Not once, did the support for our Preaching and Teaching ever run dry." Thorne let that thought sink in. "Because those people, even the ones we'd never met, were our family. Family supports each other."

Walter said nothing.

"More importantly, why would we become *less* generous to our brothers now, when we're certain to have our own homes, food to eat, and no risk of sickness and old age? Laborers were pulled from impoverished areas in your world. This is a world without disposable people." David put in. "There's your kind of 'feeling secure' and then there's ours. I haven't missed a meal in over a century." He put a few more coins in another box to make the point.

"Alright, let's come at this from another angle." Walter tried again, angrily wanting them to understand how blind they were. "When I built a new construction project, like a tower? I needed investors. They wanted to know what their money would be getting them in return. After that, there were permits, safety regulations, clearance from the city... If I wanted to build something like that now, where would I get permission?" He gestured out the door, as if to gesture at the whole world. "You guys build big things. Someone has to tell you where to build them? I've heard people talking about starting a Space Program, or an Underwater City. Who do they talk to?"

"There are Surveyors, of course. It's basic manners to make sure you aren't going to be ruining your neighbors' homes and land. Everyone gets an allotment for themselves. I've heard of three or four people trading their land allotments with someone else to get a large area for them to collaborate on." Hitch thought aloud. "Most of that is handled by the Judges, but that's administration more than anything else. Beyond that, you start a fund and make your case. If people wanna help, they will. If not, then you can still put the pennies aside over a century or three. If you care that much, sooner or later you can follow your cause."

"Just like that?" Walter blurted.

"Just like that." David nodded simply. "Almost every problem and task can be solved by time. If only two people share a dream; they'll find each other; even if it takes a hundred years."

"And that just... works?" Walter was trying to process this, and it just wasn't happening.

"It has for two centuries and counting." Hitch nodded.

"Longer than that." David added. "Talk to some of the people alive in Bible Times. They're here too. Contributions, tithing, and volunteer labor was how the Temple, the Walls; all of Jerusalem was rebuilt. And more than once, I might add."

Walter went still. It was like he'd been pole-axed, rocking back and forth on his feet, though his posture was rigid. Whatever he was thinking, it had him completely brainlocked.

"Walter?"

"It's… It's all voluntary?" Walter croaked. "No laws? No regulation? No *taxes*?"

"…oh dear." Hitch sighed, disappointed.

"People have their food and board taken care of automatically, so the old minimum wage means nothing now…" Walter breathed, his brain exploding with the possibilities. "Nobody gets sick or hurt, so Health and Safety regulations mean nothing…" A smile, the first genuine, heartfelt smile finally came across his face. "A client base that won't even age out, and the lowest cost overhead that any business will ever have! It's perfect! It's just-wait, where are you going?"

David and his father had traded a look, and turned to go. David looked back at him. "You aren't there yet." He said simply. "But you will be."

"I know you think it's all about greed." Walter heard himself say, struggling to make himself understood. "I wasn't always wealthy. I mean, I was born to it, of course, but my father was quite insistent that inherited money wouldn't get me enough respect. Not if I was going to work at the Company. So he had me start in the mail room, work my way up."

"Did you?"

"No. A year later, I had left, cashed in my trust funds, and started my own company. My point is, father was very determined that I gain an appreciation of how the whole system worked; given that he had to rebuild from his own bankruptcy once; before I came along." Walter turned away from the Contribution boxes. "So when I say that people wouldn't give pennies away, I know what I'm talking about. For people like… well, like everyone I've met here, pennies were the difference between eating, and not." He gave David a serious look. "You know what else I learned?"

"Oh please, educate me." David drawled.

"I learned that when you don't have money, life is hard." Walter said, as though it was the most important line in Gospel. "I learned that when you have money, people will open doors for you, literally. If you have money, you get offered the best rooms, the best food, people to carry your bags; bring you clothing without needing to shop for it… Even in Church, I had a reserved seat in the front row; and consultation on the Sermon; and I was an atheist. But I donated enough money to keep the Church open when God was apparently content to let it close. When you have money, people will beg for your abuse, let alone your help."

"You know that's not the same thing as real respect and friendship, right?"

"Oh, I've seen that too." Walter nodded. "People who lose their fortunes and are immediately cast out? That's what happens when you lose your wealth."

"You liked convenience." David nodded.

"Everyone likes convenience." Walter countered. "And that, I have finally realized, is the key." He grinned triumphantly. "In the old days, you made your fortune by grabbing up a necessary resource. Something people couldn't live without. You get that, they'll give you everything they've got, just to survive." He lead the way outside. "But in this world, where everyone has their needs met, conveniences are the only way."

"Has it occurred to you that if there were fortunes to be made, in any way, like the old days; there'd be some billionaires out there already?"

"A Thousand Years, right?" Walter said with certainty. "We're what? A quarter of the way through that? Less? Trust me, they'll be here. But I'm here already. So I have to move fast."

David and Hitch had that look again. Pure pity.

Chapter Nine: But Not Forever

Enough time had passed, and Atxi couldn't put it off anymore. Kasumi had continued on her travels, but after being tutored by Hannah and Irsu, she was coming to grips with the fact that this was indeed Real.

She never had gotten back to the 'anthropologist', or the 'Movie Director' about her people. She was under no obligation to do so, and everyone agreed that there would be plenty of others to answer questions.

The Classes had gone well, and she had learned how to read the local language, she had learned how to use the Technology that seemed to be everywhere. She had asked question after question, and learned things she had never imagined. Things that had just been the 'power of the gods' for all her life.

Irsu had stayed on to help her learn. At first she was grateful, then nervous. He was definitely leading her in one direction, though she could tell he was trying not to pressure her into it.

But at last, the biggest question couldn't be put off. Atxi had learned about the Solar System. She had learned why the sun came up every day, and set every night. She had seen pictures of the Sun, taken from a lot closer that her eyes could see. She had seen pictures of the Earth, taken from far enough away that she could see the shape of it, and that there was nothing underneath.

I was meant to go to the Sun. Huitzilopochtli was going to take me to The White Place, and I was to be with The Sun...

She had been crying out to Huitzilopochtli for months, trying to reconcile her beliefs with those pictures; and received no answer. If her own Gods weren't going to help her, she would have to plead her case personally.

Once she'd made up her mind, she was sorry she had waited so long. She was up early, and out of the Dorm before breakfast, looking for Irsu.

Irsu was walking with half a dozen young dogs, all of them straining at the leads he was holding. "You have pets." She observed. "You didn't seem the type."

"They aren't mine." He said with a smile, scratching one of the pups behind the ears. "Back in the Old Days, they would train animals like this for helping with the disabled. They could do a lot of useful tasks for their human friends. But here in this world, there are no disabled. So we've got a small army of creatures who are full of love and loyalty to humans, looking for a way to be helpful."

"What do you train them for?"

"A lot of things." Irsu said, as he reached into his bag and pulled out a large orange, tossing it to her. "We're a very busy planet these days. If these guys can pick up a specific person by scent, deliver a message back and forth, fetch a specific tool; seek out a specific fruit or plant… Every little bit helps." He petted the nearest one. "There's not much training to do at this stage, beyond letting them get used to people giving them direction. I help out here and there."

The puppy nearest to Atxi was up on his haunches, reaching up at her playfully with his paws, and despite herself, she was smiling back. *My mother raised animals like you for food.*

Irsu found them a place to sit, and for a few minutes, they sat in the grass, eating oranges, feeding bits to puppies, who wagged their tails happily. It was a purely innocent moment, and almost made Atxi forget what was bothering her.

"Irsu." She confronted her guide over breakfast.

"There's been a mistake. I don't belong here. I belong with my own people. I belong with Huitzilopochtli."

Irsu bit his lip. "Oh, Atxi. I was hoping you'd realize this on your own, but-"

"No, I know what you're going to say." Atxi held a hand up. "You're going to say there was never any such thing; but if you'd wound up in my afterlife, I could have said the same to you. I want to speak to whoever makes that choice."

"The word you are searching for is 'prayer'." Irsu said lightly.

"No offence, Irsu. I know you're an honest man, and I know you want to help. But I don't accept this place, and I want to ask someone…" She tried to say it kindly.

"Someone higher on the food chain than me?" Irsu guessed.

"Yes. How do I do this?"

"The Judge." Irsu said, not offended. "But I doubt he'll give you an answer you want to hear."

~oo00oo~

Walter started with the kids. They would do odd jobs for little luxuries. He could get them mowing people's lawns and scrubbing their windows; and pay them in candy. There were rules, back in OS; but here, it was a lot simpler. There weren't even worried parents watching over his shoulder every second.

The hardest part was finding customers. People did their own plumbing in this world, so scrubbing their windows wasn't a hardship they cared to pay for; but he was still as good a salesman as ever.

The currency was bland, compared to the kind of greenbacks he was used to. He hadn't seen much of it being used, even in the marketplaces, which were mostly food-based. Walter wondered how a world so focused on beauty could have such such unimpressive cash. It was practically monopoly money. The answer came to him from David, who was checking in on how he was going:

"It's because we're not worried about counterfeiting." David told him patiently. "Back in the day, money had to be made in great detail, so that it would be difficult to fake. That's not how it is anymore."

"I honestly don't know if I'm happy about that." Walter drawled. "I've only made a hundred credits or so, all week."

"Walter, that's more cash-on-hand than I've had since I was old enough to know what money was." David commented. "You know that I was serious, when I said-"

"I know. I know, you guys are all about money being the root of all evil, all that good stuff. I've heard it before." Walter promised kindly. "But I remember the people who help me out when I need help. I promise, I'll do right by you. That's how it works here, right? You take care of each other, and live forever for it."

David hesitated. "Not exactly."

Walter looked over. "What do you mean?"

~oo00oo~

Judge Dailey was young-looking, like everyone. But Atxi could tell at once that he had Authority. While the world lived in peace, it still had questions that needed answering, and matters of administration to settle. Getting a sit-down with a Judge was not difficult, but finding free time in his schedule was much harder.

"In Bible times, the Judges would sit at the Gates to a city and hear petitions, offer counsel, render judgements as needed, and mediate disputes." Dailey said as Atxi sat with him. "Here in this world, there's very little that involves crime and disputes between brothers. But when someone needs counsel, I am happy to give it." He closed his Bible, giving her his full attention. "And Irsu felt that I should be the one to speak to you, as I was a Tribulation Witness."

"I don't know what that means."

"Irsu tells me that you're still viewing this world as a form of Christian Afterlife. You wouldn't be the first Returnee to think so, but something I can assure you is that this is not an Afterlife of any kind. The way I can be certain of that, is because I was here when the world began. I did not die, Atxi. And I never will. This is not an 'other world' in any form. And at first, it needed someone to build homes, plant crops, gather resources. I was one of those people."

Atxi said nothing, though she felt a tremor hit her, deep in the gut.

"This cannot be an afterlife, if you never have to die to get here. It isn't a Heaven of any kind, or the place would have been built and prepared for visitors before we arrived. What Heaven requires you to weave your own underwear?" He looked at her. "Was yours? I'm told that when you got here, you thought it was Tialocan. Was that place meant to be anything like this?"

"I don't know, exactly." Atxi admitted. "All I know is, I wasn't meant to wind up here."

"That man who left when you came in? He is a Roman, who died in the name of Jupiter fighting against the Gauls, in the fourth century. A thousand years before *you*. Did his soul take a wrong turn on the way to the Elysian Fields?"

Atxi scowled. "Irsu said the same thing when he showed me The Tree." Atxi gestured at the door. "Why couldn't he just go where he wanted to go?"

Dailey had his Bible open. "*'Then Elijah approached all the people and said: 'How long will you be limping between two different opinions? If Jehovah is the true God, follow him; but if Ba'al is, follow him!'"*

Atxi blinked. "I don't understand."

"The Old World had a million different ideas. Whether they believed they'd be re-incarnated as an animal, or would have to Pay a Ferryman, or even the idea that they'd be in Hell, tormented for eternity. All of those beliefs, all of those billions, are all coming here." The Judge looked at her earnestly. "This world is the one described in our scripture. You ask all those people what they thought it would be like? Only one group what they expected. It's not a mistake, because it's happening to everyone who ever lived. This world was always where we were all going."

Atxi set her jaw. "You're very polite about it, but you *are* calling me stupid. A girl who died for her belief in a fairytale."

Dailey nodded. "Would it help you to know that I was in the same boat, once? I was not raised a JW. At the time, it was an unpopular opinion; and part of me always wondered: If a thousand people tell you that you're wrong, doesn't that make you wrong?"

Atxi hesitated. Those 'thousands' of people were here now, telling her she was wrong; which was surely his point. "Brother Dailey, when you were outnumbered a thousand to one, your faith was sufficient to tell you that you were right."

"This is true." Dailey admitted, opening his Bible. "But my faith told me that this world was coming, and it came. You can have faith that the earth is flat, but the earth does not change shape; no matter how certain you are."

Atxi had no answer to that.

"'I am grateful to Christ Jesus our Lord, who imparted power to me, because he considered me

faithful by assigning me to a ministry, although formerly I was a blasphemer and a persecutor and an insolent man. Nevertheless, I was shown mercy because I acted in ignorance and with a lack of faith.'" Dailey read. "A good third of the Greek Scriptures were written by a man who spent his early life torturing and executing early Christians; until he saw the Truth for himself. A truth so bright it left him blind. This verse applies to you, Atxi. And all the people who invaded and pillaged your people in the name of the Lord will say the same."

Atxi looked down. "Then why do I still believe in Huitzilopochtli?"

"Because God does not brainwash his people." The Judge was smiling. "And that's no small thing. Some of the largest religions in history have beaten children for asking difficult questions, rather than blindly obeying. I've spoken to members of religions that would drug people as part of their worship. That's not faith, that's abuse."

"What about this place?" Atxi countered, pointing at her face. "What happens to the people who don't accept your religion? Is it really any better?"

"Jesus said, *'Every good tree produces fine fruit, but every rotten tree produces worthless fruit; a good tree cannot bear worthless fruit, neither can a rotten tree produce fine fruit... Really, then, by their fruits you will recognize those men'*." The Judge said lightly. "As a rule, you know a 'good' faith because of the good its followers do."

"I got that from my faith." Atxi insisted.

"Seriously?" He pointed at her. "Atxi, you grew up *hoping* to get your heart cut out!"

Heavy silence.

"Back in OS, I took a lot of convincing. By the time all this came along, I was convinced." He reached out and took her hands. "I'll tell you what they told me: Never stop asking questions. Never stop trying to find the facts, never stop challenging what you've been taught. If your teacher is ignorant, find a better teacher, or find the answers yourself. And never, ever stop 'peering into' the sacred things of God." He looked into her eyes so earnestly. "There's no blood being spilled here. Not for money, not for war, and not for any God. The ultimate Comparison test. Jehovah is the one who provided Peace On Earth. If you can believe that this world is indeed real, and if you can accept it is a good world, then maybe you can take a leap of your own."

It was the right answer. One that made sense to Atxi, even if she didn't like it. "Judge, if all this is true… And I can't find a reason to refute it yet; then it means I've spent my life chasing someone's daydream."

"You weren't a fool, Atxi. Just misinformed. A victim of the most elaborate lie from the most powerful liar there's ever been. You were tricked. As were so many others; including, for a time, the majority of us here. But we recognized the Truth when we heard it. That's the only difference between me and you."

Long silence.

Finally, Atxi shook her head. "No."

He didn't push. "Back in the old days, the Witnesses were evangelists. There wasn't a single community in the world that they didn't try to preach to. Every door, every street, every language. Or as many as they could. Certainly more than anyone else. Because time was running out desperately for that world. In this world, there is nothing that can distract you from God. Nothing that can injure you, or take your life before you make up your mind. Time is on your side now."

"Time. But not forever." Atxi said. It wasn't a question. "That much I've figured out on my own."

The Judge regarded her silently for a moment, and pulled out his Bible again. "Isaiah 65:20. *'No more will there be an infant from that place who lives but a few days, Nor an old man who fails to live out his days. For anyone who dies at a hundred will be considered a mere boy, And the sinner will be cursed, even though he is a hundred years of age'.*"

Atxi nodded. "Sounds like a long time, doesn't it?"

~oo0Ooo~

David was having a similar conversation with Walter. "I tell you this so that you'll know where your priorities lie in this world. You heard me and my father say it: All problems can be solved with time."

"And I plan to give it my full attention, once I've established myself." Walter promised.

David looked at him pointedly. "Walter, I've been hoping you'd figure this out on your own, but it's clearly not sunk in: You're chasing after a life that doesn't exist anymore. A life that was lived in a *world* that doesn't exist anymore."

"I know." Walter said without hesitation. "Rest assured, I'm giving this world the due consideration. But when I make a decision about the future, I do so with resources. It's what I do."

~oo0Ooo~

Judge Dailey was as gentle as he could be. "Some of the heroes of our faith made the breakthrough instantly, the second they saw something new. A lifetime is more than long enough to change your mind about something, Atxi."

"If I've been praying to a fable for my entire life, I'm not about to swear my soul to another one. You don't make mistakes like that twice." Atxi growled lightly. "And I'm still not entirely convinced this isn't just a very elaborate test to see if I belong with Huitzilopochtli."

~oo0Ooo~

"You know that there are no bargains to be made with God, right?" David asked. "I just want to be clear on that point, Jehovah is not the least bit impressed by how comfortable your house is, or how full your bank account is."

"I understand that." Walter nodded. "This world is about 20% what I expected, and 15% what I hoped for the future. I know better than to think I can 'renegotiate' my life with God. But this is how I make my world better. Anyone would do it if they had the same kind of mind, the same kind of expertise that I have."

David could have argued that one, but knew there was no point.

"Once I get things running, then I can give the rest my full attention." Walter promised. "But if I don't make this my top priority, the fact is, it'll always be on my mind. I keep my focus where it has to be."

"And if you don't succeed?" David asked.

Walter finally looked at him. "What do you mean?"

"I mean, what if you *don't* make a mountain of money?" David clarified. "The world has changed; and a lot of people have tried chasing El Dorado over the course of human history. What if you *aren't* the first one pull it off?"

Walter gave him a pitying look. "You really have no idea, do you?"

David sighed, and stood up to leave. "Okay."

~oo0Ooo~

Judge Dailey didn't push Atxi any further. "It's not an easy thing to make that much of a change. It will be hard. When I made the decision back in the Old Days, I

171

thought that it was right that it's hard. Something like eternal life in paradise shouldn't come easy. It's the ultimate prize, after all." He closed his Bible, bringing the meeting to a close. "My advice? Look around. Really look at the world. Take part in things. Talk to people; listen to their stories." He smiled, eyes misting. "They are very wonderful stories." He released her hands. "But Satan's world is dead, and I hate the idea that it's still claiming victims, even now."

"That much I understand." She rose with him as their meeting ended. "Thank you for your time, Judge. I'm sorry it didn't work out better for either of us."

"It worked out fine, Atxi." He said with a warm smile for her. "What you said, about how you've been chasing an illusion for your whole life? Your life has barely begun. Take one step on the straight and narrow path, and you'll have eternal youth. What's the first few moments next to that?"

Atxi nodded slowly and left, heavy-hearted.

Chapter Ten: Where Your Treasure Is

A few months passed.

James sailed, taking work here and there, making deliveries. The world was on the move, but the people came and went from his life. It wasn't a hardship for him, as that was most of his adult life already... But he missed having a crew. Atxi had helped out with the Reconstruction where she could, but she didn't have much luck making friends. Irsu had kept in contact with her, of course; but his new assignment was further away. Irsu was the only one that respected Atxi's choice to avoid all discussion of gods and goddesses. Everyone else was determined to preach to her; and that was wearying.

Walter got to work.

~oo00oo~

The Recycling Centre was larger than Walter expected. He wasn't sure if it was a typical Recycling Plant that had been upgraded and expanded, or something started over from scratch after A-Day, but it made no difference. Hundreds of Trucks were coming in and out. A lot of them were carrying people.

There was no security, and the places with heavy equipment had plenty of safety gear being handed out freely, and all sorts of signs about using the equipment, or who to contact for training.

"A new face." A young man observed.

"Same one I've always had." Walter said to him, studying his face carefully. "You're young." He said decisively. "Everyone looks young here, but I've met people who claim to be centuries old. You don't look the type."

"Twenty six years last month." He stuck out a hand. "Ward."

"Walter." The older man returned the handshake. "So, how long you been working here?"

"Just a day or two." Ward nodded. "You ever see the place before?"

"I've seen Recycling Plants before, but this is a little different…" Walter looked around. "Way more people than I thought there'd be."

"Recycling is what they do over there in the south Campus." Ward pointed at the older looking area. "Paper and cardboard products. Over there, we've got the plastics, being sorted for Stage Two."

"What's stage two?"

"Some plastics can be recycled. Some takes five centuries to break down. We're Reclaiming and Restoring everywhere on earth that we can get to. But the stuff we can't recycle has to pass into dust on its own. If that stuff leeches into the ground, or the water table, we'll never be rid of it. So we bring it all here, and keep it stored in a place that won't be disturbed for five centuries. By the halfway point of the Thousand Years, we won't be using disposable plastics in anything. Not anymore." Ward shivered. "Plastic is made from oil. It was already running out when A-Day came. We can build clean power fairly easily now, but it's everything else we have to find new ways for. Every bag, every container…"

Walter nodded. "I must admit, garbage piles were something I never considered when thinking about eternal life." He gestured at the floorplan. "What about the South Wing?"

"South Campus isn't for Recycling, it's for Upcycling."

Walter frowned. "I don't follow."

Ward explained it. "You ever see leftover cinder blocks and planks of wood get turned into a bookshelf? You ever see an empty jam jar get turned into a drinking glass? Imagine a half million people taking apart abandoned buildings and looking for things specifically for that." Ward smiled broadly. "That's why I'm here. I like making things like that."

"Who do you sell to?" Walter asked.

"Oh, I have a stall out at the markets." Ward nodded. "It's more of a pet-project than a career. I like doing it. I've always enjoyed making things."

Walter felt his face settle into the familiar pose he would wear during a negotiation. Friendly, but giving nothing away. "Ward, how'd you like to have a list of dedicated customers for your products; and get paid a wage for it?"

"Why do I need a wage?" Ward countered. "I don't need much income, given that the stuff I use doesn't cost anything. It's out there, just waiting to be collected."

"And it's being collected by hundreds of people." Walter countered. "Maybe thousands of people. They see junk. You see potential for practicality, even beauty. And not only do you see it, you can make it happen. That's a rare talent. I have a talent for seeing potential too." He gestured at the whole complex. "These people? They're not expecting to make a profit on their labor; and there are hundreds of them. What I'm offering you will be small, at first; but it will grow." He pushed it a little further, making his tone more personable. "You said yourself, you like doing this, and you don't need a lot of income. Isn't that what Paradise is all about? Doing what you love, sharing it with more people?"

It was clear that Ward was thinking about it.

Walter was about to press him a little further, when

his Device buzzed with an incoming message. Walter checked the screen absently, not really caring, until he saw the name on the message.

~ooo0ooo~

Townsend opened the door before he could knock, inviting him in immediately. "Good to see you, Walter."

Walter came in, in shock. Townsend looked twenty years younger than the last time they'd spoken. His house wasn't any larger or more elaborate than any other he'd seen. It was tastefully appointed, with a few hints of its owner's eye for the finer things. No first editions, but there was a bookshelf with leatherbound books. Only one or two titles that Walter knew. No designer clothing, though the clothes he had were reminiscent in style of the fine suits they used to wear. No kitchen full of expensive appliances, though there was a coolroom with some fine cheeses, and a few wine bottles.

"Will it pass muster?" Townsend asked him wryly, aware of his scrutiny.

"I was stunned when I found out you'd been here all this time." Walter said quietly.

"Not that long. Less than ten years." Townsend corrected. "Why? You didn't think I'd make it to this world? I died, I came back. Like everyone else."

"No, not that." Walter shook his head. "I mean, if I could get here, you certainly could. But I figured if people like us were a part of this world, then I'd have heard your name spoken at some point." He gestured at Townsend's features. "So, you joined up."

"I did." Townsend nodded. "It was an easy choice, once I realized this world was the real thing. I have to admit, I never saw it coming."

"Neither did I." Walter admitted.

The two of them chatted for a while, with Townsend

telling his story. The food was excellent, as always; but Walter couldn't help but notice there was no apparent household staff. Townsend had always had a skilled chef… But now he was cooking for himself?

"What did you mean, before?" Townsend asked after a moment of silence. "That bit about how 'you'd have heard my name'?"

Walter shrugged. "I figured that if people like us found eternal life, we'd be running things soon enough. This world can't be that different. Two hundred years isn't *that* long."

"You'd be surprised." Townsend chuckled. "But no, I have no interest in rebuilding the old empire."

"Why not?"

"You ever hear the story of the billionaire and the fisherman?" Townsend quipped. "A billionaire meets a man who makes his living catching fish in a little boat during the day, and stretching out in his hammock on the beach at night. The billionaire tells him that if he worked harder, sold his surplus, charged a little more, bought some more boats; and then he could build a huge financial security for himself… And then settle down to go fishing all day, and stretch out in his hammock on the beach all night."

Walter snorted.

"I have a hammock out back, and the lake may not be a beach, but it's perfect." Townsend said with a contented smile.

Walter shook his head."I don't buy it. People like us don't change, Townie. We get beaten, or we get eaten, but we don't stop."

"I shared a similar thought when I first arrived in this world." Townsend said quietly. "They showed me Luke 12. It was a verse about being anxious over having enough to get by. But that meant nothing to me. It doesn't worry you either, does it?" Townsend said lightly. "Because you already know that you're not going to starve. We'd never let anyone go without clothing and shelter. You're after something else entirely."

"Food and clothing were never a measure of success, or even the bare minimums. I already had all that."

"Billions didn't." Townsend said pointedly.

"Now you're doing it." Walter scorned. "You sound like the kid they had meet me when I got here. He talked like wanting better for myself was the same thing as wanting everyone else to go hungry. I never begrudged any of the unwashed masses their chance. If they were good enough, smart enough, determined enough… or even lucky enough to win the lottery; then they deserved the good life as much as I did." Walter forced himself to calm down a bit, reminding himself that he was with a friend. "This world and ours seems to have the same opinion of rich folk."

"Except for two things." Townsend countered. "One: This isn't your world. And two: You're not rich." He opened his Bible. "For you, I think the principle is here at Matthew 6:21: *'For where your treasure is, there your heart will be also'*."

"That's not divine wisdom, that's simple logic. People spend their time on what's most important to them. David thinks I'm hooked on money. He doesn't get it."

"Money is a commodity." Townsend nodded. "Once you have enough that you can't spend it in twenty lifetimes, it becomes a means to an end." He gave Walter a pointed look. "And I know what your 'endgame' was, Walter."

"Really?" Walter was surprised. "Mister Milne was

quite serious about confidentiality. How did you find out?"

"Doesn't matter." Townsend waved that off. "You remember, when I came to see you? Your nurses were surprised you had a visitor. The only people who came to see you back then were your secretary, and your lawyer."

Walter smiled a little. "You just made my point for me, Old Man. When I went through with the Cryo procedure, I was watching your sudden giveaway on the news. What was it you said? Giving your wealth away was 'Negotiating for the Ultimate Deal'?"

"I remember." Townsend nodded.

"And we both wound up here."

"Yes, we did." Townsend nodded. "But I don't think that was my point. I asked the nurses, just to make sure, but they confirmed it. You died alone, Walter. You were in the most expensive, exclusive room in the world's best hospital, getting the best treatment money could buy, and your suite was empty. They could do nothing for you."

Walter was notably silent for a long time. "I was useful." He said finally. "It was enough."

"You can be useful here. This world values things other than money, but even if you have to change every single thing you've ever thought, there is still the potential of every single thing you might yet think in the future. That's the one resource that we can't get just by waiting. A different perspective, a differing idea. You always had a knack for figuring out what people wanted. You could use that for a good cause or two here. There's a lot of soul searching going on in the Returnees nowadays; and we are both uniquely suited to know what *doesn't* bring fulfillment."

Walter let out an epic sigh of disappointment. "I

179

would have thought that you, of all people, would understand."

"I do understand. But I don't agree." Townsend said simply.

"If you don't agree, then you don't understand." Walter answered, just as simple. "Everyone wanted to be us back then. And in time, everyone will want to be us here, too. This is a world where people can become wealthy by putting spare change aside for centuries. A world full of billionaires… Unless we get there first."

"We?" Townsend repeated. "Don't rope me in. I've got everything I need right here." He made a pointed gesture. "And so do you. You sank your wealth into cheating death. Now, you're alive; and Eternity is well within your grasp in a way that pseudoscience couldn't do."

Walter looked darkly at him. "Oh, you're really one of them now, aren't you?"

"Of course I am. Why wouldn't I be?"

Walter was about to fire back when he realized he didn't have an answer immediately on hand.

"Walter, were you happy, back then?" Townsend asked suddenly.

"What do you mean?" Walter asked, honestly confused by the question.

"I mean, were you happy, back then?" His old friend said again. "When you were in the hospital, the only people who cared were the lawyers. When you died, your money went to some Freezer Plant, the last of your personal shares went to your son, and there was less than a three percent dip in the stock." He let that sink in. "That was the sheer total tonnage of your legacy. When you exalt yourself, then yourself is all you will have."

Walter was silent for a long moment. "What's a

'Legacy' in a world where people never die?"

Townsend was quiet a moment. "Let me introduce you to someone."

~oo0Ooo~

"Franklyn?" Townsend said to a young-looking man by the lake. "There's someone here I'd like you to meet. This is Walter. A friend from OS."

Franklyn was sitting on a large rock on the shoreline, bare feet kicking in the water a bit. Pleased to meet you." He smiled serenely at them. "I'm the helpful reminder for people approaching burnout." He said conspiratorially to Walter. "Pull up a chair."

Walter squatted awkwardly next to him.

"So, I'm guessing you're having trouble fitting in." Franklyn said blandly. "The reason is simple. This world doesn't play by your rules."

"You don't know anything about me." Walter countered immediately.

"Doesn't matter." Franklyn didn't even blink. "I had the same problem when I first got here. Humans aren't a complicated species. Our weaknesses never change. It's either pride, profit, or vice. Which one's holding you back?"

The young man's certainty made Walter flinch. The people he'd met since coming here were uniformly humble, polite, unflappable… Franklyn was an Alpha. He was assertive, almost aggressive. "Where were you?"

"Heh." Franklyn looked back at the lake. "I spent my career telling people they have cancer. And then I came here, to meet all the patients I couldn't save. I wonder if Townsend wants us to talk because I know what it's like to chase the mirage of a Brass Ring, or because you knew a doctor who couldn't save you, no matter how much money you threw at him?"

Walter swallowed the first response that came to mind. It wouldn't have been polite, and he hadn't heard a single person cussing since he'd arrived in this world. "...Profit." He said finally. "I'm chasing profit. But it's not greed, no matter what these people think."

"No." Franklyn agreed. "It's identity. Saying 'I'm a billionaire' is like saying 'I'm a Doctor'. Like that's the only thing a person needs to know about you." He plucked a long blade of grass and chewed the end of it lightly. "The people here say that money and pride are traps. I knew that long before I arrived in this world."

"How so?"

"I was a doctor. A really good one, too. I knew better than most that money can't save you. Billionaires were begging me to keep death at bay for another day; and sooner or later I lost. That was the nature of the life."

"You'd be surprised." Walter said with pride. "I found a way to win... or I would have, if not for... all this."

It was clear Franklyn didn't buy that. "Yeah, well... It's jarring. Half of what these people do is education, getting people into this world and its ways. The other half is therapy, of a sort."

"Therapy?"

"People have trouble, entering a world where nice guys *don't* finish last. Or where you can leave a door unlocked. Or in my case, a world where I wasn't a doctor anymore."

"That didn't make you angry?" Walter asked, wondering if anyone had reacted the way he did.

"Angry?" Franklyn repeated. "I was furious, but not at them. Not at God, either. I was angry at my life."

"Why?"

"I was practising with medical textbooks for three

hours a day when I was four years old. I was getting tutors and private lessons before I was in any other schools, and the kids that I met with my tutors were so competitive that I never knew it wasn't normal." Franklyn saw the look on Walter's face and explained. "My father wanted to be a surgeon, and then there was a housefire. He burned his hands getting my mother out of the fire, and she held on just long enough to deliver me. My father lost my mom and his nimble hands in the same day. So he had a stethoscope around my neck before I could walk. If I took his wife and his hands by being born, then he figured the least I could do was live his dream. I'd get my allowance through spot drills. My dad would have Greys Anatomy open when I got home from school, next to a stack of singles. He'd drill me in anatomy, medications, diagnoses... Every time I missed a question, he'd take a dollar away. You have any idea how thick those medical textbooks are? I was twelve years old. Anytime he felt I was slacking off, he'd do another drill. Two hours at a time. Whenever I got sick, he'd make me diagnose myself before he'd let me see a doctor. When I disagreed with their treatment, he'd make me follow my own advice instead of the professional. Said if I was wrong, I'd learn better from the discomfort. All this before I made it to high school."

"What did you want to do?"

"He'd train me in dexterity with guitar. If I could zip through scales backwards, blindfolded, with opposite hands, then maybe I'd be worth something as a brain surgeon. I... I liked to play. But that wasn't an option. I hated that. No options... You know that the other kids who graduated medical school were celebrating? They were happy. They'd conquered Everest, and I was... I was trying to diagnose why I was ready to jump off a cliff."

"But you didn't?" Walter asked carefully. In a world

where people came back from the dead, it was never a certainty how a person died.

"No. Finally, to get away from my father, who still ran the spot drills once I was a Chief Resident, then Board Certified, then Chief Surgeon; I volunteered to work in a Mission Hospital. It was a free clinic in a warzone. Some guys came in, looking for drugs. I wake up here, where the entire medical industry is non-existent." He looked to Townsend. "You remember how I laughed like I had lost my mind? It's because I *had* lost my mind. All my thinking had been wiped out. Everything that got shoved into my brain, willingly or not, was no longer needed."

Townsend turned to Walter. "Franklyn was my charge for a while, with nowhere to land. He landed here."

Franklyn nodded. "He told me that for the first two days, my 'assignment' was to watch the sky, from midday to nightfall."

Walter looked at Townsend, perturbed. "Seriously."

"No, it turned out to be good advice." Franklyn put in. "It was the first time I stopped in years. First time, in my life, that I could remember stopping to look at a sunset, look at the stars…" Franklyn smiled. "First time, in my life, that I just… sat still and noticed things." He smiled at Walter. "There's a lot to do, Walter. But we've got a thousand years to do it. After that, we've got a lot more to do; and *eternity* to do it. If I spend a day doing nothing but listening to the breeze, watching the stars; nobody's going to disown me." He gestured at the water. "Walter, you try it."

Walter looked at the lake, frustrated at their inability to grasp the simplest point he was trying to make. His brain kept running scenarios, trying to win the conversation. What he'd say, what he knew they'd say, how he'd respond. What they might say instead, and how he'd nail them with some subtle point of logic and win them to his side. It was easy. It *should* have been easy. He was the best negotiator in…

"You're doing it again." Townsend's voice interrupted his thoughts.

Walter looked over. "Doing what?"

"Trying to conquer a world you're completely unaware of." Franklyn explained without even looking. "Your eyes are pointed at the lake, but you haven't seen it since we stopped talking, almost twenty minutes ago."

Walter was forced to admit this was true. "I don't mean to appear rude, it's just… Franklyn, I agree with your father. That world may be gone, but it was a competitive place. You had to be that good, and work that hard, from that early. If you waited until you became an adult to act like an adult, you never would have achieved anything. Me and Townsend may have put some things on hold, but we-"

"I wasn't happy." Townsend cut him off quietly. "In OS? I wasn't happy."

Walter stared at him. It wasn't a revelation, but it was an unusual admission. People like Walter and Townsend didn't concern themselves with 'happy and sad', only 'win and lose'. When someone like them was displeased with life, they took a vacation, or a mistress, or even a designer drug. Something to break up the boredom, but walking away from all of it? That was sacrilege. A blasphemy of the highest order.

"Took me a while to admit to it, but there it is." Townsend nodded, knowing exactly what Walter was thinking. "I had everything that world could offer, and I wasn't happy."

"Neither was I." Frankyln put in. "I always planned to be. I asked my father about it, and he always said:

Happy comes with success. After I graduate High School. After I get into Harvard Medical. After I pay off my debts. After I save my first patient. After I become Chief Surgeon. The goalpost kept moving. Happy came later."

"For me too." Townsend chimed in. "I asked my teachers what was most important. They told me it was getting my grades up. I asked my parents. They told me it was most important that I get into a good college. My college instructors told me the most important thing was to get a good posting. My employer said it was to secure my future. All of them, obsessed with what was good for the future, and none of them put happiness, love, or sanity anywhere on the list."

"Isn't it the same here?" Walter put in. "Happiness comes from serving God?"

"Happiness *is* serving God. Happiness isn't the Reward, it's the natural by-product." Townsend put in. "Walter, all our plans, all our blueprints for the future? Franklyn here has double our IQ points, and he never chose a single thing for himself. Ask him if this world is better or worse than the one we escaped?"

"And I'm betting you were the same." Franklyn challenged Walter. "Your career path was laid out when you were still in school. Every kid in our generations had to decide 'what they wanted to be when they grew up' and map their whole career plan, at an age when they still had to ask permission to leave class and use a bathroom. Your whole life, decided before you could vote, cook your own meals, drive a car…"

"Well, yeah, but don't say it like that." Walter stammered. "It sounds bad when you put it that way. What about you?" Walter asked his old friend. "What made you turn?"

"If you mean 'believe', then it was a pretty simple

choice, when it came down to it." Townsend nodded. "I could either spend my entire first lifetime trying to leverage back what I didn't have anymore, or I could relax by this lake in an easy chair and spend an infinite number of warm nights counting the stars. Trust me, I made the right choice."

"People like us aren't made for retirement, Townie."

"Nobody 'retires' in a world where we live forever young. Don't confuse 'being at peace' with 'doing nothing'."

Walter returned to the Lake. "I admit, if I had been in this world, 'security' would have been easier, but if there's one thing worse than being poor and helpless in the old days, it's the idea that it could last forever in this world."

"Walter, I haven't met a single person who needed a begging bowl since I arrived." Franklyn said. "I woke up to all the patients I couldn't save. People who had nothing."

"I have nothing." Walter said seriously. "I came into this world with the clothes on my back, and I still have nothing but those clothes."

"And have you gone hungry, even once? Have you slept on the ground, even once? Have you been too cold, or in fear for your safety, even once?"

"I'll concede that, but I am living on handouts." Walter said seriously. "I'm living in the Dorms, eating at a communal table. When I can establish myself, that's when I can give this world my full attention. Including God."

"Happy comes after." Townsend and Franklyn chorused with grim irony.

"It's not the same thing." Walter insisted. "I have to look to the future, if I plan to live forever."

"Just… look at the stars for a while, Walter." Townsend sighed.

Walter looked. The sun had set while they were talking, and Walter had missed the sunset completely. Walter looked up and saw a carpet of stars coming to light, one by one, east to west across the sky. A million stars. A billion stars. The night sky without light pollution, without smog. Walter had never realized it before, but the night sky wasn't black. The infinite universe illuminated the night enough that he could discern the deep blue tone, with patterns and swirls of light like a gauze. A million pinpricks of luminescence that went from horizon to horizon in a sky so all-encompassing that Walter felt briefly like they were going to fall on him.

My God. Walter thought, and he didn't even know for sure if he was praying or not. *I've never looked. Not once, in my life. Walt would have loved this.*

That last thought sent a spike through him suddenly; and he shuddered in a way that had nothing to do with the night air. "Franklyn?" Walter said finally. "What did your father think, about your 'slowing down' like that?"

Franklyn looked out over the water, face going carefully blank. "My father didn't make it through A-Day."

Walter gave a hooded look to Townsend. "Neither did my son."

Chapter Eleven: Spyglass Cove

James had been sailing his whole life. Following the wind and tide was fundamental to a sailor, but this boat could go against the wind, and even steer itself at night, which was near-miraculous to him.

On the *Stargazer*, he'd had to keep his people going without stopping at unfriendly ports. After a career of Piracy, there were very many 'unfriendly' ports to avoid. It was not a hardship, as the ocean provided everything they needed. But something even more fundamental had changed in the years he'd been gone.

The fish had gotten far too smart. He hadn't been able to catch a meal since he'd returned to the ocean. The weather had changed also, the heavy rains out on the high seas were no more. There was thick dew on the deck every morning, but his ability to harvest rainwater was long gone.

(**Author's Note:** *There is scriptural evidence to suggest that rain did not fall until the Flood of Noah's Day. There is no reference either way to describe weather systems in the New World; but Jesus demonstrated control over the elements. In earlier books in the series, I chose this route; but it's not a major plot point in any way.*)

He'd left without taking on supplies, so he'd had to pull into port once or twice. There was no effort to restrict food and water, no matter where he went. He didn't even have to pay for it. He'd clung to the idea that maybe it was still an elaborate game, and sailed as far as he could from memory. All the old coastal towns had changed. A lot of them were now long-forgotten ruins.

He'd followed some of the old routes, more out of habit than anything else. A change in the weather had affected the currents, too. He'd seen a few other craft. One was the same size as his boat, but he had no idea who would be on it. Ships like this had been very expensive pleasure craft when he was a Pirate, with the sort of owner that would be worth a Ransom. In this world, who knew? Nobody seemed to carry anything of value.

He'd also seen a cargo ship, more than a hundred times the size of anything that he could imagine actually floating, and was glad to know violence was an impossibility now. The Cargo hauler could crush his boat like a bug and not notice.

He'd stayed out at sea until his supplies ran low again, and finally settled on a destination.

Pirates were a solitary breed by nature, but they had ports of their own. Hidden Coves that were in Neutral Territory, but close enough to civilization that they could be used as a staging area for attacks, and private landings for Shore Leave. Most Pirates were just crewman fleeing trouble, and a lot of them had taken their families along. Some of those Pirate Coves had become pretty sweet spots, supplied with stolen goods; and with little rule of law.

The Coves were never on the official maps, but there were half a dozen of them that James had taken his ship to. He was following the coast from memory, landing at each one. They were all gone.

On the way to the fourth, he decided to get more information. The Terminal was connected, even so far from land. James wondered idly how people could stand to be so closely connected at any distance, but he was able to learn a few facts about the time he'd missed. The 'Golden Age of Piracy' was long dead in this part of the world, even before A-Day. He'd looked up names he knew from his own 'heroes' list. Almost all of them had come to a violent end. Most of them weren't back yet.

"What's the reason?" James asked himself aloud. "Why am I here now, and others still haven't come back? I know it's not by age or date, I know it's not by general character…"

With his 'friendly port' list in European Waters gone, James headed south, towards the Caribbean. The most famous Pirates had all been focused there, and James was eager to see what had become of it.

His ship had hunted in the north, primarily; preying on the trade routes back to the noble territories of the European Powers. But he knew of a few Pirate Coves in the warmer southern waters. Such locations were highly prized secrets; so nobody in the know ever put them in writing, or marked them on a map. James put the destination into his new ship's navigation from memory.

Even this ship, faster than anything he'd ever sailed, took a while to get across a third of the world. When James landed, he found the last thing he expected.

A familiar face.

~oo00oo~

James put the anchor down off-shore, and rowed in to Spyglass Cove in an inflatable boat. He'd never seen anything like that before, but he could see the appeal of being able to fold up a launch.

When he came close enough, he'd seen smoke from a campfire, back a few hundred feet from the beach. When he landed, and started trekking towards the trees, he realized that the smoke wasn't a campfire. It was a woodstove.

Spyglass Cove had been a Hideaway for several ships. James had never been to this one, but all Pirate-Run Ports were more or less the same. A Haven for protection, and a Trading Post; where Pirates and

Privateers could trade their goods. Legitimate salvage teams and fishermen could sell their own cargo on the black market to avoid taxes, or to get a better exchange rate for local currency, and of course there was always a place for a sailor to put in during a storm.

When James had last been to one of these places, the community was small, but enthusiastic. A bar that only served stolen or home-brew booze. A cathouse for the men who had been away at sea too long. Guarded warehouses worth killing over for all the stolen goods within…

But this place was empty. Swept clean by the centuries in between. What stood in its place was a single hut. It was timber, with a mud brick chimney on one end, trailing smoke. It was the kind of house that James could have built himself if he put a few months into the effort.

There was the sound of giggling coming from behind the house, and James followed it, to find a little boy, playing with a nimble little monkey.

"Who are you?!" A startled voice stammered.

James spun to see a young woman with darkly tan skin and sun-bleached hair looking back at him, with a basket of local fruits on her hip. The Boy also straightened up quickly, startled. They were the first people here that James had met who were not immediately welcoming. In fact, it was the first time in a while that he'd paused to wonder if he needed a cover story.

"I said: Who are you?" The woman demanded again.

"I-I'm not here to cause trouble." He said reflexively. "I was looking for… I don't know, to be honest. But I had come here before, and I wanted to see what was left of it."

The woman set down her basket carefully. "You were

a Pirate." She said with certainty. "Donnie, go inside now."

The boy scampered inside obediently.

The woman never took her eyes of James. "Keep talking, Stranger. Who are you?"

"His name is James Fogg." A voice said evenly.

James turned to stone, fists bunching. "Lancewood."

His traitorous former First Mate had come out of the trees, with a few logs of firewood being carried under one arm… and a chopping axe in the other hand. When James turned to face him, Lancewood gripped the Axe differently. It was suddenly a weapon. James hadn't seen a weapon since he'd arrived, and suddenly realized he didn't have one. The first time in his adult life he was unarmed.

"Eileen, go inside." Lancewood said, eyes fixed on James.

The young woman did so, leaving them alone.

James' eyes flicked around, looking for anything he could use to match up with an Axe.

Lancewood read his gaze. "You're new here, aren't you?"

"What about you, traitor?" James shot back. "You died before me. I recall the memory whenever I need a laugh."

Lancewood snorted. "Are you here to kill me, Captain?"

"I didn't even know you were here." James said, fingers flexing open and closed into fists. "I was exploring the old Pirate Coves, where our kind lived free. I figured if we were all coming back, then maybe…" He shook his head. "Of everyone set free from Davy Jones Locker, I had to find you?"

Lancewood studied him a long moment, before he hefted the axe, and threw it down at James' feet, blade-first. "Take your shot."

James didn't hesitate, snatching up the axe. It was swinging for Lancewood almost faster than James could think it. *I beat you once already, you-*

The axe came within a foot of Lancewood, who didn't flinch, eyes on James. The axe stopped instantly, before the blade could reach his throat. James blinked, trying to figure out what had happened. He couldn't pull back the Axe.

And then they saw it, like a curtain was being pulled back in the air. It was a man, with radiant white clothes, so bright and clean that they seemed to glow. The glow was much brighter coming from his face and hands. Hands that had caught the axe by the blade; unharmed.

And he had wings, folded neatly against his shoulder-blades.

James released the axe instinctively, expecting to be struck down dead any second. Lancewood just watched, neither of the two men saying a word, as the Angel took the axe and set it down at the woodpile. The figure faded into invisibility a moment later, but there was no doubt he was still there.

James stared at the place where it had been for several seconds, before his brain caught up and he turned on Lancewood. "You knew." He accused. "You knew that would happen."

Lancewood nodded, amused and... disappointed? "I first arrived back among the living six years ago. I went looking for my old masters. They aren't here yet. I went looking for my wife, who died from the pox, and found out she'd had my son while I was at sea." He gestured at the hut. "They came back together, eight months ago. My wife was quite insistent that we have some time alone together before… anything else."

"None of which explains the…" James rubbed his face hard and cursed fluently as a sailor could. "**&$#!**, I can't even say the *word*."

"Angel." Lancewood supplied. "Why do you think I agreed to come out here? You weren't the only pirate I was able to turn in for a reward. I made a living at it for a while."

"How did you ever get away with that more than… once…" James smirked savagely. "Ah. Because all the people you crossed were executed before they could tell others. Your cover was intact, you got your blood money; and you'd do it again."

"Until you." Lancewood agreed. "The Angels prevent any of the 'old scores' from being settled in a moment of anger." He looked James over with the same cunning grin he had when he admitted poisoning the Stargazer Crew. "I've heard some of them stop an attempted murder in a little more… permanent way."

"You were hoping the Angel would execute me." James said, unsurprised. "You haven't changed a bit; handing over an enemy to the nearest authority figure; let them do the dirty for you."

Lancewood almost laughed. "Would have been a delicious irony. The man who killed me lying dead at my feet, while I live out my time in paradise." He sent a glance upward, as though it was a private joke. "But of course, the current World Power doesn't fall for that trick quite as easily as the Spanish or the Dutch ever did."

"Live out your time?" James repeated. "So you haven't joined the Ranks, then?"

"Neither have you." Lancewood gestured at the axe. "Obviously. So how did you find me?"

"I didn't." James said honestly. "Some time before we met, my ship was attacked by a Pirate Hunter who had tracked several of my kind. I defeated their Captain, scuttled their ship... But in the Captain's Cabin, I found several Rutters."

Lancewood nodded, unsurprised. "The Pirates he caught all had their own Havens. You could remember all that?"

James tapped his temple with one finger. "I never wrote anything down. Anything put on paper could be found by, for example, a new First Mate who was secretly working for the authorities."

Lancewood nodded, conceding that point. "I can imagine how disappointed you are, traveling across the ocean from memory, looking for other Pirates and finding me."

"To say the least." James agreed. "So, you haven't thrown in with the current Authorities. And you don't plan to, do you?"

"Are you kidding? This is my holy paradise, right here." Lancewood gestured around. "Eileen hated her old life, too. Marrying a sailor was her way of escaping her family; and she never got more than a year to enjoy her life. She's as happy as I am to live here, out of touch. 'Off-Grid' the people here call it. Eat fruits right off the vine all morning, *siestas* in the afternoon, play with the kid all evening... Do it all again the next day. Live healthy right up until your time runs out, instead of slowly rotting away..."

"Runs out?"

"You didn't stay with them long, did you?" Lancewood mocked him. "We get one lifetime to make a decision. People who bow and scrape for the High Authority get longer."

"Like always." James scoffed, unsurprised. "You

don't want that? Your kind always looks out for number one."

"What? Spend eternity hanging around the world with you?" Lancewood cackled. "I've got a lot of enemies, Captain. So do you. We're safe from them, but it's not like people forget these things." He gestured. "Look at you. You saw me again and your first thought was to kill me twice."

"And failed. I don't buy it. You're a practical man." James shook his head.

Lancewood almost smiled. "I thought it was worth waiting for people to... stop looking up their enemies. This world has all sorts of delightful possibilities. And with my Patrons all gone..."

James nodded, unsurprised. "You still have a retirement plan in place, then?"

"You very nearly derailed it." Lancewood chuckled. "But if there's one thing I've learned from this world, it's that time heals everything. I have found one or two things that are sure to be worth a pretty penny."

"I don't know. What I've seen suggest that money and power matter less to the people here."

"Money and power always matter."

James shook his head, disgusted. "You never knew what I wanted those treasures for. That's why you don't deserve them. Particularly now. You don't understand, and you don't care."

"James." He scoffed. "I never pretended that I did."

Long silence. These men were enemies, but they had no way to fight anymore, and no real reason beyond old grudges. Eileen chose that moment to put herself back in the conversation. "So, is our guest staying for dinner?"

"No." Both men said in perfect unison, in full agreement on that point.

"My ship has been at sea for quite a while." James put in. "I'll need to resupply; but I can do that myself."

"Not at all." Eileen said. "There's trees all over the cove with edible fruits on them. Hundreds of them, in fact."

"There are?" James asked Lancewood in surprise.

"Looks like the world never bothered much with this island chain." Lancewood excused. "The centuries passed, the fruits that your early Brethren ate rotted away and the seeds grew wild into orchards."

"There's far more than we can eat." Eileen said. "And several freshwater streams. Take all you can."

James gave the woman a grateful nod, and gestured at Lancewood. "You're too good for him."

~oo0Ooo~

Atxi worked with the Restoration. It was good work. Honest work. Atxi had spent too long slaving for the Temple. She was busy here, and she could see good things coming from her work.

The people were friendly, and the food was excellent… And Atxi hated it. She was going through the motions. The world was a beautiful, gentle place… And she had never felt so lost.

The others made an effort to reach out to her. They always included her in conversations, and in their work and play. But she couldn't relax around them, because they were Believers; and Atxi had lost all faith she'd ever had in anything. Jehovah was the centre of their lives; in the way the Temple and Calendar had been for her.

Every single bit of the world was a reminder of her old one, and that was a source of constant anger and betrayal. Towards God. Towards the Priest. Towards anyone she could reach. Atxi was hurting, deep in her soul. On a spiritual, emotional, soulful level; she was full of anger like there would never be anything else.

"The worst part, is that on some level, you want to be like them." A voice said.

Atxi jumped, shaken from her thoughts.

The man who met her reminded her of the soldiers back home. Same ramrod posture, same steel in his gaze. "I've been where you are. You're the loneliest person in the world right now. Even your gods are gone to you."

Atxi nodded.

"And to add insult to injury, they offer you their own faith as an alternative." He said darkly. "As though we'd be so quick to embrace another, after our own has turned to smoke."

Atxi nodded. "That's it. These people… Their God is everything to them. He's the sun coming up in the morning, and the food on their table, and the clothes on their back, and the air in their lungs. I get why they want us to care as much as they do. But I just… I can't do it. I believed in Huitzilopochtli every bit as much as they do in Jehovah. I'm not that… cheap; flitting from one sacred truth to another like they were nothing."

"I agree." The man smiled, pleased with that answer. "My name is Titanus, and I come from a small community that wants what you want. To be left alone long enough to sort things out."

Atxi bit her lip.

"These people are all very polite about it, but they only think one way is right for everyone." Titanus pressed gently. "And that's just not the way people are."

~oo0Ooo~

The night sky was clear and bright with millions of stars. James crept from one shadow to another, his feet making no sound. It had been a while since his thefts had included straight up burglary, but you didn't forget such skills.

Lancewood was the first person to have a lock on his door. But locks and bars meant nothing to James, who was able to get inside fairly easily.

The small home had been hand-built, which meant if Lancewood had any hiding places for valuables, he would have installed them himself. James and Lancewood were both sailors. They were used to tight living conditions with limited privacy. So he knew where the hiding places would be.

After only a few minutes creeping around, James had found a package, wrapped in oilskin cloth; and made his way back outside.

Lancewood had apparently found one prize. It was a large emerald, cut so perfectly that even in the thin moonlight, it seemed to glow. James had heard of this stone. It was on the target list of many Pirates. How Lancewood had gotten hold of it, James had no idea. But in the same package was a roll of papers, with coded writings. But it was a pirate code, and James was able to read it as naturally as The King's Good English.

Lancewood had been trying to track down the Captain's Share from the *Stargazer.*

Of course… James thought gleefully. *All the other pirates he crossed had their plunder seized by his patrons. Stargazer went down with all hands, and Lancewood doesn't know I got my own Treasure Chest into a lifeboat first…*

James felt better. He had his old mission again, and a chance to make it right after all.

~oo0Ooo~

Atxi had missed her shift with the Restoration Teams. When she didn't show up at lunch either, Irsu went looking for her. When he knocked on her door at the Dorm, it swung open; not latched.

At the small desk, there was a note, with his name written on it.

Irsu,

I have some things to think about. And I do appreciate the effort you've put into taking care of me. I know this isn't what you wanted me to decide. But I have to get away from this. I can't see the world for what it is when I only see what you and the others point out to me.

This might turn out to be a mistake, but if it is, I'm grateful for all that you've taught me. If this goes terribly wrong, I'll have the memory of your help to guide me back. And the memory of home, to weigh against what I find.

Please don't try to find me.

Atxi.

~oo0Ooo~

James had returned to New Roma. He'd gotten a hooded look or two at the dock, but he had the papers now. The Ship was his, legally. And it was the only place in the world that he had current information on.

There were no shortage of Independent Investigators. Most people came back to life with questions. The New World was only two centuries old, and had a lot of loose ends. James knew how to track down information in Sailor's Taverns, but there wasn't really any of the gossip and information dealing. But after asking around in likely places, people directed him to Theodore Mallory.

Mallory was an investigator.

"Information ain't hard to come by." Mallory told him. "But the facts are only half the story. And the further into yesterday you go, the less facts you have on hand, until someone comes back who can fill in those blanks."

James nodded. "Where were you?" He asked. It was practically the standard question for a first conversation.

"1956." Mallory reported. "I was a Private Eye. Uncle Sam taught me good on the fine art of seein' round corners; and after having made it through Normandy, I was hard to shock when weeping housewives showed up at my shingle with the usual brand of sneakin' suspicions that their Misters were doing the two-timing mambo."

The Former Pirate stared at him blankly. "Was any of that... real words?"

"I'm a professional investigator; formerly a soldier." Mallory tried again. "After the War, I used to make my living finding out if some married man or woman was being cheated on. When I came here, I figured I needed a new racket, but it turns out almost everyone who comes back from the dead is looking for something. A lot of people are looking for some*one*. A lot more want to know how their story was told after they died."

James nodded. "Now, *that* I understand."

"So. What are you looking for?" Mallory asked. "Because I can tell you right now: If it's an object that would last that long, or a person who wasn't around on A-Day, I can find it. It might take a century, if it's long enough ago that I gotta wait for a witness to rise from the grave. But there's no such thing as a Cold Case anymore... And I don't pad my expenses like I used to."

James put the page down on the table and slid it over. Lancewood would be screaming when he found out his wishlist was gone; but he'd be looking for James to get it back; and not this man. "I was a Pirate, in what history remembers as 'The Golden Age of Piracy'. I was beaten, trying to get these things off my ship before she was sunk."

Mallory looked over the list. "What happened to the ship?"

"It was sunk, shortly after I died." James reported. "I did my best to put the pieces together myself. The area she sank in wasn't traveled real well. There was a reference in a Spanish Naval Record, which said only that a Pirate Ship with the name 'Stargazer' written on the side was engaged in heavy fog, and sunk. No survivors were found. That was the end of the story, until early 2005; when a communications company was making a survey, in preparation for laying undersea cables. Apparently, they stumbled onto the wreck. The wreck was explored, and apparently whatever was on board got sent around to various museums and private collections."

"If the treasures have already been recovered, then you probably wouldn't have much trouble finding them again... And you know that, or you wouldn't have a list of 'missing' items." Mallory looked to the page that James had slid him, and smothered a cunning look. "Because you were already off the ship, and the choicest prizes went with you."

"You're perceptive, Mister Mallory." James nodded. "I had everything on that list, except the Cross of Corinth. I went back aboard to get the last item... and then I failed to get out again. But the boat I had lowered with my own sea chest was already at the waterline... If the things in that chest weren't on the recovery list? Odds are it didn't sink. Someone would have found it when the smoke cleared."

"Mm. And if a Spanish Captain decided to keep one box a secret when reporting a Pirate ship destroyed, who'd bother to look?" Mallory studied the list. "Very well."

James looked at him sideways. "No… comments?" He probed. "Most people have something to say about my priorities."

Mallory shrugged. "I'm not your father. My contribution to the world is helping people close the book on their unfinished stories; not review how good the story is."

James gave a single nod. "Understood. There are worse things to contribute."

~oo0Ooo~

James returned to his ship, and found he had a customer waiting. "Hello, again."

"Hello." Atxi said, slinging a travel-bag over her shoulder. "I was wondering if you were heading south any time soon."

"I can be." James nodded. "But, just so you know, we'd still be the only two people on the ship. I haven't assembled a crew; and I'm not sure I'd need one, with all the shiny things on my bridge."

"It wouldn't be the first time." Atxi said lightly. "I don't think anyone's 'unchaperoned' anymore, but as it happens: There will be someone joining us."

"I'm jealous." James said promptly, with a good-natured leer. "Who else is coming?"

"Titanus" A voice said, and James turned to see the man coming, with a bag of his own. "Pleased to meet you, Captain." James shook his hand automatically, and the soldier didn't let go for a long moment, studying James' face.

It was a reaction that James was becoming used to. The signs of age were a clear signal to everyone else in the world that he was not 'part of the family', and it generally moved people to treat him like a three-legged puppy. There had been no anger, or any of the 'us-and-

204

them' that James had been accustomed to, but it happened everywhere he went. In a world full of evangelists, he was fast running out of places where nobody would preach to him.

But this look was different. This one was a look of camaraderie. The older-looking Roman apparently viewed James as having something in common with himself. The signs of age made it clear what that was.

"If you don't have any plans, Captain, you should come with us." He said with an expression the Pirate recognized from all the conspiracies he'd planned in his old life. "We have a lot to discuss. Something that may be profitable for you in the long run."

Finally, someone who speaks my language. "By all means." James agreed. "We cast off in five minutes."

Book Three: A Lifetime To Decide

1 Kings 18:21 *"Then E·li'jah approached all the people and said: "How long will you be limping between two different opinions? If Jehovah is the true God, follow him; but if Ba'al is, follow him!" But the people did not say a word in answer to him."*

Chapter Twelve: A New Plan

It had been several decades since Atxi, James, and Walter had been Returned. Atxi withdrew to the company of others who had not put their faith in Jehovah; joining their Island community where they set their own rules.

Walter worked diligently, expanding the Co-Op from Upcycled Memorabilia to include reconstructed clothing and furniture. After a few years, he expanded again. They had a core list of clients that shared all the things they were making, grateful to have several regular customers lined up.

Ward worked with him and made subtle efforts towards shifting Walter's priorities, to put Spiritual needs first. Walter had blinders on to everything else; the same dedication that he'd had in OS now in full force. But after years of work, Ward could tell that his 'employer' was not happy with what they'd achieved.

There were multiple 'colonies' of unbelievers. For the most part, they were sorting themselves out, letting time pass as they tried to get a handle on a world that had changed completely. The Island off the coast of Southern California had thrived more than any of them, with the leadership there having a different mandate; trying to make it work long-term.

James ran supplies to all these little groups. It was a relatively simple mission for him, given that the most common supply was foodstuffs, and the Witness Communities never charged or made any effort to restrict food supply. James would collect a hold full of food, and run it out to them. The Undecided felt better that their supply line came from 'one of them'.

~oo0Ooo~

"I bet you know all about making boats."

"Ships." James told the people on the docks. "Boats are the things you row. Ships use sails or engines."

"We're looking to learn how to sail. They told us to find the most experienced sailor we could; and someone mentioned you've logged a lot of hours sailing solo. Part of the classes we're taking involves ship construction. Purely the sailing method. There's all sorts of driver's ed for turbine-powered ships." The young man said. "But if you'd be willing, I'd love a day to talk about the process back in the early days. I mean, sailing is an expensive hobby for people like us, for you it was life."

"It still is." James nodded, trying to get out of this whole conversation. "Look, this is a working ship; and I may be the only crew, but I've got cargo to deliver."

~oo0Ooo~

"Walter, I've had an idea that I wanted to share with you." Ward said eagerly.

"What's that?" Walter asked, feeling like he should sigh. Ward's enthusiasm for the work was increasing, almost in direct proportion to Walter's growing dissatisfaction.

"Well, I was having coffee with Jodi the other day, and she mentioned that her brother has taken up songwriting. He's apparently always had an interest, and after decades, he's finally gotten the chance to spend some time on it. She thinks he's pretty good, but he doesn't have… well…"

"I'm not a talent scout." Walter shook his head. "Nor am I an Agent."

"You don't need to be." Ward nodded. "What he needs, we have already. A list of people who can be informed of a new product. Usually, it's something we've constructed from Reclaimed bits, or it's a tool that someone can make available for use. In this case, it's someone who can play an instrument, or a song he's recorded for them to listen to. All he wants is feedback; and a few listeners. We can do that." Ward bit his lip. "*I* can do that."

With a sigh, Walter nodded. "Go for it."

Ward looked at him sideways, glancing around the room. Walter had managed to get his home built eventually, but the whole thing was mainly a home office, with little living space. Ward had asked about it, and Walter had told him 'it was only temporary, until he could upgrade'. But that was years before.

"So, are you going to tell me?" Ward pressed. "Because there's been something on your mind for months now."

Walter sighed again and held out a spreadsheet. "We're not expanding."

"We're steady." Ward nodded.

"That's the problem. The Co-Op was always meant to be a 'first step'." Walter shook his head. "With the Recycling Campaign… It's been more than two and a half centuries since A-Day. The refuse of the old world is more or less gone. At least, what you can use to 'Upcycle' into useful things."

"Recycling helps." Ward put in. "People can't throw away stuff anymore. After a thousand years, the garbage piles up."

"Our clients can still 're-make' things, to be sure. But volume is dropping dramatically." Walter countered. "It's eating into the profits."

"Of course volume is dropping. People are 'consuming' less. That's the whole point." Ward nodded. "Walter, say what you want to say."

Walter looked at him awkwardly. "I really thought I

could make it work."

"You're closing it down." Ward said softly.

Walter shook his head. "I forget how intuitive people are here."

"You'd be surprised how intuitive people can be when they're not focused on so many personal problems." Ward nodded. He saw Walter's mouth become a thin line, and shook his head. "I refer to things like health problems, or working three jobs to make ends meet, or-"

Walter waved a hand. "Sorry. I forget sometimes that this world..." He shook his head again. "I haven't seen *one* protest march in years, Ward. No 'Great Debate', no flags being waved... I have to admit, I never thought I'd see a world with everyone on the same side. It's nice."

"Nice?"

Walter chuckled, despite himself. "Better than nice." He sobered. "Look, you know what the real problem is. It's not supply, or demand. It's not our product, or our pricing. You know what the problem is."

Ward was silent for a long moment. "When we first met, you noticed that I was 'young' by this world's standards." Ward commented. "I never told you, did I? How a person could live in your time, *and* be a Believer, all at such a young age."

"No, you never did." Walter agreed. "As I understand it, the world ended, and the Returning began, and started with the people who were... well, expecting this world. But if you were less than thirty, and a Returnee..."

(**Author's Note:** *There's no specific scripture about the order of the Resurrection. The reasoning behind the route I took can be found in 'Now on Earth'. This passage is to keep continuity with my own stories.*)

"I was raised a Christian. Knew the words, chapter

and verse." Ward said. "But when I hit eighteen… Well, out of my parent's house, I found certain things that appealed to me more. And I got in way over my head, had a particularly bad night, woke up here." Ward sighed. "You get a pretty good grip on your mistakes when they actually end your life, you know?"

Walter nodded. "Yeah, I can see that."

"My sin was Gluttony, in its way. I fell victim to certain… excesses." Ward said carefully. "Too much of anything can be lethal. You're right. We're not making huge profits. But if you think that'll change by sinking what you've got into a new idea… The world wants things in moderation."

Walter's eyes clouded. "Ward, you've been a big help, and a good partner for several years now. But you know that sermons don't interest me."

"I know." Ward sighed. "Look… If you really don't want to keep the Co-Op going, I'd like to take it over."

"Why? I told you, I'm sinking what little profits we've made into a new-"

"No, not a cut." Ward interrupted. "We've started something good here, and if it's too 'small potatoes' for you, then I'd like to take it on myself." He wrote down a number. "Knowing you as I do, I figured you'd want to work out a price."

Walter read the number. "Where did you get that? Got a second job?"

"This is every credit you've paid me." Ward said with a smirk. "I haven't spent more than about five percent of it in the last ten years. Cost of living was low enough that I could save for something worth buying, I guess."

Walter's face turned to stone. "You spent ten years setting up that 'teachable moment'?"

"I got the time." Ward said dryly. "Money in this world is meant to make the 'little luxuries' and 'personal interests' come by easier, from all across the world. Hoarding it for personal gain was never the goal." He tapped the piece of paper. "But if you're sinking what we've made into a new scheme, then I imagine having more could only appeal to you."

Walter nodded. "Well, you're not wrong."

"Y'know, the people in the Co-Op love the service, and they all use it. Why are you shutting it down on them?"

"I think this has expanded as far as it's going to." Walter sighed. "It grieves me, given how much time I've put into it, but it hasn't expanded the way we planned. You don't want to be trapped by thinking that doesn't work."

"I would say the same, but sermons don't interest you." Ward said lightly.

~ooOOoo~

There weren't many rules on 'Undecided Island'. The people there preferred it that way. Atxi had been living among them for years, and knew she had made a mistake. She had come, looking for like-minded people, but she had never felt so disconnected. Not even the Christians were so different from her.

The Undecided were all people who had chosen not to live by the New World's Beliefs. They all had their own reasons; some of them making sense to Atxi, most of them seeming ridiculous. There were patriots who refused to accept that their flags were gone. There were self-appointed God-Kings who demanded the return of their kingdoms… Some who flatly refused to accept the evidence of their senses; insisting that there was no God, and the Angels were anything from a mass delusion to subtle alien invaders.

Some of them, like Atxi, had been raised to believe in their own holy figures; and refused to betray their gods in favor of Jehovah. Atxi sympathized, but felt a certain amount of contempt for them too.

Hans, who ran the community, had told her that she should feel free to worship any god she wished, in any manner that felt 'right' to her. But after a few days of trying, she lost the will to continue. She was the only Aztec on the Island. There were several others, practicing Druid Arts, or Rituals to honor Jupiter, or Poseidon, or Loki…

The variety only served to convince her more of her newfound secularism. A hundred different believers in a dozen different gods, all of them crammed into an island, because the world would not give them a temple. Atxi could see through them all.

Just like Irsu could see through you. Just like you see through yourself. A voice nagged at her, but she did her best to ignore it.

Nobody went hungry, but they worked. James and a few others brought supplies twice a month, and brought news of what was happening in the world.

For the most part, the Undecided were left to themselves, with some exceptions.

Every now and then, missionaries from the mainland would come over. They were not received warmly, but they never quit. And they never aged. A few of them had been coming back, over and over.

"What's their story?" Atxi had asked Hans the first time she'd seen them.

"They had relatives on the island." Hans said quietly. "They came back every week, trying to get their wayward lambs to come home. And after years… they succeeded."

"But they keep coming back?"

Hans nodded. "Back in my day, we called it the 'White Man's Burden'. You see a culture that you feel is less advanced, and you just have to meddle, 'for their own good'."

"I don't agree." Atxi said plainly. She was allowed to say such things to Hans. One or two on the island would take that personally; or fire back; but Hans had a personal mission for everyone to follow their own impulses. "I spent some time with those people. I never doubted that they cared. Irsu was crushed when I told him I didn't believe in anything."

"Can I ask... Has that changed?" Hans pressed.

"Off the island, I can go to any community across the world, and sit down at any meeting." Atxi sighed. "I would know what to say to any believer, I would know what any of them will say to me. It's why they all get along so well; all of them with the same faith; if different perspectives. Here on the island, I have to juggle thirty different cultures in my head. What would be funny to one person is wildly offensive to someone else. And all of us sitting at the same table."

"As long as everyone respects each other, that's the best part." Hans said with a smile. "At least, it is for me."

But you won't be around forever. Atxi thought. *And nobody else can take over without one side or the other getting preferential treatment.*

~ooOOoo~

"Mallory!" James called through his Device. "I got your package."

"Is it authentic?" Mallory asked as James opened the box. "It was, as far as I could tell; but you're the only one I could find that has actually handled the thing before."

James beamed at the artifact. It had been centuries, and the Jeweled Staff wore several scuffs, and one or two dents. "It's real." James agreed. "I took this from another Pirate. He had run aground, and I had to get to his cargo before the Dutch got there. Where did you find it?"

"Your rowboat was found by the Spanish Fleet, as expected. Once it was out of the water, everything in that chest scattered. The Crown is in a Museum now. The Necklace, I'm still chasing a few leads. The Cross of Corinth is not likely an option at all anymore."

"How do you know that?"

"It's the only item on this list that's a religious icon." Mallory explained. "In the lead-up to A-Day, the world went berserk, attacking the religious institutions. They went a lot further than most people expected. And that cross? Made of gold and precious stones? No chance it survived the purges. Best case, it was melted down for cash. More likely, it went into the Burners, along with every other church relic."

"I don't buy that." James shook his head immediately. "I don't care if the law changed. I know from experience that people will ignore the law for a sparkly thing like that Cross. Trust me, whoever had the money or power enough to keep it for themselves, they wouldn't part with it."

"Due respect, Captain; but neither of us were there. I'm told the... mania that overtook the world was swift and brutal."

"Trust me, Mallory. Law. Fear. Rage. Prison. Greed trumps all."

~oo0Ooo~

"So why wasn't it working?" Walter sighed

tragically, out of ideas completely.

After selling off his share of the Co-Op, Walter had spent some time comparing what he knew of the world back then, to what he'd learned now. He'd been missing some meetings, but he'd promised David he'd keep up with them, so he went to alternating meetings from different congregations. The Centre hosted half a dozen of them, and Walter was able to fit them around his schedule. The networking opportunity wasn't lost on him. Word of mouth was as valuable in this world than any mass communications could be. This world was very tightly connected.

Walter worked outside a lot more when meditating on his next goal. The weather was nice, and the days of grimy cities and dangerous streets were long gone. Most people spent their leisure and working time outdoors now. In fact, Walter observed that the whole world seemed to take turns adding music and play to the already beautiful nature scenes; side by side with the most modern civilization.

Walter found a shady spot at one of the city parks, and looked over his notebooks, plucking a fruit from the community orchards. Someone was playing a tune, out of sight; and Walter could see others gathered around the musician.

Walter was engrossed in his notes; as the music changed tempo a bit; and he suddenly felt someone looking. David was there, standing over him.

Walter rolled his eyes when he saw the man; and waved for David to sit down. "Between you and Townsend, who needs a wife or mother?"

David chuckled and sat beside him. "You know me. It's been a few days, and one thing we can be sure of is that you weren't home sick with a stomach bug or something." David took a quick glance over Walter's shoulder. The notebook was full of hand-drawn spreadsheets and graphs. "What are you working on now?"

"Getting my next business together." Walter commented. "I'm comparing some data, trying to figure out what went wrong with the Co-Op. My conclusion is that it was too slow a burn. It was useful, but the sort of industry that worked best if you had something more immediate to share. Something that people needed constantly."

"Well, that's surprising. See, Lucas asked me to come talk to you." David said with a smile. "He wanted to know if I could talk you into restarting the Co-Op."

"I left that with Ward. He bought me out." Walter shook his head. "The Co-Op just wasn't working out."

"Really? Seemed to be working fine for the hundred or so people using it. It was a good idea." David observed. "Lucas in particular was thrilled. The book he wrote? He got more readers with you than anyone else, just sharing it with people on the mailing list."

"There were what? Fifty? Maybe seventy?"

"Right. Still more than he'd had before you came along." David said, unconcerned. "I took a look at it myself. Pretty good stuff." He gave Walter a look. "I never would have read it if I hadn't been on your mailing list. This world is all about connection. It's not such a bad thing, putting people in touch with each other."

Walter shook his head. "Too slow. I get that it could work, but it'd take the rest of the millennium."

"Are you in a rush?"

"I'm not the only billionaire to come back from the dead." Walter explained patiently. "You know the best time to build an empire? When there's no competition.

And even if my contemporaries aren't interested, there'll be some that are. Everyone from Steve Jobs to Rockefeller, to Croesus himself is going to get their shot."

"Empire." David repeated the key word. "Is that the problem? A Co-Op is not an empire?"

"Have to start somewhere."

"No, I mean: Is *that* the problem?"

Walter blinked. "I don't follow."

David had his Bible out. "1 Corinthians 16:14: *'Let everything you do be done with love'*."

"What's that got to do with this?"

"You were offering a cheaper option, a more efficient deal. But that's not how it works anymore. Acting with efficiency now takes a backseat to acting with love. And in a world where nobody ages, and nobody has to fear going hungry; efficient is a word with a whole other definition. We've re-written half your dictionary; and I've been waiting *years* for you to notice."

"I'm not wrong." Walter said again.

"Walter, you've known me for years. Decades, by now." David soothed. "The world changed on you. And everyone I know is happy about that, except you."

Walter was silent a long moment. "I'm not trying to sell weapons, or narcotics, or dirty magazines. I get that the rules have changed. I'm not trying to be a Crime Boss here, but people keep acting like I am." He was getting angry. "The reason I can't get any traction is that nobody wants to do business with me." Walter pointed at his aging expression. "Because I'm not 'one of you'."

"That, and because you try to cut corners on everything. You do everything on the lowest bid, you approach people who have less disposable income due to their contributions; and you don't pass along nearly as much of those savings to others you work with."

"That's how it works. I'm trying to get the best deal possible."

"Your customers want the best deal for *everyone*." David pressed. "Not just themselves. That's why they don't like doing business with you. When they find out that someone is struggling, they send their business that way, just to help out. When you find out a competitor is struggling to start their own companies, you're pleased. There's enough to go around. There always has been. Now you."

"Now me, what?"

"You want to know why it didn't work like it used to. Now you tell me why you thought it *would*. Why?" His guide asked. Not challenging, or dismissive, he was honestly asking for the reason. "Why conduct your business that way? You see that people don't exploit each other any more. People don't turn a blind eye to each other any more. Why try to squeeze them more?"

"Increases profit margins."

"How much profit do you need?"

"More." Walter said, as though it was obvious.

"Why?" The man asked again. Again, no judgement, or disapproval. David was trying to lead him somewhere.

"For expansion."

"Why do you need to expand?"

"To solidify my client base."

"Your clients won't age, won't ever die. How soft can they be, if they like your service?"

"It's not just the numbers. I told you, I'm not the only one like me out there. I've looked around, and I need to consolidate my own position. I need…" He broke off.

"Security." David supplied for him, and rose to go.

"Where are you going?!"

"You aren't there yet." David said easily. "But you will be."

"Why do you always react that way? It's been years! What are you waiting for?!" Walter yelled. A frustration he hadn't acknowledged came bursting out. "I know you don't agree. I know you think I'm a fool! Why don't you ever do something about it?!"

"Because." David said simply. "I have time."

"I'm not wrong!" Walter called after him. "I'm not doing anything immoral here! It's just business!"

But David was already gone.

"People can open their own doors."

Walter turned. There was a young boy sitting behind his bench, with a guitar across his knees. He was sitting cross-legged on the ground, leaning back against a tree, picking at the strings a little. And Walter was half certain that he hadn't been there before. "I'm sorry?"

"A while back, you said that wealth wasn't about having 'stuff'. It was about being done with the things that don't matter. For you, wealth was about convenience."

Walter nodded. "How did you know that?"

The Boy ignored the question. "But what, exactly, was inconvenience? You had a staff of people to do your laundry. You had a driver. You had people to pre-cut your cigars, and everywhere you went had doormen; their whole career was to open doors for wealthy people at restaurants, hotels… When you went to the gym to exercise, did you even carry your own gym bag?"

Walter scoffed. "Anyone would do it, if they could."

"Plenty of people thought the same, once. You need

the security. But there isn't anyone across the world, even among the Undecided, that are worried they'll starve or freeze. Security is here." The Boy said plainly. "Washing a plate is not a hardship. You know what is? Being treated badly. Being desperate for food and water. Hardship is a boy crying out to God for help when his father is drunk, or a hard working parent weeping over pennies, because that's how tight the budget is. Hardship is forcing yourself to go to work, because you can't afford to miss a shift over a fever. Hardship is wheeling your kids home in a wheelchair after an accident; and keeping a smile on your face so they won't see how heartbroken you are." The Boy smiled. "And in almost three hundred years, not one person has felt any of that fear. Not for one second." The smile morphed into a pointed look. "Nobody cried out to God in tears because they had to open a door themselves."

"Kid, it's not that I didn't care about any of those people. Back There and Back Then, if I gave all my millions away, how much of a difference would it really make?"

"To the world as a whole, likely very little." The Boy conceded. "But you weren't responsible for fixing the world, and you still aren't. Relatively speaking, it's fixed."

"Mine isn't."

"This isn't your world. In fact, it never was." The Boy reminded him. "What you said, about how someone can grow very used to convenience? It's true. You know some of the things people have 'grown used to' in the last two centuries? Eternal life. No poverty. Strangers being welcomed with love and friendship. An Authority that actually does care, and truth being more powerful than lies." The Boy suddenly looked terribly sad. "And, Walter? If you can't see that as a good thing, because it means you might have to take a turn washing your own dishes? Then you have lost something far more important than money."

Walter was about to fire back at the kid for being so superior with his elders… when The Boy faded into nothingness, right before Walter's eyes.

The man stood there for several moments, staring blankly at the empty space where someone… or some*thing* had been. He scanned around, looking for the trick, looking for anyone watching, trying to fool him… Before slowly turning his gaze upwards.

"Bah, humbug." He said finally.

~oo0Ooo~

Arguments broke out on The Island fairly often. There were just too many different viewpoints. Atxi didn't like the fact that in trying to escape the Believers, she had somehow fallen in with all the malcontents. Hans was a natural peacemaker, talking endlessly about mutual respect and practicing 'live and let live', but Atxi could tell that they were following that code only out of respect for Hans. The fragile peace he was building among the Undecided wasn't going to last without him there.

And then there was Hans' second; who was more militant about his position.

"You don't seem happy, Atxi." The Centurion observed.

"Well, if I'm honest, I came here because I didn't recognize any of the world." Atxi sighed. "But I don't understand any of this island either. You're all from different centuries, different countries… But doesn't that just prove the Witnesses are right about what's happening in the world?"

"We never said they weren't right about what was

happening, only that we didn't have a better explanation. And even if they *are* right, they don't get to decide things for everyone."

Atxi had heard it all before. She'd come to the Island to get away from all the people all telling her the same thing. But the people here, for all their variety, also shared the same opinion on the subject of God. It was closer to her own, but…

But what? She demanded of herself. *You said you didn't want to be like the others, and you aren't. Neither are these people! What's wrong with you?*

"James is back." The Roman noted, smothering a small grin. "I thought you'd be down at the dock."

Atxi hid a smile of her own. She had spent some time with the Pirate, and liked him more than she let on. James hadn't been subtle about his interest, but she'd rebuffed him gently. She knew it was going to happen eventually, but she'd heard enough stories about pirates and their ways. There were a few people who came to the island over something called 'free love' who encouraged her to go for it, and not let anyone tell her she was wrong.

Atxi knew better. There were worshipers of many eras who had tried to set up Altars to their own myriad of gods. The angels had stopped them, even here. The practicing polygamists had been 'prevented', much to their chagrin; and the amusement of the general population. The Undecided thought their little colony was apart from the world, but the Christian God was enforcing His rules in every part of the Earth.

(**Author's Note:** *There is no specific scripture or publication defining how far the 'judicial' aspects of the New System will be enforced with regards to lifestyle choices. It hasn't been a major plot point in any of the previous volumes; beyond a comment that people are* *always 'chaperoned' in the New World. It stood to reason, since the question of Sovereignty is answered in two parts: The World under Man/Satan's rule, versus the World under Christ. One of the key promises about Paradise is that we will be under the Authority of God's Kingdom. Even those in disagreement are unlikely to be <u>able</u> break laws set by a perfect and omnipresent King.)<<*

Hans came back over, looking tired, but it was clear he'd been close enough to hear that conversation. "Axti, can I offer some advice?" He said easily. "Maybe the reason you can't let the rest of the world go, is because it's not the JW's that have a hold on you."

Atxi bit her lip. "Yeah, you'd be right about that." She admitted. "There's something about the Witnesses that makes me feel awkward, but they've never been anything but kind to me. There's only one person I should have confronted."

"Everyone has someone like that." Titanus nodded. "Even the JW's. That's why they have the database. The minute their own 'unfinished business' shows up, they can confront it right away."

"When I saw my 'unfinished business', I ran away." Atxi shivered. "I've been putting it off long enough, Titanus."

Hans nodded. "So, as I said… James is back."

Atxi looked over at them. "Aren't you meant to be talking me into staying?"

Hans smiled, and gestured at Titanus. "He might. I won't."

Titanus didn't bother to deny it. "I'm a soldier. You don't send your people to the opposition, even when there's no fighting."

"That's a soldier's view. Me? I'm an activist." Hans

gave the other side. "I want everyone to have what they want. What they need. From the Free Love Hippies being told they're shameful to sleep with whomever they consent, to the growers who were told their crop were legal and medicinal one minute, and criminal threats the next, to the Founding Fathers told that there are no nations to build, to the straight up ordinary people who just want to eat a fat steak, or smoke a cigar…" He gestured at her. "And the people who escaped one destructive religion and don't want to join any other. This world is a peaceful, loving place; but it only accepts people like themselves."

Atxi couldn't help the question. "What about Ramensti?"

Hans smiled at her. "If what you need is people worshiping you, that's your choice. If nobody decides to kneel, that's their choice." He shrugged. "Who knows. Somewhere out there, maybe someone desperately wants their Pharaoh to command them again." He looked at her earnestly. "Atxi, I'm not sure that what you want, and what you *need* are the same thing. But I know that you haven't found either of them here."

Atxi looked down. "You might be right."

"This Commune isn't meant to be a hiding place. It's meant to be a place where people can be themselves. You came here because you didn't agree with the world in general. Is there one person on this Island who believes what you do?"

"I don't even know what that is anymore." Atxi confessed. "Maybe… maybe I was coming here because I was hoping to find a new 'truth'."

"It's an Island, Atxi. The only things here are what we brought with us." Hans almost laughed. "Go. Find *your* truth. Let it strengthen you. It's pretty clear by now that you haven't found what you're looking for. In fact, the only time I see you smile anymore is when the *Nicholas* is in port."

~oo0Ooo~

"So, I was wondering, could I come with you?" Atxi summed up an hour later.

James seemed very happy to learn that Atxi was leaving the Island with him. James was a well known figure on the Island, but something of a loner himself, since he spent almost all of his time out in the world too, acting as their supply line.

"It's not that I don't approve. Of the Christians, or the Undecided... I just don't fit with either of them. Not really."

"People like it when everything fits in neat little boxes." James nodded, unsurprised. "For people who are not 'all in', one way or the other, you have to find your own way. There were a few members of my crew who found their niche after sailing away from everything they knew."

"Think I'm the same?"

James smiled warmly at her. "Atxi, you haven't left everything. You've still got me here."

"Could be I'm just looking for my own Truth." Atxi murmured with a wry smile, feeling warm at his look.

"You've been talking to Hans, haven't you?" James quipped.

"I don't know why you hate him so much." Atxi commented.

"Because I know his type. You know I haven't joined the Believers either, but I can tell you that Hans doesn't have a clue what he's talking about." James scorned, even as he turned the wheel. "Every idea being equal and permissible sounds good. I was a Pirate, of course I like that idea. But I had a captain once who thought it best to shoot a crewmember now and then randomly, just to keep the rest of us on our toes. If he thought we weren't working fast enough, he'd just pull out a pistol and there'd be more food to go around the next meal."

Atxi shivered. "Sounds nasty."

"It was evil. But that was his way of doing things. Tell me again how everybody should be free to do things their way as they like?"

"I didn't say I agreed with him." Atxi shot back. "The Island isn't where I want to end up. I thought it might be, but I was wrong. I've been hiding here for too many years."

James nodded. "Well, if there's somewhere you wanna go, Miss Atxi, I'd be glad to take you…" He gave her one of those looks again. "To be honest, I've wanted to have you back sailing with me again for a while."

Atxi felt warm for a moment. James had always been nicer to her than a Pirate would be to most. She knew his love for the Ocean. He wanted to show her something important to him, and have her company while he sailed. And if she was honest, she liked it when he came back to the Island. He told her stories about the Old Days. The battles he'd been in, the places he'd seen. They were exciting tales.

"I figured it out, by the way." She said quietly.

"What's that?"

"When we first arrived, neither of us could figure out why we Returned so far north when we both died on the far side of the world." She looked at him. "Because Irsu was my best bet for a teacher. Someone who had faced the same realization about false gods that I had to. And Karen was a good teacher for you. Someone not fooled by a lot of happy noises when the reality was darker; someone who favored straight talk over 'sugarcoating' when discussing heavy topics. They were both up north." She shivered. "And so was Huitzilin and Lancewood, both people who went north to escape their pasts."

James smiled a bit. "Funny. I thought we both arrived up North within a day of each other because... Well, because we could find each other."

Atxi felt her heart give a solid thump. *Maybe Hans was right.*

~oo0Ooo~

Huitzilin had apparently moved in the thirty years since she'd seen him last. This was not unusual. A lot of people were on the move. It was an accepted part of life as an eternal, that new experiences kept you 'young'.

She found his contact details quickly, and went up to the ship's deck. "Set course for..." She checked again to make sure. "The World's Fair Expo."

"Southern California." James nodded. "It's close. Less than a day."

He went to the Bridge, and then they were sailing again, gliding across the ocean swells. Atxi prepared a meal for them after a few hours.

"I miss mutton." James sighed as he sat with her. "You're a fine cook, Atxi; but I miss meat and salted pork. I'd settle for a fish, to be honest; but I haven't been able to catch one in years."

"I'm told that eating greens is good for sailors of your time." Atxi countered. "Something called 'scurvy'?"

"Less of an issue, in this world." James admitted. "But yes, this many greens would have been a prize, in my time."

"But you prefer other prizes." Atxi guessed. "You won't find it, you know."

"You've been reading my notes." James guessed. He wasn't angry. He wasn't pleased. He was... cagey, waiting for her to declare, before he expressed his opinion on the matter.

"The other things you might be able to find." Atxi told him. "But that Cross? I've seen the historical documents. The Cross was a religious Symbol. All the icons have been destroyed, from every faith." Her mouth had become a very thin line. "Even the Temples. They're gone, James. The world embraced a madness so complete that they burned down half the planet looking for anything like that Cross. And what false icons the World spared, God finished off himself."

James regarded her. "Yes." He said, still non-committal.

Atxi looked back at him. "I know. I just declared my Temple to be one of those 'false icons', didn't I?"

"I've sailed a lot of the world, Atxi." James said knowingly. "Back then, Right and Wrong were a fact of geography. Something I learned was that everyone was completely convinced that his way was the only right way, even if he had no problem with other people living their own way even a hundred miles across water. In one nation, you were virtuous until your wedding, or you got stoned. In another, it was honorable to have six wives. In one place, you were 'noble' to stone a foreigner to death, and in the next one, you could keep him as a slave, as a sign of respectability."

"And here's me, far from my world, not agreeing with anyone else's moral code." Atxi sighed ruefully, feeling a shiver. "I had 'one way' my whole life, before here. And now I don't know if this one is any better." She looked at him. "Because if it is…"

"The more people I saw back then, the more convinced I was that nobody knew what 'Right and Wrong' were." James nodded. "It made being a pirate easy enough. I sink a French Ship, and I get a reward from the British. And vice versa. Pirates made our own places, set our own 'right and wrong'. This world… everywhere outside the Island has the same way now. I don't agree with it, but it's easier to keep track of local customs whenever I sail, considering there's only one set of 'customs' left."

Atxi nodded, looking to the horizon. "I had the same thought." She admitted. "Don't tell Hans, but I've been following the Witnesses."

"Following?"

"On the database. Every day there's something new. I've been reading everything they put out, watching all the interviews… I even agree with what they're saying. Peace and love overcoming old hates. Spiritual treasures being more important than material ones. What we owe to each other, and to the Creator… I agree with a lot of it."

"Is that why I'm taking you to the mainland?" James asked casually.

Atxi shook her head. "No. I just… I can't. I gave my life to one Altar. I can't go through that again."

~oo0Ooo~

The World's Fair Expo was a place designed to showcase all the possibilities of technology and imagination. The Expo was also a school for the most advanced of minds. Plenty of people had wasted their potential for invention and education in the old Days, trapped by laws, prejudices, or economic necessity, and now had the chance to spend eternity exploring the secrets of the universe.

The sorts of things invented by these people would have been fanciful or science fiction in any other time; but the world was remaking itself as something clean and pure and wonderful. The Expo reflected these values, with towers and meeting places that were as much art as industry. The whole city seemed to shine, like something bright and playful was living in its streets.

Atxi looked straight through it. She was going a particular way. The one part of the Expo that didn't stand out as different or particularly advanced was The Community Centre, where the meetings were held.

She'd searched for his name on the Expo terminals, and found that he had a posting at the Education Centre, teaching people about history. It was the sort of thing Atxi had been offered by Drew Thorne, but in more of a 'classroom' setting.

He also held the position of 'Elder' among the Witnesses, which meant he wasn't just teaching about the history. He was also teaching the Bible.

As before, Atxi found his name on a schedule. The meeting was already underway.

~oo0Ooo~

Ward was in Walter's home, collecting a few things. He was running the Co-Op now, and that meant he was in charge of their books, their mailing lists, and other assorted acts of management. Walter had kept all that in his home office, and with Walter out of town, it was a good opportunity.

Walter had been withdrawing more from his neighbors. Ward knew why. Walter was aging, and none of the people in the area were doing so. It made for a certain distance that Ward had been unable to break through.

These thoughts chased him when Walter's phone rang. David hesitated for a moment, and answered. "Walter Emmerson's phone. This is Ward."

"May I speak to Mister Emmerson, please?"

"I'm afraid he's not here. He's in California on

business."

"My name is Mallory. Would it be possible to get contact details for him?"

~oo0Ooo~

"Consider the early civilizations. They all had the same idea: That there were many different gods, and that you could worship as many as you liked. There were fanatics in every temple, of course; insisting that one deity was better than another; but on the whole, there were whole Pantheons that people prayed to, had icons for… And why do you suppose that is?"

Atxi took a spot in the doorway again, out of sight. Huitzilin hadn't changed a bit. He was still holding centre stage, weaving a lesson for those in the audience.

"Satan was in charge of that world. Satan was the first person to suggest that maybe there should be an alternative to Jehovah. Satan was the first person to present the idea that there could be an 'other god'. There were numerous examples in the scripture, of Jah's followers being led into worshiping idols and other altars. For the nations that opposed God at the time, that wasn't a big deal. They all had dozens of different gods. Worshiping more than one? That was normal life for them. So why did Jehovah get angry about it?"

Atxi was expecting to get angry again. Those 'nations' included the one both of them had been born to. And yet…

"Jehovah is the only God that has always demanded exclusive devotion. Right from the start. It was the first Commandment. Even in the 'last days' of OS, the churches and temples would agree that you could attend other services if you wanted; more interested in lip service and contributions than any thought of who was receiving Praise. In those days, the overriding thought was that there was good in all faiths, and that you could believe in 'a little of everything'."

And yet, here we are. Atxi thought. *Now I've got years of meeting people who followed some other deity on the Island, realizing what blind fools they all are, praying to Zeus, praying to Jupiter, praying to Ra...*

"Now we know better. People who prayed to a statue or a carving were shown to be deceived. The Universe wasn't put here by anyone else. Why should Jah share the credit for that with a carved piece of wood? The original belief that there was a practical alternative to Jehovah God came from one place only; and that is from The Devil."

Atxi stared, not comprehending what was happening to her. She had come to confront him. To tell him off. To rage against him for so easily betraying their old ways and going along with the crowd.

Old ways that you don't believe in any more. She reminded herself. *You haven't seen any sign of any other God listening to your prayers since you met Irsu...*

"Of all the gods and goddesses that anyone ever bowed to, Jehovah has demanded your exclusive devotion for the entirety of human existence; and now you can see why."

There was a round of applause at that; and Atxi took the opportunity to slip out. She wasn't angry with him. Not even a little bit.

And now she had to figure out why.

~oo0Ooo~

While waiting for Atxi to finish whatever she was doing, James checked his messages. He didn't have many. One or two members of his crew had returned, but he was ducking them, for now.

He had a new message from Mallory.

James,

*I got a new lead on that Necklace. I traced the 2014
bill of sale to a man named Walter Emmerson. You
lucked out. Not many fat-cats from that era made it here.
He was in New Roma, but I'm told he's somewhere
around the Expo, trying to do some business. I haven't
approached him yet. His contact details are included,
along with what I could find about the path your pretties
took.*

James read the message twice, and noticed Atxi was
back, reading over his shoulder. "I know you think it's
silly, but."

She shushed him. "I'm not in a position to tell people
what they should care about."

James tapped the message. "This 'Walter Emmerson'
is at the Expo."

Atxi put her arm in his. "I have no plans for the rest
of the day." She said. "What are we looking for?"

"A necklace, owned by a Spanish Duchess. My
crew… liberated it, and planned to ransom it back, in
exchange for certain concessions about sailing in their
waters."

"So, it wasn't so much a prize, as a hostage?" Atxi
drawled. "What made a necklace that valuable?"

"It was given to her by a Admiral of their Fleet, as
part of the spoils from one of their many wars in the
south." James explained, before he blanched. "Oh. Come
to think of it…"

"It was probably plundered from my people?" Atxi
commented archly. "Oh, this is going to be a fun day."

~oo0Ooo~

Walter answered the knock on the door of his
Dormitory Room, and found David. Walter sighed. "Of
course." He said, unsurprised. "Alright, come in."

David did so.

"Europe to California is a fair trip, even with the new Mass Transit. You came all this way to talk me out of it?" Walter asked, not really expecting anything else. "I'm not breaking any rules, you know. It's not gambling."

"That's not why I'm here at all." David shook his head. "I figured you might be a little depressed today. You are every year, around this time."

"I miss Christmas. It's hardly limited to me." Walter excused.

"We go through this every year, Walter." David said lightly. "Why Christmas? It's not like you're exactly 'Christmas-sy'."

"How would you know? You've never had one." Walter countered. "In fact, back when we first met, you actually asked me what the word meant."

"Well, I know *you*. A big feast? You can have one every day."

"Minus a turkey, or ham." Walter countered.

"And gifts? You never accept presents, so much as make out IOU's."

"I don't like owing people any obligations." Walter countered. "At Christmas, it's expected."

David shook his head. "I know I wasn't there, but I can't imagine a world where you have one or two days where you're 'allowed' to be generous and giving; and the rest of the year expect reciprocation."

Walter was about to answer, when his Device buzzed. He checked it. "I have a message… I don't recognize the name."

~oo0Ooo~

It took a while to arrange the meeting, but eventually, they were all in the same room. David played host, intrigued by the story. James, Walter, and Atxi. There

235

was an uncomfortable moment as they all realized they were all aging. The percentage of the population that looked their age was a very small minority, outside the Undecided Colonies.

David was more aware of it than any of them. A Congregation Elder, surrounded by familiar faces, all of them Undecided. "I remember you two." He said quietly as he put out a tray of snacks for them. "You were there for Walter's first meeting."

Atxi nodded. "James and I came back on the same day."

"So did you." James said to Walter. "I remember, because you and I were the only ones at that first meeting that looked out of place. I don't believe you saw me. That's something of a coincidence, isn't it?"

"I'd be suspicious too, but you should see the kind of improbablities that stack up when they're just building a house." Walter commented.

David nodded. "But that's not why you looked him up, is it?"

"No." James was only too happy to get them all back on topic. "Back in my old life, I was… shall we say… Freelance."

"He was a pirate." Atxi translated, not balking at his outraged look. "What? You're think you're going to fool them? Who's interested in a six hundred year old necklace?"

"Necklace?" Walter repeated.

"A Spanish Necklace, circa 1600's." James clarified with a sigh. "It belonged to a royal, and was liberated, by me. Then from me, upon my death, it was taken by Pirate Hunters, and given by the First Officer of a ship called the *Mariposa* to a young woman of the evening in a Barbados port town-"

Walter couldn't help the smile. "Alright, as much as I find this fascinating, I'm afraid I can't tell you much. I had an Antique Scout that handled that sort of thing. He would have found items that would have been good investments, and I would have signed the cheques."

"I know." James said plainly. "They were routed to a 'safe deposit box'. My investigator was able to track the bill of transit, but it was two hundred years old; so all I got was your name."

"Mm." Walter nodded. "My antiquities were in storage at a Private Security Vault in the McKellan Building in New York. I'm told the city isn't there anymore; let alone... I was trying to divest all my movable goods anyway; so it might have been moved."

"Wait." David repeated, biting his lip. "A Necklace? Jewels, gold band, locked in a safe in a New York tower vault?"

Walter stared at him. "You know something about it?"

David had his device out, and started tapping at the screen. "Give me a moment." He turned the screen around. "Is this it?"

Walter looked at the picture. A woman with greying hair, standing between David and Hitch, all dressed up for a night out at some exclusive event. Walter had seen people dress for such things, though it wasn't an everyday practise. In the picture, the woman was wearing a gold band necklace, with precious stones set into it. "That's it."

James looked at the necklace in the image and nodded. "Yup. That's the bit of shiny itself."

David sank his face into his free hand. "Well, this is awkward."

"I know that woman." Atxi pointed at the picture. "I

met her once, when I first arrived here." She shook her head at her improved memory. "I don't know how I remember that, but I do."

"She's my mother." David sighed. "I was a little kid, and working as an apprentice. We were recovering something fragile and valuable from a Vault in New York City. The place had been abandoned for over a century. Took us a while to find it, and along the way we found some other stuff. I was about ten years old. Figured mom might like a new necklace."

"Well, slightly used." James said with understatement.

"Drew Thorne is your mother?" Atxi was staring at the picture. "Yeah, the necklace belonged to the Temple Priestess. If the Spanish got it as part of their pillaging, I guess it means the temples were taken after all." She looked to James. "Well, until you got to our conquerors."

"And then Hunters got to me." James quipped. "And whoever got to them, and passed it on to Walter."

Walter shook his head, almost laughing at the conversation. "This conversation is surreal in so many ways."

"We're always the temporary custodians of all the things we own, Walter." David said lightly. "But, as it happens, I was on my way to see my mom next week. She's curating a history exhibit at the Museum of London. If you like, I could give her a message, or set up a meeting."

"Excuse you, but the last owner of that 'bit of shiny' was me." Walter put in.

James calculated. If the necklace was a museum piece, or if it was owned privately, either by Walter, or by a fully recognized, eternally-young citizen of this world, he'd be unlikely to get it back. "No, never mind.

Thank you for your time." He said politely, and mentally crossed the Necklace off the list of Treasures.

~ooo00oo~

"I know David's mother." Atxi said as they walked back to the Docks. "At least, I know *of* her. She met me early after my Returning, and asked me to sit with her a while, tell her all about my time, my people… I never did get back to her." She almost laughed. "I never would have expected to run into her son after this long."

James shook his head ruefully. "We wondered if we were all brought back in the same time and place for a reason. Could be the connections go a lot further than just thee and me."

"I'd like to go to London." Atxi confessed. "I haven't seen much of this world, and I'm starting to realize that was a mistake. I may look old now, comparatively; but I don't feel it. Not yet. Telling an expert in other cultures all about my own, keeping some of it alive; seems like a good way to spend some time."

James turned to stone. "London? Really?"

Atxi looked surprised. "Is that a problem?"

"Well…" James hesitated. "When you said you wanted to leave the Island and come with me, I didn't realize that what you meant was 'I need a personal carriage to take me places'." He cleared his throat hard. "And London? I've been to London-Town only twice in my career, Atxi. Both times, I barely made it out alive."

"You know that's not an issue anymore."

"Of course I know that, but… Who knows how much time either one of us has left?" James' fist was clenching and opening as a bit of a nervous habit. "You sure you want to spend your life on something like that?"

Atxi stopped, startled by that. "As opposed to what?" She countered. "You've been chasing the wind yourself,

239

James. And I'm not talking about the weather. Are those trinkets what you want to spend your time on? Because if I wasn't here, you'd be doing that, right?" Her gaze narrowed slightly. "Or is that the problem? That I'm coming to other ports with you this time?"

"Meaning?" James asked, annoyed at her tone.

"Well, you're the first Pirate I've ever met, but I hear they have a reputation for being... possessive with things they want. And also for having a girl in every port... I imagine the island might be the only place in the world left where you *could*, now that 'every port' isn't quite so-"

"HEY!" James snapped.

"Well, am I wrong?" Atxi pressed. "Are you saying if I stayed on the island, you'd have stayed with me? For what? For company? You take off every time your supply run is unloaded. Why should I build my life around your boat?"

"I'm not saying you have to!" James argued. "But I had a course of my own charted, and I would have liked your company along. Now, it seems, I'm heading to London; a place I actively avoided for much of my life, because you have someone you could chat with there. I don't know if you noticed, but the world is full of ways to talk to people on the far side of the horizon, luv."

Atxi settled through sheer force of will. "You're right. I'm sorry." She said tightly. "But the point of leaving the island was to look for something I couldn't find where I was. So I will be going to London." She took a deep breath. "I'm told the Aircraft haven't had a single accident in over two hundred years. It's probably time I tried one."

James looked down. He'd pushed too far. "I know the world isn't quite so predatory as it was, but you've never been to a city before. Not a modern one, anyway. It may not be like it was, but it's still a city with many, many people in it. The noise alone... All seas are treacherous when you get lost. Do you have someone to... escort you?" *Ask me, please.*

"David offered to make sure I reached my flight, if I decided to go by air." Atxi bit her lip. "Irsu would meet me on the other end, if I asked him to."

Somehow, from his reaction, Atxi got the sense that this was the worst part yet.

She pulled her head in a bit, feeling awkward. "I don't really have anyone else outside the Island to call; and he's been trying to get in touch since I left, every few months. I've been ducking his calls and... well, he was the first person I met when I got here. I'd like to see him again. It's been years."

James nodded, withdrawing. "Of course."

"What are you afraid is going to happen?" Atxi asked him, suddenly angry at him. "Irsu and I aren't-" She almost said it. *Like you and me.* "But I don't have anyone else to call. No family, which is a nightmare, no friends beyond you and him. So yes, I'd like to see more than this ship, which I have seen and traveled on before."

James' mouth became a thin line. "Of course. My apologies for the... presumption."

~oo0Ooo~

Atxi had little, but the people in the Dorm were quick to supply her with things she needed for a trip to London. She had made no announcement to the people at Dinner, but in her room, she found a travel bag with maps of London, a new change of clothes, contact details for all the public Dormitories and Community Centres in the area; and some food for the trip.

"I have no idea where it came from." She remarked

to David. "Someone left everything I'd need and didn't even stop for me to say 'thank you'."

"Most of the human race is on the move at some point." David was unsurprised. "You leave in the morning. Were you planning to get an early start?"

"I usually do." Atxi admitted. "It's strange, but one of the lifestyle habits I never shook was the way I always got up with the dawn. Don't know why I bother. Transit like planes and trains are usually on time, but nobody else seems to take schedules seriously. I've met people in this dorm who honestly don't know what year it is."

"Yeah. I couldn't tell you when my birthday is to save my life." He agreed. "How long have you been back in the world, Atxi?"

She froze. "Huh. I'm honestly not sure. Decades, at least."

"Some people keep a journal, day to day. Some people just don't worry about time anymore." David checked his Device. "I have a stop to make between here and the Airport. If you don't mind a slight Detour to the Community Centre…"

~ooO0Ooo~

"How did you find me?" James asked as he sat down. "I woke up to a note waiting at my ship. Are you still tracking her somehow?"

"Nono, try that again." Karen said lightly.

James took off his hat. "Apologies. Good morning, Miss Karen. It's been some years; and wonderful to see you again. You haven't changed a bit; wish I could say the same about myself."

"So do I." Karen said under her breath.

The cafeterias weren't the only place to eat. There were small cafes, open plazas where vendors found regular customers; and the off Diner. The entire spectrum of where people went to meet and dine together was represented somewhere in the world. Karen had invited him to a small cafe that catered to people that had just arrived at the dock.

"So, how did you find me?" He asked again.

"I got a call a few days ago from your Investigator." Karen reported. "Your phone was off, and you weren't responding to your Holo; so he started looking for a contact point. It didn't take much to figure out where you'd docked; and I knew you wouldn't be staying in the Dorms."

James shook his head. "All this 'instant communication' would have made being a Pirate impossible."

"I found the *Stargazer*."

James' eyes flashed. "What?"

"Your old ship? I tracked her down."

"I did the same myself, years ago. She was found by a surveying team-"

"They found the wreck. The news you didn't find, was that they salvaged more than the cargo."

James nearly dropped his cup. "WHAT?"

"The *Stargazer* was rediscovered by Surveyors some years before A-Day. Treasure hunters took the cargo. Most of the wreck was unsalvageable, but what was recovered was sent to the Museum of London. A structure that survived A-Day, and is still in operation, I believe."

James was intrigued. "What parts did they keep?"

"Hard to be sure. A lot of the records were wiped out by the passage of centuries, but there are Restoration Teams cataloguing everything."

"Well then." James said with dark irony. For a

moment, he looked upward, as if to pose a question, but he said nothing until meeting Karen's eyes again. "London. Of course. To London, then."

Karen didn't stand up. "And then what?"

James paused. "What do you mean?"

"You're going to London to look for the fragments of your old ship?" Karen repeated, clearly not believing it. "Come on. You can come up with something better than that if you want to fool me, Pirate."

James paused, looked to her, and sat down again. "Back then, there was a difference between 'legal' and 'right', wasn't there?"

"I'd say yes." Karen nodded.

"It's… not that I'm not repentant, about the things I did." He said finally. "Some things more than others."

Karen's eyes flashed, intrigued that he was finally opening up about his past. "For example?"

James fought all his survival instincts for a moment. Sharing information about the Crew was dangerous, for him, and for them. But deep down, he knew they weren't his crew anymore, and probably never would be again. "Smitty." He confessed. "He was my friend. My brother." He rubbed the back of his neck. "I get the idea that 'all men are brothers' here, because I already had that with some of my crew. The Pirate life isn't a safe one. I lost a few to attrition, some more to combat. Smitty… I killed him myself."

His eyes flicked to her, expecting judgement, or at least some disapproval. She just gave him a steady look and gestured for him to keep going. "Tell me about him."

"Well, he caught me-"

"No." She interrupted gently. "Not how he died. Tell me about him. This world is a place for the living."

James hesitated. "'Smitty' wasn't his right name. He never actually told me what is was; and it hardly mattered. He was born Dutch, but the Ocean is home for Independents." He said finally. "He was younger than I was. We met on our first tour. He was selling pages out of his Bible."

"Selling pages?" Karen repeated. "Why?"

"He was…" James shook his head at the irony. "He was a believer. Was raised by a church-run orphanage, I suspect his mother couldn't admit to him. So he was raised by a Vicarage, and he was in training to join the clergy."

"You put together a Pirate Crew with an ex-Vicar?" Karen found that very amusing.

"Something happened, he wouldn't say what, and he decided to go elsewhere." James pushed at his breakfast, not really seeing it. "Seemed to me that he did it for the same reason I did. You saw something you couldn't stand for, was told that was how the world worked, and decided you're rather rebel. He sold pages out of his Bible, so that some of the men could roll their tobacco into a shape they could smoke. That was how I met him."

"And you stayed friends?"

"Our Captain, on the second tour, was a monster. I took him down. Smitty supported me, and… Yeah. That was how we started." He looked away from her, out the door of the cafe. "How we ended, was at the end of each other's swords."

"And you regret that."

"I regret all my sins, Miss Karen. The point was that in some ways, the rules of this world are not at all unlike the rules of my own. The things that those in power considered 'wrong' and what I considered 'justice' have never been in agreement."

"And sometimes they are." Karen pointed out. "Like Smitty."

"Yes." James admitted. "I was very much in the wrong that day."

Karen sipped her juice slowly, letting that hang in the air for a moment. "James." She said finally. "Your first day here, I remember the meeting was on the topic of how 'we could do nothing against Jehovah'. You disliked that idea. But what you didn't consider is that all the things you *regret* were wiped out too." She smiled a bit. "I remember when I made a really bad screw-up, my mom used to tell me: 'In a hundred years, who's going to care'? Well, I died way too young, and A-Day came a lot sooner than a century after that." She pulled out her device. "On the subject of regret, let me show you Romans 6:21. '*What, then, was the fruit that you used to produce at that time? Things of which you are now ashamed. For the end of those things is death.*' And you, James; already died. What more can one ask?"

"You don't understand." James said plainly. "I wasn't exactly *there* for any of that."

"Oh, I'm sorry. Would it be more merciful if God boiled you in a lake of fire and brimstone for a few centuries first?" Karen scorned.

"I'd feel like I owe Him less. Him, or my crew." James returned. "I know they'll be back too. I know that's the whole point. So I had better be prepared to make an accounting for my sins towards my people."

"What about your victims?" She shot back. "You're still trying to find the treasures you stole. Are you prepared to give them all back? Because I don't think you're trying to find these 'priceless relics' you lost to return them to their rightful owners."

"The people I stole from weren't the 'rightful owners' any more than I was. Not by any measure, except for the laws *they* wrote for their own convenience." James scorned with real hatred. "But now, in a world where everyone can live forever, they can keep what they have, at last. You have any idea what that would mean?" James pressed, getting more excited again. "After centuries and centuries of changing hands, the truly priceless things stop moving. We'd be the eternal owner of what we actually deserve. I saw Smitty's eyes when he… I can give it all back to him."

"And then maybe he forgives his best friend for a sword through the heart?" Karen said with sympathy. "You know that isn't…" She trailed off, knowing he wasn't there yet.

"I know." James told her with unshakable confidence. "In this world; the only things that exist are the things that matter. Trust me, what I was trying to do was far more important than make money."

Karen looked over, surprised. "Then… What were you trying to do?"

He gave her a sideways look. "We find my ship, maybe I'll tell you."

Karen smirked. "That works for you, doesn't it? 'Get what I need, and maybe you'll get your cut'?"

James chuckled. "I know. Not exactly how it works here, but it's how things go when you're a Pirate."

She nodded. "You can play your cards as close as you like, James. It's not my business." She sipped the last of her coffee. "But don't think I didn't notice you changing the subject. You aren't going to London for the pieces of your ship. I mean, what would you do if you found them?"

James hid his response behind his cup. "Come with me, find out."

"To London?" She seemed surprised. "I have final

exams on some of my classes; but I can meet you there. I assume you'll sail your own ship. I take a flight, I might even beat you to London."

James kept his face even, but was glad to hear it. *Unsupervised? Better and better.*

Chapter Thirteen: The Museum

Walter was looking around the empty Room with barely restrained frustration. There was nobody there. A dozen tables, thirty immaculate chessboards, a nice spread of food, and no players.

Walter checked the door, as if it had somehow been locked without his knowing it. But there was nobody there.

Finally giving up, he decided to get breakfast. Before he could turn out the lights, the door opened, and in walked a man with a large tray. "Good morning." The man said. "I'm Brett Colbert."

"Oh, yes." Walter recognized the name. "I meant to get back to you."

"I heard you were here already, and thought I'd meet you at lunch." Colbert said, holding out the tray. "Then you didn't show. I'm told you rarely do."

Walter was hungry enough not to care, and took the tray. "It's… Frustrating." He allowed. He munched for a few moments. "You know, back in the day, the kind of food they put out in Refugee Centres and Homeless Shelters… Sandwiches. Cheap sandwiches. This is not 'cheap food'."

"Well, I wouldn't compare the Dorms to Refugee Centres of course; and 'homeless shelter' isn't quite right either, since the majority of people in them are merely on their way to somewhere else. 'Guest Accommodation' is more accurate."

"Yeah." Walter sighed, not really interested in pursuing it. "Sorry, you were trying to reach me because…"

"I was hoping to use this room in the afternoon." Colbert explained. "The Community Centre is appropriate for teaching classes, but I got more students than I anticipated. I wasn't sure how long your own function would continue, so-"

"You may as well take it." Walter sighed. "My 'Function' never started."

Colbert looked around the empty room with the chessboards. There was a poster on the wall, advertising the event, and he studied it a moment. "Hundred credit entry fee?"

"It was a tournament. Two thousand credit prize for the winner." Walter nodded.

"Thirty sets. Sixty players. Six thousand in entry fees, minus two thousand for the prize, that's…" Colbert tapped his chin elaborately. "Let me just do the math here…"

"You think if I made the prize bigger, someone would have shown up?" Walter pressed; knowing the answer. It would have made no difference. "I don't get it."

"Your look says you've been back a while. You ever seen a casino in this world?" Colbert pointed out.

"This isn't gambling. Chess isn't a game of chance." Walter said immediately. "I know. I checked."

Colbert actually laughed. "You figured if it was a competition instead of a random draw, it'd be more acceptable to people. Hey, you might be right. I entered a competition or three back in OS."

"Then why is nobody here?" Walter demanded.

Colbert wandered over to the food table and got himself a cup of coffee. "Look, poker is a game of skill too. You chose Chess because you figured if people weren't used to money being involved, you'd get away with it. You chose Chess because you figured, this close to the Expo; there'd be at least sixty competitive geniuses willing to pay for the privilege of beating each other. You think genius-level people can't see through that?"

"That why you didn't sign up?"

"Chess isn't really my game."

"Of course not." Walter sighed. "You think I'll ever get over the 'Culture Shock'?"

"It's not my business, sir." Colbert said evenly. "But I know all about Culture Shock. Back in OS, I had a few semesters abroad. You get over Culture Shock by immersing yourself in the local one."

"I admit I haven't done that." Walter confessed. "I traveled a lot in OS too. I handled it by finding something I recognized. A favorite movie, a familiar food…"

"McDonalds was the same everywhere, as I recall." Colbert quipped.

"I would kill for a good burger." Walter said wistfully, more nostalgic than actually angry.

"I know they were working on 'meat' without slaughter back in OS. The project was set back almost to scratch after A-Day. The Expo is working on something similar now."

(**Author's Note:** *In 'Just See Yourself' I had this technology being used to create meat without slaughtering animals at the 500 Year mark. In the two years since writing that book, I've discovered that the technology is actually available now, though moderately cost-prohibitive. The 'Clean Meat' industry is growing, for financial and ecological reasons. This isn't likely to become a major plot point, but I added this to explain why my characters went 500 years before anyone in Paradise made it work.*)

"Assuming anyone's interested." Walter shook his

head. "I tried loopholing the rules for Christians today. I've found they're not willing to settle, even for fun, even for profit."

"Depends on what you count as 'profit'." A woman's voice said. Both men turned, and found Atxi and David wandering over. "I saw your tournament. Chess? Even the Undecided don't bother with cash prizes for such things. If people love playing chess in this world, they can find five or six other people who love it just as much, and spend all day playing. They'll compete for candy. Why would they pay for the privilege?"

"For the prize."

"Walter, for one person to win big, a dozen people must lose." David told him. "Or a hundred. Or a thousand. This is a world where nobody cares for that to happen to their neighbor."

"How do you capitalize on that?" Walter thought out loud.

"Why do you need to?" Atxi asked suddenly.

"Because I don't believe in a Paradise that rewards the idle, and the hard working, with the same prize."

"You know it's not like that."

"I know, but… Where are the exceptional people? Where are the captains of industry? The ones that make the decisions? The Elite?!" He was annoyed again, face wrinkling with frustration. "If people like me are all coming back, how can they all be convinced that money is the root of all evil?"

David put a hand up. "Actually, that verse says that 'the *love* of money' is the problem." He said kindly. "Walter, take a look at the heroes of our faith. Solomon had a mountain of money greater than anything you ever had. But his treasure was his relationship with God. When he lost that, his money was nothing in comparison. Some of God's most faithful followers lived in tents, others in palaces, some in prison cells. The measure of a man is not the control he has over his life. We never had control of anything. Not really."

With a growl, Walter stormed off; looking oddly like a child throwing a tantrum. Atxi stayed behind with Colbert.

"Sad." Colbert said quietly, looking after Walter.

"It is." Atxi nodded. "I haven't quite accepted this world either, sir. But even I can tell he's chasing after the wind."

Colbert smiled a little at her vaguely biblical quotation. "And you? What's holding you back?"

Atxi sighed. It seemed most conversations, with very well-meaning people, kept leading back to the same question. "I have trust issues, where Gods and Demons are concerned." She rolled her gaze to look at him. "Care to try convincing me of the error of my ways?"

Colbert chuckled. "Sorry. I doubt I could come up with anything you haven't heard before. I'm smart, but less creative than some."

Axti scoffed. "It's better here than we had in my world, but…" She shook her head. "I don't know how to say it. Did nobody get it right? Was there nothing of my people worthy of anything in this world?" Kevin started to answer, and she held up a hand. "No, I know what you're going to say. I've heard it before, and more than once. I just… I just wish I could be sure."

Colbert nodded. "I had the same thought, once. I was taught to 'throw my anxieties on Jehovah'."

Atxi bit her lip. "I haven't… prayed, since my Rising. Not to anyone real, anyway." She confessed. "I prayed real hard, real often, back in my old life."

Colbert almost smiled. "My first prayer was after my

mother died. I wasn't a Witness then. I heaped all the rage, all the frustration, all the hurt... I let God have it; before I ever knew his name. Then I reminded myself that I didn't believe in him; and went about my life. Not long after, I got a knock on the door. Take my word for it, sister. God can handle whatever you've got to throw at him, and he'd rather you talking about your problems than ignoring him completely."

David recognized a good point to leave the matter, and quickly checked the time. "Atxi, you've been kind to indulge my detour, but you do have a plane to catch."

~ooO0Ooo~

As they made their way towards the Airport, the conversation turned to the flight, what it would be like, what she would find in London... But once they reached the Airport itself, Atxi couldn't help but bring up the subject again. "What he said, about prayer... Do you really think your God would hear me?"

"He's your God too, Atxi." David said gently. "It's not a question of Who He Is, only a question of what that means to you. There have been times in history when people would open their wrists, or whip themselves with chains to make their prayers heard. God doesn't ask any of that. He *wants* to be closer to us, Atxi. That's the whole point."

She hesitated, as the announcement came to board her plane.

"You have to go." David said quietly. "So I'll just say this. The name 'Jehovah' means 'He Causes To Become'. Whatever it is you need, He knows already. I've heard stories about people praying to understand God, and have a knock on their door come in the same instant. Whatever you're waiting for, God can provide. Not because He changes to suit you, but because He recognizes that everyone is looking for something in particular. If it hasn't come yet, He's waiting for you."

"I know." Atxi said quietly, and picked up her bag.

~oo0Ooo~

Old London was visible out the window of the plane Atxi flew in on. The city looked... dusty. At first she thought it was falling apart with the passage of time, but as the plane turned, she looked closer and realized the 'decay' was too precise. It wasn't falling down, it was being dismantled. She had heard tell of how London was nearly choking on coal fumes for much of its history. That time was long behind them, but she supposed that the dust must have caked into the old buildings after all that time.

But New London just... shone. She'd never seen a big city before, not counting the Expo. It looked like they were taking Old London, scrubbing it up, and putting it back together, a piece at a time. The place looked happy, if a city could describe an emotion. Atxi had spent the flight reading about the sights. The one in particular that she came to see was The Museum.

She only caught a glimpse of it as the plane landed. It was a huge building, with glass dome ceilings and marble pillars out front. It was extravagant by modern standards, but Atxi knew that the permanent, public structures were made to be beautiful. She wondered if it was a new construction for this world, or something taken and adapted from the old. Either way, it was the largest structure that she'd ever seen. The Museum alone was almost bigger than Tenochtitlan.

~oo0Ooo~

Until now, Atxi had always traveled with the *Nicholas*, which was technically a cargo ship; or at least being used that way. Passenger Liners were always given a huge welcome by the locals. Atxi found that strange and amazing, given how many people were moving, that they'd always arrive to a huge group of people offering little mementos, hugs and kisses, music playing...

Atxi had done some traveling before. Not a lot, but enough to know that this sort of thing was normal. She rolled with it. As much as she loved the warm welcome, she had something on her mind, and the huge crowd was making it harder to think.

The conversation with Kevin, and the counsel from David, had stuck in Atxi's head all the way to London. Prayers were part of the life for an Aztec. Part of the life for a Christian. Atxi didn't know what she was anymore, but she wasn't someone who prayed.

And after many years in Paradise, she started to realize that she wasn't getting any better by refusing. She was long overdue.

~oo0Ooo~

Atxi went off to be by herself, uncertain of what to do, but sure that she didn't want an audience. It took her a while to find an isolated spot, halfway between the airstrip, and the town itself.

Should I kneel? Should I close my eyes? She shook her head. It had been years since she'd prayed to anyone.

"So. God." Atxi began awkwardly. "Um… You know me. You know why I'm not joining your people. The reasons matter to me. That's all." She bit her lip. "Amen?"

Even she knew that was pathetic.

With a hard sigh, she tried again. "I miss my sister." She said. "I heard about people being returned from the dead, and even when I was with the Undecided, I would check for her name… I want to see her, before I die of old age. Is that the point? Are you keeping her away until I'm gone? What are you going to say to her?

'Welcome to Paradise, where everyone gets to live forever, except your family'?"

Silence.

Atxi's scowled so hard she felt her world go red for a moment. "Or are you waiting for me to die so that she knows better? Plenty of 'Christian' leaders who came to my lands made examples. I was dead. What more could a god ask of me? It wasn't enough to believe, I had to believe all the way to my death and then get told to believe something else, or die again?!" She came to her feet violently. "Never! I've wasted enough of my life begging gods for attention. More than enough begging for my life! I hate all of you. You hear that?!"

She turned to storm away from the spot and found she was not alone. Irsu was suddenly there, like a magic trick. He'd heard enough, it was clear.

Atxi looked down, unable to meet his gaze. "I wasn't expecting you until tonight."

Irsu nodded. "From what I heard, you had some ground to cover before coming to meet me." He said quietly. "Or anyone else."

Atxi looked down, unable to match his gaze. "I heard you're a Judge now. I guess you have a… problem, with…"

"Everything I just heard you rage at the sky?" Irsu finished. "No. You're angry. You don't need me piling on to that. I do have a question, though."

Atxi still couldn't look him in the eye. "Ask me."

"If your sister came back yesterday, what would *you* tell her?"

The question caught Atxi off guard. She would have to tell Patli that their world was gone. That The Temple was gone…

And then she'd tell Patli that this world was different.

A place where people didn't fight, where nobody went hungry, or was carved up on the Stone Altar. She'd tell Patli all about the animals, all about the aircraft making it possible to fly across the world, about the food and drink, better than anything they could have dreamed of before...

"You, my dear Atxi, are in a unique position." Irsu said lightly. "Your faith was strong before you got here, and seeing Paradise is what broke it. For most people, the opposite is true."

"I've lived in a world where everyone I met was convinced of something, and they were all wrong." Axti said quietly, not looking at him. "For all I know, when we die here, we go to the paradise of some other God."

Irsu actually let out a bark of laughter. "Oh, Atxi. Tell me that's not why you're holding out?"

"No. Maybe. I don't know." She still wasn't looking at him. "The Temples are *gone*, Irsu."

"Atxi, your temple was a building. What do you really miss?"

She looked down. "I miss the belief. I miss the certainty. I miss knowing about God. I miss being part of it. I miss being part of something holy. I miss-"

"You miss having what everyone in the world has right now." Irsu summed up.

"I fell for that once!" Atxi said, not for the first time. "I know this is real. I know the difference. But I haven't changed. How can I say that this world did what my world could not? How can I live a life of faith and devotion again? It would make me like Huitzilin, and I don't know if I can do that."

"After you left, I tracked down Huitzilin and spoke to him for a while. He lost the same thing you did: He lost the lie. Some of the heroes of my faith began their careers by attacking True Worship; and made the change when they saw the reality laid bare before their eyes." Irsu pressed. "And by the way, Atxi: So did I."

Atxi felt her stomach lurch, and she reached out a hand to him immediately. "Oh, Irsu. I'm sorry; of course you did." She covered her face in her hands. "I don't even know why I'm fighting it."

"You don't know how to say it, but I'm betting the reason is there; if it's this ironclad." Irsu counseled. "When you think about your old life, before this, what strikes you as most important, in comparison to this?"

"I don't know."

"Well, take a minute and think it over. Not counting your worship; what was most important about your old life?"

Atxi bit her lip, thinking. "My sister."

"Keep going."

"My last conversation with her was before I went to the Altar. My sister was hoping to go first, but my mother... She persuaded the High Priest to let me be offered as Tribute, while my sister fulfilled her other duties in the Temple."

Irsu was listening patiently. "Keep going."

"My sister, she was so… eager. To serve. To nourish the gods. But I got there first. I still don't know if my sister ever did the same." She looked at Irsu. "She loved the Temple so much, Irsu. And it's gone. The Temples are gone, and she loved them, and…"

Irsu nodded. "Keep going."

Atxi wiped furiously at tears that threatened to fall. "How do I tell my sister that we were wrong? That even Huitzilin believes we were just wrong? That we were killing ourselves for nothing?"

"Far easier to tell her that the people 'in this land'

simply worship a different way." Irsu put in. "A problem that wouldn't budge an Aztec, who thought there were many gods a person could follow."

That idea had not occurred to Atxi. Her eyes bulged as it hit her in full. "And if I was able to tell her that I still believed what she did, and that nobody could convince me otherwise, that'd be a far easier reunion, wouldn't it?"

Irsu nodded, non-committal.

Atxi was silent for a while. "Huitzilin was talking about how Satan worked in the beginning. As angry as I was at him back then… This time I realized. He wasn't bragging about getting away with anything. He was confessing."

"I can relate." Irsu nodded. "My birth culture does not have a popular position in the Bible Story, Atxi."

"And mine isn't mentioned at all." She murmured. "Was there nothing of our people that was worthy? I know that I'm here, and so is Huitzilin and so will be all the others, in time. But were we that unimportant? That… insignificant?"

Irsu considered a moment. "Atxi, would you come with me tomorrow? I'd like to show you something."

~ooOOoo~

The *Nicholas* arrived at the Port of London. Karen had flown and landed ahead of him. Karen had called and said she had gone on ahead to verify an appointment; and get a copy of the Museum Guide.

James spent the time watching the empty city skyline with suspicion. There was an odd sense The Old City migrating, as parts of the old world were made shiny and eternal. James knew this was no accident. Much of the world was in such a state.

James thought about trying to contact Atxi. The

world was not a hard place to get in touch with someone. But to be truthful, he didn't know what to say. He knew he'd overreacted, and blindsided Atxi with his annoyance. But James was one of the few people in the world counting his days, and he wanted to spend them with her... Only to find out that he was her taxi service.

You know that's not true. The thought came to him. *And you're only counting the days because-*

James shook his head against that thought. He'd made his choice.

~oo0Ooo~

The Museum was huge. Atxi felt like she'd been walking forever. It took Irsu a while to explain to her how it all worked. The Museum was laid out by century, and by continent, with a different land in each wing of the Museum. There was overlap in some of the exhibits, of course, as all human civilization had been changed by migration. Irsu had shown her the Directory. The way every exhibit connected. By year, by wealth, by location. The Rise and Fall of every Empire, and the Origins and Collapse of Various Religions, financial institutions, political philosophies, the path of technological advancements...

"When we first met, I told you that Jehovah stepped back to let the human race try and manage themselves." Irsu said as she struggled through the Directory. "The usual question I get is 'why so long?' Now you know why. The argument could easily be made that we needed time to sort out the winning combination."

"Combination of what?"

"Everything. Type of government? Democratic? Monarchy? Fascist? Type of Economy: Capitalist? Socialistic? Religious Order: Monastic? Ministerial? Technological superiority? Favorite recreation? Every combination was tried, and the world just devolved as we went."

"Which is the point of the Museum." Atxi guessed. "Most people only see what's right in front of them."

"And assumes others have it better." Irsu agreed. "Also, the Museum lets people get a proper look at the… impact that got left behind. It's all here. The animals, the ecosystems, the good days, the disasters, the kings, the criminals… We haven't forgotten anything, Atxi; I swear."

Atxi shivered and went to the Directory again. "Alright. Can't put this off anymore."

~oo0Ooo~

"Drew Thorne was right. It's mine." Atxi murmured.

"Are you sure?"

The Aztec Exhibit included relics from that era. Including the tattered scraps of a ceremonial robe; worn by one of the multitude of human sacrifices. "Positive. See that pattern on the collar? It's barely recognizable, but I was there when my sister wove it on our loom. Mother added it to my robe. She'd stayed up all night making it for me to wear. She wanted me to look my best."

Irsu watched her. "Are you okay?"

Atxi nodded compulsively.

Irsu and Atxi had found the exhibit on the Aztecs. It was smaller than some; larger than a few others. What was there was accurate; but there were several important omissions. Enough that Atxi thought seriously about asking for a job.

~oo0Ooo~

"Lot more kids than I thought." James observed. "In fact, now that I think of it, there are always a lot of kids about."

"Children have a higher ratio of people awaiting a Returning." Karen told him seriously. "Infant mortality was a serious concern for most of history. Miscarriages and abortions get their chance too."

(**Author's Note:** *This is a hugely controversial topic, and it's covered more closely in 'Just See Yourself'. The decision of how to handle unborn children is not directly mentioned in Scripture, but we can be sure it will be done with love. This route was one I chose in JSY, so for continuity, it remains that way in this book.*)

"That would indicate that there's a huge number of children without parents."

"On the contrary, they all have parents. They also have a huge number of aunts, uncles, cousins, brothers, and sisters. Our whole world is based around the idea that it's not genetics that make a family." Karen told him. "You've been here this long, and you haven't noticed?"

"Well, I don't spent a huge amount of time among people." James admitted. "Oftentimes I land at night, when the littl'uns are tucked away."

"Remember, James; whole generations of those Lost Boys and Girls have already grown up to adulthood and have kids of their own to raise. Family is at the heart of what it means to be human."

James said nothing, but inwardly he felt a spike. He had no family of his own. Nobody but the Undecided would marry 'outside the Lord', and James had little interest in the Undecided, except for Atxi, who wasn't speaking to him.

"Anyway, your *Stargazer* was salvaged, and some of the pieces were sent here." Karen got them back on topic. "I'll track down a Directory, and we'll see what we can find. Feel free to browse, in the meantime."

~oo0Ooo~

What startled Atxi out of her thoughts, was how close her Aztec exhibit was to one about Pirates. Her fight with James had been weighing on her, and this was an uncomfortable reminder of how things had been left.

"Okay, say it." Irsu told Atxi gently.

"James has been chasing some of his best plunder." Atxi said quietly. "But even if it was melted down, turned into Crosses and Crowns and who knows what else, that Gold was pillaged from my lands, wasn't it?" Atxi sighed hard. "The Spanish slaughtered my people looking for gold, and all they found was shipped across the world." She pointed at the piracy exhibit. "Waiting for someone to steal it. What a world this must be, where my people, the Conquistadors, and the Pirates are all in the same room."

"For all James' talk about how much he pirated from them, one man couldn't carry the *crumbs* from a whole nation." Irsu noted. "Don't give him too much credit."

"I adore James. I really do. He's been a source of great friendship and support since I moved out to live with the Undecided. But seeing his... his kind, on the timeline here, it suddenly seems so small."

"Large enough to take up his entire lifetime."

"And barely a drop in the bucket compared to what was out there." She glanced at Irsu. "It just occurred to me that I must seem equally laughable to you."

"Atxi, be honest. You haven't believed in Huitzilopochtli for quite some time." Irsu countered. "You're refusing the truth because you're angry about the lie, and it's hurting you. There's nothing laughable about that at all. This is the reality of the predatory system, Atxi." Irsu said kindly. "The entire human timeline, from Eden to A-Day, was just like this. One tribe fed on another, until they get fed on. But that doesn't work anymore. Even the animals don't think like that anymore."

"No, only people do." Atxi said grimly.

"Very few of them." irsu reminded her.

Atxi shivered. "When I left California, I spoke briefly with a man who was like me, 'Undecided' and trying to make his fortune." She gestured at the coins on display. "I have a different view of 'gold and silver', Irsu. With the blood of two different armies all over the same gold trinkets I handled, to say nothing of his own; what would James say about this?" Atxi pointed at each part of the room in turn. "From my people, to them, to- *James*?!"

Sure enough, pointing along the different exhibits, she suddenly found herself pointing at a familiar face.

~oo0Ooo~

James had felt icy cold fingers go up and down his spine as he walked through the Piracy Exhibit of the Museum. His ship, the Stargazer, was in pieces. Cut apart and put on display for people who were walking through the relics of centuries.

Like me. James thought numbly. *I belong in a Museum.*

"Hello again." A man's voice said kindly, and James turned to see a familiar figure. A huge, heavily muscled man with dark skin. "You probably don't remember me, but I was there the day you Returned."

"Trust me, you're hard to forget."

Irsu gestured. "And I believe you know Atxi."

James smiled with irony. "We've met, yes." He pointed at one of the Museum exhibits. "I've been wandering around this Museum for a while now, and one thing I've realized is you chart the course of history by the order of who loots and pillages whom." James gestured around. "In fact, I was looking for-"

"James! I found it!" Karen called over as she returned

to his side. "I was right. They did have... Irsu?" Karen smiled. "Wow! What were the odds? It's great to see you."

"And you, sister." Irsu clasped her hand briefly.

Atxi's eyes never left James. He was openly staring back at her. Irsu and Karen read the room enough to know they needed a moment, and pulled back, talking to each other quietly.

Which left Atxi and James alone for the first time since their fight.

Atxi made the first move, and stepped forward to give him a tight hug. "I'm sorry." She whispered.

"You didn't do anything wrong." James rasped back, returning the hug.

"No, not for that." Atxi looked down, trying to put it into words. "I hadn't realized when I boarded the *Nicholas*, that you would take it as... what? An invitation?"

James shook his head. "You don't owe me anything, Atxi. I shouldn't have assumed."

"You had every reason to assume." She told him firmly. "In truth, I've been waiting for you to return to the Island with every supply run. Even Hans said he only saw me smile when you were back. I mean, you must know why, by now?"

"I do." James held her hands, kissing her fingers tenderly. "But this trip was different, and I should have known that, and I'm sorry that I snapped at you."

"I snapped back." Atxi murmured. "What you said, about 'who knows how long we have left?' Well, I don't know, but I do know that I don't want to spend it fighting with you."

"Me either." James promised. "And I wasn't really mad about you with Irsu. I felt like I should be jealous, but I'm not. Something else that's different about this world, men and women can be friends here. And… to answer your accusation, my days of wenching, smoking, brawling, and drinkin' are all long done. In all these years, I haven't found a single appropriately immoral woman in any port, nor a place where you could buy pipe weed or cannon. Not for love or money. Not much left to being a sailor, let alone a Pirate, eh?"

Atxi smiled and let go of his hands. "Did you come to London to tell me that?"

"Actually, I'm here looking for something myself." He smiled at her. "But if I came to London looking for treasure, and I found you; I'd call it a good day."

Atxi smiled warmly, feeling young again for a moment… before she gave him a swift kiss on the corner of his mouth. "I'm glad we're 'us' again."

"Aye. Me too."

~oo0Ooo~

"He's trying to track down the money's and wealth he died over." Irsu commented to Karen. "Why are you helping him do that?"

"Because I know it won't lead him where he needs to be." Karen shrugged. "And the places it will actually lead him? It might be enough to get through to him."

"I hope so." Irsu agreed, and the two of them returned to their charges. "Atxi, is James coming with us, then?"

"No, he has his own things to do." Atxi said, happy. "I'm going to meet him when we're both done."

Karen looked about. "Where'd he go?"

Atxi pointed to a different exhibit, and Karen gave chase.

~oo0Ooo~

James was looking up in disbelief at the largest

exhibit he'd seen yet. His jaw was hanging open, arms slack at his sides.

Karen sidled up behind him, already bringing the display up on her Device. "It's a dinosaur skeleton. A Tyrannosaurus Rex, to be precise." She said lightly. "They were extinct for some time before either of us. The first Dinosaur bone was found in the 1670's, which is why it's up this end of the Museum, but nobody knew what they were until they found a whole lot more of them, and assembled a skeleton in the 1800's. A number of years *after* you died." She chuckled. "You should see your face."

"It's... big." James said finally. "When we were chartin' our maps, there was always a few places out past the edge of the map that we knew nothing about. Some of the Navigators refused to go past what was known, because... Well, on those parts of the map, they would write-"

"'Here there be monsters'." Karen said it with him. "I know. I heard that in history class."

"I had thought that... well, if the map was completely filled in now, then maybe it meant there were no more myths and legends." James said quietly. "But there are, aren't there?"

"There are many mysteries yet to be found, sailor." She promised him, and showed the Manifest. "It looks like the *Stargazer* treasure was sold at auction. The ship itself had a few pieces that were still in good enough condition to be auctioned. The maps and charts survived, sealed in a sea chest. The cannons went to an Historical Society for display. The ship's flag went to a different museum; the Cutlass that was thought to be your own was sold to a private collector in the States..."

"And all this was all two centuries ago, of course." James felt the despair creeping in. "Who knows where it went in *this* world. If it's not in the museum..."

"Huh." Karen was still glued to the manifest. "This is interesting. The Ship's Wheel and the figurehead went to an Art Restorer when A-Day was about to hit."

James looked over sharply. "Where would they be now?"

"I have no idea. But I have the address for the Art Restorer. We can try and find out." Karen told him. "It was in New York, so it was probably a high end place."

"What's New York?" James asked, having never heard of it.

"Doesn't matter. The city doesn't exist anymore, but I know someone who made a living in restoration work. They started with what was left after A-Day." Karen pulled out her Device. "That's part of the reason we came here. London is the best place for locating such items. They have most of the records that survived this long."

~oo0Ooo~

"Penny for your thoughts." Irsu said quietly.

Atxi looked over. "What's a penny?"

"A coin used by people long after us. A coin of very little value; but 'penny for your thoughts' was a saying people used."

"Not sure my thoughts are worth much more." Atxi sighed. "James isn't hunting the gold because he wants profit. He's after something money can't buy."

"Oh?" Irsu was surprised by that. "That wasn't the impression I got."

"You only know him as a Pirate." Atxi defended him immediately. "But he hasn't been a Pirate for at least as long as I haven't been a Priestess; so you and Karen barely know him at all."

He was looking at her face, calculating something, coming to a realization, but wisely decided not to push it. "Okay."

"But what he said, about how you can tell the story of the world by who consumed who, and in what order… In so many years of human suffering, was it really for no greater motive than self-interest?"

"You're asking the wrong person." Irsu commented. "My ex-King thought that his wealth was needed in the next life, and took it with him. I know, because I was part of his fortune."

"What?" Atxi blinked.

"I was a Cupbearer to Pharoah." Irsu said lightly. "I told you that I was likely your Greeter because I know what it's like to live your entire life according to false gods. What I didn't tell you was that one of the gods in question was my direct employer."

Atxi blinked again. "Really?"

"The King was considered a living god, and I was part of his entourage. It was a highly coveted position." Irsu explained. "I saw the effort put into making the humble members of the public believe that they were in the presence of something Mighty, and it never occured to me that a true God wouldn't have to work that hard."

Atxi shivered. "Why did you bring me here, Irsu?"

Irsu smiled. "I knew a man who was horrified at the idea of living forever. He thought that the reward for a faithful life was eternity in heaven. A Paradise Earth was a massive disappointment to him. He wanted heaven or bust. To live forever on earth is to be denied a chance to enter heaven." Irsu sighed, looking out at the view with her. "And that man was part of Christendom. He had more of the truth than you'd have ever heard, and he'd drawn the opposite conclusion."

Atxi nodded, waiting for his point.

"In that Museum, we got a look at so many different facets of human history." Irsu explained. "For a long time, people didn't understand most of the natural laws. My people had whole Pantheons of Gods to explain how the sun rose and set, how the tide came in and out, why the rain fell on one field, and not on another. As humanity learned the facts of things like the sun and the moon, or how the tides came in and out, people stopped giving the credit to a Sun God, or a River God, or a thousand other things. The more we learned, the less we needed fairy tales to explain them away."

It had made sense. Atxi had seen the pictures, the video, heard the testimony of people who studied their whole lives to prove it.

"And then people made the leap that if a Sun God wasn't needed to explain the sunrise, then maybe there was no need for any god at all. Confusion and half truths filled the old world, there were a thousand variations on how to pray to the same god; or whether He existed at all."

"And all those people arrived here." Atxi finished for him.

"I don't want to restart the old point of disagreement, Atxi. Everyone came to the same paradise. A lot were expecting something different, and a lot more were expecting nothing at all. But we're all here; looking for our place." He gave her a sympathetic look. "You've never felt like you have a place in Paradise. I had hoped that maybe if you saw just where your people, and everything else you recognized fit into the story, maybe it would help."

"We weren't much, were we?" Atxi said bitterly.

"*None* of us were, is the point. This world is only a few hundred years old, but it's already achieved more than anything all our empires put together could dream of."

Atxi shook her head. "You don't need to convince me, Irsu. I know this world is something different to whatever came before it. My problem isn't with the world, it's…"

"It's with you. The old world left scars, and you don't feel right in your own skin anymore."

Atxi nodded.

Irsu had his device out, and called up the scripture. "1 Corinthians 10:13: *'But God is faithful, and he will not let you be tempted beyond what you can bear…'*"

Atxi shook her head. "I did take more than I could bear. I died."

"And *that* wasn't enough." Irsu said simply. "Jehovah was able to undo death. Not just yours and mine, but everyone's. Death, poverty, war, sickness… None of these things were so terrible that God couldn't undo it all and replace it with something wonderful. Every tear that you ever shed has been undone, except for the things you hold onto. Everything bad that the human race has ever gone through will eventually fade into memory, the way you don't even remember stubbing a toe when you were a toddler. Walk through this museum, look at every soldier ever killed; every Pirate ever sunk, and know that they all have a happy ending. In a thousand years, a million; these fears and doubts will be long forgotten."

"Because I'll be forever young and faithful, or because I'll have 'aged out' and you'll have forgotten me and my doubts?" Atxi drawled painfully.

Irsu put his device away. "That, sister; is entirely up to you."

~oo0Ooo~

"Elizabeth!" Karen called brightly.

"Karen! So good to see you again." The two women embraced, and James looked the workshop over. Aside from the Expo, there weren't a lot of huge-scale laboratories or engineering done. James had seen the way construction was done in this world; and it was clear whoever's workspace this was; they were not inventing things, so much as preserving them.

Karen turned away from her friend and made introduction. "James, this is Elizabeth Bagley-"

"Sommers." Elizabeth put in quietly.

Karen reacted to the use of her Maiden name, but had grace enough to blow past it. "This is Elizabeth Sommers. She's part of the Reclamation Teams for New Paris." She gestured around the place. "Her job is to catalogue and identify everything left after A-Day for determination."

"A career path that has taken me from Paris, to the Expo, to London, to Jerusalem, and most of the places where ancient records and art treasures are still in safe keeping." Elizabeth put in. "A lot of it will have no use in this world, but some of it does. And some of it has a 'rightful owner' to be returned to."

"Ahh, good." James took off his tri-corner hat. "I have just such a list of items to locate."

"A list?" Elizabeth and Karen said together.

Karen knew what Elizabeth was thinking. "James, you realize that you may not be the 'rightful owner' on a lot of that stuff, right?"

"In fact, a lot of people are trying to figure that out." Elizabeth put in. "For the most part, people don't care; but there are some family mementos, keepsakes… The sort of thing you hand from father to son through a dozen generations, you know? Only all those generations are back, so 'who gets what' is an interesting question." She straightened her shoulders. "One that I can cheerfully help you with." She picked up her Screen, ready to work. "So, what are you looking for in particular?"

~oo0Ooo~

The Search had gone on for several hours. He'd spent a few hours in one archive or another, following clues, and references in old letters. Elizabeth had a huge collection of old documents, right alongside her Screens. It was a microcosm of the world now, with ancient tomes and disturbingly advanced technology side by side.

"Liz is trying to scan all these documents in." Karen explained as she carried a bundle of sheepskin documents over for James to pore through. "Once they're all recorded, it's easier to search. Not a complicated task, but a time consuming one."

"How do you know Ms Sommers? She doesn't seem like your type." James observed quietly.

"Elizabeth and I were in the same Class." Karen explained. "Like you and Atxi, we were both Returned close to each other. We also died within the same decade; which is all the common ground most of us had back in those Classes.

"Found something!" Elizabeth called, coming over. "The Art Restorer in question did not survive A-Day, but his workshop did. Our guys found it, and made use of what we could. Back then, the tools were worth more than any of the artworks, but there were more than a few Art Lovers that thought to see what could be saved. The works that were in good condition were stored until someone could decide what to make of them, including the pieces of your ship." She checked again. "The Wheel, and the Figurehead, yes?"

"Where did they end up?" Karen asked, interested now.

"On an Airship." Elizabeth turned the manifest to show her.

Karen froze, eyes flicking to James. "Captain Diaz. The *Stargazer*."

"Stargazer. That was my old ship." James said in disbelief.

"Not a surprise. We recycle ship names; especially when we go from ocean craft to aircraft... Come to think of it, I know Diaz." Elizabeth told them. "Back when he was at the Conference, my ex-husband was part of the team that built the first modern airships. Sister Diaz was one of his students. I can contact her, if you'd like?"

"Thank you." James agreed, though he couldn't help the question. "Does it seem... coincidental? I come here, and that leads me to you, who happens to be based in the same area, and you happen to know the next person we're looking for..."

"You'd be amazed how often that happens." Elizabeth smiled at him. "Divine help or not, it's what happens when you spend a lifetime with people who share a connection." She pointed a finger upwards. "We've all got something in common, nowadays."

Almost all. James moved past that topic quickly. "Do you mind if I keep looking through some of these files? There are some items that I was curious about."

Elizabeth looked at him, and she had it too. That tiny hint of pity for him. James was really coming to hate that look.

~oo0ooo~

"You're the only person who doesn't look at me that way, y'know." James observed as they walked away.

Karen waved at a truck in the distance when they

reached the road. "It's hard for people not to feel sorry for the terminally ill; and you're one of the few people in the world that still fits that description."

"I think that's why I like you, Karen." James scoffed. "I don't believe I've ever seen you feel pity for anyone yet."

"I'm well trained in hiding my horror at the sight of wrinkles, Cap'n. It's the one skill from the Old Days I held onto." She said with grim sarcasm; when the truck she'd waved at pulled over. "Afternoon. Can we get a ride to the Docks?"

James climbed into the back of the truck next to Karen, fingering the page in his pocket. He'd lied to Karen and Elizabeth. He didn't care about the figurehead of his sunken ship at all.

The next step would be to escape Karen's attention long enough to get the most important possession of his old life back.

~ooO0Ooo~

Townsend opened the door to find Walter, looking annoyed. "I take it that the Chess Tournament failed?"

"Nobody even showed up." Walter groused.

"I told you, people don't take a gamble like that."

"And I told you it wasn't a casino. It was a Tournament with a prize. How many of those have there been? It's not gambling, technically."

"When you have to say 'technically', you're on shaky ground." Townsend reminded him. "But that's not the 'gamble' I mean."

"What did you mean?" Walter asked as Townsend lead the way inside.

"Scripture says: '*be determined not to put a stumbling block or an obstacle before a brother*'." Townsend explained. "We followed that principle ourselves, back in OS. When Addison was at the club with us, we always ordered club soda. And why? Because we didn't want to tempt him." Townsend let that sink in. "Nobody is certain if the Tournament is gambling or not, so most of them don't risk it; until they get a clarification. There are a thousand places people can meet to play chess. There are world rankings available on the Database. Correspondence games, online games…" Townsend shrugged elaborately, spreading his hands wide. "If people love something in common, they find each other."

"It's not gambling. Chess is a game of skill." Walter insisted. "I could have started a poker tournament; but I didn't. Why would people have a problem with that?"

"I really don't know how else to say it." Townsend sighed. "Money doesn't matter in this world. Fame doesn't matter in this world."

"Money and fame always matter." Walter said firmly.

"Not. Here." Townsend said seriously. "The reason you can't figure out this world is because the people here aren't interested in anything you have to offer, and aren't scared to lose anything you can take away. What other tactic have you tried?"

Walter had no answer to that.

"We told you that we didn't have to defend this world, and how it does things? That's because the world makes its own case. Time was, JW's had to knock on doors and defend the Kingdom of God as being real, and being worthy. Now the rules have changed. Believers are behind all the doors now. The Truth can take care of itself. If you can't find any traction, the problem isn't the market, or the economy, or anything else but what's in the mirror."

"But why?! Why doesn't it work?!" Walter raged. "What am I doing wrong? I'm not offering a bad service to my consumers!"

"There it is. You remember what we used to call them all, back in the day? Consumers. 'Customers' if we were feeling generous."

"I remember."

"You know what JW's call people they haven't met yet? The Brothers. The Friends. That's the difference, Walter. You're still trying to make things work like they did in a time when nothing worked."

"You're one to talk. You haven't held down a straight job in years."

"Yeah, and look at the result. I work a four day week like everyone else, and I have quality of life at home too. I have a wife, two kids, we all get along, and I live on a lakeside. Back in the day, to get a week off to stretch out beside a lake without any sound of traffic, how long did it take to organize? How long did we have to book our vacation in advance?"

"Months."

"I can do it every other week, if I want." Townsend said, and Walter could hear the smile. "There is power in patience, Walter. You're spending everything you've got, trying to get more. Me? I get money in smaller amounts, but I don't spend much; and need even less. In time, I figure about five hundred years, I'll have savings enough to take an extremely long sabbatical. One that can last a long time. There's banks, and savings accounts. Most everyone is working hard, but everyone has a dream to chase. And after living on my savings for another decade; chasing personal interests, I'll want something more relevant to do. Work is satisfying, when it's not holding you hostage."

"This *is* a necessity, Townsend." Walter said intensely.

Townsend looked at him a moment. "You see that bookshelf?" He pointed. "All of those books are favorites. I have spent decades reading, and putting together a collection of my favorite novels. And that collection will not stop growing. Now, with a library card, I could read all those books just as often as I could from owning them. They aren't a necessity. It isn't a matter of life and death that I own them. It took some money. It would cost me nothing to use the public library instead of building a bookshelf. But I love them. I love my books. They… enrich me. They make this room feel like my home, because they are things that I love."

Walter nodded.

"Franklyn, whom you met? He's built his own home. He found he loves the outdoors. He's working to become a landscaper. So he built his home to have good views of his bit of allotted land, which he will spend a century planting, tending, and landscaping to make it 'just so'. Because he loves it. We used to pay people minimum wage to keep our yards trimmed and bushes pruned. He does it out of love, because he sees beauty."

Walter nodded, listening.

"A friend of mine, Heinrich. You haven't met him. But his favorite thing is Music. He built his home with something like a small concert hall. A room that's acoustically perfect for playing his recordings, with a huge collection of rare music, on vinyl, CD, Digital… His audio equipment rivals a professional studio, all to give him incredible sound quality when he listens. These things are all luxuries, but they aren't status symbols, or the excesses of rich kids with time on their hands, like our old lives used to be." Townsend gestured at the bookshelf again. "Heinrich could care less about books. And while I have some favorite music, as everyone does, I could never see myself putting that much effort into listening to it. Everything we fill our lives with now is chosen because it brings us joy, or because it brings us fulfillment."

Walter said nothing.

"Now, I'll take a bet." Townsend said seriously. "I'll wager that your house has nothing but spreadsheets and ledgers, and notebooks full of ideas on how to make your fortune." He saw Walter's face, and pressed further. "Including all the ways you can exploit the fact that people live forever, and all the loopholes you can find in scripture to make your vices more acceptable."

"I'm not wrong!" Walter snapped. "Anyone would do it, if they could! It wasn't easy, to build what I had built in OS-"

"Walter." Townsend cut him off. "You miss the point of everything I just said. This is a world where things are valuable because they are loved; not the other way around. Including the people. You value your business skills. But what do you *love*?"

~oo0Ooo~

Irsu had excused himself to take care of some other matter. It had been some years since Irsu was assigned to meet her at her Returning, and in the years since, he had become a Judge for this area. Atxi was very aware of how much of his time she was taking up.

The Museum was huge, covering half a town. In its way, it was the natural opposite to the Expo. The Expo was about the future, with some history. The Museum was about history, with some mention of how it lead into the future.

Atxi had spent a whole day wandering through the different phases of mankind, before she decided she had to leave. On her way out, she heard a familiar voice, echoing through a quiet marble hall, and she followed it. The classrooms were always in use. Atxi was far from the only one with questions.

When Atxi found the classroom in question, it took her a moment to recognize the teacher. The last time they'd met, Atxi was young, and the teacher was old and grey. Now the reverse was true.

Drew Thorne, young again, recognized her at once, and waved for her to sit in an empty seat, not breaking off from her lesson. "The question I get asked again and again, is how come secular sources didn't have far more information about the biblical events? The answer is, history gets to decide such things; but never with the future in mind."

Atxi looked around the class subtly. There was a fairly uniform cross section of people. Something Atxi had realized was that people from all backgrounds were interested in all sorts of topics, but it was a relatively new thing for them all to pick whatever field they wanted.

"I know, you're thinking that there should have been something more left." Drew told them. "Well, let's try this another way. How many here have heard of Eva Peron?"

A few hands went up.

"Eva Peron was the first lady of a country called Argentina. She was also a hugely popular figure with the public. So much so that she was declared the 'Spiritual Leader of the Nation'." Drew explained. "When she died, over two thousand people were sent to hospital from the crush of people trying to be closer to the body during her funeral procession... But a few years later, there was a Military Coup in Argentina, and a new government came to power. Her legacy was such a problem to the new leaders, that they stole and hid her body; and made it illegal to own a picture of her, or even *say her name* out loud. They struck her from the record for almost a decade. Other nations knew her story, so it didn't work for long; but it happened. In the 1940's."

Atxi shook her head in disbelief. She knew the point Drew was making. She'd lived it.

"In ancient times, if a King was embarrassed, it would be within his right to destroy every record, execute every witness." Drew told them. "I had a man here last month, who was an official Scribe to one of the Egyptian Pharaohs. He misspelled the King's name on a Temple wall; and was tortured to death. The Temple wall was razed and a new one put up. The places where the Kings and Armies of the Ancient Earth came into opposition to Jehovah? It didn't go proudly for any of them." Drew smiled. "I was there in the last part of OS. Trust me, you couldn't get a *modern* politician to accept they'd said something wrong, even if you had it recorded in HD-Video. What hope for Bible Times?"

The polite chuckle went around the room.

"The Bible kept all these moments recorded, including the most embarrassing mistakes and crimes committed by the most respected and honored men in the Bible Record; and there was a copy of that book in almost every home in the western hemisphere." Drew summed up. "And now, at last, we're getting eyewitness testimony to things that were deliberately struck from the history books. So, with that in mind, I'm going to hand you over to Brother Fargo; and he'll instruct you on the project, and how to fill in all those blank spots that the history books were left with. The Bible is the story of God's relationship with mankind. What we're starting here is something far more complex: The story of mankind's relationship with each other."

There was another round of applause as Drew handed off the lecture to another man, and swept out of the room. Atxi followed automatically. The moment they were alone, Drew turned and gave Atxi a tight hug. "It's good to see you again."

"And you." Atxi said automatically. "You look different."

Drew ran a hand through her reddish-brown hair. "I suppose I must, yes."

Atxi bit her lip. "Quite a project you're starting in there. Being Curator suits you."

"Mm. It's a project that's been a long time coming." Drew admitted. "You remember the book I wanted your help with? Well, imagine the book being a thousand volumes longer. Everyone in history will be coming back. The more we know about them and their lives, the more common ground we can find during the Returning."

"What…" Atxi struggled to say it. "What made you believe?"

"It finally clicked that I don't get to judge." Drew smiled. "It took me so long, because I never thought of it that way, but it's what I was doing. I judged that the Egyptians were great builders, and that the Romans were civilized, and the Spartans were honorable… And most important of all, I judged that I was right to make those choices, because I had a doctorate, and I was accredited, and I was smart." She shook her head. "What an idiot, I was."

"You're far from an idiot, Mrs Thorne."

"Drew." She waved that off. "My stupidity wasn't that I didn't understand the facts. It's that I understood them from a distance. I got to talk about the fervor of Aztec worship, to a woman who actually died on the altar. I got to talk about the wonders of Egyptian Construction with the slaves that made bricks or died under a whip." Drew shook her head. "I was so hung up on what was missing from this world, that I didn't realize how much of a Paradise this world is to everyone that I've spent my life trying to understand."

Atxi said nothing to that. She'd spent most of her time in Paradise fighting the comparisons too. Here was a woman who had seemingly agreed with her, and aged like Atxi did… only she was now young again, and apparently had changed her mind. Stricken, Atxi turned away from her.

Drew caught her shoulder, turned her around to bring them face-to-face. "No." Drew said. "I won't make you feel bad about yourself, Atxi. I spent enough time putting people on the spot. I *do* know what it's like, because even when I was convinced this world was wrong to leave behind all the things I wanted it to have, I couldn't deny it was really happening."

Axti sighed. "Neither can I."

"So?"

Atxi felt brittle. "I've wasted enough of my life begging gods for their love. And I'm still so angry about the last time I just can't… I don't even know."

Drew looked sad for her. "I never asked Jehovah for anything." She said quietly. "I didn't even know the name until I got here. I never asked him for my husband and son to find the Truth after I died. I never asked for them to be protected as the world fell down around their ears. I never asked for my husband to join the Conference, or my son to become a respected Elder. I never asked to be Returned to a world where nobody has so much as used harsh language against me or anyone I love."

Atxi winced. "I didn't mean to suggest-"

"Back then, I never knew it was an option. If I had, I would have prayed day and night." Drew cut her off. "I never begged Jehovah to give me eternal life in Paradise, where my kids will never be scared or alone or unloved.

And I never begged for my mom, my grandfather… to see all of them, young and healthy and with all their faculties back." Drew wiped a tear away absently. "But I was given all those things anyway." She pointed to her own face. "And it still took decades for me to say 'thank you'."

Atxi looked down. "I'm not blind. I know I'm one of the few people getting older. I know I'm one of the few people who isn't happy. And I know it's my fault, but I can't do it. I just can't take the *games* anymore."

Heavy silence.

"Y'know what?" Drew said finally. "When we first met, I was worried about what we'd lost as a people. It never occurred to me how much was saved. Neither of us were there at the end, but apparently it came really close."

"Close to what?"

"To losing it all. Your nation came crashing down almost a thousand years ago, Atxi. But all the world was on the brink at A-Day. All the billions of people."

Atxi said nothing. The words washed over her. What was the world? She hadn't seen it. What were billions? She'd never even heard a number that high until she came here, after the war between Good and Evil was won.

"Matthew 24." Drew had her device out. Atxi noted that nobody went anywhere without the Bible in some form. "*In fact, unless those days were cut short, no flesh would be saved; but on account of the chosen ones those days will be cut short.*" She read. "Think about that for a moment. <u>Nothing</u> would have survived. I wasn't there, but my husband was, and he says it was exactly that bad."

"I have heard a similar story." Atxi nodded. "But it's hard for me, because everything I knew was long dead before it got that far."

Drew nodded. "We would have lost popcorn." She said profoundly.

Atxi blinked.

"And we would have lost French Fries." Drew added. "And playing the music too loud when you drive, and singing along even louder, just because it's fun. We would have lost climbing in trees, and nighttime bonfires on the beach-"

"And ice cream." Atxi added, out of nowhere.

Drew smiled broadly. "And ice cream. And taking our kids to their first day of school, and playing with kittens, or even Tiger Cubs. And sleeping in on days off, and the smell of cut grass in your front lawn, and learning how to make cookies with your grandmother, and a hundred other happy things that everyone got to do without thinking much about it." She had tears in her eyes. "Now think bigger. We would have lost Beethoven's Sonatas, and the words of William Shakespeare, and the voice of Billie Holliday, and the ideas of Stephen Hawking, and the art of Leonardo Da Vinci. All of them, lost to time; and their legacy would never have lasted past the rot of OS... Until this world began, where they all can live again." Drew wiped her eyes. "We have to say thank you, Atxi."

Atxi was silent a long moment. "How?" She whispered helplessly.

Drew regarded her a moment, glanced around, and then led her back inside.

~oo0Ooo~

Drew took Atxi to her private office, guided her to a chair, and then shut the door. She pulled over another chair, sitting with the grey haired woman, and took both her hands in her own.

"Thank you, Jehovah." Drew said softly. "Thank you for not keeping your very best qualities all to yourself. Thank you for giving us creativity, and laughter, and courage, and love. Thank you for a beautiful world, and an awe inspiring world. Thank you for sifting through all our sins to find something good. We know that we're insignificant next to you, and that you are without flaw. Thank you for seeing us better than we saw each other."

Atxi watched all this through eyes that she pretended were closed. She was observing, not taking part. *She could go on forever, couldn't she?* Atxi asked herself. *We could spend eternity finding more and more things to thank the Creator for. 'We'? Did I really just think that?*

"Thank you for my family. Thank you for bringing me back from the dead so that I could be with them. Thank you for being patient enough that I could be with them forever. Thank you for every happy thought; because it was you who made us able to feel joy. Thank you for giving us beauty. Thank you for saving it before it was gone. Thank you for David; and for seeing him through the years without his mother. Thank you for Hitch, and for seeing him through the scariest days anyone's ever had."

This is a prayer. Atxi thought to herself awkwardly. *This is giving thanks. This is being content.* Atxi looked at Drew's face. *This is being happy.*

Chapter Fourteen: A Good Day

What do you love?

The question stayed on Walter's mind for a long time; because he couldn't think of anything offhand. Nothing he'd find in this world, anyway. He loved spending time at his Bistro. The Club. He loved his job. He loved making things happen.

He'd never put it into words, but he loved the exercise of power. He hadn't had a moment of 'power' since he'd come back from the dead. And he'd been so focused on getting it back, he'd never stopped to consider why.

He'd given that question some thought over the last day, and come to one conclusion: He wasn't altering his plan. He'd gone into the Cryo Deal with no clear idea of what he'd find, and a very clear ledger of what he'd have available on the other side to rebuild with. When he came to, he'd had neither.

The realization made him feel better. If the world he knew had held on, he would have landed soft; with his whole fortune at his disposal. It had taken an act of God, literally, to keep his plans from playing out as he'd expected them to.

As to the question of how he would deal with God… He wasn't concerned. There was business to be done under anyone's rule. Democratic, Fascist, or Theocratic; there were still opportunities to excel. God should understand that, It had been the staple of many religions that God rewarded his people with prosperity.

Walter had heard enough lessons about humility and 'daily bread' to know that the world wasn't overly concerned about such things. Walter had no desire to dominate or rule the world, only to excel in it. And if other people didn't respect that, it would be far more their problem than his.

He'd spent the morning away from the others, walking the edge of the community he lived in. There were small orchards on community property; and he helped himself to a snack from one of them. He'd tried his luck building a new business in three different communities, wondering if the problem was local culture. It wasn't. The culture was similar everywhere he went.

He understood how other people could be dazzled by the idea of Resurrection. He'd been one of the few people who'd planned a scientifically proven, genuine reality of an afterlife, but-

A low growl made him jump, and he spun back towards the tree he'd just plucked a fruit from. A large, lean form jumped down smoothly, and Walter let out a bark of shock. He'd apparently woken a full grown lioness from a nap in the treetops.

Walter had seen exotic animals three times since his Returning. At least, what *he* considered exotic. They simply didn't travel that far unless someone transported them. That wasn't a common event, given that most of the animals were considered 'community property', like the parks and orchards. But every country had its zoos or wildlife preserves, as well as a few privately owned or illegally smuggled animals. The passage of years had caused some animals to live out their lifespans, while others found each other and thrived.

But it was still a rare event for Walter, and it sent a thrill though him. He hadn't seen a lion in person for years, let alone one close enough to reach out and pet. And then the lioness came over and rubbed the side of her face against his hip like a housecat, before turning and padding away.

Despite himself, Walter followed.

~oo0Ooo~

The Lioness pushed through a hedge maze, and by the time Walter had gone around it, he couldn't see her.

What he could see was half an Ark's worth of domesticated animals.

There were hundreds of them; at least. With a large house in the middle of the space, more like a multi-room gazebo than a regular house. And every space of it was filled with animal feeders.

The animals themselves were varied. There was a high proportion of dogs and cats, but some more exotic creatures like foxes and horses. Some sheep gathered over on the far side of the house; and some more wild species like Wolves and Hawks were lazing comfortably.

"Howdy." A voice called. "Looking for a friend?"

Walter turned. There was a woman there, with the same eternally young features. She had a lion cub in her arms, which was squirming around, trying to get loose. "How many lions are there?" Walter asked reflexively.

"As of last month, eight." She said. "A lioness had her litter. We're actually trying to figure out where she's gone."

"I saw her over there…" Walter gestured. "If there isn't more than one adult lioness."

"This little tyke has a habit of running away and getting into scrapes. Earlier today, his mother… and I swear this is true… carried her cubs over to me and dropped them, literally, in my lap; and then stalked off. I'm a lioness' babysitter now."

Walter found himself laughing. Something that was very much out of character for him. "I read somewhere that cats domesticated themselves. I'm not sure that holds true in a world where you've got people that can tell you the origins of such things; but I have no trouble believing it." He held out a hand. "Walter Emmerson.

She smiled broadly and stuck out her free hand. "Mickey McQueen." She introduced herself. "You don't remember me, do you?"

Walter felt his heart give a solid thud. "Um…"

"S'okay. No reason you should." Mickey told him. "You were a contributor to the animal shelter I worked at, back in the 80's." She ran a hand through her dark curls. "I barely recognize myself. I was quite a bit different then."

"Animal shelter…" Walter mused. "I remember that…" And Walter followed the woman as she returned the cub to the rest of his siblings. They were rolling around with a large rubber ball, full of the same energy that young animals always had. "The mother doesn't mind you being this close?"

She just smiled at him.

Walter rolled his eyes. "I know, I know. That's how it is here. What can I say, I've never been this close with a lion before. At the very least, these dogs should be barking."

Mickey set the cub down gently and made her way towards the gazebo. Walter went with her. As they walked, Walter looked at the animals. They all seemed to be getting along, sharing food, or cuddling together, napping in the shade. McQueen seemed to know instinctively which one was a 'good boy' or a 'clever girl' and once she reached the Gazebo, she checked a few Devices. "Feeding schedules. Not all these guys eat the same foods, or at the same times. Best not to let anyone get lost in the mix."

Walter nodded. "You run this place?"

"Me and a half dozen others. Animal care is a full time job, even these days. I worked in a shelter back in OS, but back then you needed a lot of medications, cages… Trust me, this is better; until we can find a more permanent home for them."

"As I understand it, animals just come and go."

"Well, not exactly. They are *free* to come and go, but animals now have an instinctive need for each other, and for humans. We're all part of the same team." Mickey went to a nearby fridge and pulled out a drink bottle, tossing another to Walter. "It's a good thing the animals knew that right from the start, too."

Walter followed her back outside. "What do you mean?"

"After A-Day, there were a lot of people who had to start over. Imagine being the only Believer in your family. The Day After, you're the only one left." She sat down on a bench, and her lap was immediately filled by a young doe, coming over and resting her head on Mickey's knee. "The animals were all turned loose; and while they could mostly fend for themselves in a world where 'lion will lay with the lamb', a lot of them followed the people around."

"Assistance Animals." Walter translated, sitting with her. "I've heard of it."

"People will accept affection from a pet that they just won't from a human. I'm not sure if that's a blessing or a failing, but these guys all knew where they were needed." She stoked the Deer, and the creatures eyes closed contentedly. "To say nothing of some animals who had waited their whole lives for someone to be nice to them." She gestured at the lioness, reunited with her cubs. "There was a time when that mother over there would have to fight tooth and claw to keep her young alive in a hungry world. There's no such thing as an endangered species anymore, praise God."

Walter still had half the orange he'd picked in his hand. A puppy had noticed, coming over and rearing up on hind legs to sniff at it. Without thinking, Walter reached down and hauled the puppy into his lap. "Except animals don't live forever." Walter pointed out. "Are some animals exempt from old age just because they are specially loved?"

"That's the point, Walter." Mickey said as she reached over and gave a particularly vigorous scrub to the puppy's ears. "Having pets isn't an answer to *our* prayers. It's an answer to *theirs*."

"What?" Walter barked out a laugh. "You're not serious."

"Well, maybe prayer isn't the word for it." She conceded. "But do you have any idea the life that animals had back before A-Day?"

"To be honest, it's a question I didn't much consider."

"Before I came here, I worked in an animal shelter." McQueen said. "That was in 1973. Thirteen million cats and dogs went into shelters per year; in America alone. By the time it ended, a change in the laws got that number down to eight million a year. Three million had to be put down per year, because they kept coming in, and they had nowhere to go. Three quarters of all animals put down were perfectly healthy. And that's not even counting animals that were penned in and slaughtered, pumped up with drugs to keep the meat sanitary, fed bad diets to make the meat thicker… And all that was legal. Consider the animals neglected and beaten by thoughtless owners. Or deliberately abused until they were savage enough for dogfights. Or the ones poached and gunned down for trophies, or for fun?"

Walter winced. "I… I went on safari once, with a few

members of my club. Two of them knew a man who could take them hunting. They came back with a few trophies."

"But not you?"

"No, I never thought of killing animals, even other predators, as a way to entertain myself. You want a trophy, you can buy one." Walter shook his head. "But with all that, you focus on domesticated animals?"

"Well, first of all, those are the ones that are in this area; save a few that are descended from zoo animals. Secondly, they're *all* domesticated now." McQueen told him. "Well, all tamed, anyway. The line between domestic and 'harmonious' is non-existent." She lifted the pup from his lap. "A fella like this one? His view on Paradise is to be a good boy and have someone love him for however long he lives. If his litter had been born back in OS, he'd be a roll of the dice, between being given to a good home, being given to someone who would have beaten him when having a bad day, or being dumped on the side of the road somewhere. He never has to worry about starving to death or being beat up, any more than we do. None of them do."

"That's the good ones." Walter quipped. "What about the bad ones?"

Mickey didn't even blink. "They're *all* good ones, Walter."

Walter was about to answer… When the lioness padded up to them again. She reared up on her hind legs, and promptly lay across McQueen's shoulders from behind with a low, rumbling growl.

Walter felt his heart in his throat, even after this long; wondering if the lioness was about to go for a neck-bite. It was a fear that faded instantly, as the lioness started nuzzling Mickey, rubbing her nose across the back of her neck. By the time McQueen turned to look at the lion, she had already rolled over onto her back; paws the size of frypans waving playfully in the air.

"She is so greedy for belly scratches, this one." McQueen said with affection. She glanced over at Walter. "If you don't mind my saying, my friends all told me it was a long shot, coming to you in '83. Charitable donations to animal shelters isn't what you were famous for."

Walter was silent for a while, staring down at the puppy gnawing on the orange in his lap. "When I was little, I found an abandoned litter of kittens in the woods behind my school. So young their eyes were still glued shut."

"Abandoned." Mickey sighed sadly.

"Not by their mother. I found them all in a shoebox."

Mickey scowled hard enough that the deer in her lap recoiled and trotted away.

"I took them to a shelter, of course... And if I'm honest, I knew, almost immediately that they didn't have a chance; and I sort of... kept one."

Mickey smiled broadly.

"My family was slightly appalled, but I kept my grades up so they couldn't begrudge me a pet. He had this white stripe that covered the end of his tail, so i named him 'Tux', after the white tailed tuxedos. I bottle-fed him long enough for him to grow up... It was nice, having him on my side." He sighed. "Animals were something of a weakness at that age. Simpler times."

"At *that* age?" Mickey repeated sympathetically. "What changed?"

Walter looked around the reserve. "When I was seventeen, my uncle took me to a racetrack. My father told me that gambling was for consumers; and the only way to win at it was to be 'the house'. My uncle didn't agree, and placed bets all the time. I remember, there was this one horse… absolutely beautiful, but *I* could have run faster. His owner had just bet his last dime and lost; and was taking it out on the horse…" Walter shook his head at the memory. "I flew at him, took the crop out of his hand and broke it in half. My uncle told the authorities, and that man got kicked out of the business, cited for animal cruelty. The Horse was going to be sent to the glue factory, or wherever they discarded horses back then… So I asked my dad to buy him for me. Dad said no. Said I was too old to ask for a pony."

Mickey was watching him carefully. Walter suddenly looked ten years younger, talking about these moments from his past. "So what happened?"

Walter licked his lips. "I forged his signature, went to the bank and cashed in one of my trust funds early. Bought the horse myself. I visited him every week; and he… I swear this is true, the animal knew my routine. He'd be waiting at the fence when I arrived."

She smiled. "That's a great story."

"That Horse started my career, in a way." Walter nodded. "When my father found out what I'd done, he told me I was cut off. If I wanted to waste scratch, I could only waste my own. He sacked me from my job in his company; I took what was left of my trust fund, and started my own business. In ten years, I'd bought my father out. He retired with almost nothing."

She said nothing, but it was clear the story had just lost some of its shine.

Walter nodded grimly. "I know. It was how my dad and I talked, in the old days." He bit his lip. "You think he'll forgive me?"

"I've seen a lot of things be forgiven here." McQueen told him, eyes flicking over Walter's older features. "Is that what's holding you back?"

"No." Walter admitted. "But it's on my mind, today." Walter took a blue envelope from his pocket, as a Labrador puppy flopped down in his lap. "I… I've never gotten one of these letters before." Walter opened the envelope, petting the puppy absently. "It's my father. He's back in six hours."

McQueen let out a low whistle. "Well now. That's going to be an interesting reunion." She looked at Walter sideways. "If you don't mind my asking… What will you say to him, when he asks you what this place is?"

"I'll tell him everything." Walter said quietly. "I'll tell him the truth. All of the truth."

Mickey could have asked the obvious follow-up, but she didn't need to. The question was plain on Walter's face: *When I tell him God is running the world now, what will I say when he asks why I haven't made my own dedication?*

The Labrador in his lap was aware of the shifting mood, and decided Walter needed some attention, rearing up on his hind legs to nuzzle the man's wrinkling face.

"You've made a friend." Mickey observed with a smile. "Take him with you. He'll make good company for the reunion."

"No, thank you." Walter said politely. "Horses aside, my last pet was when I was a much younger man. I've stopped with 'temporary' companions."

"Walter… look at yourself." She told him gently, with open pity on her face. "I think there's a real chance that the dog may outlive you."

It was the first time anyone had addressed the matter with him out loud; and it was so unexpected and direct that Walter was left mute for a long moment. "Everyone... and I mean everyone in the world… has been giving me sideways looks, like I'm a little kid with some terminal illness. You're the first person ever to give me the ultimatum."

"I work with animals." She didn't blink. "Almost all tof which are the fourth or fifth generation I've raised in their line. I plan to keep going forever; answering doggie prayers. Animals love their babies same as we do. Back in OS, we prayed that our kids would be safe and loved after we weren't there anymore. Animals feel no shame at not living forever. Original Sin, and the Ransom alike never applied to anyone but man. Still these creatures know how to have a happy life together, full of love and play. To them, we are angels. We are ageless, super-brilliant creatures that have existed for generations, taking care of them and loving them unconditionally. If a dog can figure out what a good deal he has here, why should I pretend you're just not paying attention?" Her face relaxed back into a smile. "Too bad. If memory serves, you cut quite a dashing figure in a suit."

Walter rolled his eyes. "Don't flirt with me, lady. I'm old enough to be your grandfather."

"No, you *look* that old." Mickey shot back. "You're a toddler next to me."

The puppy yipped, as if to agree.

Walter pet the dog a little... before reaching out to scratch the lioness under the chin too.

Mickey smiled at him. "Listen... When you're telling your dad all about this world, mention the bit with the horse. Then tell him that the Co-Op you started is still running, and providing me with feed and volunteers for the whole Reserve."

"Really?" Walter blinked, and found he was smiling. "Well. I'm glad to hear that it helped."

"You helped." She said gently. "All the animals here? They wouldn't have starved or anything; but... They wouldn't have found this place. All the lives they touch?

Who knows if they ever would have found each other. You made a difference to a lot of lives back in OS, even if they weren't human. You made the same difference here. I'm sorry they didn't pay back a loan, or whatever; but…"

"Thank you." He said softly. Walter came to his feet. "I have an appointment to keep."

"Hope it goes well." She called after him.

Walter paused. "Um… If you like, I could come back. Help you out a bit? There are a lot of animals here."

Mickey smiled broadly. "I'd like that."

Walter nodded and headed off. The Labrador gave chase. Walter looked down and found the puppy at his ankle, keeping pace eagerly. With a sigh, Walter walked faster. The dog kept up, undaunted.

Okay. I guess I have a dog now. How long is that likely to last?

The answer came to him as he walked. *For the rest of my life.*

~oo0Ooo~

"So, that's the *Stargazer*." James observed, and his voice was slightly awed. "I saw a few of those crossing the oceans while I was sailing… I've never seen one docked before."

Karen smiled. "You'll really enjoy the Tour then."

"Tour?"

"You're not the only one who predates air travel by centuries. Airships didn't get that popular until after A-Day. So when they're between flights, they often open the ship up to the public."

James had seen a tower in each major community. They always stood out, since most of the world was townships now. But now that he was seeing an Airship Dock for the first time, he understood. The towers weren't just buildings, they were docking ports.

Karen had led him into one such tower, and the elevator had gotten them higher than James had ever been, almost fast enough that he hadn't been aware of it happening.

And they just open it up to the public. James almost felt sorry for the world. It was a good thing they had divine protection. They didn't have a clue about protecting themselves from bad people. *Bad people like me.*

~oo0Ooo~

The Blue Letter told him to be at a park. It was a similar place to where Walter had been Returned; and Walter had learned that most people came back in quiet nature spots.

But the park wasn't that quiet this time. There were dozens of people in the park, gathering around the park tables, setting up an event of some kind. Walter could see more people threading in. They all had red hair, which seemed like an outrageous detail, given how many of them there were.

Walter checked his Device clock for the fifth time. He was early. Despite himself, he was nervous. He hadn't seen his father in decades.

And if he takes to this world... I shall have to make an account for myself. Walter thought darkly.

He lost himself in those thoughts for a moment, when a young man came running up to him. "Mama's side, or Da?"

Walter jumped, startled. "I'm sorry?"

"Were you on-" The man noticed the Blue Letter in Walter's hand. "Oh! Sorry, I thought you were here for this." He waved back at the growing crowd. "We'll stay out of the way. We're setting up, but the guests of honor won't be here for another hour or two."

"If you don't mind my asking, what's the 'event' in question?"

"Family reunion." He explained, and stuck out a hand. "Connor."

He shook it automatically. "Walter."

Connor gestured back at the crowd. "We've got five generations of the family here for the first time. We found out that Great-Gram and Great-Grandpa are back, they were Returned together. We pulled members of the family from all over the world to have ourselves a family reunion, introduce everyone to the people we've only heard stories about. Mam and Da are very excited to meet their kin."

Walter felt the nerves hit him all over again. "Yeah. I'm sure they must be. I have a reunion myself, coming in just a few minutes."

"I'll get out of your way." Connor promised. "Hey, Walter? Don't stress. Family reunions can be nerve wracking, but they're also the very best part of Paradise, getting loved ones back. This is a good day." Connor's eyes flicked to Walter's aged face and white hair. It was clear he knew what that meant. "It *can* be a good day."

Connor left him then, and Walter took a shuddering breath.

Should I pray? Walter asked. *Funny. Last time I thought that, I was dying. I have no idea what to ask for, even if did.*

Instead, he pulled out his Device and made a call.

"Walter?" Came the surprised response. Hitch Thorne hadn't spoken with him for quite a while; but everyone's memory was razor sharp now, Walter included. "This is a surprise."

"I got tapped." Walter reported. "My father arrives back from the dead in five minutes." He shook his head, laughing ruefully. "I sure don't sound like a skeptic."

"You believe. You just don't agree." Hitch blew past that. "Are you worried?"

"Terrified." Walter admitted. "My father and I have a difficult history, to say the least. Mom was the one that knew how to handle him. When she finally left him... I didn't step up. I avoided him. His health wasn't the best then, so it was easy to... well, leave him in the care of others. He was not grateful."

"Remember, your father will need to sort things out too. Baggage with each other is something we all have. But I've discovered that when you take people away from trying circumstances and give them something huge and wonderful and interesting to learn about, it helps. A lot of the old grudges starve, once they're made irrelevant."

"I've found the same thing." David said. "But I've also found that family is the exception. He hated the Retirement Home; and my buyout meant he had nowhere else. Tell you the truth, Hitch; it was my mortal fear, having that happen to me." His watch beeped. "Two minute warning. Any advice?"

"Be honest, and seek to make peace, more than getting the upper hand. Whatever your issues are, you could very easily have eternity to sort them out. Do you have anything with you? Study aids or something?"

"I have a copy of the videos you use to welcome people back." Walter offered. "Though I wasn't shown one when I got here."

"Would it have made a difference?"

"No." Walter admitted. "But it'll help with my father.

I think he'd take the word of a video made and narrated by a total stranger over that of his son."

Walter disconnected the call and turned to see he was no longer alone. His father had been an old man when he died, but so had Walter. His father had the same mature features of his age, but with a new kind of vitality to them. After so many years, Walter was now adept at telling the difference between someone who had lived a long time in this world, and who had lived a long time in the last one.

"Hello, dad." Walter said, proud that his voice hadn't cracked. Most people were weeping at Reunions. Walter was just nervous.

"Junior?" His father breathed. "Is that you?"

"I look different, don't I?" Walter admitted. "So, um… You have questions."

"Where am I?" His father asked.

"Right. That would be a good place to start." Walter agreed, and held out his Device. "Here. I'm no good at this sort of thing, but they've planned for that."

"Welcome, our dear brothers and sisters." A voice came clearly from the device. *"You are privileged to be freed of the last, greatest enemy that mankind has ever had. In an expression of his love for us, God has returned the world to the way He had always intended it to be. A paradise. A utopia. A united family of man. For thousands of years, human rulers have made the same promise, and been unable, through inability or personal failings to live up to it. But now, as he always promised he would; Jehovah God has freed us from the clutches of suffering and death."*

The image on the screen was showing a quick series of animated shots, some of them appearing like an exquisite hand drawing, some of them just fading in and out of view. The narration continued with eager anticipation. *"These promises include many wondrous things, such as an end to hunger; an end to hatred, an end to violence. Chief among these promises, was the glorious hope that death itself would no longer trouble humanity. Jesus himself resurrected people who had died, and promised those watching that 'the hour is coming when all those in memorial tombs would hear his voice and come out'."* The image on screen showed that moment, when Lazarus embraced his sister again for the first time. *"If you are watching this video, then you are one of those who have heard his voice."*

"Oh wow…" His father breathed. "We're really here! He was right! They were all right! I never really thought it was possible! But here it is!"

This was unexpected, and for Walter; 'unexpected' was not appreciated at all. "Wait. Who was right?"

His father smiled broadly at him. "The Witnesses."

Chapter Fifteen: Forgiveness

There was a Welcoming Committee of course, and James and Karen had to wait for people to step off the airship, lugging their bags and their cargo. James was impressed. The Airship easily carried as much cargo as his yacht could, plus a lot more people.

When they got aboard, he was even more impressed. The interior was so luxurious. Captain Diaz was showing a small group of people around. "The idea of these airships was to provide an experience halfway between a luxury train and a small cruise ship. The technology was around in the 1930's, and was refined for the modern day after A-Day changed the rules. Once aloft, these ships never need to come down, provided they are treated right. Since hazardous weather is no longer an issue, and nobody's in a hurry; that makes an airship the ideal way to travel the New World." She smiled at them. "Of course, I may be slightly biased."

~oo0Ooo~

The Tour of the Airship was informative and interesting. It was kept aloft on technology and chemistry that James had no hope of understanding.

The Tour included a brief stop on the bridge. James noted the crew was still working, even as people walked through their workspace. "Look." He nudged Karen. "That old steering wheel mounted on the wall? It's the original steering wheel from the first *Stargazer*. I recognize the pattern of the wood like the back of my hand. That's the same wheel I steered her by."

Karen let out a low whistle as the tour moved on, not noticing James subtly checking for signs of security.

James noted that the ship was designed to be plush and comfortable. It was a leisure craft as much as a working craft. There was a small gallery along the Starboard Promenade, with the observation windows on one side, and a row of models and artworks on the other side. James recognized one of the models instantly. It was the Man-of-War *Stargazer*. His old ship. And right next to it was the figurehead, painted up and looking brand new.

Karen observed James staring at the figurehead earnestly. "Usually, it's supposed to be mounted on the prow, but…"

"It's more a Museum Piece than an actual part of the airship." James nodded, not offended. He just kept gazing up at it. The figurehead was of a woman with long hair, swept back. It had been underwater for centuries, dug up and restored beautifully. It almost looked brand new.

Karen noted his reaction. "Who is she?" She guessed the question. "I mean, I assume the carving was based on someone…"

James blinked hard, realizing how long he'd been staring. "My mother." He said quietly. "She died before I got my own ship, but…" He shook his head. "Nearly started a mutiny against myself."

"Why?"

James smothered a grin. "Sailors were a superstitious bunch back then. The sight of a woman's bare chest was believed to calm angry seas, so figureheads mounted on the prows of a ship were… well, topless."

Karen smothered a laugh. "But this one was based on your mom, so you painted clothes on her."

"I didn't want to forget her." James whispered. "It's unbelievable, seeing her face again. This 'statue' went ahead of me every course I charted. She's been sunk, forgotten, rediscovered, restored, lived through the world ending and being remade…"

"You know that the real thing will come back too, James." Karen said quietly. "We don't understand the order, but sooner or later, your actual mom will be back."

"We all will."

James felt his heart stop, then start to race as he turned around to face… "Smitty?!"

His old friend came over, his face unchanged by the passage of years. His clothing said he was part of the airship crew. "Good to see you again, Cap'n."

James took a step back automatically as Smitty came within reach, and the other man settled, recognizing that this was not going to be the happiest of reunions. His eyes flicked to Karen. "Miss." He bowed. "Gerret Van Beek, at your service."

"Gerret?" James repeated. "I… I would have looked you up, but you never gave me your right name."

"I would have looked you up too, Cap'n; but… well."

"You didn't think I'd be here?" James guessed.

Smitty shrugged. "I didn't know for sure, and I figured if you wanted to see me, you would." He almost laughed. "I forgot to put 'Smitty' in the database. My fault."

James watched carefully. Smitty was *happy* to see him? "I'm… I'm sorry, Smitty."

His old friend was immediately at his side, embracing him. "Me too, James. Me too."

~oo0Ooo~

"I only know a little about the Witnesses. I met one, back in the day." Walter's father nodded as they walked. "There was one in the Retirement Home. His name was Martin; and he noticed that I didn't have many visitors; so I sat in on a few studies with him. He had people coming to take him to his Meetings."

The implication was subtle, reminding Walter that he'd never so much as called his father once putting him in the Home. But the conversation had gone in an unexpected direction. After an hour of rehearsing what he'd say, how he'd say it, what his father would respond with, and how Walter would use his responses; this was a direction that had never occurred to him. "So you know about... All of this?"

"Well, I know they were expecting something like this." His Senior nodded, head on a swivel as he tried to take everything in at once. "I never believed it, of course, but... Here it is." He looked sideways at Walter, making comparisons silently between the rest of the people in view and the sight of his elderly son. "How long have you been back?"

"A while." Walter told his senior, not wanting to go into it.

Senior nodded. "I should start here. I owe you an apology."

Walter blinked again. Two unexpected statements in one minute. This was getting serious. "Apology for what?"

"Biting your head off over your trust funds. It was your money. I was just..." Walter Senior shook his head, and bent down to pet the puppy. "I worked so hard to get you that start in life. I started out with nothing. You know the story, I told it to you enough times. Living on hand-me-downs, scraping for work..."

"I know the story, dad." Walter said sullenly. "I made it work. I made something of myself."

"Yes, you did." His father agreed readily. "But I had thirty years on you, and I knew what you didn't. When you're at the end of the movie, you only dream of fixing a few bad moments. I took out my own issues on you when I cut you off. I'm glad you rebounded; but I hate the way we left things. And don't pretend that's why you suddenly got so 'busy' when your mother took off. I would have given anything to make that right."

Is that why he kept calling, at the end? Walter felt a lump in his throat. This wasn't going the way he planned it out at all. "Well…" He said finally. "While we're on the subject, I'm sorry too. Mom took off because you weren't rich anymore; and that part of it was my fault. You did work really hard. Harder than even I knew. You know how thin the line is between accepting a little help, and being someone's prisoner."

"I do."

"A mistake I vowed never to make. And I never did." Walter said proudly. "I made the Dean's List; then Valedictorian, then I-"

"It's beautiful here." His father said suddenly. "Look at that!"

Derailed, Walter followed his father's finger; to where he was pointing at the Labrador puppy. The young canine had run ahead of them, and was now playing with a large cat. "Is that a Mountain Lion?"

"A Lynx. The animals tend to come and go as they like. I never appreciated how much of the climate was comfortable for animals, even in civilization. They aren't in any danger anymore, so they tend to come and go."

The pup barked and came back over to Walter, crouching in front of him, front legs out; asking to play. Walter-Senior laughed and found a stick to throw. The dog took off after it instantly.

Walter looked over. His father was crying. "Are you okay?"

"I feel like a fool." His father admitted. "Rightly, and happily so. I spent a week with the Witnesses because I was so cosmically lonely, just marking time in an old age home. I liked them. They were nice. But I figured I was too far along to make such a total change, and I didn't really know if I believed a word they were saying... But it got me to thinking. About my death. My soul. I had no clue of what was next. Wondering if I should pray for heaven, or expect hell; and no idea of who I should pray to. I just never gave it much thought. Life was so hard and took so much time to survive that I never gave much thought to an afterlife. It took everything I had to keep my head above water, leave any kind of helping hand for my son... I literally had nothing else left."

Walter nodded. "I knew you'd understand. Why it's important to look out for yourself; take care of business first and make sure to plan long-term for your security. I didn't say it enough, but those have been my guiding principles for my entire life. Making a decent stockpile in this world is harder, since everyone's so relaxed about it, but-"

"You must be glad you can stop, huh?"

Totally derailed, yet again, Water had nothing for a long moment. "Glad?" He repeated. "What do you mean?"

"The pressure is off now." His father said, tears in his eyes. "I admit, I don't know much; but what I heard about this world in three meetings suggested that everyone would live forever." He looked at his son again. "I guess 'forever' doesn't mean 'forever young' necessarily-"

"It does." Walter corrected automatically, and immediately wished he hadn't.

Silence. His father took that in, processing, looking at Walter, then down at himself, then over at the family reunion taking place, calculating everyone's relative ages, working something out… until finally it hit him.

"Oh, you've got to be kidding me." His father scorned.

"It's not what you think!" Walter insisted, feeling about five years old again. "You always said 'religion is a fairy tale for grownups'."

"Yes, I did. And I believed that, right up to the moment I *died*. And for me, that was ten minutes ago. But a lot's happened since then." His father returned. "I've been in this world ten minutes. I had three lessons to prepare me for it; and the one thing I already know for sure is that if God raises you from the dead and offers you eternal youth, the correct response is: 'Thank You'!"

Walter erupted. "You've been back ten minutes, and already you're ashamed of my life choices! I don't expect other people to understand my reasoning, but I did think that you, of all people, might have a clue. You spent thirty years working like a dog just to keep your head above water! I would think that you, of all people, would understand what real life is like."

"I looked back on thirty years of working like that, and I realized one thing." His father snapped. "That's *not* a Real Life."

"And you're so sure this is?" Walter scorned.

"Walter, if I could have had a week when the water wasn't rising anymore, what do you think I would have done with it?" His father demanded. "Because I tell you this, I wouldn't have spent it working! Money opened all the doors back then. If God opens all the doors in this one, to say nothing of the fact that He's **Real** *at all*, and created a *Paradise…* How does that not change everything?"

It was enough. Walter's face had turned to stone, and he withdrew into himself; the way he did with everyone else who had preached at him over the years; telling him something he didn't want to hear. And now that his own father was the same, Walter was finally past the point of caring, completely fed up; alone in the world. "Yeah." He said flatly. "Anyway, I'm your Welcoming Committee. Follow me. I'll show you where to go next. So you can catch up on the 23rd Century."

His father slumped a bit, knowing he'd pushed too far. It was an old argument with a new coat of paint, but they'd fallen straight back into old patterns.

~ooO0oo~

The Reunion between James and Smitty was tense for a few minutes, but Karen was there; and that kept the peace. Aware of the tension, Karen made sure to get the conversation moving. She had questions about their adventures; and it was enough to break the tension. Once they got talking, and trading war stories, the two men were suddenly old friends again.

It took James several minutes to realize why they fell back into old patterns so quickly. After an hour, Smitty had to excuse himself and return to his duties on the ship; and James had a chance to talk about it with Karen.

~ooO0oo~

"You'd think Diaz would let him have the day." Karen commented. "The sudden reunions are a universal event now. Everyone will have a few."

"It's the life." James wasn't bothered by it. "The Ship always comes first. This thing may sail the skies, but a ship is a ship." He sent Karen a glance. "And to be honest, it might be best to take this one minute by minute. Thank you, by the way."

"I can read a room well enough to know what's not being said." Karen nodded. "In time, observation is a talent you can raise to near telepathy. It seemed a good idea to keep the conversation moving."

"And it worked, too." James observed. "But it took me a while to figure it out: Smitty isn't angry. He was nervous, he was worried; but he isn't holding a grudge."

"Why do you think he was nervous?" Karen asked.

James scowled at her.

"No, really." Karen pressed. "He's been here long enough to get a job on Diaz's ship. He can see you're growing old and grey; and there's nobody alive who doesn't know what that means. I'm betting he also knows you can't hurt him, at all; not even by accident. So what was he nervous about?"

James scowled a little harder; the guilt gnawing at him. "Not everything we lost with the last world was bad."

~oo0Ooo~

Walter had taken his father to the Dorms; and set him up with a more experienced brother to teach him about the world. Walter felt sick as he walked the street. There were people playing music, kids playing games; and the dog keeping perfect pace with him, but he barely registered any of it. He and his father had never been close. There were harsh words and hard feelings between them, like many other families. And yet within five minutes of learning that Paradise was real, his father had asked forgiveness for his part of the feuds, and taken the same position as everyone else in the world; telling him off in a way that nobody else had... But Walter knew they had all wanted to.

"The Lord helps those who help themselves." A young voice said.

Walter jumped, and spun around. A face he hadn't seen in years looked back at him. "You again. Why are you here?"

The Boy pointed at the people down the street,

playing music. "Just enjoying the tune."

"Can you enjoy our music?" Walter asked curiously. "When you and the others like you hear our music, our jokes... Do you like it?"

The Boy's head tilted. "There's a little girl in the Far East. She's realized that tapping her mother's rice pot with a wooden spoon creates a note. She will not become a musician, or have any interest in music. But right now, she's put together a series of seven tones that makes her crying baby brother sit and listen. I can hear the baby making the first connections in his brain. At two months old, he's intrigued by a 'song' that has big sister just made up. There's a man climbing one of the mountains along the Appalachian Trail. He's whistling a tune to the birds. He thinks he heard the song somewhere and forgot most of it. He doesn't realize that he imagined it himself. It will take him many decades to turn that bridge into a full piece of music. He doesn't even know how to play, yet. But he just conceived the first notes of his magnum opus. Any other point in history, that song would stop there. He'd go back to work, and he'd work hard every day, without ever thinking about taking up an instrument ever again, because he just doesn't have the time."

Walter had nothing to say to that. "The Lord helps those who help themselves." He repeated finally. "That's not actually in the Bible, is it?"

"No." The Boy said simply. "But you knew that."

Silence.

"It wasn't greed, y'know." Walter said finally. "Everyone thinks I was greedy, but I wasn't."

"No." The Boy agreed. "But for the record, that wasn't your sin."

"Then what was it?"

"Convenience. You expected God to look the other way, just as you did; because it was convenient for you that He do so."

"It's not as simple as that." Walter countered. "You of all people should know that." His tone was accusing, but that was a facade. "Before you get off telling me that I was a moral failure, just remember I've got a few years of Sunday School with me on this; even before coming here. Maybe I exploited a few people, but it was *your* kind who did so much damage to the world that a Flood was needed; just to break even."

The Boy gave a nod, conceding the point. "Granted, but when a Flood was needed, God didn't hesitate."

"The Bishops, the Cardinals… They all came to me to plead the case about helping the poor, looking for sponsors for homeless shelters." Walter scorned. "I signed my name, and those shelters took in thousands of people a year. The Social Groups and Charities? They came to me to plead for the sake of the hungry. I signed my name and Soup Kitchens opened. God didn't make that happen. I did. Even the Churches knew that. They tell their rubes that prayer helps, but they came to me when they wanted something to actually get done."

"What about Walt?" The Boy asked.

Walter froze.

"Your son wanted to know how he could help, in a personal way. Signing your name fed the hungry and clothed the cold, but it was as simple to you as writing your name. Did you even listen when those people came and told you how bad it was getting?"

"My son did." Walter sighed, conceding that.

"Your boy wanted to see a world that billions of people lived in, instead of the life he'd been born to. He looked for someone to show him how to do good in the world. And you told him-"

"I didn't want my little boy in those churches. When the Holy Men of the world wanted to help the poor, they prayed real hard. But nothing changed, until they prayed to me for help!"

"Prayed to you?"

"*Asked* me for help." Walter clarified quickly. "And then... Ugh, then one day they came in to talk about liability insurance."

"Because there was a class action against the hundreds of priests who were abusing children, and you signed your name again, showing them how to hide the pay-offs, hide the assets they really had..."

"It was my job. The Churches were a firm worth billions. If I didn't take it, someone else would have." Walter argued. "I had a responsibility to get my client the best deal I could and keep them happy with the service I was providing! So did the other side!"

"And when Walt came to you and asked what could be done about the victims, and the desperate, and the unemployed?"

Walter stopped short suddenly. "I... I told... I said..."

"You told your sixteen year old son that 'The Lord helps those who help themselves'. Your sin was to expect that God should look the other way; just as you did." The Boy finished. "When you first came back to life, did it even strike you as odd that you searched for your Bank Accounts before your son?"

Walter said nothing. There was nothing to say.

The Boy nodded. "Say it. Commit to it. You want credit for your victories; you have to do the same for your mistakes. It's not like you can keep it a secret from Him. It's not about the money. You're too practical to obsess for decades over something that barely matters anymore."

Walter did a slow burn and finally said it out loud. "I don't agree with Him."

"Yes." The Boy nodded. "Finally. Welcome to an honest conversation."

Walter sat down. "You remember the story of Jonah?"

"The Story? I was there."

Walter scoffed. "God gave Jonah an assignment he didn't want. Jonah made a choice. He used his 'God Given Free Will', and he was promptly *eaten* for making a choice that God disagreed with. Why does God act like things are our choice if He gives us only one choice to make?"

"Because He knows better." The Boy said simply.

"Not the point. I knew better than Walt on many occasions. My father took ten minutes to decide my life was a waste. I gave my kid life; but I don't get to pass judgment on his choices. Why does God?"

The Boy was silent a while. "Jonah ran away because he was scared of his assignment, and he spent a few days learning that God could keep him alive and safe even *after* getting *eaten*. With that kind of protection, why wouldn't you want to be on His Side?"

Walter snorted.

"Walter, is it better to reign in hell, than to serve in heaven?"

Walter's head tilted. "Milton. Paradise Lost."

The Boy nodded. "Is it so terrible to be in service to the ultimate Good, and live forever in His Kingdom? Especially given what the alternative was? Walt thought so, at least when he came to you that day."

Walter's face hardened. "Listen to me, you little thug:

I didn't end my son's life. You did that on A-Day."

"He was a grown man, capable of making his own choices." The Boy stared him down. No anger, no judgment, only calm certainty. "As are you."

"And anyone who makes a choice you don't agree with, they die." Walter scorned.

The Boy sighed. "There was a time when anyone could make a choice that disagreed with God. The result was certain extinction. If A-Day hadn't happened, this planet would be a ruin now, never to recover. Does that really seem like there's a huge problem with the *world*?"

Walter bared his teeth. "I'm dying. Slowly. *Again*. That seems like a problem to me."

"There was a time, not that long ago, when people came to us because they saw something terribly wrong, and wanted to be made better. They could do that because there were people who devoted themselves to spreading that message. How would you have run the Preaching Campaign, Walter? It's not like the Truth has ever been 'cost effective' in anyone's bank account. But there are people alive today because someone made those investments. Jesus invested something as valuable as the Truth in humans; and came back to check on the result. The result was millions of lives being saved. If you had been in charge of that campaign, would you have focused on reaching people's hearts, or would you have been looking for a way to turn a profit?"

"I haven't done anything wrong!" Walter raged.

"And what have you done right?" The Boy shot back, as sharp as Walter had ever heard him speak. "Romans 12:21 says: *'Do not let yourself be conquered by the evil, but keep conquering the evil with the good'*. Belief and Acceptance is not a passive state. You have to take a stand, one way or another. The claim that you've done no evil since being Returned to Life with a totally Clean

Slate is tenuous at best; and what of the good?"

Walter said nothing for a moment. "Mickey thought I had helped. Here, and in OS."

"Yes." The Boy let him chew on that a moment before he spoke again. "You speak of your merits, and the value of what you have done. The Truth is a responsibility and a privilege, even more so than material power." The Boy let him think on that for a second. "What would you think of a wealthy man who was wasteful, who was frivolous, and threw his fortune away on foolish diversions?"

Walter looked down. The puppy was looking up at him earnestly. "I would think that he'd run out and be left with nothing, soon enough."

"Yes." The Boy said simply; and he faded from view before Walter could argue the point.

~oo0Ooo~

Once the Tour was over, The Stargazer put up a dinner for their passengers. Smitty had quietly given James a table pass. "So, do I get the truth now?" Karen asked after a discreet interval.

"What do you mean?" James had picked at his food.

"I asked you what this was all about, really. You said getting those trinkets back wasn't about the money. I asked you what you really wanted; and you said if I came to London, I'd find out."

"Oh. I guess I did, didn't I?" James sighed.

"Why is it so important?" Karen asked pointedly. "I've been listening to you and 'Smitty' trade war stories for an hour. You guys got all kinds of shiny things; but you weren't interested in recovering any of it. You know that money isn't an issue anymore. And if it was, we wouldn't care about Royal Trinkets like crowns and necklaces. Of all the treasures you were trying to track down, why was that Cross so important? Smitty tells me you killed yourself trying to get it back when the *Stargazer* sank. Why did that one matter to you enough to go back for it?"

James considered his answer, before deciding it didn't matter anymore. "The cross was my final move."

Karen clearly didn't understand.

James looked around. "Come with me."

~oo0Ooo~

He led the way back to the bridge of the Stargazer. At that time of night, there was nobody there, while it was tethered. James lead the way over to the old steering wheel, mounted on the wall. There was still a notch in it from Scarlett's sword; and James ran a finger over it as he spoke.

"If I'm right," James drawled. "And if nobody found it…" He produced his knife and started poking around at the base of the steering wheel support, before he found what he was looking for and plunged the blade deeply into the wood.

"What are you doing?" Karen hissed.

James worked the knife, until something cracked, and he levered the wood apart. "Hundreds of years of salt water and retouching have sealed the compartment shut, but it's still here." He withdrew an oilskin rag, and very carefully drew out a rolled parchment in a thin metal canister. "It's held up remarkably well."

"What is it?" Karen was intrigued.

"My Original Sin." James said quietly.

~oo0Ooo~

They had left their clandestine visit to the Bridge and returned to the common area, choosing a place where they could speak, unobserved. It struck James with a sense of Deja Vu. He'd had dozens of private conferences like this with clients and conspirators.

Karen had unrolled the parchment carefully, and pressed it gently in a protective plastic coating. "Where did that come from?" He asked.

"They have nametags for the crew and VIPs. There's a laminator kit on board." Karen explained, smiling impishly. "I'm sure nobody will notice me borrowing one sleeve." She rolled her eyes. "Well, 'Borrow', in the less traditional sense."

James grinned. "Pirate." He teased.

Karen was looking over the parchment, able to study it closely now that it was protected. "I can't read the words. Whatever Translation Magic we enjoy here, it doesn't extend to 'ye olde writing' languages."

"It's a commission." James explained. "You asked why I wanted that Cross back in particular? Back then, the Church decided who got Salvation or Damnation. But they could be bought. I know people who did way worse than I did, but every now and then, a job would come along. A local Lord who wasn't paying the proper tithe, or knew something a Cardinal would rather not get out. A man could buy his soul back if he had something-"

"Something to Ransom it with." Karen said with grim irony. "You stole something you knew the Church would want back."

"The Church, and whatever feudal lord happened to be begging for their approval. It wasn't just the Cross. The Cross of Corinth could make me a prosperous Land Owner in any Dutch territory. The Necklace would fetch a full pardon from the Royalty of Spain. The Scepter was a personal prize, craved by several English Dukes, who would have had no problem offering me a title if I could bring it to them…"

"And 'the truly precious things stop moving'." Karen

laughed, quoting the conversation they had before leaving for London. "You were ransoming your freedom."

"Freedom is everything, Miss Karen. Freedom is life. Money was just a means to get that. Money gave you options beyond working to death like my family did." James said seriously. "I turned criminal, because I could see how every law, every lawmaker was only interested in their own personal pleasures and profits. The world was divided up by Kings and Popes and money changers; and they drew lines on a map to decide who got what. People who lived in those places died at the whims of powerful people they'd never heard of. Whenever the lines shifted, people like me died for it."

"And you bleed for no flag." Karen finished. "You know, back in OS, we talked about the big three tools that the world used to put pressure on people. False Religion, Big Money, and Political Powers. That woman we met today, Atxi? Her burdens are what false religion left with her. I thought your thing was money. Turns out it's Political instead."

James nodded, unconcerned. "You asked me once what I'd do with any of the things I'd taken. It's not what they were, it's what they were worth. Everyone wants their own back." James shook his head, rolled his eyes skyward, looking askance. "I've been chasing it since I was old enough to Mutiny against my worst Captain. Trying to beat the Kings and Nobles at their own game, and win my own piece of their Kingdom, where I rule and they don't." He looked over at her. "But none of them are here. I can have my own Piece given to me."

"No charge." Karen confirmed. "You're doing better than I thought you would, just getting that far in your reasoning. That does raise the question, though. What's holding you back? By now you must know for sure that there's no Kings and Popes left. No borders, or warrants. You can sail anywhere you like, make your home in any port. There isn't even a language barrier anymore. You can go in peace, end up wherever leaving takes you; and do it forever."

"And all I have to do is kneel and say 'please'." James scorned.

"You know it's not the same thing. You hated the way 'power' played games with the lives of people. God doesn't play dice, James."

"I know. But he wants the same thing every other King and Prince wanted: My submission." He shook his head. "I'll never do that. Not even for this beautiful world."

"Even the Kings were brought low before God, James." She quipped back, also not pushing the argument. They settled for a while, saying nothing; until she finally broke the comfortable silence. "By the way… I know why it was me."

James blinked. "Why what was you?"

"Why I was assigned to meet you when you returned. It wasn't what I could offer you. It's what I could learn from you. My first time on a boat with you, and I saw the whale..." Karen looked off at something only she could see. "I went looking for more information about the Humpback we saw. And while I was looking at that species, I found out a few things about other types. And as long as I was learning about ocean creatures, I decided to look a little closer at ocean ecology…"

"And all free of charge." James said in dull awe.

"The world is a better place if people are educated. Why would we make that prohibitive?" Karen asked rhetorically. "I learned something pretty interesting about the world, and about myself. I went back to school just to see how interesting it could be."

"The Ocean can do that to a person." James said with experience.

Karen grinned. "I love it, James. I had no idea that I would, but I love the ocean. I never even saw one back in OS. Plenty of pool parties, plenty of Yacht Parties, but we never actually went out past the dock." She shook her head. "Who would ever think that I'd be interested in Oceanography?"

"You'd be surprised the people who wind up on the Ocean, luv." James wasn't surprised. "You wouldn't be the first heiress who wanted something strange and wonderful."

"'Strange and wonderful' was what I could say of the whole world when I first arrived here." Karen said lightly. "And I didn't like it."

He looked over. "Why? I mean, you've already told me that you had trouble fitting in, as I have…"

"James, all the things a person couldn't do anymore were far outweighed by all the things we could suddenly do without limit. Once I got past my initial… Uncertainty, that was my main problem. I had absolutely no idea where I wanted to go with my life."

"But you joined up?"

"My career and hobby options were hugely varied, and hard to choose from. Eternal life to work it out seemed just barely long enough." She smiled at him. "You were an answer to my prayer, James. I never would have looked at the Ocean if not for you."

James said nothing to that.

Karen leaned in, speaking more earnestly. "You say you don't understand this world, and can't see a place for yourself. But look around. When you were busy chasing treasure, you had people asking you about your skills. You were practically handed a job as a shipwright. Half a dozen people who grew up hearing stories about Pirates wanted to know if they could be your new crew; even if you aren't part of the brotherhood yet. Transport and Construction are the two biggest industries on the planet right now; and you know how to build ships and sail clear across the ocean."

James gestured at the sky. "They make Airships, Karen. You think anyone's going to care about a six hundred year old design for a Man-Of-War Replica?"

"Why not? They care about six hundred year old people who sailed on them." Karen shot back. "Are you telling me, that given the choice, you wouldn't rather sail on your old ship? Even if it's slower, and sticks to the sea, you wouldn't want to take that route anyway?"

James hesitated. "I suppose I would. More time at sea is not a hardship for me."

"You won't be the only one. Some people refuse to fly, even though there hasn't been so much as a stormy ride in centuries. But one thing I've learned about this world: It takes all kinds. There will always be some who want to sail on a Man-Of-War."

"I'm one of them." James nodded.

Silence.

"When I was twelve, I went on a ship for the first time." James said finally. "I never wanted to be anywhere else." He took a deep breath, finally opening up. "I went on a tour, got paid the lowest wage on the ship, and went home. I had been gone six months. In that time, the local Mayor had raised taxes enough to put half the township in a workhouse, which the local Pastor owned. They buried my family, and dozens of others, squeezing them dry for every last coin, working them until they died." He took another breath, fortifying himself. "When they saw I was back, my parents told me to run, before I got put to work with them." He rubbed his eyes. "The lawman said they were working off a debt, but any time they got within ten shillings of being free and clear, they'd suddenly find another debt put on top of their ledgers, clapped in irons every night."

"So you ran."

"I went back to my ship, asked to do another tour. They said yes, because I was small, and that meant I didn't need to be fed or paid much. I found out as I grew up that the story was the same. The Lords, the Nobles... They could make whatever rules they wanted on a whim, and the rest of us could either starve, or go to prison and work forever." He smiled. "But when you were out on the water, the only people were the Crew; and they all knew each other. The only people you ever see. Discipline and Authority were something of actual use when you were a sailor."

Karen just listened, letting him pour his story out.

"I was bounced around ships for a while. Wound up as a Privateer, which is a Pirate that sailed under a national flag. Came home when I was eighteen, found my mother had been flogged for asking for an extra serving at dinner. She was giving it to the children. She never healed right, and was gone by the time I got back. My father had been executed for trying to get her medicines that he couldn't pay for."

"I'm sorry to hear that." Karen said quietly. "You look them up?"

"Listed as 'Pending'." James returned to his story without missing a beat. "I went back to the ship, which sailed under the Dutch flag. The new Captain was a miserable old miser. It took me five minutes to organize a mutiny, and we went independant. I went through his papers, found out who his Patron was. Someone who owned the ship, and took a cut of the profits. I went to his Patron, and offered to take my late Captain's place. This Patron was an investor the East India Trading Company, which were the deepest pockets in the world back then. The Patron in question had us running jobs, which weren't strictly legal. But he owned the ship… We made a major score, enough to buy the ship off him, free and clear; and he responded by having us all arrested on some trumped up charge."

"So he could get the money, and keep the ship for the next crew." Karen nodded. "Cold."

"Wasn't even an unusual story." James nodded. "I was Captain then, so I broke my people out, we retook our ship, and became straight up Pirates. Three different Navies put a price on my head large enough that someone finally claimed it." James finished. "I lived my life on ships, sleeping in hammocks with sixty other guys. If I was interested in an easy life, I could have been a farm hand at any point since coming here." He drew himself a bit taller. "But my whole career as a Pirate was based around the idea that my life, and my death, would not be decided on the whim of any Authority that proclaimed themselves to be the Last Word on what was Righteous."

"Your career has been building to the idea that little people with a little power would give you your own idea of 'freedom' if you found the right trinket to dangle at them." Karen said without mercy. "What you got, was a swift and brutal death after a life of crime trying to make it happen." Her voice softened, suddenly gentle. "And what you're being offered now is a world run by a legitimately all-knowing being of benevolence; who made his opening offer of eternal life and world peace, before you knew he existed."

And James had no answer to that.

"For you, and your parents, and your crew. Including

the ones you saw die." She finished. "Forever doesn't seem like such a long time, put like that, does it?"

~oo0Ooo~

James didn't sleep that night, considering her words. Instead, he wandered the area for a while, taking in the night. He could feel this world pulling at him. As much as he didn't think he could measure up, he found he hadn't been that far off. The Angels kept anyone from duelling and violence, and there hadn't been a woman who gave him any indication she was willing. At least not yet, which was patently unfair, given how flawless everyone looked.

Everyone but you. He reminded himself.

Nobody cared for money, and there were no flags at all. *No flags, no kings, no nobles.* That thought played on a loop until he reached the Tower again, with the Stargazer still tethered to its peak.

"So, what now?"

James turned in surprise. He was impossible to sneak up on, but he'd been so deep in thought, he hadn't seen Smitty coming out of the building. "What do you mean?"

Smitty lifted a dusty bottle. "Drink?"

"Oh yes." James nodded, almost relieved. "Finally, something I recognize." He took the bottle and they went into the building and found a quiet spot near the kitchens.

"I know that look. I had it myself, when I got here." Smitty explained as he poured for both of them. "I wasn't one for duelling and wenching, Cap'n; but I recognized that this world was the end of how we did business, back in the day."

"Smitty... or *Gerret*, I suppose... You never gave me your right name, but I knew your background. A Vicar, turned Pirate? Seems to me this is exactly the sort of place you'd like. Where hypocrites can't get away with lies, let alone run the world."

"Bleed for no flag." Smitty threw back his glass at the old vow.

"Bow to no King." James said reflexively, before he suddenly remembered the last time they had said those words to each other, not long before they had fought to the death.

Dead silence. James pulled the small parchment from his pocket, and gave it to his friend. It was faded, and ruined in spots; but it was enough for Smitty to read it. "Seriously?"

"The Cross alone would have been enough to make us all honest men again. You were a Vicar. Tell me they wouldn't have forgiven us of all our sins for that particular bit of treasure back."

"They would have promised our immortal souls, and deeds and titles to whatever land we wanted in a Dutch port." Smitty didn't hesitate to nod. "Bought and paid for." He smirked. "Not that they could have actually provided eternal salvation."

"They could have provided land, title, and a clear record, right enough." James said quietly. "And for all the rest, our haul from that last run would have made us prosperous men. I wanted that for our team…" He shook his head. "Then Kent died. Twynam and Preston on the next raid…"

"You know that they'll be back too, Cap'n." Smitty pointed out.

James said nothing to that. "If they hadn't been killed, I never would have needed a new First Mate. In fact, I probably would have just promoted you."

"Nah, I'd be wasted on Command." Smitty said,

unconcerned. "Besides, we can't say it didn't turn out alright."

"Turn out alright?" James repeated. "I *killed* you, Smitty. My best friend, and I left you to face the Spanish bas-"

"Bite your tongue." Smitty told him sharply. "There are no more flags, no more kings. There are no Spanish, no Dutch, or French, or-"

"The people are all here, it's the same thing." James dismissed that instantly.

"No, Boss. No it isn't." Smitty insisted. "By now it's dawned on you that everything's different here." He held up the preserved parchment. "Including this."

James spoke over him. "Lancewood is here."

That caught Smitty off guard for a second, before a sad smile. "You saw him before me. Ouch."

James said nothing to that.

Smitty sipped his drink. "So if that was the goal…"

"Lancewood confessed to me that he'd sabotaged the cannons. Powder, fuses, one or the other." James explained. "So we were sitting ducks. I figured the Spanish wanted prisoners, so I told you guys to go to the useless cannons, and then I took that Captain's Chest with me for an escape." He tapped the Parchment. "Because if I was arrested, I'd lose all those bits of Treasure, and the Mission was over. But if I got away-"

"If you escaped with the King's Ransom, then you could come back and buy us all out of prison the next day."

"It was a race, to see if I could get to those Lords and Dukes before the Courts got you to a Noose." James admitted. "I figured the odds were about one in ten."

"We beat those odds all the time, back in the day." Smitty agreed. "And then I rumbled your escape, and drew on you."

"It's not like you would have believed me." James excused. "And it was all for naught, in any event. If our cannons didn't work, then it means the Galleons came in, guns blazing. I guess they pulled a double-cross of their own, decided not to give Lancewood anything they had promised him, even if I hadn't got to him first."

"Lancewood is the point." Smitty said finally. "We didn't have a single King, Prince, Duke, Bishop or any other blue blooded barnacle that we respected. We got the worst of them, to the point where we all swore ourselves to piracy over living under their laws." He gestured at the parchment. "I found those kings to be an affront to honest men, and the spirit of God." He smiled. The same smile he'd had back in the days of sailing under no flag. "Then I came here. This world has a King that can't be corrupted, can't be bought, can't be cruel, can't even lie, or be lied to."

"You really believe that?" James asked, not angry, just curious.

"I didn't at first, but I do now." Smitty nodded, pouring another round. "Remember what we always said about that miserable old crow we used to call 'Captain', when we first started out?"

"I remember he was my first kill."

Smitty nodded. "There wasn't a single one of us on that ship who so much as shed a tear for him. Because he was a terrible Captain, and a worse person, and Leadership Leads. Working on that ship was a brutal beating; and the second you took over, life became better. You have a good Captain, a good King, it trickles down." He picked up his glass. "Diaz is a good Captain. I hope you'll take it in the right spirit when I say that I count myself lucky to find two excellent Captains, even six hundred years apart."

James smiled and drank. "Cheers."

James poured again. "I asked myself, what would a world look like, if God Himself was in charge of it? A loving, benevolent, all-powerful and all-knowing God; suddenly stepping in to give all the gifts he'd ever wanted to give anyone; down to and including bringing people back from the dead, so that they could receive all these blessings?" Smitty threw back the glass and poured again. "Sounds impossible, but I sat down and seriously asked myself: What would it be like, to live in a world like that?"

"And this is what you came up with." James guessed.

"Pretty close." Smitty nodded. "It's a good world, James. And I'm looking at the grey hair, and the…" He trailed off. "You wear it well, but there are people here who have lived for almost three centuries and wear it a whole lot better. Know what I mean?"

"I do." James conceded.

"Is it possible, we've found ourselves in a world where Justice and Peace and Goodness and Freedom of Choice is more than just a point of view; or a privilege for the wealthy?" Smitty put it to him. "Even if we had to die to get here?"

That comment made James cold dead sober again instantly. "Smitty…" He croaked. "I killed you."

His old friend nodded, becoming somber.

"You're here, pouring a round, asking me to gain eternal life and paradise; and the last time we spoke-"

"I drew first." Smitty offered. "And now, it seems, for the wrong reason. I've never forgiven myself for that night either."

James thumped the parchment on the table between them. "All my plans, all my ultimate goals to live like Them, and the second the noose tightened, I left you all to…" He grit his teeth hard for a moment against the drink, and the spike of emotion. "Why don't you care?"

"Cap'n, I've lived for a number of years in a pretty sweet world. I can't even remember losing the duel; it all happened so fast. That was the world we lived in, and we don't live there anymore."

James gripped the glass so tightly he felt it crack. "This world is everything you ever wanted."

"And a few things I didn't dream were possible." Smitty nodded. "Cap'n, just tell me one thing. Am I the reason you're holding out?"

James hesitated, and gestured at the Parchment again. "This was what I wanted for my crew. And when I found out you'd all be back, I knew sooner or later, one of you would look me up. I felt like I had to finish the mission. If I couldn't actually give you a title and a clean slate, then I at least had to come back with more an excuse. But with the pledge, written and sealed, in one hand; and the stated price in the other..."

"And that's why you've been chasing these treasures." Smitty realized. "Because if we got here and came for you… You wanted to show us what it was all for." He sipped. "You could have squared things with God first. It's not like any of us could have done anything… unsavory about it."

"Death doesn't frighten me." James said plainly. "I've even done it before. Running out of time was our entire life." He threw back his drink. "When we became outlaws, we knew there would come a time we'd die for it. But I abandoned my crew. I had to make it right. Having the King's Ransom to give you was the only way left." He barely met Smitty's eye. "It's not like I could bring you back to life."

"I was wondering why you never looked us up." Smitty nodded. "I had no idea. I've been working on this airship since they installed the wheel and figurehead, and I had no idea that you had a hiding place in there."

"Nobody did. I installed it myself." James admitted. "Never would have expected to find *you* here at the same time."

"Surprise." Smitty quipped. "But if you're telling me that-"

"It should matter." James snapped, suddenly furious. "It should matter, dammit! I drew a sword on my best friend, and cut him down! I betrayed my private and public oaths, and left my crew to die. That should matter! There should be some consequences for that!"

"It's not like you escaped, Cap'n. You've been dead for centuries."

"So were you! At the very least, it should be enough to ruin a friendship! You should hate me! You should be *allowed* to hate me!"

"I am allowed." Smitty said seriously. "It's a big world, and plenty of people have run into old foes. Some of them handle it by agreeing to stay on opposite ends of the earth. Some of them handle it by agreeing that what they fought over is no longer valid." He made sure James was looking at him before he said the next thought. "James, the list of 'no longer valid' is extremely long and varied. I haven't seen you in twenty years, and I spent most of that time learning things and seeing things that I could never have imagined back in my old life. There hasn't been a warrant out for either of us in seven hundred years; and there gets to be a point where you stop looking over your shoulder. It's not a bad life, Captain."

Silence.

James pushed the parchment over to him. "Sorry it took me so long." He stood up to go. "Thanks for the drink."

Book Four: Welcome Home

Joshua 23:14: *"Now look! I am about to die, and you well know with all your heart and with all your soul that not one word out of all the good promises that Jehovah your God has spoken to you has failed. They have all come true for you. Not one word of them has failed."*

Chapter Sixteen: Every Ninety Seconds

After so long trying, Walter was forced to admit that he had failed. His businesses had never grown beyond the local level, and his idea for Competitions and Tournaments had failed miserably.

But Walter's life hadn't been changed by any of it. He'd seen the journey his contemporaries had taken in the old days, from Rags to Riches, and back to Rags again. He'd seen when someone like him had gone from a mansion to a hovel. What he'd been living in was better than that, but it was never going to be a mansion.

"And the truly gut-wrenching thing?" He'd confessed to David one night. "I take a look at how much time and money and effort I've invested in these things. If I'd saved it all up for now..."

"You might yet have had that mansion?" David quipped, unsurprised. "Come on. Let's go to the meeting."

"I'm not in the mood."

"I know. That's why you should go."

~oo0Ooo~

And so, Walter found himself in the audience of a Christian meeting, once again, listening to commentary on Bible Passages. This world had a four volume Bible instead of two. The Witnesses were the only religion he'd heard of that valued audience participation to such a degree; and yet Walter would confess to only half-hearing it, until the speaker said the magic words.

"It was a great deal of money." The Speaker said. "*That is why the Kingdom of the heavens may be likened to a king who wanted to settle accounts with his slaves. When he started to settle them, a man was brought in who owed him 10,000 talents. But because he did not have the means to pay it back, his master ordered him and his wife and his children and all the things he owned to be sold and payment to be made. So the slave fell down and did obeisance to him, saying, 'Be patient with me, and I will pay back everything to you.' Moved with pity at this, the master of that slave let him off and canceled his debt."* The Speaker looked up from his Bible. "Now, that amount of money was more than a working man of the time could see in thousands of lifetimes. And the Master just forgave it. Like it was nothing to him. But that's not the end of the story. You see, this slave had debts to collect also. We read on, and find out that this slave knew a man who owed him much less… And tore him apart when he couldn't repay it."

Walter winced. He'd had people who owed him and his company more than they'd ever hope to see in their lifetime.

"What we owe to a perfect God who has given us eternal life is a billion times more than anything we could owe to small, still-imperfect creatures like each other."

Was this deliberate? Walter asked himself. *Did David know what they were going to be talking about?*

"But here in this world, where money is no longer an issue; the parable takes on a whole new meaning. The important point of that Parable was how easily the kind Master forgave the enormous debt, and how angry he was that his servants couldn't extend that same forgiveness to others. A debt of ten thousand Talents would take a thousand lifetimes to repay. But remember the Source. Jesus knew this world was coming. A world where people would live forever. If you had a marker for that much crippling debt today, would you forgive it, or would you live happily in the knowledge that your debtors would be able to work for a thousand lifetimes to repay you? Jesus knew this world was coming. Did he ever promise to make you work off your sins for eternity? Did he ever suggest that God was keeping a Ledger of everything we owe to him due to the sins we committed? No. He just forgave us."

David didn't even have to look. Walter was already walking out.

"Jesus closed that Parable by saying: *'My heavenly Father will also deal with you in the same way if each of you does not forgive your brother from your heart'*."

Saying a quick prayer, David started to rise, but felt a hand pulling him back into his seat. His father gave him a look, and went after Walter himself.

~oo0Ooo~

There was always foot traffic outside a Conference Centre now. It was the central part of any community. But the people walking past were careful not to disturb whichever congregation was using the space. There were meetings running every night.

Walter had stepped out, and wandered through the lobby to get some air. Hitch followed, staying a respectful distance away, letting the younger man with pale grey hair gather his thoughts.

Walter turned back, not surprised to see him there, and scowled. "I just figured something out." He explained. "And it frustrates me."

"Dare I ask?"

"I haven't forgiven any debt." Walter admitted. "All this time, I assumed the problem with my business was that nobody wanted to work with someone who wasn't 'one of you', but the real reason is that everyone else keeps an accounting of what is owed… But nobody demands it back. Because it will come with time.

Nobody charges interest on what they offer others anymore; because the whole point of the world is to give free."

"Yes." Hitch nodded.

"But that only works if *everyone* plays by that rule!" Walter raged.

"Everyone does." Hitch nodded plainly. "David and I have been waiting for you to notice, but the whole point of a utopia is that everyone has what they need, and that what they want should only be what's good for everyone."

Walter sighed hard. "Doesn't. Make. Sense."

"You're the only one around who thinks so." Hitch sighed. "You aren't there yet." He said regretfully. "You're running out of time. I had hoped that by now you would have opened your eyes and seen the world for what it was. The only thing stopping this from happening is you, Walter."

"Then why do you keep coming back for more? You or David?" Walter asked in a very brittle voice. "You're not responsible for me."

"No, we're not. But we're hardly the only people speaking to you about this." Hitch shrugged. "I come back for more, because I am a servant here. And it is a very patient cause to be in service to. Noah was telling the world that the Flood was coming, and after decades of telling people to be ready, not one of them went into the Ark. Not one. After *decades*. I'm pleading for your life, and you won't listen."

"I'm listening. You're just not making sense." Walter bunched his fists, hard enough to feel his fingernails cutting into his palms. "I'm not wrong." He insisted hotly. "I know what I'm doing, and if this world would just see sense for five minutes, I'd have what I needed; and be able to do what you've all been telling me to do for… I can't even remember how long anymore."

"Yeah. It's easy to lose track of time when nobody ages around you." Hitch sighed. "One every nintey seconds. "

"I'm sorry?"

"I did the math once; when I was a far younger man. I wanted this world to come sooner. I wanted to stop... the fear. I wanted to be in this world where I wasn't scared for my kid, and where my wife would come back, and I'd see her again. I found myself getting angry about it. After a bad week in the ministry, I found myself hating the whole wait. I wanted to get here. It felt like keeping the Old Days going even a minute longer was just cruel to us who were waiting, being faithful."

"And?"

"I did the math on it. When the world was at its worst, there were hundreds of thousands of new brothers per year. One of a very few religions where the numbers were going up instead of collapsing. It shook out to a new brother in the world every minute and a half. As bad as my day was, if I held out another *minute*, someone would gain eternal life, and be part of my family."

Walter said nothing.

Hitch just looked at him. "It's not like the old days. The only people hurting now are the people like you. The Undecided. The world is going through a Second Revelation. Every single person in the world has had to take a long hard look at what they believe, and make a choice. Every. Single. Person. There's no pretending that 'There Is No God' or that something else is more important, or any of the things people told themselves back in OS. Back then, I couldn't change anyone's mind. All I could do was tell them what I knew of the Truth, and help them look on their own. And here in this world, that's still all I can do. Twenty thousand a day come back. How many become part of my family per minute? How many gain eternal life every ninety seconds now?"

Walter said nothing.

"The worst part is... I can see you finding a place in this world so easily." Hitch sighed. "When you first got here, you organized kids into mowing lawns and helping out. You found them regular customers, and paid the young ones a wage. That's still going without you. The kids in your old Circuit? They're building arcades, skate parks... Their parents are thrilled to have kids learning about sharing and improving community spaces. Those Co-ops you put together? You launched a few careers. A lot of people wanted to make their living with writing, or singing, or painting... You got that going for a dozen people, and you walked away because your cut wasn't big enough. But you have a talent for it; you really do."

Hitch went back into the Meeting Hall. Walter stood at the doorway, glowering at nothing. He almost didn't notice another man walking past him. The other man was wearing a tri-corner hat, straight out of a pirate movie. For a moment, they regarded each other. The only two men with grey hair and wrinkles for a hundred miles.

Nothing was said, but Walter turned to walk away from the Hall quickly. Unable to meet his gaze, James went inside, sweeping his hat off.

~oo00oo~

James and Atxi had agreed to meet at a Meeting Hall. Attending the current Meeting was not a hardship for them. Even after decades of avoiding The Choice, they had both been to many such gatherings over the years.

The talk hadn't finished by the time James came in. "Jesus was once asked: 'How many times should I forgive my Brother?' and he essentially said that it should be as many times as requested." The Brother on stage continued. "God gives repentant ones his forgiveness freely, regardless of how often, or how large the debt."

James noted he was getting some long looks. His age was making him stand out. It made Atxi stand out too. He scanned the audience, and quickly spotted Axti, sitting near the back. The only pale grey head of hair in the whole auditorium.

"That forgiveness is something we all need, and it is an act of love. You've heard it many times: God Is Love. Look around, and this whole world is a sign of it. Almost all of us had lives in OS. That world was all about Greed and Cruelty. And these are the properties and behaviors of The Other Guy. The Devil ran the last world; which is why it reflected his personality. Anger, Selfishness, and a complete opposition to God. Scripture referred to Satan as '*A Roaring Lion, seeking to devour someone.*' Nobody can deny he had power to control the world. Jehovah, by contrast, is described in the Bible as '*The Happy God*'."

James circled around behind Atxi. They were meant to meet here, simply as a rendezvous, but she was listening with close attention, as interested as everyone else.

"What defines Jehovah's Rule is not His power. What defines a world ruled by Jehovah God is his Love. Power is nothing compared to that. We've seen what happens when supernatural power rules the world according to anger. A God without Love is Satan."

Atxi shivered as she felt someone leaning a lot closer. "Interesting thought."

"Yeah." She smiled at bit at James' voice in her ear. "We should go."

~oo0Ooo~

They returned to the *Nicholas* and set sail. The

minute they were out of the dock, Atzi spun around and wrapped her arms around him tightly. He returned it, burying his face in her silver hair. "I know we've forgiven each other, but after that talk, I want to say it again. I hate fighting with you." She said softly. "We've only fought seriously once, and I didn't like it at all."

"Nor me, luv." James agreed immediately as he set the controls, taking them out to sea.

"I was a pirate." James said quietly as the ship rocked. "You have any idea how many people I killed in my career? At least a dozen ships; and they all fought to stop me. My last act in the Old World was to kill one of my own. They're all back. None of it meant a thing. But that's the problem, isn't it? They're so willing to forgive each other. If I went back and set that whole Centre on fire, what are the odds they'd apologize to me for having such a flammable meeting place?"

"Are you angry that they're not trying to hang you?" Atxi asked, perturbed.

"I drew a sword on my best friend. That should matter!" James insisted.

Heavy silence.

"The worst part is…" James said finally. "I was so glad to see him. My worst sin, brought to nothing. My worst guilt, and it turned out to be fixed, without my ever knowing it."

"On the Island, there's a constant struggle to keep the different factions from killing each other." Atxi observed. "I come back here, and there's no… anything. No old rivalries, no old grudges. They just… make it work. I feel like I'm seeing a side-by-side comparison."

"You are." James admitted. "And I admit, the world outside the Undecided is… better. I've been sailing from one end of the world to the other, and I've yet to see a storm. I've walked into a hundred different communities, and they've all had a meal and a bed waiting before I can tell them my name."

"Hans is barely keeping the Undecided together." Atxi gave the other side. "Even when the people are openly defiant of the Scripture, the 'Wings' don't allow violence. There's a fierce rivalry over everything else. Games. Resources. Food. Shelters. Even the women. Hans has been smoothing it over, trying to build some bridges, but he's getting older too. We can all see it… James, there was an argument last week, over a trade. One man traded crops he'd grown for some help with a home repair. The JW's would have the entire town out to help fix a damaged house, and they'd put out enough food to 'feed the five thousand' as Irsu would put it. No trade, no price, no questions asked."

Silence.

"Atxi, I don't understand this world." He said finally. "I mean, I know why they do the things they do, but how do they get there? I know what they say, but… You should be *allowed* to hate things. Bad things."

"Some do." Atxi offered. "I asked Irsu about that once. He said that back in OS, the Witnesses practised a form of Exile from their congregations. They call it 'disfellowshipping'. I was curious, so I asked a few other people about it. It's crazy, but the meanest, hardest, last-resort thing they do is not talk to someone."

James rubbed his eyes. "I'll never fit in with them."

She looked over. "Do you want to?"

"I honestly can't say anymore. All the people I want to see again are either with them, or on this boat right now." He didn't want to talk about it anymore. "How about you? How did your thing go?"

"Can't believe I'm about to say this… But I'm not sure either." Atxi actually groaned. "I spent decades rehearsing what I'd say when I finally got to confront the man who told me the gods wanted my heart. By the time I found him, he'd joined the Witnesses, and I don't know how I feel about it."

"Been my experience that the bad guys always land on their feet." James commented.

"Not here." Atxi said immediately. "James, you were the bad guy back then. My bad guy was a Holy Man. Now we're in this world, and the bad guys can't get away with anything. And if he's… I mean, I'm told that Angels are the police force now. If he was just playing along, or trying to con people into giving him a position back… Maybe he can fool people like me, but he can't fool the Angels, can he? He has to have *genuinely* changed."

James regarded her. "You talk like one of the Bible-Bashers."

"I do, don't I?" Atxi was tearing up a little, though her face was calm. "I wanted so badly for him to be terrified. For him to be as confused and angry and hurt as I have been since I woke up and found out the whole thing was a lie. He was the one that taught it to me, so it made sense that…" She trailed off. "I wanted him to have trouble fitting in here."

"Of course you did." James said. "Smitty was a Vicar. He taught me a few lines of scripture. Enough that I had some idea of what this world might be. But you? You were taught a lie, but the man who taught you was smart, compelling, certain… Just like the people here. Would have been an interesting conversation to watch."

Atxi nodded. "That's it. When I came back, I felt completely unable to match my beliefs against those of the people here, because they were logical, reasonable, persuasive… But in my heart I was convinced; so I wanted *him* to be here, to argue the case for Huitzilopochtli. He convinced me, and if I wasn't quick enough, or smart enough to find the right words to prove my gods were real, then maybe he could."

"And then you find out he fell into this world easily." James snorted. "You must be ready to strangle something."

"You'd think so." Atxi nodded. "But I'm not." She looked at him. "Why aren't I furious? When I found out about him, I was angry. When I saw him the first time, I was so mad I didn't come back for decades. Why am I fine with it now?"

He thought about it for a long moment. "I don't know." He admitted. "What do you think?"

Atxi thought about it for a while. "Maybe… Maybe it's because I'm in a larger group than I thought."

"How so?"

"Back on the Island, with the 'Undecided'? There's plenty of people who follow the Old Gods, and didn't want to change. But back among the Witnesses, there's a much bigger number of people who followed all the gods I've never heard of, and *did* make the change. In fact, I heard Huitzilin talking about some of them. He was talking about a man named Paul, who stoned the early Christians to death, also in the Name of the Lord. Then he saw something that proved he was wrong, and he became an apostle so widely respected that he actually wrote about a third of the Greek Scriptures that you grew up with." She looked at him. "How does a person sincerely look at the evil they've done, and then decide they can just move on and be holy?"

"Maybe I'm not the one to ask." James said quietly. "I can't move on yet. When I started my campaign against people I hated, I was working towards a pardon from half a dozen different Kings and Bishops. I died without achieving any of it. But if I had lived long enough to finish my plan… I would have declared victory, taken my ransomed full pardon, and lived like a gentleman."

"You could have that here, y'know." Atxi said.

"Could I? In the old days, living 'honestly' meant keeping all your backstabbing a secret. I could do just fine in that arena. In this world, it means being legitimately good. I'm not sure I can do that."

Long silence.

"Ask you a question?" James spoke finally. "What if he *had* been broken by this world?"

"What do you mean?"

"You wanted him to have trouble with this world, because in your opinion, he's the reason you were so confused and scared and messed up when you arrived. If he had been like that? What would you have done?"

Atxi blinked. "Huh. I honestly hadn't thought of that."

"Could it be, that if your teacher was forced to admit that he was wrong and this world was right, then maybe you could finally declare victory, and do the same?"

Atxi said nothing to that for a while, before she turned to him, took his face between her hands, and gave him a deep, loving kiss.

He kissed her back happily for a long moment, before they broke for air. "What was that for?" He asked. "Tell me, so that I can do it again?"

Atxi smiled a bit. "James, what I'm feeling right now? When I saw all those people, listening to him talk about letting go of the Old Ways and Living the Real Life… I realized something that honestly never sank in before."

"That it was a good thing? That our world being gone was perhaps the best thing that could happen?" James guessed. "Yeah. I had a similar realization a few days ago. Our story isn't that unique, really."

"Back on the Island, nobody's interested in healing the old wounds, or letting go of the Old Ways. They're on that Island because they refuse to change." Atxi said. "If I'm honest, something changed for me this week. I suddenly stopped feeling so... lonely." She held him tightly. "The only other time in this world when I haven't felt alone was when I was on this boat. With you."

James held her close. After a little while, he smiled at her. "Alright, it's time you learned how to pilot this thing."

"What?" Atxi almost laughed in disbelief. James was famously protective of his ship. To date, as far as she knew, he'd never let anyone else touch the controls; and now he was giving her lessons? It was oddly flattering, and a better expression of love than anything she had said.

The ship had engines, but James still used sails more than anything electric. Atxi had watched him steer and tack into the wind. He was more than relaxed about it, he was extraordinary. It was like he was part of the ocean, moving with it. It had been some years since Atxi had been taught to dance, but this had the same feeling. James was teaching her how to move along with a rhythm that she didn't control; and do it so naturally that she didn't think of it.

~oo0Ooo~

"Not bad." James smiled at her after an hour or two. "You've got to feel it, in a smaller boat like this. Let the ocean show you how it's going to move. Everything affects it. The wind, the temperature, the speed, the location... But when you've been on the water, and seen what each of those things can do... It all comes together in your head, and it's like the ocean is moving with you.

Like it's part of you."

His voice was melodic and full of affection. He'd been more generous when speaking of her ability than was honest. Atxi wasn't even close to what James was telling her. *It's the sort of skill that takes a lifetime to master.* Atxi smiled with endearment. "It must be nice."

It's home. He almost said it. "I'm always glad when you sail with me, Atxi. It's just better with you."

She felt warm inside, against the cold sea breeze. "I feel the same." She bit her lip. "James, I plan to stay with the Witnesses. I'm not like them, and at this point I doubt I ever will be, but I like their world more than the Island. But I'll still be here for you, every time you come into port, and every time we sail together. I promise. We'll be together..."

"...for the rest of our lives?" James finished with biting understatement. But the mood stayed soft and warm, as she came over to lean back against him, looking out over the ocean by night.

"James?" Atxi said finally. "I'm running out of reasons to say no. You won't lose me. Not even to God. I just wanted you to know that its taking more effort for me to keep saying 'no' than it might to say 'yes'; because you've done more than anyone else to put my heart back together after false gods broke it. If I'm going to be your... anything, I need you to know where my soul is at."

"Okay." He put an arm around her, and she leaned into it, letting him hold her as they sailed away.

~oo0Ooo~

Walter was tired. So when there was a knock at his door, he didn't feel like answering it. But he knew who it was.

David and Townsend had brought food. Walter

barely bothered to greet them as they came in and set up. "We're told you haven't been to the market in a few days. Figured you'd be hungry."

"Thank you." Walter said automatically, not really caring. "I don't like the market. Same with Mickey's Animal Reserve. I go there, and parents point me out to the kids. I'm the handy reminder of what 'Aging Out' is."

"Walter, we've been waiting for you to come the long way round on your own." Townsend said crisply. "But by now it should be clear that you need a change of strategy. You haven't made a decision. You've withdrawn completely from the rest of the world. So let's have this out, once and for all."

"You're done being patient with me?" Walter quipped.

"We can afford to be patient. I don't think you can." Townsend said without pity, and ignored David's sharp look. "David here was born in a world where every conversation is done with restraint and gentleness. You and I are more direct. If you want to pretend the rules haven't changed, then I'm game to keep playing around; but I'll last longer than you."

Walter snorted. "I remember when we both found out we were dying, back in OS. You called it 'Negotiating the ultimate deal'."

"I remember." Townsend agreed. "So, what deal are you working on? I lost track of you after you tried hosting that Tournament."

Walter shook his head. "Nothing. I got nothing after that."

"That Tournament was some time ago, Walter." David pointed out. "Clearly, you haven't starved, or been turned out of your home."

"I know." Walter said sullenly. "Trying to make a worthy profit wasn't just because I wanted to support myself. Nobody goes hungry in this world. I had that much figured out fairly quickly."

"Speaking of not going hungry…" David started portioning the food. "From my wife. She is very much of the opinion that hard conversations are improved with good food."

Townsend produced a bottle. "And if not food, then perhaps a eighty year old Port?"

Walter squeezed his eyes shut for a moment. "Well played, Townsend. Well played, indeed."

"I'm not sure I follow. 'Played' how?" David asked, providing glasses for them all to drink from.

"Back in OS, a dusty bottle of fine liquor was a sign of luxury." Townsend explained. "An antique piece of furniture, or a first edition novel, signed by the author? All signs of extravagance. But every home designed for the last century or two has had a cool room or a wine cellar. Everyone has a favorite book they first got new, or their first hand-crafted chair. We all get this brand of opulence now, with time."

"A subtle reminder that if my efforts to become wealthy were because I had a taste for luxury, I came at it the wrong way." Walter put in. "But it wasn't that, either."

David was carefully trying to keep the conversation moving, while at the same time, distracting them from getting caught on any exchange that would lead to an argument. "And on that note, dinner."

The three men ate. David and Townsend prayed over their food. Walter did not.

"I remember the first time we met after you returned, I told you that this world had different priorities."

Townsend commented as the meal drew to a close. "I remember I said to you: 'Back in the day, we had to establish our wealth first, because money opened the doors in OS'. In this world, it's faith, and it's time. Those things go hand in hand. Life without end."

"I could have gotten that on my own." Walter countered.

"Walter, you wouldn't be the first powerful man to think the universe owed him better than anyone else-" David began.

"This isn't ego, David. I was one of the privileged few with a legitimate shot at immortality, if I'd had the chance. I could have done it."

"No. You couldn't have." Townsend said simply.

"Hang on a second. That intrigues me." David held a hand up. "Why do you think that, Walter?"

Townsend answered before Walter could. "He poured his fortune into a company that was meant to preserve his body, like meat in a freezer. He was gambling that science would be able to conquer the death barrier and bring him back to life in some far-distant future; with his ready-made fortune waiting in storage."

David actually let out a bark of laughter, though it only lasted an instant. "Oh, wow. I have to admit, that never occured to me." He said to Townsend. "They spent a century training us up to talk to people of any background, from any century. This one never made the list."

"It's not a new idea, David." Townsend said back. "I met a man last year who was a Middle Ages Alchemist. Thought he could find the Elixir of Life and turn Lead into Gold if he kept at it."

"Hey! Hey! Am I invisible?!" Walter demanded. "I could have made it work, is my point."

"No, Walter. You couldn't." David put in. "Death and Old Age were not illnesses that could be cured. They were a direct act of God, as punishment for what happened in Eden."

"And that's the God you want to Worship? A few hundred generations later, he still held the grudge?"

"You think it was spite? Walter, look around. Death is yesterday's problem. We know that, because everyone in this room has been dead before. A temporary life in a place without God, for an eternal one in Paradise where people get the truth. You couldn't have done that with your 'immortality' experiment."

"YES, I COULD!" Walter nearly screamed.

The explosion came out of nowhere, and blew up so fast that it had clearly been building for a while.

"I had it all! I even had a plan to handle my own death!" Walter raged. "Why the hell couldn't they have just let well enough alone? I didn't need anyone else to make that choice for me! Not even God! He had no right to decide my fate! I choose my fate! I choose! Nobody else does! ME!"

Townsend sighed hard, looking sad and resigned in the face of a volcanic eruption. "I thought so." He admitted. "You're too practical for it to be procrastination all this time. Greed dies in a place that doesn't care about wealth. Pride? That burns forever."

David was leaning back in his chair, blindsided.

Walter got himself under control. "Never once in my life did I ask anyone for rescue. Even death was a temporary setback for me. I had a plan, Townsend. A way to cheat death, and live forever."

"You can do that at any time, right now. Like everyone else. Is that the problem? Eternal life isn't a prize if everyone else can do it too?"

"Not the point. I had it sorted. God took that away from me." Walter hissed. "It's just not fair. I worked really hard on my success, and it was all a zero sum when I woke up. This world isn't fair!"

"Isn't fair?!" Townsend repeated in open disbelief. "One of the Elders in my congregation was an Assyrian Slave before he came here. He died because his Master's Daughter was bored one day, and asked the household slaves to fight to the death for her entertainment. If they said no, or were not eager enough, they'd all be killed. She was fourteen years old. And you're angry at God for bringing you into a world where you have to change your own sheets?"

"No, this isn't that." Walter shook his head. "I know that this world is better for a lot of people, but none of those people are me. Everything I ever set out to do, I did it. Until I came here." Walter said feeling himself start to seethe. "And I tried to play ball. I really did. But this world, so caught up in it's own view on 'perfect', won't so much as do business with me anymore."

"What are you talking about?" Townsend scorned. "I spoke to Ward last week. The Co-Ops are still running, adding new members. You got that running. You bring people together and give them a place to share something they love to do with like-minded people. In this world, that's *everything*!"

"That wasn't success, that was a book club." Walter snapped. "They were drops in a bucket. Does that really seem like a consolation prize?"

"Unbelievable." Townsend almost laughed. "After decades, you still haven't figured out that other people matter." He shook his head. "I finally get it. You honestly don't care who's running the playground. Jehovah, Satan, or Men from Mars, just as long as you get to be the biggest kid in the sandbox."

"I spent my entire life making my life as I wanted it. And I succeeded. Just because other people didn't have it in them to-"

"To what?" David demanded. "What's the end of that sentence? I've met people from all along the timeline, and they were all tormented by the same questions. Questions like: Why? Is there a reason? Why do we suffer? Do I matter? Since coming here, nobody has those worries anymore."

"I never did." Walter countered. "That's no great miracle for me."

Townsend blew past that. "And that's not even counting food, and water, and shelter, and security, and leisure time. Billions of people couldn't get so much as a cup of clean drinking water. And I don't mean across history, I mean while you and I were *personally* dining at a Five Star Bistro, ordering champagne infused caviar."

"None of that was my fault. I don't judge people for where they were born, and I understand people who were sick and weak being grateful; but not me. I had all those things, and those questions never bothered me. I had everything I needed already!"

"And billions of people did not! Billions. Every. Day." Townsend pressed. "Does that really mean *nothing* to you?"

"Those people were not my responsibility."

"If God felt that way, we'd all be dead right now." David put in.

"Not. Me." Walter said harshly. "God is like an overbearing parent. He wants you to be happy, but only in the life he picks out for you. Anyone who doesn't enjoy that life, it's their problem!" He pointed at his face. "But not for long."

"You can't possibly believe that anymore." David said in a hushed tone.

"I succeeded. God didn't give me anything. I did it. I did!" Walter was raging now, the frustration boiling over after decades; hammering his fist on the table. "I never asked anyone for a handout. I was all I ever needed! Home, family, property, prosperity, and finally beating death? I did all that! Without God! I'm the only God I need!"

David blanched. "You really just said that, didn't you?"

"Well why not? It was my will that determined if the hungry ate, or the homeless were cold, or if the unemployed had work. I decided! And I'm sick and tired of pretending that I didn't!"

"Walter, if you say the word 'I' one more time, I'm going to start getting angry with you!" David finally snapped back.

The room was silent a long moment, while Walter got his breathing back to normal from the outburst, and the other two took a moment to let things cool. "Well." Townsend said finally. "You've been holding that in a lot longer than you needed to." He stood up and spoke in a voice so calm and reserved, Walter almost didn't hear him. "Walter, your tax write-offs didn't end homelessness, or mass starvation, or disease, or death. God did that. He's already done that. There's nobody left who's starving, or afraid to catch a disease. Your crumbs didn't save anyone; and you took way more than you gave."

"My 'crumbs' were worth more than any of those people out there ever saw. They could have saved me just fine if God had let it play out."

"No, they couldn't, Walter." Townsend sighed hard. "After you died? Your son contested the will, demanded he inherit the full fortune instead of whatever was left over. The Cryogenics people fought it in court, but your boy found out who the other Rich Popsicles were, and went looking for other jilted relatives. The Trial turned the other way once the lawyers were all on the other side, and the Cryogenics company went bust. All their 'preserved' people were shipped to the nearest morgue to be cremated. Your stab at immortality ended in a family courtroom drama that nobody noticed; and A-Day wiped out the winners not long after. If Jehovah God had treated you the way you just asked to be treated, you'd have never come back."

Walter felt a little bubble of hot rage pop in his brain. "Get. Out." He said with an anger so deep he could feel it quivering in his bones.

David was actually trying to show sympathy. "Walter, you're not the first Returnee to find out that you've built a mansion on quicksand."

"GET OUT!" Walter howled, enraged.

~ooO0oo~

Townsend nearly dragged David out of the house, and they could hear things smashing behind them.

David didn't say anything, but Townsend answered him anyway. "If we'd stayed a minute longer, You-Know-Who would have had to step in any second, and I honestly don't know where he'd be after that."

"I know." David said quietly, head down. "Nothing we've said, in all this time, has made a difference."

"David, living in Paradise for *decades* hasn't made a difference. Our words are worth nothing compared to what he's seeing. But no matter what he sees, he doesn't observe. That's not on anyone but him."

The two of them walked for a while, letting the moment cool.

"What would it have been like?" David asked philosophically. "If they could have eliminated death and old age back in OS?"

Townsend shook his head. "It would have been a disaster. I was a wealthy man in a place where poor people had to join the military get an education. Or turn to crime to buy food. Or go to prison to see a doctor. Trust me when I say, if they were able to turn eternal life into a marketable product back then..." He looked up at the sky. "Having more Time is the least of what makes this world a Paradise."

~ooO0oo~

After spending a perfect night riding the waves, James had dropped Atxi back at civilisation. She wasn't returning to The Undecided. And in truth, James didn't want to go back either. He promised Atxi that he would return to join her back on land soon enough, but he had a stop to make first.

With the *Nicholas* to himself, James went to the cargo hold, and pulled out his Treasure Chest. Mallory had been able to track down a few more pieces over the years. He only had a few of the items. Most of the others were gone, lost to history, scrapped and melted down.

Meeting Smitty had changed the rules. The treasures he had hunted and guarded so jealously were worthless to him now.

There was only one place left to take them.

~ooO0oo~

Spyglass Cove hadn't changed much since he'd last been there. He arrived as the sun set.

Eileen was walking the beach as he came ashore. She took one look at him, then to his ship; and turned up the beach to shout for her son. James noted that she hadn't changed since he'd seen her last; but her eyes said that she was tired of being patient. "Take us with you." She said quietly. "You can drop us anywhere."

"I will." James promised, not even surprised at the request. "Where is he?"

"Back at the house, where he always is."

James made his way deeper inland, as Lancewood's son; now a young-looking man with that same eternal gaze, made his way towards his mother, carrying a satchel.

~oo0Ooo~

"Donnie looks like you." James said to his old foe by way of greeting.

Lancewood opened his eyes. His hair was ghost-white, skin grown slack. He was rocking in a hammock-chair, with a fire-pit smoldering low flames beside him. "He looks like I used to." The old man said, unconcerned. "They've been waiting for you. My wife and son declared ages ago. And she's fed up with trying to reason with me."

"Nobody reasons with old sailors." James admitted dryly. "But most of the people I know have given up too." He tossed his satchel down next to Lancewood. "An apology, for taking that list, last time I was here."

Lancewood reached out and opened the bag. He saw the Scepter, the Crown... And burst out laughing. A sick, empty laugh when nothing was funny.

James sat down next to him roughly, suddenly exhausted by his whole life.

"I'm glad you came." Lancewood coughed a little. "You'll take them with you, of course."

"I will." James promised quietly. "And you?"

Lancewood shook his head. "I may not make the voyage. This is my place now, and if my kid doesn't have to watch, that's fine with me." He rocked in the chair a moment. "They're young again, James."

"I saw."

"Y'know, I've spoken to some people. At least once a year, someone comes by." Lancewood said. "I'll never watch my wife grow old. I watched my father and mother turn grey and lose each other, a piece at a time. To me, my wife is forever young." He looked over. "You don't have kids, do you?"

"No." James admitted. "Not on the cards."

"Not for our kind of life." Lancewood agreed, and produced a bottle. "My last one. Only a little left. Care to have a drink with me, James? If memory serves, you never tasted the last one I poured you."

"Why not?" James almost laughed.

"I'll say this for the New World." Lancewood commented. "It leaves you with your dignity."

"Mm." James grunted, not wanting to say anything.

"I watched my old man go from old age. His teeth had rotted, hair was gone, lost control of his... functions. He could barely hold a tea cup by the end." He gestured at himself. "I have none of those things. I can feel it coming, James. But I don't feel shamed by the process."

James couldn't help himself. "You still think we made the right choice?"

"I don't regret it. Last time we spoke, we both knew a long life and a comfortable old age was more than people like us ever hoped for. A lifetime on a beach with my family? Paradise. I asked for much less, but that lifetime is what I got. I made my deal with the universe a long time ago. My boy lives in a world that offered him a different deal, and I couldn't be happier that he took it. For people like us, children was our stab at immortality. I remember my father once said to me that as long as I was around, he'd never really be gone. My kid will live

The Undecided

forever. Old age scared me more than death ever would. But after a lifetime of refusing, God's giving me my dignity, right to the end." He waved at the sky. "I'll say this for Him: He's a Class Act."

James took a deep pull off the rum. "To going out with Dignity."

"Here here!" Lancewood agreed, and took the bottle back to drink the last of it. "Thank you for coming back, James. It's nice to see a familiar face."

The familiarity of it sent a thrill of horror through James, for reasons he couldn't really define. "I should go."

Lancewood didn't try to stop him.

James walked up the beach, back towards the *Nicholas* in a daze... Until he broke down sobbing for the first time since his parents died.

Atxi. Get back to Atxi. He told himself. *You wasted enough time.*

Chapter Seventeen: Next Best Thing To Demons

Atxi and James didn't have a set home. James still took odd jobs, though for the most part, it was an excuse to keep sailing. Atxi went with him most of the time; sometimes she would stay on land to see what the world was like. When they were together, they clung to each other tightly. Neither of them said it, but it was clear they were reaching the twilight of their lives; and they loved each other fiercely enough to be okay with that.

Atxi had adapted completely to shipboard life. Seasickness was never a factor anymore; and she was the most content she'd ever felt.

Today, however, was different. She woke up to the distant sound of his voice; and padded up to the Bridge, following the sound of his conversation with someone.

James saw her and held out a Device. "It's for you."

"For me?" Surprised, she took the call.

"Axti, this is Karen." A familiar voice said. "Apologies, but James was the only point of contact I had for you. To be honest, calling James was kind of a desperation move. I wasn't sure either of you were still… Well."

"Alive?" Atxi supplied the magic word. "This isn't about either of us, then?"

"It's about Irsu." Karen reported. "We can't find him."

Atxi blinked. "What does that mean?"

"It took us a while to figure it out, because he wouldn't talk about it, but it looks like he was inspired by your attempt at confrontation with Brother Huitzilin. He told me once that you felt inspired by him because

362

The Undecided

your stories were so similar; and I don't know if he ever told you, but apparently that feeling was mutual."

Atxi blanched. "Irsu looked up his old King."

"Looks like he's back, but Irsu couldn't find him."

"No, he wouldn't." Atxi said darkly. "But I already have. Ramensti lives with the Undecided now."

~oo00oo~

James turned the *Nicholas* towards Southern California, and sailed at top speed. "Why are we in such a rush?"

"If Irsu has found his old King at the Island, then he'll be looking for a ride to the place." Atxi explained. "Karen's worried about her friend; so I want to get there first."

"You plan to intercept him."

"I do."

"And do what?" James countered. "It's been some years since I've taken prisoners. And even if the Authority doesn't stop us from doing it, I think Irsu can take me. Have you seen that guy?"

Atxi bit her lip. "I don't plan on stopping him. Well, I mean, I'd like to, but there's no chance that I'll be able to, if his mind is made up."

"So what are we doing?"

"Finding out if his mind is made up."

~oo00oo~

Irsu was at The Expo, looking for a ride out to the Island. There were constant people coming in and out of the World's Fair. Their Dockyards were extensive; but working on a schedule. He knew he was going to have to charter someone, but thus far there was nobody willing to take him where he needed to go.

"Most people don't go out to the Undecided

363

Communities." A familiar voice said.

Irsu spun, and found Atxi had crept up on him.

"If you really need to go, I have an 'in' with a privately owned yacht now." She told him, smiling tightly.

~ooOOoo~

They boarded the *Nicholas*. Atxi installed Irsu in a guest cabin. "James, you remember Irsu."

"I do." The Captain shook hands with the huge man. "It would be hard to forget. I've set a course."

"Thank you. Why do you have passenger cabins anyway?" Irsu asked him.

James shrugged. "I run supplies to the Undecided Communities. Every year at least a few of your people want to go out there to try and bring righteous wisdom to the heathens. Now and then, they bring someone back." He looked over. "You think that's going to happen this time?"

"I do not." Irsu admitted.

~ooOOoo~

The voyage wasn't a long one. But long enough for Irsu to spend some time on deck. Atxi joined him. James could see them from his bridge, and had the good sense not to get in the way.

Atxi said nothing; letting Irsu decide if he wanted to talk about it or not.

Finally, not looking at her, Irsu spoke. "The Priests told us that the Dead were powerful. They told us that the way the Dead were treated in this world mattered in the next one. When my King died, we were all walled up to go with him. Even his cat was mummified, to keep him company." He said with tight menace. "I spoke to someone a month ago, who told me that almost every single Tomb and Burial Chamber in Egypt had been raided and pillaged before the western archaeologists got to them in the modern times. It was why the find of some artifact or death mask was such a huge event." He scowled at Atxi. "It was my people who did that. My people, who were *supposed* to have such awe for the powers of the dead. And if it wasn't my people, then it was the dozen or more invaders that took apart the Pyramids, the Temples…" He shook his head.

"Hey." Atxi cupped his face with one hand. Smooth skin against wrinkles. "I know what you're going through. When my people were rediscovered, nobody even remembered what gods the temples were built for; but there they were, dusty and covered with vines. They're history. You and I, we remember the power of them. The awe, and the fervor, and I still haven't…" She couldn't keep going. "Why did you come here, Irsu?"

"I don't know." He said, not looking at her.

"Yes, you do. If you don't want to tell me, you don't have to."

He still couldn't look at her. "I heard he was back. I heard he was here."

Atxi nodded sadly.

"I don't want…" He shook his head hard. "I had to see him again. I had to face him. I… He was my god for my entire life, Axti. There were statues and Priests and chants and music and stories about all the Gods of Egypt, but the King was someone I could see, hear speak, someone I could touch."

"Someone who could touch you. Tell you he was pleased. Tell you that you had been good, done well, shown loyalty." Atxi said, almost in a trance of her own.

"I have to see him again." He said seriously. "Because if he's-" He struggled for the words. "If he's here, and… I don't even know how to say it."

"You want to see if he's still a god." Atxi said quietly. "Your life is split between the days he was a god, and the days where he wasn't there at all, and you knew he was just a man. You have to know if your New Eyes will still see him like they used to."

"He's just a man." Irsu hissed. "I know he's just a man. I've been a Christian for almost twice as many years as I worshiped him, and never once did I look back. If he's here now, it's because Jehovah gave him his chance. I know him. He won't take it. But…"

"I know, Irsu." Atxi said forgivingly. "There's still that little bit of superstition in everyone. People who were born and grew up in this world are afraid of nothing. Everyone who lived Before, no matter when in history, are still nervous about something, even if it's something as simple and childish as the dark."

"I know it's foolish. I know it's crazy. Maybe even a little dangerous. And all for an answer I already have, really. But I just have to know what's happening with him, now. If he's got questions. If he's… Like Huitzilin. Even if he's just an ordinary man."

Axti nodded, and threaded her fingers through his. "I'm going with you." She said quietly. "We both gave our hearts; literally, our hearts; to false gods. If seeing him again is what it takes for you to get yours back completely; then I'm going with you."

~ooOOoo~

Irsu returned to his cabin. James came up on deck, and found Atxi at the railing, looking out at the ocean by night. "The ocean's so calm these days, I sometimes feel like I can see the stars twice. Like we're sailing in the sky."

"I went on an Airship once." Atxi offered. "I'm told people have walked on other worlds in the sky. Centuries ago. Leaving the *planet* is ancient history in this world."

James shivered. "Does that seem as insane to you as it does to me?"

"Yup." She finally got to the point. "What do you think? About Irsu?"

James shook his head. "I think this is a terrible plan." He admitted. "I've seen what happens when people come home after a long time. I've seen what happens when people come face to face with their demons. And even if there are no demons anymore, the human race has always been the very next best thing."

Atxi shivered in a way that had nothing to do with the sea breeze, and stood closer to him, wrapping herself tightly in his arms. "I hate the thought that this might stumble him." She admitted. "I lost my faith long ago. But I liked that Irsu was certain of his. My story and his aren't that different, and I liked... I don't know. Even if I never joined the brotherhood, I liked knowing they were there, and that they'd last forever."

James said nothing to that, and she was grateful. They both knew she was being hypocritical; but they also knew it wasn't likely to change.

But then, for the first time since they'd met; certainly for the first time since they'd declared their love for each other; James decided to push back on this most forbidden topic. "I went and saw Lancewood, some time ago. He was at the end of the road; and he declared victory because his family had become believers. I finally understand why that thought made me want to cry."

Atxi leaned back against him, rolled her head back to look up at him. "Tell me."

"Because I like the idea of you living forever so much I feel like my chest could explode at the thought." James said, matter-of-fact. "I only ever knew you after your faith was broken. But I get the sense that you're at your best when you're…" He trailed off, unsure how to say it. "You said you were running out of reasons to say no."

"What about you?" She returned instantly. "I like the idea of you living forever too, love."

Long silence.

"Actually, I always thought you and Irsu would wind up together." James admitted.

"What?" Atxi laughed.

"You two have far more in common than we do." James nodded quietly. "He's ageless. I'm not."

"Neither am I."

"Atxi, I don't know how to tell you this, but you're a believer already. It's why you wouldn't marry me. Because you knew that one day you'd 'run out of reasons to say no'."

Atxi pulled away enough to look at him, stricken. "James…"

"S'okay, I'm not angry." He said quietly. "Hate to say it, but Lancewood knew the score. If God won't hold us accountable for what we did; and even our victims don't care; then my last act of being an honest villain is to live with the consequences. A Pirate got the noose; and I knew that, back when I became one. Dying, after a long life, and with full dignity? That's far more humane than anything I ever expected." He squeezed her hand. "I don't know what you're waiting for; but I know you'll be at your best when you get your faith back."

Atxi was silent a long moment. "When we first got here, my faith is what stopped me. But when faced with the truth, it gave way to such… awful bitterness. That guy we met, Walter? He came to this world full of pride, but I could see it. There was rage simmering under all that ego. Anger enough that he'd choke to death on it. For you, I thought it was greed. You still wanted what you always wanted. But now-"

"Now that I am faced with the truth about how I used to live… That has transformed too." James agreed. "It's guilt. I won't deny it. I have victims, Atxi. I made an effort only to take from the people who could afford to lose; but I knew that none of those privileged people would miss a meal. They had victims of their own to feel the pinch. And my sword took its due. With all of them back, and the system suddenly fair to people…" James looked down. "All that moral outrage I felt at the unfairness of life. And I wake up to find that it's just… stopped. God just stopped it. Like that." He rolled his eyes to Atxi. "At your most fervent, your faith in false gods never took lives; except your own."

"Don't be so sure. Those obsidian daggers took thousands; and I was part of the show." Atxi said seriously. "I love you. And I don't believe you're a bad person. A killer? Perhaps. A reformed criminal, certainly. But a 'villain'? I wouldn't love you half as much as I do."

"Of course you would have." He returned blandly. "I'm charming and handsome; and love makes you stupid."

Atxi snorted and kissed him lightly. But as they both turned back towards the ocean, Atxi thought of Irsu, walking a knife-edge of his own, and shivered hard. If both Irsu and James were pushing her in the same direction...

~oo0Ooo~

As they sailed and the sun set for the night, Atxi did something she hadn't done before; even after decades. She appealed to Jehovah in prayer.

"I don't know if you will hear me. It is hypocrisy to

ask you for something; given how I have acted in your house." She said to the stars. "Back Before, the Priests let us Pray to all the gods we needed. They said if one wasn't answering, then what we were asking for was the responsibility of another god. I asked him why they couldn't just pass the message onto each other for us. It did not go well." She rubbed her eyes a little. "Irsu was so certain, before he found out about his King. I want you to know that I do not believe his faith has wavered at all. But he has to confront his own demons, and the only way to do that is to to face his old gods. Something I will never get a chance to do. I don't know if you will hear me, but please don't let Irsu face this without you-"

"You know how to interpret the appearance of the sky, but the signs of the times you cannot interpret. A wicked and adulterous generation keeps on seeking for a sign, but no sign will be given it except the sign of Jonah."

Atxi jumped, as a voice suddenly interrupted. The Boy was perched on the railing, swinging his legs a little. He looked about twelve, with a Bible across his knees; and had seemingly appeared from nowhere. 'Who are you?" She asked, stunned to see a stranger. "I didn't know James had other passengers. You're looking for passage to somewhere?"

"No, I'm just here." The Boy didn't seem concerned. "Apologies for listening in."

"It's okay. I'm not entirely sure that…" Atxi gestured upwards. "Back where I come from, it was permissible to pray to any and all gods who may be listening, but I know that Jehovah doesn't think so, and…" She trailed off, suddenly wondering why she was pouring her heart out to a stranger's little kid.

"Once, long ago, when it was His Purpose, Jehovah's Temple was where Heaven and Earth overlapped." He told her. "That's why Jerusalem never fell, as long as the Temple was there. But when Christ died, something better was put into place, and the Temple was just a building." The Boy looked so sympathetic, almost heartbroken. "They thought the same thing you once did. That the building was what mattered. The trappings. The dressings. The image of holiness."

Atxi nodded. "And what was a holy place, became another idol to the people who were warring over a building."

"When The Day came, no small number of honest-hearted believers were in prison. Their Interior Rooms were cages. But anywhere that two or more of His people stood, there He was in their midst." The Boy said. "The world is full of His people now. Every inch of it. That's the whole point, Atxi. If Holy Places and People are exempt of evil and pain, then we have to make all places and people Holy."

Atxi bit her lip. "I admit, I haven't done my part."

"You fought so hard to embrace your false gods. And you fought so hard not to be fooled again." He reached out and held her hands tightly in his own. "Atxi, you guarded your soul so jealously that you never saw it."

"Saw what?"

"That nobody was trying to take it from you." The Boy said simply.

Atxi looked out over the water. "Can I be honest with you?"

"I hope so."

"I don't know why I'm having so much trouble getting there." Atxi admitted. "How can a person deny what's right in front of them? I wanted so much to see the gods when I lay on that altar. I've seen Angels now, and I still haven't… Why does having the proof not prove it to people?"

"The Eternal Question. Even in Heaven. Remember, Satan chose to defy God, while being in His presence. He took a third of Angels with him, and they were actually *in heaven* for so long… But you're closer than even you think, if you're praying for someone else's faith to be strong in a difficult time. Even some Spirit Creatures didn't do that." The Boy admitted. "When Jesus was Raised from the dead, Thomas was the last of the Apostles to see him again. *'So the other disciples were telling him: 'We have seen the Lord!' But he said to them: 'Unless I see in his hands the print of the nails and stick my finger into the print of the nails and stick my hand into his side, I will never believe it'."*

Atxi nodded, listening.

"That man was one of Jesus Apostles. He had seen everything Jesus could do. Even talked about his Resurrection. So why did he need to see one more miracle before he had faith in something he already believed in?"

Atxi thought for a moment. "Because he wanted to be made sure again. After."

"After." The Boy agreed. "Thomas' heart was in the right place. He'd followed the Son of Man for three years, and his heart was broken to watch that most wonderful man being tortured to death, of all things, for a charge of Blasphemy." The Boy smiled a bit. "It's not an easy thing to fill up a heart when it's full of holes."

Atxi put a hand over her heart unconsciously. "Or taken away."

"God doesn't hold back what people need. Some need to see loved ones returned to them, some need to see their wrinkles fade into youth."

"What do I need to see?" Atxi asked, voice small.

"Not see. You need to Know. To know what you longed for so much that you begged to be chosen for that Stone Table." The Boy said, and Atxi felt her heart give a solid thump as he turned to face her fully, giving her his complete attention. "You need to know that you are His Creation. In all the universe there has never been, and will never be, another quite like you. You are wanted, and beloved of God, and the fact that everyone else has that offer doesn't make it any less miraculous. This is a world made of nothing but Miracles."

And then, Atxi heard her own voice, younger, a little bit scared. But she heard it, clear as a bell, as though she was speaking in her own ear. *"Any Gods who may be listening, I pray that you are good, and that you know how much I want to be good too. I hope that what I have to offer is good in your eyes, and that you can forgive me for all the wrong things I've done. Thank you for all the good things I've seen and felt; and I hope one day to understand the bad. Because if you can hear me, I know that only good things would come from whoever's listening. Because a cruel or bad God wouldn't hear me."*

The Boy smiled. "Did you think He had forgotten something like that?"

Atxi felt herself tearing up a little. "Oh... You're..."

"Yes." The Boy nodded. "Atxi, you've given your heart away, quite literally, to lies. Here now, is truth. There is, and has only ever been, One God, and He is Good. This world was always His Plan, but important questions raised by lies forced a small delay. He would never let anything happen to the world, or to you, that He cannot put right. He wants you to be one of His people. He wants you to be happier with every passing day, more loved than you have ever been, more content than you have ever felt. And He wants that to last forever and ever. Without violence, without judgement, without sacrifices or bloodletting of any kind. Just honest effort."

"He wants that for everybody." Atxi whispered weakly.

"Aren't you part of 'everybody'?" The Boy asked with a smile. "He loves you very much, and He is here, being part of this conversation, right now; watching with hopeful anticipation, because He can see just how close you are."

Atxi sniffed, unable to look at him.

"Everyone you knew once lied to you, a lot of them quite sincerely, and you believed them." The Boy said, so gentle that Atxi felt warmed by his voice alone. "So now you're far less trusting. That's perfectly understandable. But Jehovah God not only took the lies away, he undid all the damage those lies did to the world; starting with the very first lie ever told."

Axti wiped her eyes, looked up, and let out a gasp so loud the entire ship probably heard her. The Boy hadn't moved... but he suddenly had wings. Huge, white, flawless angel wings.

The Boy smiled. "Jesus said to Thomas: *'Put your finger here, and see my hands, and take your hand and stick it into my side, and Stop doubting, but believe'.*"

"Oh, God..." Her voice could barely get past the lump in her throat, or the tears in her eyes, but it was the most heartfelt prayer she'd ever spoken. Atxi wept, reaching out and touching the wings as they extended towards her. "Oh, God..."

The wings brushed her face sweetly, and the Boy was suddenly gone.

Atxi rocked, arms wrapped tightly around herself. She rocked back and forth with the gentle motion of the ship; for what felt like an eternity. Finally, she noticed she wasn't alone. Irsu was there, standing a respectful distance away. She went over to him. "Why now?" She asked him. "If that was all it took, why wait so many years to send me an Angel?"

Irsu shrugged. "Because now is the right time."

"That's the sort of answer my old Priest would have given."

"Heh." Irsu chuckled. "Atxi, Moses left Egypt in disgrace, and spent forty years tending sheep before he was ready for the assignment he wanted. Joseph spent over a decade in prison for a crime he didn't commit; Noah waited over a century for the rain to fall. God has his own view on time. And now, at long last, we're starting to get that same view. You've been in Paradise for more than fifty years. You've seen miraculous things every day. Seeing was believing, but not accepting. The decades you've spent getting into a mental place where you could accept what you just saw? Are nothing compared to the eternity you could spend on the right side of this question."

"Irsu…" Atxi said softly. "I came with you on this trip, because I know what it feels like, to need to see something with your own eyes."

Irsu nodded. "I do appreciate it, Atxi."

"I know why it took until now." She said softly. "It's because of you. He heard me, when I was a child. He sent you the Blue Letter. It's because your story means so much to me, given how I got here. And then, when you have a dark day; a weak day…" She smiled. "Well, the truth is I ran out of reasons to say no a long time ago. Because there is one thing that always encourages people like… people like us. And that's when someone you care about has been through it themselves."

Irsu looked at her swiftly. "People like 'us'?"

And Atxi closed her eyes. "Jehovah God…" She said aloud, before rolling her eyes up to the stars. "Jehovah, *My* God."

Irsu smiled suddenly, tearing up instantly. She reached out and clasped his hand automatically, glad he was there for this. "I know you are here with me, and that you love me." Atxi said softly. "I was once told that I had to give to the gods. Give my blood, my life. My everything. It was a price that I paid eagerly. And then I got here, and wondered what was the point of paying that price at all. And what could I offer to You, if my life wasn't it? But I see it now. What I have to give you, is exactly what you keep giving me without end. Life, and love, and thanks. And if you'll have me, I promise I always will." Atxi looked to Irsu, smiled warmly, and suddenly remembered. "Oh… Amen."

She wiped her eyes, and saw James at the doorway, watching the whole thing. His face was unreadable, as he turned away from them, and went back to his cabin.

~oo0Ooo~

They arrived at the Island, and Atxi led the way with long experience.

"Are we likely to face… opposition?" Irsu asked her. "I'd prefer to be quiet like a mouse."

"You're with me; you'll fit in fine." She told Irsu. "It's not uncommon for people to leave the Island. But it's a lot more likely that they'll come back. There gets to be a point where you just have nowhere else to go."

"I didn't plan to bring you back here." Irsu reminded her.

"I know." She sighed. "Stay away from the Soldiers. You're a big guy. Like seeks like on this island. You'd fit right in with them, built like you are."

"Soldiers." Irsu observed.

"It's a lifestyle." Atxi excused them. "They're mostly good guys, but they're more devoted to 'their kind' than anyone else in this world, including the Christians. Remember, you don't want to get dragged into the games here. There are factions on this island. I know you don't plan to stay, but if you choose a side, on *anything*, they'll all know it."

Irsu nodded, and a horn sounded. "What's that?"

"Our cue." Atxi said grimly. "It's the Parley. Ramensti is sure to be there. Because he always is. Every. Single. Time."

~oo0Ooo~

There wasn't a huge crowd on the Island, but almost all of them were threading their way to the middle of the Island. Irsu almost laughed when he saw it. It was a natural amphitheater, not unlike the open speaking places that the Witnesses used during their outdoor sessions.

Hans was centre stage, hosting the event. "I've always told you guys that as long as we keep something alive, it's never gone." He said grandly to those assembled. "Even if the world we loved is long gone, we are here."

Atxi had heard this speech with every Parley, and took the opportunity to glance around. She had been away for a while. Some faces she knew had 'Aged Out' while she was away. And comparing to others around her. She knew she was close to doing the same.

Irsu leaned in. "What are we looking at?"

"Everyone on this Island is here because they don't want to live like this world does." Atxi explained. "Hans is of the opinion that as long as you keep an unpopular thought spoken aloud, it will endure."

"Well, he's not entirely wrong." Irsu admitted.

"Hang on just a minute longer." Atxi told him. "The man you're after can't resist an audience."

"You knew he was here." Irsu observed. "You knew, and you didn't tell me."

"I didn't know it was the same man. Your nation lasted almost a thousand years longer than the Christian Era. That's a long line of God-Kings; and you never did tell me his name."

"If you had known for sure, would you have told me?"

Atxi hesitated. "I don't know." She looked over for Hans, wondering if he'd noticed her. She found him quickly enough. Hans was talking to someone new. *A new face.* He was older, like she looked, with grey hair and wrinkles growing on his face. *Which means he's probably one of the younger people in the world now.* She observed distantly.

Ramensti had taken centre stage for the Parley. Irsu was at the back of the crowd, staring at him, somewhat transfixed. Atxi gave him a bleak look. Irsu looked like a believer. Atxi had no doubt it was the same expression he'd worn back in his early life, before Paradise. The centuries in between had vanished at the sight of his old King.

Ramensti spoke. He had a voice that was full of power and grandeur. It was not unlike the way Huitzilin spoke; spellbinding and persuasive. "I Am Egypt." He intoned. "The Gods have granted me a vision of the whole Earth, and burdened me with Purpose to raise Egypt to its rightful place as Master of the world. Though my Leadership is in Exile; I know that this path leads only to my Glory. I know this, because of all the Great Pharaohs to Come and Go over the passage of eternity, I am the only one who still holds the Esteem of Egypt in my hand. The Sun God Ra has returned me to this land of Mortals; because His purpose requires it. " His chin was up imperiously, his gaze fierce and unyielding. "Some have suggested that The God of Slaves could hope to match Me in combat. Some have even suggested that the Ancient and Unknowable Gods were but specks in the sky! I am Pharoah, and if I decree that day is night, it will be written as Law. What could those stones and 'planets' hope to say back at me? Do they have my mind? Do they have my heart? Does a 'planet' have my will?"

The spellbound look on Irsu's face had gone slack, and he drifted back to Atxi. "He's a joke." Irsu said, as though just realizing it.

"He's a complete joke." Another voice said in full agreement.

Atxi glanced over at who had spoken. It was the newcomer she had noticed. He had made his way away from the parley without anyone noticing him leave.

"There's nothing here." The greying man said, mostly to himself.

Atxi answered him anyway. "No, there isn't." She drifted back a bit to stand next to him. "I'm Atxi."

"Nick. Nick Alman." The man introduced himself. "You're new here, aren't you? On the Island, I mean."

"I was here for many years. I left for a while, just came back this evening. How can you tell?" Atxi asked, impressed. She looked older than he did.

"Your shoes." Nick said. "One thing they don't seem to have on this island is a cobbler that can make a shoe anything like what they have out in the world."

Atxi noted he had similar footwear. "You must be new here yourself."

Nick nodded. "I was over at the World's Fair Expo just yesterday."

Axti gestured at him, with his greying hair, and weathered face. "You looking to move here?"

He gestured at her own signs of age. "Are you?"

"No." She said seriously. "I made my dedication just a few days ago, while I was on the boat coming here. We're here for Irsu."

"Really?" Nick looked at Irsu. "He looks far too young to be as young as we are."

"He's not. He's here to answer his own unresolved questions."

Nick bit his lip. "And you can still have personal demons, if you join up?"

"I suppose you must." Axti guessed. "I'm rather new to being a Christian; but I figure all those warnings and reminders in the Bible went to the early congregations; so they must have been needed. When have righteous people not had demons to fight?" She smiled a bit. "Or at least, the memory of demons; which is a much harder battle than I thought it would be."

Nick was silent for a long moment, watching Irsu, who was watching the speech. "I was… I don't know, I guess I wanted to make sure." Nick said at last.

"Make sure of what?"

"Exactly." Nick laughed at his own foolishness. "I've been trying to put it into words for almost forty years; and nothing I can come up with sounds quite right."

Atxi nodded, as though that made perfect sense. "This world runs on its spirit. This world runs on its soul, and on the soul of humanity in general. Such things we have never found proper words for."

"Soul of Humanity. That was it. I was afraid that all this might have taken something from the Soul of Humanity. I was worried that Peace and Tranquility might also mean atrophy." He gestured around. "I came

here to see if being less content also made you more...
fierce. Not in a bad way, just with more energy, more
drive."

Atxi looked back at Irsu a moment. "Does it?"

"A week ago, I might have said yes. But I've spent
the last few days at the Expo. I finally figured it out.
Necessity was never the mother of invention. Curiosity
is. Necessity just changed the priorities."

Atxi smiled. "I was an Aztec. The more I learn about
all the history that came before and after my time? The
more I think that the policy of the human race was to fix
things one at a time. Put out fires by making even larger
fires that would burn the next day."

"I'm starting to see that myself." Nick nodded. "Now
that I'm here... I'm only seeing half of what I expected.
Three different 'factions' on this Island have offered to
let me join them. There's more passion here, but there's
anarchy too. Sort of a collective Anarchy. Even for
people like me, the Angels prevent anyone hurting each
other. The rule here is Do As You Please."

"How is that different from out there?" Atxi asked. "I
haven't found anyone doing something they hated."

"With basic needs met, I guess nobody has to." Nick
agreed. "But it just... It works better out there. People
work together better, y'know?"

"I know." Axti nodded.

Ramensti was still going. "Millions of people once
bowed to me, recognizing me as The Morning and
Evening Star! But this world has lost its way, seduced by
the promises of... some other god. Rest Assured that
when Ra reveals his design to me; and I accept my
reward as rightful Ruler once again; you will all be
rewarded, for you did not accept the smooth words of
this God of Slaves!"

Irsu came back to join them, looking disgusted. "Let's go."

"You don't want to talk to him?" James asked, gesturing at the old King, still making his grand speech."

"What is there to say?" Irsu scorned. "He's a fool. And I was a fool for ever believing in him."

"You weren't foolish, Irsu. But for a time, you were misinformed." Atxi said.

"We all were." Nick added. "And so's he. Either he's a great actor, or he's actually certain of what he's shouting at us right now; even when anyone with five minutes work can prove him wrong."

"Five minutes is more than most people would need, looking back four thousand years at him in a history book." Irsu nodded. "You have any idea what it's like to know that your gods and Kings were just names that nobody remembered? We built Pyramids that stood longer than empires and nations ever could, all in honor of men that history forgot."

"I'm going back to the Mainland, and telling my brother I'm a Christian now." Nick agreed. "I've got a boat back to the mainland, if you need a ride."

He said it so easily, so casually, that Irsu almost didn't register it at first. "Just like that?"

"To be honest, the decision was clear a while ago, I just needed to test it."

"Test it against what?" Irsu asked.

"My brother showed me this verse once from the First Volume. About how the Demons believed."

Irsu already had his device out. "James 2:19. '*You believe that there is one God, do you? You are doing quite well. And yet the demons believe and shudder'.*"

Nick nodded. "That was it. For me, becoming a Christian is less about what you believe, and more about how you live. I wondered if living under God's Rule could really give people everything they needed."

"You mean, other than eternal life?"

"I was killed in the Second World War, Miss. There are worse things than dying." Nick returned. "I've seen day-to-day life under the wrong kind of rule. There's no initiative, no mercy, no compassion, and the only kind of energy was fear. This world has mercy and compassion, but I needed to know if the initiative and energy was still there." He gestured around. "My Brother brought me to the Expo, and a day later I saw this. The energy of both places is just so different."

"And this is worse?" Irsu guessed.

"Not about better or worse. It's about what it's built on." Nick pointed back at the centre of the stage, where the Pharaoh was finally stepping down. "You know why people are clapping? Nobody believes in him. He's screaming at the void about how he had it better back there. So why are they clapping for him?"

Silence.

"Because they have something to say too." Atxi guessed finally.

"And not one of them are any more willing than that Pharaoh to admit they were just wrong." Nick nodded, and the look on his face said it was a revelation ripping apart his whole world view. "What's missing from the Paradise World is the lie. And I had no idea how much it was a part of me. So much so that when I didn't have the lies anymore, I was scared that we'd lost something fundamentally required by human beings."

Atxi had been listening to them quietly for a few minutes, and finally spoke. "I wonder if it's that we need the lie, or need the excuse."

"What do you mean?"

"If there is no God, obeying Him doesn't matter. If He's real, then nothing could be more important."

~ooOOoo~

Walter hadn't even tried to get another business going after his argument with Townsend and David. He hadn't attended a meeting, or really spoken at length with anyone else. His attempts at studies were full of barely concealed rage and frustration at what he'd lost.

David had tried again, and again; and Walter had sent him away each time. Mickey stopped by a few times. She brought him baskets of food from the market. Walter rarely left the house anymore, his age making him an object of pity by the general population.

But then, one day, as Walter felt the weakness filling his bones once more, he had a visitor.

"Well." Townsend said grimly as he sat beside Walter. "Here we are again."

Walter nodded. The irony was not lost on him. His only visitor as his time ran out. The last time, he'd been able to offer Townsend a five star meal. At this point, the only thing left in the house was a basket of apples. The last time, there had been a Penthouse level view, even from a hospital. This time, they were on the ground floor, with the curtains pulled closed, because Walter couldn't stand to be seen.

"Your father made his choice yesterday." Townsend said quietly. "He's on his way here, hoping to reconcile with you." He held out a letter. "He sent this ahead, since messages travel faster. He asked me to deliver it."

"He's going to live forever." Walter snarled. "After everything…" He took the letter and scrunched it up, unopened.

Townsend sighed.

"I know you think it's spite, or ego." Walter coughed.

"Some personal failing that you can wag your finger at, and tell me off for. But it's not. I'm not wrong. Seriously, what was my sin? What did I do that you haven't done a hundred times yourself?"

"I'm not here to pass judgement, Walter." Townsend said softly.

"Of course not, because there's nothing to judge. You can't think of anything I did that you haven't done. So what? I was a few bucks shy in the contribution boxes? Didn't pray to an empty room often enough? Can't remember enough verses?"

"It doesn't work that way, and you know it." Townsend said. "In all the time I've known you, you've never treated people like people. You called them 'consumers' or 'clients', 'customers' and 'employees' if you were feeling generous. 'The unwashed masses' or 'clock punchers' when you had your blood up. Your sin was that you didn't show them love."

"Why do they need my love?"

"*They* didn't need your love, Walter. *You* did. Loving God and Loving Others are so tightly entwined that they are the same thing; especially in a world where God runs the world by loving even his enemies into eternal youth. You only ever looked for ways that others could benefit you and what you wanted. Even Jehovah God was your 'Retirement Plan'. Low Priority. I don't know how to convince you that other people have value. Your sin was that you thought God and His Kingdom needed you, more than you needed Him."

"You have any idea what I could offer this world if it would just…" Walter trailed off.

"If it would just think like the last one." Townsend nodded, having just had his point made for him. "If only this world would treat you the way the Old System did, then you'd be happy to live here with us."

Walter turned his head away from Townsend. "Please go. I don't really want people around for this."

Townsend rose, squeezed his hand, and left him then. The labrador, older and slower now, rested his head on Walter's knee; offering what affection he could.

"Do I count as 'people'?" A voice asked after a moment.

Walter turned his head the other way. "Oh."

The Boy was back, this time without his guitar. But he had a Bible with him. "*Skin in behalf of skin, and everything that a man has he will give in behalf of his soul.*"

"Job." Walter recognized the quotation. "A man who refused to break, no matter what evil threw at him."

"Is Jehovah God evil in your eyes?" The Boy asked, sounding genuinely curious. "Because even now, he wants you to come to him. Be his friend, and live forever."

"Beg for my life." Walter countered.

"Walter, Jehovah God isn't wrong. He can't be wrong. He genuinely does know what's right for you, and for everyone. That's the whole point. This isn't like a rigid, fallible ruler, demanding one inflexible standard for a huge variety of differing souls. If you needed some special treatment, you would have gotten some. You act like your life is being held hostage, but it's not. You were offered Eternal Life in Utopia... and still felt like you needed to demand a better offer."

"I'm not wrong." Walter insisted, falling back deeper into the chair. "I'm not! I didn't... didn't do anything... anything wrong. I'm not cruel of unfair to anyone..."

He was gone. Walter was alone again.

~oo0Ooo~

Nick had accepted the ride back to the mainland. His

brother was expecting him at the Expo. Nick had made his dedication on the boat, and Atxi and Irsu celebrated, spending the night eating and drinking and giving prayers of thanks. The only one on the ship who wasn't a Christian, James retreated from the party, feeling more alone than he had in some time.

The Captain's Cabin was dark, shades pulled and lights off. James was in his chair by his desk, bent over by age. His white hair nearly glowed against the darkness of the room. Atxi came no further than the door. "James." She said quietly.

He straightened a little, but didn't turn to face her. "Well, go on. Say it." James said darkly. "Tell me I've made the wrong choice, and that-"

"James." She cut him off with a sigh. "My love."

He stiffened. It was the first time she had expressed her feelings for him since becoming a Christian. Part of him had expected that to change.

"I don't want to make you feel bad. I don't get to judge. Heaven knows I've taken a long time to get here myself. I don't even know if good and bad enter into it by this point. All I know is that I found what I was looking for. Took me decades to admit it, but I found what I needed." She took one step closer, paused when she saw him turn his wrinkled face further away, not wanting to meet her eyes. "I would like to be with you for a lot longer than we've had. Eternity might just be long enough for that. But if you don't see anything in this world that outweighs what you see in yourself; then who am I to tell you off about it? I love you. And I promise I won't think less of you when you're gone."

He gripped the arm of his chair tightly. "Atxi." He said finally. "I want you to take the launch back to Dock. Leave the ship at sea."

"I had planned to-"

"No. Go with Irsu. Be happy. Be safe. Live forever, young and strong." James spoke his last request. "And spare me a thought now and then. Once every thousand years or so?" He chuckled at his own comment, and broke down coughing. "But I don't want you to be here to watch this."

"Funny. I bet Lancewood said the same words to his wife."

James closed his eyes miserably.

Atxi nodded. "I think you're wrong. But I said I wouldn't judge, and I think this counts."

"Thank you."

"I love you, James. So, so much." She said softly, and shut the door, letting that be the last word between them.

"Love you, too." He said, without turning towards the door.

~ooOOoo~

Sailing on the ocean. Usually, it felt like a holy thing to him. He'd heard some of the scholars talking about God, as something eternal, and infinite. They'd talked about the compassion of Him, giving such tiny little specks his attention, when he was vast enough to be beyond comprehension.

James already had that feeling, every time he sailed out of sight of land. The ocean had that same sense of eternity, and he was a speck, touching it and gaining life and motion. The ocean was untouchable by anything he could do, but it gave him everything he had.

The ocean was like a prayer to him, but today it did nothing.

He could feel it. He was too old to sail. This world was kinder in old age than the one he understood, but he was far older now than he had been in the Old Days.

I'm dying. The thought came to him suddenly. It almost made him laugh. *I'm an old man, and I'm dying.*

"Permission to come aboard."

"ACK!" James nearly fell off the boat. Below him, on the water, was a face he hadn't seen in years, and she hadn't changed a bit. She had just emerged from the water like a mermaid, with something vague and mechanical below her. "Karen?"

"Hullo, James." She smiled up at him. "What do you think of my ride? It's called a submarine."

"I've heard of them." James nodded. "Never seen one before. I didn't realize they were available for one person to go sailing."

"She's new." Karen said proudly. "I'm part of a team trying to build something entirely new for an expedition to clean up the bottom of the ocean, instead of the surface. It's proving to be surprisingly difficult. We have to invent all sorts of new tech just to have a shot. It'll take us decades to see it out, but…" She stopped herself before she could finish that sentence.

"But you have decades to spare, and decades more to relax; take your time and do it right." James said it for her. "Not like me."

Karen didn't respond to that. "Can I come aboard? I've been below for almost two days, and would like to see the sun again."

James nodded and went to get a rope ladder for her. "So, what made you look me up today, as if I didn't know?"

"Atxi called me." Karen nodded as she lashed her submarine to his motionless ship. "Her exact words were: 'I don't want him to be alone'."

"That's it? Nothing to say." James gestured at himself. "Most everyone I meet has something to say about my poor life choices."

"I told you years ago that there was a very real chance you wouldn't make it." She didn't blink. "What more do I need to say that I haven't said?"

"Hasn't stopped anyone else."

"And you sailed out across the horizon to get away from them." Karen shot back. "Their hearts are in the right place. But you and I know differently, don't we, Cap'n?"

"We do." James nodded. "Old age is nothing to be ashamed of."

"It was denied to both of us, once upon a time." Karen nodded. "And I suppose it always will be, unless I do something royally stupid one day."

James snorted, and they both watched the horizon for a while. He'd known her for almost seventy years, and here she was, looking achingly young and beautiful. She hadn't changed a bit in face or body since he'd first met her. The comparison was not lost on him.

"I'm a little surprised Atxi couldn't convince you." Karen observed. "True Love does it for most people. Atxi's seen you at your best and worst-"

"She's never seen me close." James cut her off. "This world stops you from being the worst of anything. If she'd known me back then, she'd get it."

Karen shrugged. "If you say so. I wasn't there."

Silence.

"I used to think of God as the Ocean." James said finally. "No deals to be made with it, because it's so much bigger than you. Show respect, or get rolled."

Karen grinned like a little kid. And without a word she made a quick jump, landing flawlessly on the railing, and making a neat swan-dive into the water. She didn't come up for several moments, but was still smiling when she surfaced. "Just because it's bigger than you can see? That doesn't make it something to fear." She called up to him.

James couldn't help but smile at that.

~oo0Ooo~

Atxi had finally returned to look up Drew Thorne and get to work on 'filling in the blanks'. The project had evolved as Drew had taken over part of the Museum, but there was still more than enough work to do. Atxi's mind drifted constantly towards James; and Drew was kind enough to realize it.

In fact, Atxi wasn't the only one dealing with just such an issue.

"David's home with his father and I this week." Drew said quietly to Atxi. "I understand you met Walter Emmerson some time ago? Well, we received word this morning through a mutual friend named Townsend. It looks like Walter isn't inclined to make the Truth his own, and his time is nearly up."

Atxi shivered. "You live with Undecided, you sort of forget what a Minority we are. But we are, aren't we?"

"What's this 'we'?" Drew joshed her. "You made the same choice I did, Atxi."

Atxi flushed. "I guess I did. It's still new, so it hasn't really sunk in yet; that I'm growing younger right now, or that I'll never die…"

Drew hugged her tightly. She was old enough to be Atxi's mother, and looked young enough to be her granddaughter; but they were sisters now; in all but name.

"I know you're worried about James." Drew said quietly. "David is worried about Walter. We've been praying all night. And David's very touchy on the subject, given that his own mother waited a pretty long time compared to most."

"I'm living proof that as long as there's life, there's hope." Atxi offered. "At least, that's what I keep telling myself whenever my James comes to mind."

Drew bit her lip. "In fact, I should get back to my boy. Perhaps you'd like to come with me? Join us for dinner?"

~oo0Ooo~

Atxi knew she'd be intruding, but somehow found herself at the Thorne household for dinner anyway. It was the most uncomfortable she'd ever been in the company of believers. There was a cloud hanging over the table. Drew and Hitch made no effort to pretend it wasn't there, or to keep the conversation moving, and Atxi suddenly realized she wasn't there to distract David from his thoughts. She was there to empathize; because she was in the exact state David was in.

Over a meal that they barely ate, Atxi and David put each other in their respective stories.

"I only met Walter once or twice, but we've been walking similar roads for our entire time here." Atxi said quietly. "The same could be said of James. I have no idea if…" Atxi shook her head. "Karen was the first person to meet James when he got here. Maybe it'll make a difference, coming full circle."

"I made the same argument about going to see Walter." David commiserated. "But he was quite adamant. He didn't want company."

A Device started chiming as a call came in. David and Atxi looked sickly at each other, both checking their Devices.

"It's mine." David said quietly, and answered. "Townsend? Give me good news?"

Atxi couldn't hear the other side of the conversation,

but she could read the way David's shoulders slumped. Drew came over to her son and rested a hand on him sympathetically.

~oo0Ooo~

Atxi withdrew from them, went out into the air; sitting on the front step for a moment.

Atxi started to pray. *Dear God, I know it's his choice. But please... please, please... Save James. If there's something I need to do, something anyone can do, tell me now...*

"Give Karen the bad news."

Atxi jumped. Hitch had stepped out to join her. "I'm sorry?"

"You sent Karen to James, right? That means she's in the right area. David just called Walter's father, and apparently he doesn't want to know about it. But Townsend needs transportation; and ditto for the body."

~oo0Ooo~

Karen swam for a few more minutes, and James heard a chime from a distance. He followed the sound, and came to Karen's device, resting on the deck with her jacket.

On the screen was a message, from Atxi. *'Tell James that Walter died this morning. David just got the message.'*

James checked to see Karen was still out of earshot, and picked up the device, tapping out a response. *'Atxi, this is James. Why are you calling Karen about this?'*

The answer came quickly. *'I'm with Irsu and David's mother, working on that book. David is here. He's miserable. I know you're in the area, since I sent Karen to meet you. We need someone to bring the body back.'*

James jumped as Karen suddenly appeared, reading the conversation over his shoulder. "Funny thing about the world. The people in it find each other often. Too often to be a coincidence."

James shook his head slowly. "I've had one conversation with Walter, or David; or David's mother... And yet..."

"And yet here we all are, praying for you; pulling together on bad days." Karen nodded. "You're part of our story now, James. And we're part of yours."

~oo0Ooo~

Walter had lived in a form of self-imposed exile, fed up with the world. Those that lived in the area were glad to know that someone had made arrangements; and Karen and James collected the body without ever leaving the dock.

"He's... He's like me." James said. "He died of old age."

Karen nodded, and looked sideways at him. "How you doing over there, James?"

James said nothing. "It just dawned on me... I've never had anyone die of old age before. My parents were worked to death. Most of my crew either outlived me or died violently. One or two went overboard in a squall... The Undecided 'age out', but I come and go from there. I've never been there for it. I've never seen anyone die of old age before."

Karen tapped at her Device for a few moments. "His name is Walter Emmerson. He was a big money type in OS. When he came here, he apparently didn't make the truth a priority, since he wanted to make his fortune first. According to Brother..." She checked the name again. "Brother David Thorne, who was his Welcoming Committee, the way I was for you, Walter looked at this world and saw a chance to make major profits, with few taxes and regulations."

James snorted. "I could have told him that was never going to work."

"Oh?"

"I lived in a time *before* there were Regulations. The result was Children being put to work the second they could walk. The result was having workers paid in gruel till they dropped dead from exhaustion, like my parents. The result was narcotics available over the counter, because nobody cared to check what they were doing to paying customers." He shook his head. "This world was never going to tolerate exploitation." He almost laughed. "Human nature has changed, Miss Karen. Maybe that's why I don't fit in. Humanity has left itself behind."

Karen smiled a bit. "We never really knew for sure, how much influence the Devil had over individuals. I don't know if human nature has changed, or if it's just had a chance to become the best it could become. If that's what it is, then we're still seven hundred years short of the finished product." She pulled a large sheet from the guest rooms' locker. "But I guess, some of us are finished early."

The Pirate started to say something, and then turned, stalking back to his cabin.

Karen let him go, wrapping Walter's body for transport.

~oo0Ooo~

James felt the ship turn. Karen was sailing them back to land. There was a time he would have given someone the lash for changing course without the Captain's permission.

But James didn't come out of his room for hours, until the sun grew low on the horizon. Finally, he smelled food cooking outside, and came to join her. She didn't say anything, which was starting to grate on him more than the sermons he'd been hearing on land. She just pushed a plate at him. Bread and cheese. The same sort of food that he'd eaten back in the day, minus the salted pork or fish. She had eggs cooking on his hotplate. But she didn't say a word.

Finally, he brought it up himself. "If I have to give up every single thing about myself, am I still me?"

"You are always you. There's a reason we move from milk to meat in life. We are never what we were."

"That's not what I mean." James said. "This place has taken every vice I ever indulged in, and everything I ever wanted for myself. I took a lot of blows in the Old Days. I had to fight for my right to have a *name*, Karen. I fought for it, and I came… so close. So, *so* close to having what I always wanted. And in all that time, I bled for no flag; and I bowed to no King. If I-"

"If you bow to God, you think that's surrender?" Karen sneered lightly. "If you had pulled it off, and lived out your life as a wealthy man with a title and lands; you'd still be here; having to sort yourself out in a world you didn't expect. What, you think Walter won some moral victory by having the last word? Because he doesn't have the last anything. We're all still here; and so is God."

"You know why a Captain goes down with the ship?" James argued. "It's because if it gets that bad, someone else went down first. The Captain is responsible for all of it. My crew was all brought back before me, because God decided I would be a bad influence if I got here before them."

"You don't really know what God was thinking, James; and neither do I." Karen pointed out. "If you're expecting pity, you won't get any. You got what everyone got. The truth, a clean slate, and a whole lifetime to make up your mind."

"I ask for nothing." James said simply. "I see no

point discussing it further."

"Okay." Karen said without blinking, and returned to the hotplate, where the eggs were ready. They ate in something of a charged silence; like they were screaming at each other without making a sound.

"I don't know why it unsettles me suddenly." James confessed finally.

"It's because I'm here." Karen counseled without blinking. "You've known me for decades, and my face hasn't changed at all. You run supplies to that Island of Undecided; but you get those supplies from many different ports. You haven't watched other people stay forever young because you keep moving. Atxi got older with with you. You never saw death as a defeat, because we all had to go through with it. But if you learned Smitty had some terminal illness that would take his life too soon; and then found out you had it too… Well, that would be a tragedy."

James nodded, suddenly getting it. "A disease that you're immune to."

"Not immune, just protected from." Karen countered. "If I ever stepped out from that protection, and didn't make things right, I'd be just like Walter."

"That doesn't bother you? Your God has you on a leash that you'll never get free of."

"It's not a leash. It's loyalty. He made the universe; and I'm smart enough to realize that should count for something. Besides, back in my old life? Time, age, and the world in general had me on a far worse one. And it was crueler and harsher than anything you've had to face since you woke up on a beach and met me." Karen fired back with heat. "And that's not even counting the constant war I fought for every last inch of everything I had… until I just didn't have any fight left in me anymore." She glared at his fiercely. "And don't pretend a pirate doesn't know what that's like."

James had to nod. "I'll give you that, I guess."

She didn't push him further, clearing their empty plates away. The table clear, she went out on deck. He followed, and they looked out to the ocean, where the sun was getting low.

"I'm dying, aren't I?" He said finally. "I've waited too long, and I've… used up my time."

Karen nodded, not unkindly. "Yes."

"That's why you changed our course, instead of taking Walter back with you in your submarine. Because you don't have room for all three of us; and you can take back possession of the ship you bought me."

Karen said nothing for a moment, but she had tears threatening to spill from her eyes. "The boat? You really think that's why I'm here?"

"No." James admitted. *Those beautiful, ancient eyes in a young and perfect face…* He thought, gazing at her. He was feeling cold and weak in his bones, and she was so alive it hurt to look at her. *She could care less about the ship. She's here for me. She was the first face I saw when I got here, and she'll be the last…*

"Do you think Walter feels victorious?" Karen asked, out of nowhere. "Do you think he believes he won?"

James was silent, looking at his last sunset. He was leaning heavily on the railing, strength failing him. "I've been dead before, Miss Karen. He don't believe nothing anymore."

"Yes." Karen agreed. "What about you? You feel like you won some prize?"

"If I saw this face in the mirror, back in the day; I would have declared victory. Old and settled by a fireplace somewhere, relaxing in an easychair… It was the kind of dream that kept you warm on cold nights at sea."

"What about now?" Karen asked. "Look at him, James. He's in your cargo hold. Look at Walter, and tell me he did something romantic and noble, refusing to accept what his own senses were telling him."

Silence. The sky was filled with glorious red and yellow, fire that blazed across the whole horizon, end to end. The ocean was calm enough that it shone with the same reflected glow. A far better sight to end on than a body in the hold.

"Back in the day, when a Pirate was captured, he could sometimes save himself." James croaked quietly, finding it harder to breathe. "If he gave up his mates and licked boot convincingly, he'd be stuck for good, but maybe escape the noose. None of us had any respect for them. Didn't your Witnesses have to make the same choice once, to renounce their Way, or die? How many of them bowed and scraped?"

"What are you dying for, James?" Karen asked. "You rebelled once, because the world was unjust; and you refused to play by its rules. What are you dying for now? Walter isn't a Martyr. He had no cause to give his life for besides his own stubborn insistence that the world should be his way."

"I don't know why it eats at me." James said again. "Most everyone I knew back then was hoping to die that way. Old age was a final victory to my kind."

"Most everyone you knew back then? They're alive, and look like me. Or they will, in time." Karen said simply. "Now ask the question you're not game to ask."

"Would God accept me, given I waited so long?"

"So long? I'm over fifty years older than you, Captain." She scoffed. "What's time to God?"

"What I mean is, if I ask now, is it just because I

can…" He put a hand to his chest. "Because I can feel it coming? I have no tolerance for deathbed repentance. It's cowardice to think it still counts."

Karen looked at him carefully. "You've been running supplies out to that Island of Undecided. You know why we call them that? Because you can still take back your choice, right up until the moment you've died. Walter can't change his mind, because he's wrapped in a shroud now."

"Guess that's true."

"Now, my turn to ask a question." Karen pointed a finger upwards. "If you *did* dedicate yourself, right now; and God said yes… Would you laugh, and say 'fooled you' or would you be grateful for the sheer *compassion*, after waiting so long?"

James' vision dimmed, just for a moment, his back bending, losing strength. "I… I wanted to be one of the good guys. Really, I did. I knew the difference between 'outlaw' and 'villain'. Even when I was straight up pillaging, I never wanted to be a bad person."

Karen squeezed his hand. "I know."

He didn't let go of her hand as his eyes closed. His head felt heavy and he rested it on her shoulder. She was practically holding him up. "Jehovah God, I am a Pirate, a criminal, a killer, and a Sinner many times over. I have walked this world for decades, and I still don't understand the rules. I have seen the wealthy shake their fist at you, and fall into death. I have seen naive boys become wise leaders of men, and my own pirate crew become righteous. I know that nobody beats the ocean, because it's just too big for man to master. But I love it so. And that's how I know it's possible to say the same of You. If you'll accept an old fool; I ask that you come into my life… And make of me whatever you can make of me."

"Amen." Karen said in his ear.

"Amen." James agreed. Even as he let the breath out, James could feel his breath coming easier, feel the strength flowing back into him.

Karen was still holding his hand, smiling gently. She could have said something, but she didn't. There would be time for that later.

There would be time for everything.

~oo00oo~

Atxi and Irsu were waiting on the Dock when the ship came back in from the Ocean. Axti was craning her neck, trying to see who was at the wheel, but the angles were all wrong…

She saw James walking down the gangplank once the ship docked, and she ran to him, tears in her eyes. One look was all she needed. His back was straighter, eyes clearer, and his stride stronger that she'd seen in years.

She slammed into him the second his foot hit the wharf, nearly knocking him over. He put his arms around her tightly.

"So." She said softly into his shoulder, nearly blubbering. "What do you want to do tomorrow?"

"As it happens, I have a few ideas." James said back, soft as a prayer. "But what's the rush?"

Chapter Eighteen: Amen

There was little room in the world for something as unnecessary as graveyards. People put up markers for loved ones that made the wrong choice. Walter had little family left after A-Day. Even fewer who would miss him. His father had made no arrangements, so they fell to David.

David had claimed the body when they docked. The drop-off was seen by everyone at the Dock, and the normally constant chatter dropped significantly. David thanked them, and Karen and Irsu prayed with him for a while. In the next room, Atxi and James did the same.

Walter's dog had come along, and now kept pace with David. The aging Labrador had gravitated to David at every step since padding down from the *Nicholas*.

"My boy knows what it's like now." Hitch observed. "Back in OS, they told JW's not to get too tight with worldly people. At first, it was to protect us from their way of thinking. But by the end, it was to protect us from their sudden absence." He sighed hard. "Oh, and while I have Atxi here, there was a delivery for her this morning." Hitch reported, and handed an envelope to her.

Atxi blinked hard. He had handed her a Blue Letter.

~oo0Ooo~

"I don't envy him the task." Karen said as they watched David walk away with his family. "He got the Letter, but he was never meant to be Walter's legal guardian."

"David got the Blue Letter because he was the best option." Irsu said. "Sometimes that means being the one who stands to grow the most as a teacher. Sometimes that means someone who'll be a lifelong friend to the

Returned. Sometimes it means the person who'll have the most appropriate answers to the individual questions… And sometimes it means the person who can bear the difficult days best. Walter rubbed a lot of people the wrong way with his obsession. David was raised in a world without any of Walter's particular problem. His father was a Tribulation Witness, his mother very nearly 'Aged Out' herself. Walter had all the pieces he needed within a week; and he couldn't make the decision in a lifetime."

"David will handle it." James said with certainty. "If he couldn't handle this day, he never would have gotten the Letter." He squeezed Atxi's fingers.

"David and Townsend are to be commended. They were still trying, right up to the last." Irsu commented. "Some would have bowed out early, when they saw the way he was going; to spare themselves the heartbreak."

James headed for the gangplank, leaving the others behind. "This I know. Believe me, I know."

"Where's he going?" Karen asked Atxi. "I thought we were all heading back out."

"We are." Atxi said quietly, still staring at the Blue Letter in her hand. "But he has to talk to someone first."

~oo0Ooo~

Eileen saw James as he came along the dock. "Ah. So, you made it." She said quietly. "I'm glad."

"Are you?" James asked. "I wouldn't be offended if you weren't, you know."

Eileen shook her head. "I never even met you until we came here, sir. Of all the things I have to live with, good and bad… Please don't take this the wrong way, but-"

"I don't register enough to make the list." James nodded. "I understand."

"It's time for a fresh start." Eileen said. "When I heard about your offer, it was an answer to a prayer." She pulled out her Device. "It's a fairly easy process these days. Last chance to back out."

James tapped at her Device, and their business was done. When James turned back towards his ship, he saw a familiar face. "Smitty! Glad you could make it."

"Wouldn't miss this, Cap'n." Smitty said with a huge smile. "And if I can borrow you a moment, I have a package for Karen."

~oo0Ooo~

Atxi had finally worked up the courage to tear the envelope open. "I knew it!" She whispered. "It's my sister."

Irsu rested a hand on her shoulder. "I'm happy for you." He said. "Where do you meet her?"

Atxi read the page twice, and almost missed James coming back aboard. "I don't know. I haven't heard of this place."

Karen looked. "I have. Trust me, you'll get there in plenty of time."

"Someone give us a hand with this?" James called. "I'm still an old man, y'know."

Coming up the gangplank was James and Smitty, each of them carrying a huge wooden crate. Irsu stepped forward quickly to take James half of the load. "What's this?"

"No idea. It's addressed to Karen." James wiped his brow. "Who's sending you things here?"

"I ordered it." Karen said lightly. "But you can't open it yet." She turned the blue page towards James. "Our next stop?"

James looked, and smiled at Atxi. "Our next stop."

~oo0Ooo~

Spyglass Cove was more or less unchanged by going empty for a while. White sandy beach, with a large, half-moon cove. The sort of place you could park a fleet that didn't want to be found. The treeline was at the very edge of the beach, and the water so blue it could make your eyes hurt to stare at it.

"Beautiful spot." Karen observed as James dropped the anchor. "With the trees so close, I feel like there's someone watching."

"That was the point, back in the day. Deep shadowy trees meant the Pirates camped out here could observe newcomers without ever being seen."

Atxi came up on deck when she felt the boat stop moving. "So this is Spyglass Cove." She looked to the Blue Letter, though she'd long memorized it. "Why would my sister come back here?"

"I have a few ideas." Karen said blandly, sending James a saucy look as she jumped up on the railing, and made a perfect swan dive into the water; not bothering with the inflatable boat James unpacked.

~oo0Ooo~

The Hut was still there, though the insects had moved into it. There was a layer of dust over everything… and a skeleton stretched out in the hammock. It was wearing the tattered remains of homespun breeches.

"Lancewood." James sighed, and tied the ends of the hammock together, making it easier to take his worn out bones away from the camp.

Digging a grave was relatively easy. Lancewood had plenty of tools around. James said nothing while he worked. He sent a glance back towards the beach, but the others knew this was something he wanted to do alone. He dragged the whole hammock, and its burden, into the grave, and filled it in. He used the axe as a marker, and put Lancewood's hat on top.

That done, James swept his own hat off, and bowed his head… before realizing he had no idea what to say. Lancewood had nobody there to say a word for him; except an old enemy.

"Irsu once told Atxi that if you asked everyone here: 'What Convinced You?', they'd all have a different answer. What changed my mind wasn't the offer of eternal life. I've been dead before. It's not like I suffered any when I was gone. What kept me back was the same thing that convinced me. It was you." James almost laughed. "The only people I could relate to in this world were the people I truly despised back in the Old Days, and that was a reason enough to believe, and more reason to say no."

James hesitated, realizing this was becoming less of a eulogy, and more of a prayer, but there was nobody there to counter his claims.

"Have you not read what was spoken to you by God, who said: 'I am the God of Abraham and the God of Isaac and the God of Jacob'? He is the God, not of the dead, but of the living."

James turned. The Boy was back, the one that had spread his wings for Atxi.

"When Jesus said that, Abraham, Issac, and Jacob were all dead more than a thousand years. It was another two thousand years again before they were Returned." The Angel said. "But to Jah, they were always alive; because they were His."

"He could bring Lancewood back." James said to him. It wasn't a question.

"He doesn't get any special treatment, just because you have to say goodbye when he can't hear you. He made his choice. You made yours." The Boy said without pity or judgement. "God gave him the breath of life, twice, and he never said 'thank you', even once."

"I always knew how to handle my enemies. When it was an enemy I could defeat, I attacked. When it was one too strong, I lay in wait, and watched for a chance, looked for a weakness." James looked down. "This world has only one way to deal with enemies, and that is to show them love and friendship; until there's nothing left of them to love. Not nearly as satisfying as I would have liked it to be, but things are different now."

"Better now." The Boy said, and gestured at the marker, then back at the Ship. "Walter Emmerson once asked if we liked Human Music, their plays, their movies… We hear all of it. Shakespeare once wrote: 'What is Past, is Prologue'. And that takes on a whole other meaning for you now. Everything that has come before, from the events of the first page of the Bible to the moment you made your dedication, is still the very first page of your story. Lancewood's story has ended. There will never be another page written for him. Your story is just beginning, and it can go on forever and ever. Every horizon is yours to sail. Jehovah is a God of the Living. And you are alive."

~oo0Ooo~

"Are you sure you want to do this here?" Irsu asked as James returned to the group. "I mean, you just came back from… well, burying someone."

"Lancewood and I were never exactly friends." James explained. "Besides, that's the best reason of all to do this here. Two lives are just getting started here. And two people left this place to start fresh. This is the place where one life ended, and four began anew."

"A good metaphor for the day's proceedings." Irsu agreed. "I take it Eileen had no objection?"

"She signed the Cove over to me before we left."

James reported. "It was a straight up swap. The place I was allotted was landlocked."

"I knew that wouldn't keep you down for long." Irsu agreed with a smile.

James looked around. "Where's Karen?"

"Right here." Karen called, coming back from the ship. "I had to take a call. David's mother wanted to know if Atxi was still interested in helping out with that study about older cultures, and how they're adapting to the New World. Except that the 'book' is now an exhibit at the Expo." She sent James a glance. "Apparently, David is part of the project now."

"David is going to need a lot of attention. I know he's an Elder, but guilt is the one purely destructive force left in the world." James agreed. "And it's not my place to offer help."

"No, see: That's the thing. David was the one making the call. He wants to go with Atxi, and knew she'd be here." Karen explained, waving her Device. "I think he's looking for a new project he can throw himself into; and his mother's career has always interested him. So he wants to know if he can hitch a ride with you, next time you go in the direction of the Expo."

"As it happens, I'm heading that way soon." James told her. "A man named Nick Alman is chartering my ship. Apparently, he's organizing his first Ministry, out to the Undecided Colony."

"Nick?" Irsu repeated the name. "He was there the last time we went out to the Island. He won't be popular there."

"No indeed, which is why I'm going with him." James explained. "I've been their supply line for decades. Seeing me losing the grey hair will make a difference."

Karen smiled. "I hope so."

"So do I." James admitted. "Because I have no natural talent as an evangelist, and there are some people there whom I would like to see live forever." He took a corner of the tablecloth and straightened it. "This world isn't a big enough proof for them as it is. Maybe seeing it happen to me will help."

"I hope so."

James bit his lip and looked at Irsu. "They aren't bad people, Judge. Not really."

"I don't know if good and bad are the point anymore. It's about trust. Walter never trusted God to give him security; and you decided you could."

"I've never needed security." James shook his head. "I lived my whole adult life without it. Before coming here, it was actually the most interesting part of being me. But there was one thing I couldn't live without. And Eternity was just barely long enough for it."

"What's that?"

James cast a look towards Atxi, who was emerging from the trees, with a large basket of freshly-picked fruits.

Karen smiled sweetly. "Well. A happy ending."

"If there is such a thing as an ending anymore." James acknowledged, and left the picnic to head towards Atxi.

Smitty smiled, so glad for his Captain. "So. If Atxi's Blue Letter is arriving here, I'm guessing we'll have company soon. Shall we put an extra place at the table for lunch?"

Karen nodded. "Why not?"

~oo0Ooo~

"This is a nice spot." Atxi commented, breathing

deep. "I was a fair way from the ocean before coming here. A beach was never exactly part of my world view. But I have to admit, it seems little more like 'Paradise' here than it does back in the cities."

James chuckled. "You ask any of the people at the Expo, they'd say the opposite."

"I suppose so." Atxi nodded. "But there's a favor I'd like to ask."

"Anything."

"Can my sister stay here for a while?" Atxi asked awkwardly. "I know you just got this place signed over to you, but you spend most of your life on the ocean anyway. The sheer size of the world scared me when I first got here." She ran a hand through her hair, still grey. "Watching me grow young before her eyes will help. She'll have the same trouble I had, accepting The Truth. I want to bring her around to it in pieces, tell her what to look for."

"I've got a charter to do, which will take a week or so." James nodded. "After a week, I'll be back. You can show her the *Nicholas*, let her get used to technology, to seeing her sister grow younger instead of older…"

"There'll be time." Atxi nodded. "To die of old age was a dishonor among the Aztecs. My sister will have no answer to my looking older, or to my getting younger."

James nodded, and took a deep breath. "Atxi, I had given some thought to… well, the future. Our future. But if your sister has to be the priority, I can stay on the ship. I've done it most of my life. If you want to wait for-"

"James." Atxi interrupted. "If there's one thing we know about, it's wasting time. Especially on the important things. I'm not doing that again. Yes, I will marry you. Today, if you want."

James chuckled. "Well, we do have everyone we'd

invite here already. Including your sister, if you can wait till after lunch."

Atxi was giggling. Then James was too. She stepped forward and took him in a tight hug, their laughter growing stronger and more joyful; tears streaming down their faces. It wasn't just happiness. It was the sheer joy of being safe and in love after such a near miss.

~oo0Ooo~

Atxi and James stood at the edge of the ocean, with the others gathered around them in a semi-circle, a few feet back. In front of them all, Irsu beamed at them both. "When we read about the millions coming back, it's easy to see numbers. But each and every person who returns to life has a story. A personal story, that's unique to them, and nobody else. Even if there are a million people who lived under similar circumstances, there's nobody who thought about what you thought about, and who felt what you felt when it happened." Irsu looked to the small audience. "But Jehovah does. He who reads hearts and minds can know us completely. Jehovah knows each hair on our heads individually, but for the rest of us; it's easy to see only part of the story. Never ever forget that these are people, and they are precious and unique. Because Jehovah never forgets that; not ever. We all come to God from different places, but we all come to the same place. Every person who comes to Jehovah brings a lifetime of unique thoughts, and that makes the world a little more special and interesting. It may not be what we expected, but it's what's good." Irsu smiled broadly. "Speaking for myself, I'm glad to have eternity to get to know you all."

James and Atxi were both at the water's edge, holding hands tightly. Karen and Smitty were there, watching the proceedings with big smiles on their faces. "Amen."

"Atxi, I told you once, that if you asked anyone: 'What Convinced You?' then they'd all have an answer." Irsu gave the two of them his full attention. "Do you have one, now?"

Atxi nodded. "It was a long road. I went from expecting something very particular, to being told those promises were false. I met a woman who knew more about my nation, after they had all gone to dust, than I knew after living with them. I lived with a hundred people who were all desperate to keep things the way they knew, and saw through all their lies once I bothered to look. I was taught how to spot the truth by someone I felt was the worst liar I'd ever met, and learned how love could be eternal, from someone who had little interest in eternity." She clutched James' hand tightly. "But most of all, I learned that Jehovah was the True God; because he'd heard my prayer, even before I knew his name, and He'd patiently waited centuries for me to hear his answer."

Irsu smiled, so happy for her. "And you, James? What convinced you?"

"What did it for me was that when my time came, people came looking for me. They all knew I was making the wrong choice. Even as I died, there was no yelling, no anger." He looked in the direction of Lancewood's marker. "The people who lived here made their choices long ago. Lancewood's wife knew he wouldn't change his mind, but she stayed out of loyalty, until whatever love she felt for him was gone. But when my time came, I had several people who were sad to see my clock run out, and that meant my life had value to them. Something to ransom it back with. They never gave up on me. I always thought that Power and Evil were the same thing, but if a flesh and blood person could forgive that much wasted time, then surely someone as almighty and all-knowing as Jehovah God could do the same."

Irsu nodded, eyes shining. "A long path, indeed. When you first came back; we told you that this was what Jehovah had always intended the world to be. In fact, we aren't there yet. There are still billions more to be raised and taught, and hundreds of years of work to clean up and restore the world to a true physical, and spiritual Paradise. But now that you're here; we're a little closer than we were yesterday. Welcome Home, brothers and sisters. Welcome Home."

Everyone cheered as Irsu lead them into the water, and baptized them both.

~oo0Ooo~

There was a celebration. Right on the pristine white sand, those who came to see the ceremony had laid out a picnic, complete with tablecloths and torches. There were hugs and kisses in every direction, tears on every smiling face. James and Atxi hadn't let go of each other's hands since stepping out of the ocean. As everyone expressed their joy, the two of them traded a look. They'd come closer to the edge than any of their friends had wanted to admit.

"When I was a girl, I thought the Gods decided things for reasons I couldn't comprehend." Atxi said quietly. "Part of me still wonders, even now, if maybe the reason it took me until old age before I finally figured things out is because my sister will waste far less time, watching me grow younger."

"Mm." Irsu sipped chilled juice, enjoying the day. "I stopped looking for reasons over every choice and consequence long ago. Free Will isn't subject to whims of anyone; and you'll make yourself crazy looking for justification. But lessons? Lessons can be learned from almost everything, if you have a mind to look. I hope your sister learns fast. Time is a limitless resource now, but the world isn't a place to waste such priceless gifts."

"Amen to that." James admitted as they ate. "We still have a lot to learn."

"You do." Irsu wasn't concerned. "But you finally got the most important lesson into your hearts. Everything else is just time and study."

"Study was never my strongest skill." James admitted.

"Me neither, but we have time." Atxi smiled at him, and put a kiss on his cheek as she stood up. "And speaking of time, I have an appointment."

"Don't be nervous." Karen told her.

"I am nervous. But not about this." Atxi said seriously. "I came close. I don't like the idea that my family might do the same. My sister is... like me, in many ways. I look back at my life, and if I'm forced to admit: I wouldn't have been half as patient with anyone as God has been with me." Atxi told her friends.

"Me neither." James said with grim understatement, trading a look with Smitty. They knew what 'trying someone's patience' would cost pirates, back in their day.

Atxi checked the time again and looked upwards briefly. "If my sister takes the same path that I did, I hope that I can be as patient and as compassionate with her, as God and the rest of you have been with me."

"We will, and He will, and you will, too." Karen promised her.

"And, without wanting to start the 'destiny' debate again," James added. "Patli will have something you didn't have. She'll have her sister there to meet her when she arrives."

Atxi glanced in the direction of where Lancewood was buried. "I hope it's enough." She said quietly as she left the table.

~oo0Ooo~

Atxi walked deeper into the trees. "Father, I pray that my sister learns the lessons that my life has taught me. And after her, my mother; father… All the souls that I have loved." Atxi prayed aloud quietly. "Thank you for bringing her back to me, and thank you in advance for all the others… And thank you that James and I can be together forever now. It's funny, but back when I first got here, a lifetime seemed to be long enough. Now I know it isn't."

She arrived at a clearing. The birds in the trees and the press of the green, leafy foliage was almost like the places they had hidden together as children, while their parents were trying to get them to help with the harvest. The Blue Letter didn't specify more than the cove, but the second she saw it, Atxi knew this was the place.

She checked the time again, and-

There was a sound, like a gentle breeze, like the air was inhaling and exhaling at the same time; and suddenly Atxi was not alone. Her sister was there, lying peacefully on the grass. She opened her eyes and blinked, as though waking from a nap.

Atxi swallowed back the sob, and started towards her. Almost immediately, she was running.

Patli turned at the sound. "Atxi?!" She couldn't believe her eyes. "Is… is that you?"

Atxi nearly tackled her sister into the hug. Even as she did, she knew she had some explaining to do. Atxi had been little more than a girl when she died. She was older now.

"Patli…" Atxi said with a smile so wide it hurt. "I'm so happy to see you again!"

"Atxi! Sister, it is you!" Patli hugged her back

tightly. "We made it! Thirteen Heavens, and we're in the same one!"

Atxi almost wanted to laugh, but instead started to cry. "Well. We're together. For now, that's what's important."

Epilogue

The gathering at Spyglass Cove lasted late into the night, with eating, singing, and a lot of conversation. Patli had many questions, and everyone was happy to answer them.

Karen had brought a surfboard, of all things. James and Atxi had never seen one before. Neither had Patli; but seeing Karen riding the waves had thrilled her. Patli had never even seen an ocean before, or learned to swim; but there was plenty of time for that.

James had lit a fire on the beach and they'd roasted snacks as the stars came out. The night was mild and Irsu produced a guitar. James and Atxi had danced for a while, eyes locked on each other. They could see the youthful energy there, slowly coming back; ready to last for eternity.

Finally, the night came to a close. James had slept on the beach, lulled by the ocean. He hadn't slept so well in years. Irsu had done the same. Smitty had strung his hammock between some trees. Atxi, Karen, and Patli had returned to the ship for sleeping bags and cots.

~oo0Ooo~

The next morning, James had awoken to find Karen already holding out coffee. "Morning."

"Good morning." She told him. "Listen, as much as I'd like to stay and keep this party going, I have to head back to the Expo. We finally got the go-ahead to start work on the *Nemo*, and I've been invited to sit in on some of the planning sessions."

James was digging around the ashes of the previous night's fire, wondering if he could coax it back to life for breakfast. "It'll be another hundred years before they get the thing built. Have you even started on the designs yet?"

"That's what we're meeting about." Karen explained. "Captain Diaz isn't that far away, heading towards the Expo. I called from your ship, had her divert here to pick me up."

James nodded. Karen said nothing, just sitting and looking at James earnestly, as though waiting for him to say something.

James took a deep sip of the coffee. "Karen, I promise, if Atxi and I decide to jump the broom today, and we'll do it before you leave."

"I would have thought you'd make that a priority."

"We discussed it. But remember, to Patli, Atxi is still a Temple Priestess. We agreed not to overload her too much, and…"

"And the wedding will bring questions aplenty for a while." Karen nodded. "If you want to ease the new girl into the world gently, we better warn Atxi that there's an Airship arriving in a few hours." She took the cup back and sipped herself. "Y'know, James… It'll be years before the *Nemo* is ready to launch. If you were looking for a goal to chase…"

James shook his head. "No. Going under the water was code for 'death and destruction' in my time. The Ocean is my world. The Ocean Floor may well be yours."

"I hope so. Because I plan to do more than just build this thing. I want to be on it." Karen said. "And just so you know, I never would have looked twice at the waves if it wasn't for meeting you." She held his hand tightly. "I know you've only been part of our family for a day, but you've made such a big impression on my life. You've changed the course I was on for the next few centuries, possibly a lot longer. And before I go, I just wanted to say thank you."

James didn't realize she meant more than just offering sentiment, until a few minutes later when Smitty and Irsu came back from the ship with Karen's huge cargo crate between them. "What is that thing anyway?" James asked again.

"Well, it was going to be your wedding present. But I suppose you can open it now." Karen smiled secretly as they freed the lashings. James pulled the crate open, and actually gasped. It was the figurehead from the *Stargazer*. Pinned to it was a small note:

Compliments of Captain Diaz. Welcome to the Family.

"How did she know?" Smitty asked.

"She didn't. But she knew that if things had gone the other way, I'd have wanted Karen to give the boat to you, Smitty." James said with a smile. "Sorry to snatch it away from you at the last minute."

"I'll live, Cap'n." Smitty said with biting understatement and a smile on his face.

~oo0Ooo~

Beyond the beach, beyond the small house, there was a natural orchard of fruit trees. Atxi had collected a basket the day before, but there were still plenty of fruits ripening on the vine.

Her sister was with her, taking a bite. "The food is amazing." She said. "Are you very sure we aren't in Tialocan?"

Atxi almost burst into hysterical laughter at the irony. "Pretty sure." She squeaked.

After they had refilled their basket, Atxi linked her arm with her sisters', and led the way back. "Patli, I very nearly made the wrong choice. But I'll tell you the best advice I got when I arrived here, and I pray you'll actually take it instead of looking the other way as I did:

Look around. Experience everything. This world is proof positive of the one who provided it."

"And... That is good?"

"That is very good." Atxi said emotionally. "The things you'll see, sister... I envy you. I really do. You're just at the start of something wonderful. There's so much to see."

Patli was looking at her, eyes wide at her sincerity. "Like what?"

Atxi smiled eagerly. "Like ice cream. I like the choc-mint flavor most. And all sorts of extinct animals back. And conversations with Kings and Paupers alike; and eating honey straight from the beehive without fearing a sting. And sailing fast on an ocean so still you'd swear it was the sky above; and friendships that last forever. And being able to run all day without getting tired. And hearing music of every kind in every place you go. And rolling around in the grass with a leopard cub. And popping bubble wrap, and-"

Patli was lost, a little disturbed at the intensity. "What's 'bubble wrap'?"

"-and falling in love. And knowing that you're loved in return, and seeing them gain eternal life." Atxi had tears in her eyes. "And seeing your family raised from the dead. Oh, sister; you're just at the start of the most incredible story."

~ooO0oo~

It had been twenty years since their baptism, and in that time they had built their cove into something that would last forever. They were not alone there for long.

Atxi had studied with her sister for almost a year, and after enough time had passed, she had taken Patli to see Huitzilin. The meeting was long overdue for all of them. In fact, many members of older, forgotten religions were having the same re-entry trouble that Atxi's family did, and the Cove was being talked about in some circles as a good place for such devout followers to visit first. Atxi knew how to lead them gently to the Truth, both secular and scriptural. Over two dozen such persons had been convinced by Atxi and Irsu, working together in their private little island Haven.

"It's not exactly Thirteen Heavens." She had told James. "But it's what I always wanted. To be closer to God, to be part of Him. Prosperity and Joy for my family; eternal service to a loving creator. The God in question was one I never saw coming, but he heard my prayer and answered it."

"I get the feeling that Jehovah has been waiting for a chance to answer a lot of prayers." James had agreed.

James had cracked open some of the old caves where stolen goods had been hidden in the Old Days; and converted them into proper warehouses. With so much cargo and so many passengers on the move, there was always work for a well-placed storage depot; and an experienced ship captain. James had taken some time to teach a class on shipbuilding, and had found himself a good crew in the process. With The Depot gaining a small list of regular customers in the area; James had settled into a management role in Spyglass Cove, and let ships and crews come to him for instructions.

"It's not a title and mansion on a large acreage; but it's a prosperous enough life for a gentleman." He had told Atxi. "The ironic thing is, if I'd managed to become a Patron myself, and build a shipping company of my own back in the day as I planned; I would have had to be wary of pirates and thieves."

The rest of their own families had been returned, one by one. As time passed and the two of them had grown young again, Atxi had expressed a desire to have the whole family together; and to update the wedding album to reflect how they would always look from now on.

"I know we don't 'renew our vows', any more than we get baptised twice." Atxi had said. "But our appearance in those pictures isn't accurate anymore, and to be honest, I don't like reminders of how close we came."

"I would think it'd be important to remember." James had countered.

"It is, but… Can you even tell that the woman in that photo is me?"

James had agreed, and made the call. It took almost no effort to throw a party anymore. The sun coming up was usually reason enough. Getting their families and friends together for a reunion was an annual event in many households.

"And I think Irsu might want to talk to my parents." Atxi had teased quietly. "Just a hunch."

"Oh, is that the reason we're in such a rush to pull this together?" James chuckled. "You still trying to play matchmaker for Irsu and your sister?"

"Mmmmaybe." Atxi drawled.

"You know that people need a better reason to get hitched than just having the family all in one place, right?"

"I know, but Patli's been talking about it for a while, so it's not so terrible a reason." Atxi smiled hugely… before pulling James' hand to her stomach. "Besides, if we put off the pictures for another two or three months, I won't fit in the dress anymore; and we'll have to do this all over again."

"A third time would be pushing it." James nodded automatically; before his jaw dropped open and his eyes bulged out. "Wait. WHAT?!"

~oo0Ooo~

Smitty had taken over command of the *Nicholas*, and ferried cargo and passengers out to the Cove. For the party, he'd have to add on an extra trip and bring the extended family.

"And of course, we'd want you to attend too." James had told his best friend. "You were my best man at the Wedding, so it stands to reason you'd be there. You still have that suit?"

"I do. You're hardly the first people to retake your Wedding Photos, you know. In fact, there's a whole Industry for it now. There have been dozens of those photoshoots done on the Stargazer. An airship's view makes for nice pics."

"Really?" James was surprised. "With the 'photographs' only being around for a century or two…"

"Yeah, but there were still plenty of them taken." Smitty nodded. "Anyone who's settled on a different hairstyle, or hates what they wore on the day. Or for that matter, needed glasses or a cane. To say nothing of all the reunited couples who married before there were such things as 'cameras' and want to have one of their own."

"To say nothing of looking forty years younger since we wed." Atxi put in lightly as she came up behind her husband. "People want a 'timeless' moment captured on film, they can have one now. It's why we're doing it."

"That, and it's time our families met each other at last." James returned, smooching her warmly. "Happy anniversary, luv."

~oo0Ooo~

At the head of the table sat James and Atxi, smiling at everyone they knew. Huitzilin was there, smiling back at Atxi. After far too long, she had finally sat down with him and sorted things out. James had been with her the entire time. James had done the same with each member of his old crew; and life went on.

"So much of the old world feels like a bad dream now." Atxi said quietly to her sister. "In another thousand years, we won't think of it at all anymore."

Patli shivered. "I still don't know what the future will bring, but I'm not afraid to find out. And I'm glad you're here."

On a perfect beach, framed with trees on one side, and ocean on the other, with an elegant sailing ship docked, and an Airship parked overhead, the extended family gathered around long tables piled high with food and drink. Almost a hundred eternally young people, raised to a world full of love and family and friendship, gathered to tell each other wonderful stories of all they had seen and done.

Atxi caught her husband's hand, and made him stand with her a moment. She pulled him a bit away from the table, giving them privacy. James was about to ask why, when she bowed her head, eyes closed.

"Jehovah, thank you." Atxi prayed quietly, just for them. "Thank you for everything. I look around and I see everyone I love, and everyone they love too."

James took up the prayer automatically. "Atxi and I both had things we would have given our lives for back in OS; and now we have those dreams, fulfilled to a degree we never could have imagined. After a lifetime of ignoring, opposing, and screaming at you; we are so grateful to you for being so willing and ready to forgive us; and bring us into your world."

"Your wonderful, beautiful world. We vow always to be grateful to you for your generosity and abundance. Forever and ever." Atxi agreed. "Amen."

"Amen." James agreed.